OVERTHROW

OVERTHROW

A NOVEL

CALEB CRAIN

VIKING

VIKING
An imprint of Penguin Random House LLC
penguinrandomhouse.com

The author thanks Allison Lorentzen, Ben Nugent, Christine Smallwood, Peter Terzian,
and Ben Wizner for their insights into an early draft and their suggestions for improving it.
He thanks Sarah Chalfant and Jacqueline Ko at the Wylie Agency, and Allison Lorentzen,
Norma Barksdale, and the rest of the team at Viking for shepherding the book into print.

LIBRARY OF CONGRESS CATALOGING-IN-PUBLICATION DATA

Names: Crain, Caleb, author.
Title: Overthrow : a novel / Caleb Crain.
Description: [New York] : Viking, [2019] |
Identifiers: LCCN 2019003204 (print) | LCCN 2019005390 (ebook) |
ISBN 9780525560463 (ebook) | ISBN 9780525560456 (hardcover)
Classification: LCC PS3603.R359 (ebook) | LCC PS3603.R359 O94 2019 (print) |
DDC 813/.6—dc23
LC record available at https://lccn.loc.gov/2019003204

Printed in the United States of America
1   3   5   7   9   10   8   6   4   2

BOOK DESIGN BY LUCIA BERNARD

To Peter

You may my glories and my state depose,
But not my griefs; still am I king of those.

—*Richard II*

OVERTHROW

1.

It was a few days after the clocks had fallen back for the end of daylight saving time, during the interval when people have adjusted their schedules but not yet their habits. A graduate student in English named Matthew Fisher was walking home from the subway. Dusk had caught the houses along the street with their blinds still undrawn, and living room after living room was exposed, glowing in bright display. Was it wrong to look into them? It was like looking into lives that one wasn't going to get to live. Matthew saw a toy sailboat on top of a television. He saw a sweater folded over the back of a chair. When he saw a pinecone on a mantelpiece, for a moment he seemed to see the room that contained the pinecone from the pinecone's point of view, as if he, too, were surrounded by the bright yellow cheer that belonged to the family that lived there.

And then he was himself again, outside in the dark, walking.

He had a beard, which he had grown after he had turned thirty, just over a year ago, in the hope that it would make him a little harder to read. He was pretty sure that he did now look a little bearish. In one of his online profiles he claimed to have a boxer's build, which wasn't completely misrepresentative. According to a man he had recently picked up in a bar, he looked like the sort of person who could work for a long time without getting sick.

He hadn't called the man again, afterward. He was a little alone in the world at the moment, as it happened. He had fallen behind in writing his dissertation, and his close friends in the program, including a man he'd been seeing, hadn't. They had finished in the spring and then left for jobs and fellowships in other parts of the country over the summer. He had stayed in touch with some of them by email, and he and the now amicably former boyfriend talked now and then by phone. He hadn't foreseen how hard it would be to replace a number of friends at once, exactly when one was supposed to be conserving one's energies for research and writing. Nor had he foreseen that not having people in one's life would make it much more difficult to take in new ones. Under the circumstances, any single new person seemed to carry somehow too much presence.

Tonight, though, he noticed that he seemed able to send some of himself out into the world. Halfway down the block, he became aware of a young man on a skateboard, pushing down the sidewalk toward him. Twenty-three? Twenty-four? The boy was wearing a gray toggle coat. Against the dim evening, his face and bare hands were almost luminous. He had a sort of elfin beauty, Matthew saw as the boy came nearer. A fine nose. Thin lips. Eyes like little candies. A few yards from Matthew, the boy kicked up his skateboard and carried it. The dismounting might have been no more than urban politeness, but when his eyes met Matthew's, they had a sly look, and Matthew heard himself saying hi.

"Oh, hi," the skateboarder replied, stopping in his tracks.

It was always startling that it turned out to be so easy. For a moment Matthew didn't know what to say. The boy was taller than Matthew was.

"You can say it," said the skateboarder.

"Say what?" Matthew wondered aloud.

"I'm on my way to a friend's. Do you want to come?"

"Is he a skater like you?"

"She. No."

"She."

"She's straight, even."

"I remember straight people," said Matthew.

The boy continued to carry his skateboard, and Matthew, reversing direction, fell into step beside him. The skateboarder said his name was Leif. He had been skating at the late-nineteenth-century monument at the park entrance a block away. Matthew was familiar with it. A marble ledge at the back served as a bench, and skaters liked to pop their boards into the air and surf along the bench's edge, as if filing it down by skidding along it. The marble was soft, and Matthew had noticed that they were in fact filing it down, unevenly. He always felt a little protective of a thing if it spoke of the past.

The city had trained him to be a connoisseur, and he could tell that this boy, with his nonchalance and moonglow complexion, outclassed him. Still, he was used to getting more than he deserved, and there wasn't any evidence of unwillingness. In a few minutes, he might be grabbing the tousled hair at the back of the boy's head and kissing him.

He was aware, however, that as they walked, his own apartment was receding behind them, along with the prospect of dinner.

"Where are you taking me?" Matthew asked.

"Down the rabbit hole."

"Uh-oh."

"No, not really."

"'Drink me,' I hope," Matthew hinted.

"Subtle!"

"I mean, drink *you*, as it were," Matthew clarified. "That you're a tall drink of water or whatever."

"'As it were,'" the young man echoed.

"Not that that's any more subtle," Matthew admitted. He didn't believe in dignity, at least not where the pursuit of boys was concerned. The skateboarder, for his part, accepted the compliment without acknowledgment, and Matthew realized that he knew he wanted the boy without knowing yet whether he liked him. The boy might be stringing Matthew along merely for the pleasure of manifesting the power of his own beauty.

"You're sweet," the boy offered.

"No, I'm not," Matthew replied.

In pickups, there were always small frustrations and disappointments, such as delay, that one had to decide what to do with. If they added up too quickly, one could decide to set against them not only the pleasure that, if all went well, one was about to have, but also the revenge of never seeing the man again, afterward. In case he might want to see the man again, however—in case the latest boy might turn out to be the one for whom he was willing to break the pattern of solitude that he had fallen into—Matthew always tried, for as long as he could (for a while, anyway), to turn aside any verdict that negative impressions of the boy might have led him to by sorting them, along with positive ones, into a picture or story that was, at least tentatively, worth holding on to. That is, he tried, as he assembled the picture or story, to see in it someone he might be interested in or even able to fall for. Someone he could imagine looking back at the picture with.

They turned onto one of the quiet residential avenues.

"What do you do?" the skateboarder asked.

"Do you skateboard a lot?" Matthew countered, because he didn't feel like explaining about kingship in early modern English poetry yet.

The boy coughed. It began almost as a hiccup but sank quickly into a rough hacking, low in the chest, and the boy had trouble mastering it. "Sorry," he said, when he had his breath again. "I meant to *laugh* at you, not cough at you." He took a plastic water bottle out of his coat pocket and swigged from it.

"Do you smoke?"

"I caught pneumonia at Occupy. I'm just getting over it."

"Should you be out in the cold? Are you even wearing a sweater under that?"

"I thought you weren't sweet. Here it is."

They had come to one of the stolid corner-lot apartment buildings—prewar, gray stone, with elegant cornices—that were still just a little too large for the rich to convert to single-family residences and persisted therefore as refuges for young strivers. The best part of picking people up, Matthew sometimes thought, was seeing the insides of strangers' homes, the apartments of people that a grad student in English might otherwise not even get to talk to.

"It's me," the skateboarder told the intercom.

At the back of a black-and-white-tiled lobby, a staircase twisted up tightly and steeply, and on the first landing, Matthew caught up to the skateboarder—his name was Leif, Matthew reminded himself—and kissed him. The boy gave more than the porcelain delicacy of his looks suggested that he would. Afterward, his face was flushed, Matthew saw; they kissed again.

"You're perfect," Matthew said.

The boy smiled with concern. He had a girl's eyelashes and very faint freckles. "Are you drunk?" he asked Matthew, unseriously.

On the third floor, a door had been left ajar, and the skateboarder walked in without knocking and without waiting to see if Matthew followed him. "I brought someone," he hollered as he strode down a dark, narrow corridor, which, according to a paradoxical layout typical of prewar buildings in the neighborhood, revealed the private spaces of the apartment before the public ones, leading past the open doors of a bathroom and three bedrooms—onto the dainty pink-and-white quilt of one of whose beds, carefully made, the young man possessively threw his toggle coat—before reaching a dining room and a parlor. The skateboarder and Matthew paused on the near side of the threshold between the two rooms, which were connected by pocket doors trundled away into their pockets.

Beyond the threshold, a petite young woman with straight chestnut hair unfolded her legs from a lotus-style perch on a sofa. She was sitting next to a scruffy, fair-haired man who seemed to be her boyfriend. She rose to give Leif a hug.

"Matthew here wanted to see what we're doing," said Leif, by way of introduction. "He's perfectly safe."

Somewhat sheepishly, the woman inspected Matthew. "He looks safe."

"Elspeth and I went to college together," Leif told Matthew. "That's Raleigh," he added, of the man still on the sofa. "He's a skater like me. I mean, not like *me*, not in my league."

"Why are you such a dick?" Raleigh said. Then, looking Matthew over, "Does this guy skate?"

"No!" Matthew admitted.

"Did you just pick him up?" Raleigh asked Leif.

"I think actually he picked me up? Can I offer him a glass of water without you giving him the third degree?"

"Oh, there's juice, too, I think," said Elspeth. Speed-sliding in her slippers, as if they were cross-country skis, she took Leif with her to the kitchen.

Left alone with the straight man, Matthew nodded, as if to acknowledge that the man had a right to be suspicious, and became aware of holding his winter hat in his hands and worrying it as if he were a Dickens character. He shoved it into a coat pocket. How embarrassing to be older and to be here so obviously as a supplicant.

He looked around in what he hoped was an innocuous manner. The dining room, behind him, was bare, somewhat severely so. The only decoration was a black-and-white photo-poster, blown up so large that grains of half-toning were visible. In the photo, a chair had been knocked over, on what seemed to be a stage. A microphone lay on the floor beside the chair; a black cable snaked away.

By contrast, the parlor, where Elspeth and Raleigh had been sitting, was a jumble. It was in the cluttered style, reminiscent of respectable Victorian living rooms, that had become fashionable among people with somewhat unconventional ambitions. There was a smoke-damaged oil of a landscape. There was a birdless subfusc birdcage. On a coffee table, a glass pitcher held half a dozen dried hydrangea clusters, of a mothlike grayish lavender. The sofa had been reupholstered in white and chartreuse stripes sometime in the past decade, but cracks in its dark, carved frame had been repaired with a glue that had turned mustard and opaque and had begun to crumble. Only in a listing Ikea bookcase was fresh color visible—red, orange, and blue on the dust jackets of essay collections and volumes of poets' correspondence, the fogeyish new hardcovers that young people who work in publishing are tempted into bringing home from the giveaway table but then never read. In such a setting, with its allusions to a tradition that it hadn't quite inherited, Matthew thought he knew where he was. He might know even better than the people who lived here, he thought, with a confidence whose force triggered in him, as suddenly, a reconsideration: What if his confidence was a way of keeping from himself an awareness of how out of place he really was?

When Elspeth and Leif returned with a glass of water, Elspeth waved at Raleigh, as if shooing away his vigilance. "It's *fine*," she insisted.

"I thought we were supposed to try to find people," Leif said, in his own defense. "I actually do think he has . . ."

"Has what?" Matthew asked.

"If that's what this is about," Raleigh said.

"Sometimes we do experiments?" Leif said to Matthew. "With tarot cards?"

"Tarot cards," Matthew repeated.

"I know, right?"

"No, no," Matthew said. Magic was a thing that one had to reckon with when trying to understand kingship. It existed in Spenser's fairy world; it existed in Shakespeare in even his earliest plays, the ones not really much by Shakespeare. In the course of his reading and note-taking, Matthew had been learning the scholarly way of discussing it, which neither reified nor underestimated.

"Leif," Elspeth pleaded.

"It's tarot cards not because we think we can predict the future," Leif said. "It's tarot cards because Elspeth doesn't have any feelings about card cards."

"I don't understand why anyone would have feelings about them," she said.

"If you'd had a childhood, for instance."

"We used to do it at school," Elspeth told Matthew, "and when we started going to Occupy, it seemed like we should take it up again. As an alternative means of communication."

"A new world is possible," Leif said. "You don't have to tell us you don't believe because we've already read your mind about that." The irony in his voice suggested that he was setting up a test less of Matthew's credulity than of his willingness to be carried along.

"It's not *really* a joke," Elspeth said.

Matthew was bewildered, but he nodded. Sometimes during a pickup it was advisable to be as parsimonious as a diplomat with statements of how much one believed or didn't believe.

Through the cotton of the skateboarder's upper right shirt sleeve, Matthew thought he saw a figure, and he pointed at the boy's arm. "Is this a tattoo?"

Leif rolled up his sleeve to show off the image: a small thicket of lightly stylized trees, somewhere between depictions of trees and emblems of them. While Matthew was admiring the trees, Leif did, too, looking over his own right shoulder at them while his left hand held back the fabric. "A green thought," he said, in explanation. The lines were drawn so boldly that Matthew wondered if they were legible by touch.

Elspeth dropped onto the sofa and pulled Raleigh down beside her.

"Like it's so hard to read this guy's mind," Raleigh commented.

"Does he have a boyfriend?" Leif asked Elspeth, as he let his sleeve fall.

"No," Elspeth answered tentatively.

"True," Matthew admitted. Maybe it was a game. Or a way for the girl to keep a hold on her gay friend, or vice versa.

"Is he trouble?" Leif asked.

Elspeth paused. "Yes."

"I'm not trouble!" Matthew said.

"He's sad," Elspeth said. "He's that kind of trouble." She was willing to look at him only dartingly. Under her eyes there were shadows that appeared to be part of the structure of her face, as in the face of a child born prematurely who hasn't quite, as grandparents say, "filled out." She closed her eyes for a moment. "I think actually you're right and he knows. That's why you brought him, isn't it."

"Don't freak him out," said Leif.

Elspeth shrugged. She looked at her boyfriend, who gave no sign of either approval or warning, and then back at Leif. "I don't think he's stupid, is all I'm saying."

"Do you want to try?" Leif offered to Matthew.

For the first time Matthew noticed a deck of cards on the coffee table. Perhaps the hydrangeas had been hiding it from his angle of vision. On the backs of the cards was printed a yellow sun on a black background—sol d'or, on a field sable, the symbol of sovereignty, which almost never appeared in the arms of a house except in exercises of the imagination.

Matthew looked again at Leif. There was something unstable in the air between them. He stepped, and Leif stepped with him, from the dining room into the parlor. They took seats across from the straight couple.

"I don't think I have any feelings even about tarot cards," said Matthew.

"You don't have to," said Leif. "All you need to do is feel Elspeth's feelings. Just say what you feel, and I'll tell you what card it is."

"What I feel?"

"The feeling you get from Elspeth." Leif leaned back as he lazily shuffled the deck overhand in his long fingers. "Actually, you better shuffle," he said to Elspeth, "so he doesn't get the idea it's a card trick or something." He delivered his instructions to Matthew as if giving the rules of a parlor game: "It'll be that thing that for you is always right there but that you've learned not to talk about because you've come to realize it's not there for other people. You know what I mean, don't you? You can still feel it, right?"

So the boy was a kind of shaman. A pretty, casually seductive shaman. Cautiously: "Yes."

"Most people can't anymore. That's why it's easier for them."

"Why what's easier?" asked Matthew.

"You know. Everything, really."

"Now you are creeping me out a little."

"Three cards?" asked Elspeth.

Next to her, Raleigh fidgeted. "Why do you guys always do three, anyway?"

"Makes it easier," said Leif.

"It does triple your odds," Raleigh growled. He glanced at Matthew as if to make sure that he was being credited for his skepticism.

"I can't really do the number cards," said Elspeth, "and if I draw three, there's almost always an *atout* or at least a face card in there."

"A what?" asked Matthew.

"The Moon or the Papess or a card like that. A picture card. The instructions that came with the deck are in French. I guess I could have googled for the English word, but I wanted us to be using the cards in our own way. In a made-up way."

"A scientific way," said Leif. "Numbers are kind of our Achilles' heel."

"Why do you need them? Do you want to work the casinos?"

Leif frowned. "I wish."

Elspeth drew a hand. "Aww," she murmured, as if the cards she had pulled were somehow endearing. Then she flipped them facedown onto her lap.

"What do you see?" Leif asked Matthew.

Did he see anything? Nothing had happened. He had heard Elspeth's soft exclamation, and he had watched her compose her face afterward, for the sake of the experiment, into a pleasant neutrality. Had there been anything else? He tried to revisit the sequence of his perceptions. He had also been aware of a strength that Elspeth seemed to draw from the proximity of the man beside her on the couch, and it had occurred to him, very briefly and somewhat inchoately, that the apparent contrast in the demeanors of the two, the disparity between Raleigh's truculence and Elspeth's readiness to accommodate, probably reflected a deeper harmony, the basis of which he hadn't yet seen but without which they wouldn't have felt comfortable being so unlike each other in the presence of a stranger. They were awfully young to have achieved such a harmony, but Matthew's own parents had been even younger when they had met, he knew. He didn't know the basis of his parents' harmony, either. He had always associated it with concern for his brother and him, but it must have been something more general; it had preceded his brother and him, after all. For a long time, it had seemed to enable his parents to look out at the world with a kind of doubled attentiveness. As instruments of perception, they seemed to have been calibrated, or maybe a better word was tuned, by their contact with each other, though lately the process might have begun to falter a little.

"Parents?" Matthew said aloud. "But that doesn't make any sense."

"What are these parents like?" Leif asked.

"Mild-mannered. A little worried."

"Are they kind of . . . ?" Leif folded his hands and leaned forward, as if he were playacting the word he was looking for. "Organized? But that's not what I mean exactly."

"Sensible," said Matthew, accepting Leif's image.

"The king and queen of money," Leif guessed.

Elspeth turned the cards over onto the coffee table. The third card was a three of cups.

"But my parents aren't rich," said Matthew.

"Tarot isn't like that," Leif said.

"I always think these two cards are so cute," said Elspeth. "They're so tidy. Look."

The man and woman had large eyes and dainty fingers. They looked nothing like Matthew's parents. They wore royal robes, and each carried an enormous coin. "The rulers of this world," Matthew commented.

"Because the suit is money?" Elspeth said. "I hadn't thought of that."

"Marxist tarot," Raleigh said appreciatively. "There could be a reference to Britain, since it's a French deck."

"Oh, I think the designs are older than—," Elspeth began.

"Than British capitalism?" Raleigh asked, cutting her off.

"Maybe you're right," she conceded.

"'Phlegmatic' is the word I was looking for," said Leif, shuffling the deck again.

"For the king and queen of money?" asked Matthew.

"Or for you. You look like you sit down and read whole books."

There was a compliment in having been studied. "Don't you read books?" Matthew asked.

"I try not to give the impression of being someone who reads them."

"I'm pretentious, you mean."

"No, phlegmatic," Leif insisted. "So do you believe now?"

"No," Matthew replied. "How does it work?"

"By metaphor?" Leif hazarded. "But it's a funny kind of metaphor, where you know the tenor but not the vehicle."

"It's shut-eye," Raleigh interrupted. "He's cheating, but he's so into it he doesn't realize."

"Raleigh believes in his own way," said Leif.

"I believe it works. I just don't believe there's anything to it."

"Can I talk to you a minute?" Matthew asked Leif.

"We're going to have a homo moment," Leif told the others.

"Of course," Elspeth replied, to excuse them.

Matthew rose first, and in the dance that he and Leif fell into, he was expected to lead, though since he didn't know the apartment, he had to look over his shoulder to Leif for guidance. In this awkward fashion, they made their way back into the corridor where they had come in, until, beside a row of coats hung on pegs, Matthew rounded on Leif, pushed him against the wall, and kissed him again.

"Can I see you?" asked Matthew. "But not to play cards."

Leif looked away. "Are we going to be fuckbuddies?"

"I thought we could go on a date."

Leif shrugged. "Okay."

"What?"

"You're good at it," Leif said. He looked Matthew full in the eye.

Matthew called his phone, so they would have each other's numbers. Leif's phone was as dumb as his. In another clinch, Matthew felt his cock stiffen, but he broke away. As he turned to descend the stairs, he heard Leif shout back along the corridor to his friends: "So was I wrong about him?"

It was a case of exactly the kind of boy he liked to fuck, was the way Matthew put it to himself as he unlocked his dark apartment. He liked to think through such matters a little brutally, in order to keep clear the distinction between what he wanted and what he thought he ought to want. The latter had a way of creeping in. While he was being brutal, he had to admit that even though he wanted Leif, he wasn't sure, now that he was beyond reach of the spell cast by Leif's immediate presence, that he was going to call him. There was an etiquette conformed to in most hookups, and in the months since his cohort of friends from grad school had moved away, Matthew had become used to the way it rendered disappointments as well as rewards foreseeable. Leif didn't appear to be the sort of person who would abide by even an ungentleman's agreement.

There was only one window—as, aside from the lavatory, there was only one room—to Matthew's apartment, but it was a generous one, a bow window that spanned the front wall and looked out, from the fourth story, over an avenue block; below were a bodega, a dry cleaner, a pizzeria, a tattoo parlor. The window faced southwest, and by day it was lit fiercely by sun. Tonight it was no more than faintly salted by a glare reflected upward from the pavement, and the room lay in a blue darkness, out of which were resolved, as Matthew crossed it, the familiar shadows of the card table where he ate his meals, the futon that he folded up every morning and unfolded every night, and the desk, just beside the window, where he didn't write his dissertation. In the darkness his things looked impersonal, as if he were returning home to them after a long stay in a hospital and had forgotten, or at least misplaced for a while, the roles they played in his life.

Because he used the windowsill as a shelf for library books, he had to guide the blinds, as he lowered them, into a channel that he had left open between the backs of the books and the window sash. As his desk lamp flickered on, the spines of institutional buckram shifted from apparent grays to actual olives, crimsons, and browns, the white impress of the call numbers remaining constant. He sat down to check his email. There were only the usual notifications from his department, which he was free to delete because it was his writing year and he wasn't teaching or taking any classes.

It was too late to do more than wash greens for a salad and scramble some eggs, and as he began to tear leaves into his colander, he thought about the game that he and the boy had played with the tarot cards. Seeing into other people's minds was something a literary scholar tried to do every day, hoping to perceive, across centuries, meanings that in some cases people might not even have been aware that they were giving away. But to read a living person's secret thoughts, while sitting in the same room with him . . . That was impossible, and Matthew had been asked to believe he could do it, which was the sort of game that only a young person would insist on. A test for lovers. In their first years of adjusting to an open sexuality, gays seemed to like to tell stories about themselves that were elaborate. Matthew's explanation was that it took time to learn to do without the machinery of hiding, and for a while one's story remained encumbered with unnecessary structure. He guessed that Leif's myth of himself had such a character. To protect himself, Leif had probably accreted a layer of self-regard, like a shell, which he was soon going to find it convenient to break. It would fracture along the seam of its implausibility.

If the guess was accurate, the future that was possible between Matthew and Leif was less likely to resemble a conversation than attendance at a performance, a division of roles that Matthew didn't ordinarily have much patience for.

But the boy was so beautiful. Maybe Matthew could muster up a week or two of patience.

The next morning, with a promptness that most of the men Matthew knew would have avoided as a defect of strategy, Leif called.

"I said I would help out the Kitchen with serving lunch today at Occupy."

"Is this a date?" Matthew asked.

"You and dates."

The protesters were encamped across the river, Matthew knew, in a part of the city he rarely went to. Though their camp was almost two months old, he hadn't yet visited. He agreed with most of the reforms that the protesters were demanding—or rather, making a point of not demanding—but he had the usual aesthetic problems with the left, and he didn't think of himself as political. He may have been writing on kingship, but in twenty-first-century America, he told himself, kingship was merely historical. If he gave the puzzle in his dissertation the name sovereignty, he couldn't as easily justify his lack of curiosity, but no one pressed him to justify it, and if they had, he would have pointed out that graduate students with unfinished dissertations are famously vulnerable to distractions that take the form of purposes. To give even a little of oneself to a cause so undefined would bring too many questions too close to the surface.

But now that a pretty boy had invited him . . .

He rode his bicycle into the city. It was one of those late fall days that the warming of the world has rendered so temperate and brilliant. An undeserved mercy. On the bridge, the wire diamonds of the suicide barrier fluttered past like frames of movie film, and he looked down through them at the water below, which was jade in color that day and textured like alligator skin with white caps. The sight of salt water always brought a kind of equilibrium to some inner part of him. So much water was so unfakably a thing of nature. Danger was part of its appeal. He felt alive.

Before leaving, he had looked at a map on the internet for the specific block and for a way to approach it on the downtown's one-way streets. He locked up to a street sign while still a few blocks away.

He had been too cautious, he saw as soon as he walked a block further. There were plenty of empty posts to lock a bike to. Was he nervous? He tried to check his reflection in a store window but saw only a hollow shadow in the center of the bright street scene. The crowd around him on the sidewalk didn't seem too unusual. Ponderous tourists. Straight men in shapeless suits. Maybe there were a few more of the city's young people than were usually to be found in such a charmless neighborhood. *Is there a reason they're all walking so slow?* he wondered with reflexive urban irritation.

There was; he had reached the encampment. There wasn't a vista. In fact, all he could see, at first, was a row of half a dozen people, in ordinary dress, some cheery, some solemn, holding up sheets of oaktag painted with facts and slogans. A few, instead of holding their signs, had laid them on the cement and were squatting or kneeling beside them. The important thing, evidently, was to have a human face next to every sign and a human hand ready to touch it. Police were trying to hurry pedestrians through a narrow defile between the sign holders and a mirroring palisade, a few feet away, of tourists and businesspeople taking photographs with their cell phones. It might have been a diagram in a biochemistry textbook, Matthew thought: a transfer of ions along the osculation of two membranes.

A few steps down, and Matthew was standing on the granite pavement of the occupied park, which in this corner was sunk a few feet below the sidewalk that ringed it. The occupation was surrounded, Matthew realized upon looking up. Policemen stationed along the bordering sidewalk were scanning the park's interior. Matthew watched as one shifted his gaze from spot to spot in a professional simulation of curiosity. In a far corner, a crane had raised a white metal observation cabin, which had the gleam of a new device. It must have been bought with the city's share of antiterrorism money. Its windows were darkened with the apparent intention of preventing those on the ground from knowing exactly when they were being observed.

Well, so Matthew would show up in a database. To mind too much about the surveillance would be a form of surrender to it.

Leif hadn't specified which part of the encampment, and Matthew was a few minutes early, so he went for a wander. There were signs about student loans, carbon emissions, and a recent case of police brutality. At the People's Library, which was an array of transparent plastic bins full of books and hand-stapled pamphlets, he didn't see any scholarship on Renaissance England. Further along, under the kind of square canopy that Latino families bring to the park for quinceañeras, a few protesters were working at computers. Otherwise the infrastructure seemed to consist of tarps, pizza boxes, folding plastic tables, duct tape, and the granite pavement of the park itself. He had expected to be one of many lookers-on, but most people were in conversations that supplied them with a visible and ongoing context of belonging, in twos, threes, or larger circles, and Matthew felt the absence of such a context in his own case. The longer he went without speaking to anyone, the more aware he became of his isolation. He saw people signaling with frilly hand gestures that he had read about online, which meant "Agree," "Disagree," or "Louder, please," and he admired their shamelessness but didn't think he would ever be able to make the gestures himself. Similarly, when he walked across the path of a speech being transmitted by human microphone—a relay of people amplifying a speech by shouting it, phrase by phrase, as it reached them—he couldn't bring himself to participate. He had a history of not joining things. He hoped his reticence wasn't registering with the people around him. He didn't want to seem unsympathetic. He didn't want to be mistaken for a cop.

He came to the drum circle, but on the matter of aggressive noise-making, he was for better or worse a conventional homosexual, and he moved on.

In one zone, nothing rose higher than his waist. Though it was midday, young men and women lay resting on sleeping bags, their hands mittened, their necks scarved, their eyes intermittently closed. A few were spooning each other, indifferent to observation. Many had waterproofed the underside of their sleeping bags with blue tarps or with black plastic garbage bags that they had cut open and unfolded into sheets, and a number of them lay beside a roll of clothes and possessions wrapped in a matching sheet of blue tarp or black plastic. Here and there a roll was the length and shape of a person and resembled a bagged corpse. While Matthew was watching, one of these apparent corpses uncovered a living face; a man was shifting in his sleep.

As Matthew stood at the edge of this dormitory, he noticed Leif sauntering toward him, shading his eyes in the sharp sun. *Come here*, Matthew silently summoned him. In Leif's company Matthew wouldn't feel so cut off from the people around him. What he was standing in the middle of was a kind of celebration, but until he spotted Leif, he hadn't been aware of wishing so badly to be able to respond to the invitation to join it. What a dangerous wish.

"How old are you again?" Matthew asked.

"Twenty-four. But I never told you."

They studied each other. It would have been less awkward if they had already gone to bed together, Matthew thought. There was a reservation in Leif's manner, and it was probably the reservation usual with attractive men who think of themselves as serious—a hunch that Matthew wouldn't be. In most cases, Matthew knew from experience, the reservation was little more than a pretext for shifting onto Matthew the responsibility for light-mindedness, a burden Matthew was happy to shoulder. But the attraction of Leif, perhaps, was something in him that was genuinely re-fractory to routine.

"For the record," Leif said, "you're fairly transparent to me right now."

"We could go to my place."

Leif took up one of Matthew's hands in both of his, in a manner that suggested that Matthew's assertion of lust was a gift that he found over-whelming and was therefore going to put off. He turned Matthew's hand palm up, and Matthew opened it. "You have a long lifeline," Leif said. "That's how the reading always starts, isn't it."

"You would know."

"I actually wouldn't?"

Matthew tightened his hand around one of Leif's.

"Ow," Leif said without meaning it. A text arrived on his phone. "It's time to go unpack the lunch of the revolutionaries. Do you want to come?"

Leif led Matthew across the park to three folding tables that had been lined up end to end. A black woman in a quilted sleeveless traffic-orange down jacket was spraying the tabletops and wiping them. When Leif greeted her, she merely paused, while still bent over the table, and craned her neck to exchange kisses with him until she noticed that he meant to introduce a friend, at which point she drew herself up to full height and pulled off a latex glove. "Diana," she named herself, as they shook hands. She seemed to be Matthew's age. Behind her, in a work space protected by a tarp strung between two trees, a heavyset woman with pronounced eye-glasses waved at Leif, twinkling her fingers.

"Where's the dolly?" Leif asked Diana.

"It's been a while since you've been here, hasn't it."

"I'm a bad boy."

"No, no, no. Not unless you want to be. I just mean, you don't know the latest. The police have stopped letting them in."

"Dollies? Are you serious?"

"They say they're vehicles. No bicycles, either." She let Leif enjoy a few moments of outrage. "Exactly," she said, of the faces he made.

"I should have brought my board," said Leif.

"They're vehicles, too, now."

A hatless man with close-cropped hair and green eyes had approached them, and he now struck Leif on the shoulder. "I'll carry one, you carry one," he said.

"Uh, no?" Leif replied.

"What are we carrying?" Matthew asked.

There were two large insulated plastic tanks—a brown rectangular one for hot drinking water and a yellow barrel-shaped one for cold—that had to be filled up in the back kitchen of a diner with an indulgent owner a block and a half away.

"Chris is in our working group," Leif said of the green-eyed man.

"The food group?" Matthew asked.

"The other one."

But the man didn't look like someone who would be interested in the interior of another person's mind. He looked confident rather than sensitive, and so radiantly and abundantly straight that in an earlier era, Matthew imagined, his was the type who would have been happy to let you blow him so long as he had a chance to beat you up for it afterward. "You helping us out?" the man asked.

"With lunch?" Matthew asked in return. He had to hope that the man couldn't in fact read minds. "Between you and me we could probably carry one of these," he suggested to Leif.

In fact, the tanks when empty weighed little, and Matthew was easily able to carry one by himself while the green-eyed Chris carried the other. "Coming through," Chris warned. The visibility of their task, Matthew felt as the three of them edged gently through the crowd, conferred a distinction. Pride in it wasn't perhaps a very Occupy sentiment to be having, but considering that Matthew had been insisting to himself a moment ago that he never belonged to groups of any kind, it seemed forgivable to hold on for a minute or two to a pleasure not quite orthodox. There were several elements compounded in it. There was the glamour of usefulness—what a child feels when asked to fold cloth napkins into hats for a party that his parents are throwing. There was the clemency of an arranger of a picnic who forbears to lord it over the mere picnickers; they were performing their errand gladly and mildly. And then there was the simple tension of muscle. Matthew felt as male and as strong as Chris and as gay as Leif, identification between the three of them, however brief their acquaintance, having become unfussy through collaboration.

In the steel-and-white-tile kitchen of the diner, the cooks didn't attempt English and only Chris attempted a few words of Spanish, but meaning was evident. The cooks were brusque, jolly, and magnanimous. The palm of one held the boys off while with practiced aim the grip of another deftly tipped a pot of boiling water into the square brown tank as it sat in a deep sink. Once the cook had poured the water, he clicked the lid shut with fasteners whose mechanism Matthew hadn't yet had a chance to understand, and when Matthew and Leif bent to pick the tank up, he tapped on a brim just under the top to show them where it would be easier to get a handhold.

"You got it?" Chris asked. Matthew and Leif shuffled in order to be sure of the synchronization of their steps. Chris, meanwhile, having fist-bumped the cooks, held his tank by its strap with one hand, canting against its weight, which he arced his arm and his shoulders to distribute. "You got it?" he repeated. To watch the parade that the three of them were making, the patrons of the restaurant looked away from their conversations and up from their coffees. To watch the clowns, a.k.a. the heroes of the moment, go by. Chris and Leif sang out thanks.

Hurried by the strain of his burden, Chris soon left Leif and Matthew behind. Once he was safely out of earshot, and Matthew and Leif were tottering together alone, knocking the tank into the sides of each other's knees with every third step, Leif asked Matthew where he grew up. Matthew described the suburb to the northwest of the city where his parents still lived and where little ever happened, apart from the coarsening successions typical in such places: a bank building converted into a drugstore, a church at the town's old crossroads pulled down for the sake of a mall, and then the mall falling into neglect upon the advent of a second mall positioned, more strategically, next to the throughway.

"Your parents are still together?" Leif asked.

"Yeah."

"It sounds nice," said Leif. "Snug."

The comment didn't seem to be ironic. "What about you?" Matthew asked.

"Oh." The weight of the tank wouldn't let him shrug. "My mother lives in a little ranch house with vinyl siding in Vermont. It's on top of a hill." He seemed to glance at the landscape with his mind's eye. "So we didn't spook you last night?"

"You don't seem to have," Matthew said.

"Would you be willing to try it again?"

"Maybe."

"Not here," Leif said. "Almost everyone here has it a little. If you tuned in on all of that . . ."

"You make it sound dangerous," Matthew said.

The boy didn't reply.

They set the tank down, to rest for a moment. Matthew realized that he was hoping that the implausible fantasy was something he could wait out. Matthew's advantage, in being older, was that he was more familiar with waiting.

The boy combed his hair with his fingers.

"Is Chris really in your mind-reading group?" Matthew asked, as they picked the tank up again.

"He's not any good, but he's really into it."

"He's something."

"Raleigh knows him from New Orleans," Leif replied. "All us girls had a crush on him at first." He glanced at Matthew. "You don't like that, do you."

"That you think he's hot?"

"No," said Leif. "'Us girls.' But you're not allowed to be square about gender identity here. At the start of an assembly, when a person says their name, they also say their pronouns."

"Which ones do you ask for?"

"I don't usually get all Ursula K. Le Guin about it." They set the tank down to take another break, and Leif shook a finger at Matthew: "It's a matter of human dignity, you know."

"In the *Arcadia* . . . ," Matthew began. At this point he still hadn't disclosed that he was a graduate student.

"In the *Arcadia*," Leif prompted. "Go on."

"After one of the heroes dresses as a woman, Sidney calls him by his new name from then on."

"Her new name," Leif corrected.

"Have you read it?"

"No, but."

"It's a little confusing. He's so consistent about it. The least he could do is slip up."

"Slipping up can be fun, too," said Leif.

It was another of the boasts that Leif's beauty allowed him to make, Matthew decided. Any quality that went so high would partake of both aspects.

By the time they returned to the Kitchen, as the serving area of the encampment was somewhat aspirationally called, Chris's tank was in place and Chris himself had moved on. Matthew and Leif sat down with the women, and after rubbing their hands with sanitizer, flapping them dry, and slipping on latex gloves, they prepared lunch. It was the least impressive meal of the day, Leif explained. A local pizzeria usually delivered pizzas that strangers had donated by phone or online—the number ebbed and flowed with the mysterious tides of news coverage and of the internet generally—but the rest of the meal was often cold, unlike breakfast and dinner.

The health department required the volunteers to wear hats, and they had agreed among themselves—*consensed*, as they called it—to minimize, in their presentation of the food, the number of surfaces that were communally touched. Leif stood an array of small paper cups on the table in front of him and into each one placed a single baby carrot and a single cherry tomato. Matthew set about making peanut butter and jelly sandwiches on grocery store bread, and with assembly-line efficiency, the glasses-wearing woman tucked these sandwiches into plastic baggies, which she sealed with red twist ties. There was a debate about a large bowl of popcorn, the kernels of which Leif saw as just so many fomites and lobbied for portioning into paper cups like the vegetables, but there wasn't enough time and there didn't seem to be enough paper cups; instead, one cup was deputized scoop. There was no time even to debate a carton of cheddar-flavored goldfish crackers, and at the very last minute, a woman in a bandanna ran up with an enormous plastic tub of what she identified as tuna salad with sauce gribiche, along with half a dozen loaves that she called peasant bread. The peasant bread had a thick, almost black crust. It was to go with the tuna gribiche, the woman said, in the voice of someone whose suggestions were customarily followed. The volunteers were able to find a ladle for the tuna, but no one had a bread knife. To the woman donating the tuna, the members of the Food Working Group were all smiles, but "I sometimes think the bane of my existence is unsliced bread," was Diana's mutter. A young man stepped up, fortunately, who was willing to have his hands sanitized and to hack away at the tough loaves with an unserrated, not very sharp knife, which was all they had, and he did hack away at them, just as the hungry were precipitating out of the crowd into a line behind him. The consequences were no worse than raggedy, distorted slices.

For a while the line seemed to bring almost as much food as it took away: apples in an orchard's white-and-green paper sack, a family pack of individual-size bags of corn chips, a bowl of pink-shelled, hard-boiled eggs. Matthew and Leif made plates for themselves and seceded a little, finding a few feet of empty ledge.

Matthew felt the cold of the stone through the seat of his jeans while, on his face, he felt the touch of the sun as its light fell through the tracery of a tree's bare branches. When one thinks about how far away the sun is and realizes that one is feeling its touch nonetheless . . . He took off his wool hat and tucked it under his butt. "Have you slept out here?"

Leif nodded. "I learned that water-resistant isn't actually the same thing as waterproof."

Matthew imagined the boy on his side in the dark, twisting in a sleeping bag wet with the plaza's runoff. The Leif who sat presently beside him, meanwhile, sprinkled goldfish on his tuna salad and fastidiously matched exactly one goldfish to each forkful of tuna. "It means something to you here," Matthew hazarded.

The boy coughed and then pounded his own chest to clear it.

The place was another test for Matthew. Was he passing? Did he need to believe in it any more than in Leif's psychology experiments? He had felt uncomfortable when, for a few moments, Leif had spoken of unfastening his gender identity, but he knew that in any environment where such an unfastening was imaginable, they were safe. They were protected here by the only bulwark that homosexuals ever really believe in: a temporary rebellion of pleasure against order. And there was something else here, too, the scent of which Matthew recognized from having hunted for ideas about kingship in seventeenth-century pamphlets and transcripts. The scent of new governance, it might be called. People here felt that they were getting in at the beginning. Everything was going to be rebuilt from scratch; there was so much to be done. Acts had to be fresh and arbitrary, like a gardener's with seedlings, tender at one moment and cruel the next. Free of history and also pregnant with it. In this sunlight it seemed like it could all be done without money. Without the Democratic Party. Without proper names, even. It was so early that one recognized that there was no place for personal ambition, yet one felt the excitement nonetheless of one's almost personal recruitment by the new power. The growing power. Whether one was an idealist or an opportunist—and maybe one was still too young to know which career one was looking forward to—being here might make all the difference.

A great menace to the writing of dissertations.

"This place makes me feel like I'm not wrong to think that it's all coming together," Leif said.

Matthew set aside his plate. He leaned back on his arms to catch a little more of the sun as it came through the tree and to show himself off a little.

"It's one thing," Leif continued, "to keep it to yourself that you're aware what other people are thinking and feeling. It's another to hold in upon yourself that the world is ending."

It was pleasant to hear the end mentioned so matter-of-factly, as if they were dispensing with preliminary arguments that most people never found their way to the other side of.

"I don't necessarily mean a meteor hitting the earth or anything," Leif went on. "It might just be ending the way it ended in 1914 or 1939. But I think it's because the world is ending that what's different about people like Elspeth and me has become so hard for us to ignore." He had a musical voice, and despite the banter and cachinnation near them, and the drumming and chanting in the distance, his words took up an unassuming but distinct order in the air, as if they were sparrows assembling in the empty branches of the tree that Matthew had been looking up into.

"I don't get it," Matthew said. "What does knowing how people feel have to do with knowing that the world is ending?"

"It's ending *in them*," said Leif. "They have feelings about it."

"Why don't they know, then?"

"They do know, in a way, just not a way they can talk about."

"You're going to talk about their feelings for them," Matthew said.

"We're going to talk about *our* feelings, which have a *relation* to theirs."

"How do you get politics out of that?"

"You don't, maybe? I just want to understand it a little. To help people understand it. I get worried that it becomes overwhelming for some people. For someone like you, for instance."

He was honest about not knowing, Matthew saw. And the power that Matthew was curious about must exist, even if, as Matthew had to believe, Leif himself misunderstood the nature of it. Matthew could feel its real force as it acted on his own person; he was being seduced by it. Into antres vast and deserts idle. Matthew had wanted to go to bed with the boy, and he was being led to a plane even more tenuous than utopia.

It was a strange gift. Matthew was meeting Leif just as Leif was in the process of discovering what it was. He was still trying it out. How it would develop, what he would do with it, what it really was, and what he would come to think that it was—those were in the future. At present Leif's gift was as fluid as the congregation in the park around them. A potential rather than a quantity. It was hard to give a name to, but Matthew suspected that it would be even less nameable later, once Leif had finished talking his way out of the framework of expectations that he had been born into. At the moment it was still early but not too early. Maybe Matthew was even in time to save Leif from it.

When, in the artificial gloaming of Matthew's room, an hour or so after midnight, Leif got up from Matthew's futon, it was the sight of the boy's pale shoulders, seen from behind as he loped away into the blue darkness, that brought home to Matthew his innocence.

"Do you have to be up for anything?" Matthew asked, the alarm clock in his hand, when Leif returned.

"Rich people have always been tacky, haven't they," Leif said, as he stalked ahead of Matthew into a room of eighteenth-century panels. Women with doll-like faces and all-too-human bodies were sitting in bowers and in swings, accompanied by men with complexions as sugary as theirs.

Over breakfast, Matthew had taxed himself to come up with a parallel to Leif's invitation to Occupy: a city sight that Leif ought to have seen but hadn't. They were as a result visiting a mansion and art collection that had been left to the public by one of the point-oh-one percent a century ago.

"It's just ladies and their beaux," said Matthew. "I don't think they're as tacky as a glitter skull." A human skull sequined with diamonds had recently been auctioned as an artwork for a very high amount.

"Are they whores?" Leif asked.

"You know, it's the French Enlightenment. Everyone looks like a whore, everyone talks like a philosopher."

"Can I tweet that?"

"One night together, and you want to tweet me?"

"Only the funny parts," said Leif. He took out of a back pocket a pencil stub and a little red notebook the size and shape of a passport. "Don't look."

"Why not?" Matthew made as if to look anyway. "That's so cute."

Leif turned his back. "It's private. There are other things in here besides the table talk of Matthew Fisher."

"Is it for your poetry?" Matthew asked in a more tactful voice.

"If a line comes to me."

They had had their confessions. Matthew had admitted to graduate school, and Leif, to writing poetry, or, as he preferred to characterize it, "poetry." He worked in a coffee shop by day to pay his rent, but he had published in a few journals. It was part of Matthew's snobbishness as a scholar that he didn't believe real poetry was still being written, but the disbelief wasn't too serious, and he was willing to suspend it. They were having such a good day. And at least Leif wrote his poetry, which was more than Matthew could say for his scholarship. Today Matthew even felt willing to read the poetry, and he had said so, not too convincingly.

"This is the room," Matthew said, as they walked into what had been the millionaire's parlor.

Leif followed Matthew's sight line. "Is this it?" he asked.

Matthew had told Leif that his favorite painting in the world was in the museum. Faced with Leif's question, the painting, when Matthew himself looked at it, seemed flat and, if not small, because it wasn't small, then limited. Contained. Matthew hadn't seen it in a while. It was just a painting. A saint in a rocky landscape. The rock, which might have been limestone, was green for some reason. Matthew had permitted himself to have a favorite painting because he didn't know much about art, and he had chosen this one probably because it didn't have anything to do with what he studied. There were no kings and no parliaments in it. It was early modern, but it was Italian. It looked as if it was set somewhere in Tuscany. There was a rabbit hidden behind the saint, watching—the rabbit was something Matthew could point out, if he had to find something to say—and small plants were painted against the pale jade rock so distinctly that one felt one ought to be able to recognize them and say their names. Matthew didn't know the names. Nothing in the painting was the sort of thing that he was supposed to know or care about, and he was far enough along in grad school that for him his ignorance made for a feeling of liberty. In liking it he was being a bit of a tourist. And maybe, since he was taking pleasure and perhaps even a kind of pride in his ignorance, a philistine. Was it a good painting as a painting? He didn't really know.

He checked on Leif. Leif was still studying the work.

The saint was alone. Was the solitude what Matthew liked about it? On the saint's desk, just outside the cave where he slept, there was a book. The Bible, probably. Near it was a skull, the traditional reminder to pay attention. One had the impression that the moment before, the saint had been reading the Bible, in the sunlight. Maybe the implied scene of reading was what Matthew liked.

"It's beautiful," Leif quietly said.

Matthew knew that he had set himself up for the feeling he now had, but he was surprised by it anyway: a sense, in sharing an image of solitude, of no longer being alone.

"It's a green sunlight instead of a green shade," Leif continued.

"I think it's the rocks that are green."

"But somehow the light is coming through that laurel."

"I didn't know it was a laurel," Matthew admitted.

"Well, he was a poet."

"Who was?"

"Francis. It is Francis, isn't it?"

Was the saint looking at the laurel? He seemed actually to be looking through it. The viny branches of the laurel, which held together like a gathered bouquet, were bending down toward the saint, responsive to him as nothing else in the painting was. The saint wasn't alone, Matthew realized. He was seeing and feeling the sun, the way Matthew had felt it in the park yesterday. Its touch. Every other thing in the painting stood still in its place as if giving testimony of its independent being. Even the skull on the saint's desk registered a distinct life.

Not knowing exactly what it was was part of the charm. Not knowing what it was, not having to say, not having to justify oneself. To do something that no one had managed to define yet and to do it without permission— to represent the potential for that was what it was for, to a great extent, Matthew saw.

It lay between them, though, something of an embarrassment. Matthew hung back for a while from asking about it, because he didn't want to focus Leif's attention on it any more than necessary. Left untouched, it might fall away like a crush gone stale. Matthew could hope, anyway.

The trouble was that Matthew found it difficult to keep even his own mind away. There was something noble about exactly its silliness—about exactly the part that Matthew found most embarrassing. Moreover, to show no curiosity at all would have been, in this case, as awkward as the repeated turning away of a compliment, because Leif understood some of his attraction to Matthew in terms of it. Matthew had a share of it, Leif believed, and he kept repeating that he believed in Matthew's share. Maybe Leif was too young to be able to understand attraction more simply; maybe this belief made it easier for him. It really was how he saw the world, at any rate, and it had the merit, even in Matthew's eyes, of being distinctively Leif's own way of seeing it. As such it called out to be answered by Matthew somehow. Met by him.

If Matthew could see lower motives for their going to bed together, there was no need to be cruel about higher ones, even if they might be imaginary. That much was simple diplomacy. Not that diplomacy was going to be enough.

Matthew found himself wanting to ask a question about it the afternoon of their third day together. They had put their boxers back on and were sitting up on the opened futon. Leif hadn't volunteered his own apartment yet; roommates, was his excuse. The bare skin of their backs was clammy against the white paint of Matthew's wall. They were playing a game where Matthew would pick up with his left hand a hand of Leif's, drop it into his right, and then pick it up with his left again. It took a few iterations before Leif understood that he should let his hand fall freely. It would have been tactless of Matthew to ask what he most wanted to know, namely, how much Leif himself actually believed. For purposes that even Matthew was able to see, Leif didn't need to believe everything. Instead, Matthew therefore asked when it had started.

"Didn't you ever play with a Ouija board when you were a kid?" Leif countered.

"I didn't believe it," Matthew answered.

"But it said something."

"It wouldn't shut up. My friend was cheating."

"What if he wasn't," Leif suggested.

"Then I should look him up right now on Facebook and apologize. It was a big fight, and we stopped speaking. Edward Rocket. I used to make fun of his name. Irvine, California. We were in second grade. It would have been 1987."

"I was born that year."

"Oh, fuck you," said Matthew.

"I was," Leif insisted. "Were you scared?"

"Well, dead people."

"It wasn't dead people."

"Uh . . ."

"It was my fetus, trying to reach you. Let me try something. Close your eyes."

Matthew closed them. Leif climbed astraddle him.

"What are you doing?"

"Keep them shut. Do you feel it?" Leif asked.

"What are you doing?" Matthew asked again.

"Do you feel it?" Leif repeated.

"You're holding something in front of my forehead."

"But how do you know?" Leif asked. "Your eyes are shut."

It was as if Matthew were feeling an indentation or a concentration of some kind in the air half an inch in front of his face. "X-rays," Matthew said.

"It's your third eye," Leif said, mock-significantly, as Matthew opened his two worldly ones again.

"What are you talking about."

"That's where your third eye is, you know. In the middle of your forehead. That's the kind of game I played in second grade."

Leif stepped off him, knee by knee. Matthew felt that he ought to give Leif a confession in return. He thought of the mistake he sometimes made, at the front door of a building, of saying the greeting that another person was about to say to him. *Hello, Matthew.* Or *Thank you*, even when he was the one holding the door. It came, he thought, from a wish to meet the other person halfway that somehow overreached.

Leif tried another way of explaining himself: "What if the thing you always hear—'Oh, his wife says she sort of knew, all along'—is true? Of every feeling. Dislike. A crush. Mistrust."

Was Leif trying to say something about the two of them? But if he sensed Matthew's reservations, he must also have sensed Matthew's reluctance to talk about them.

"If we never really fool anyone," Leif said, "why not just say?"

"I have these, by the way?" said Leif, before he left on their fourth morning. "I didn't have time to wash them."

The two of them had had a long weekend, a movable one that hadn't coincided with any weekend recorded in the calendar, as is possible when a poet-barista gets together with a grad student in his dissertation year, but now they had to return to their separate storylines, at least for a while. Leif had a double shift at the café coming up, and Matthew had reading to do, as a grad student always does.

Leif was offering up a plastic grocery bag. Inside were a T-shirt, a pair of underwear, and a pair of socks that he had borrowed the morning after he first stayed over.

"Why thank you," said Matthew.

"Is it pervy?"

"Not on your part."

After Leif was gone, when Matthew was unwrapping the clothes to throw them into his hamper, he did wonder and he brought them to his nose. The only perversity was in his thought that if Leif were hit by a car while the two of them were apart there would be no other way to experience his presence one last time. The smell was of cotton that has been against skin. Like bread, but less than that. Like a drawer that one used to keep bread in.

It occurred to Matthew that in his finicky wish to pin down the right metaphor, he was like a courtly lover refining his sonnet about the sweetness of his lady's breath.

Southeast of the park that was near Matthew's apartment, a broad nineteenth-century avenue ran to the sea, and about a mile down it, there was a campus of the city's system of colleges. Sometimes Matthew worked in its library when he needed a quiet place away from home and didn't have the patience for the subway ride to his own university. He put a Samuel Daniel volume, his current notebook, and two pens into his shoulder bag, and he unlocked his bike from the basement.

The elms and plane trees that raised their branches above the bike path were still losing the last of their leaves. Wind, or at any rate eddies from the cars rushing angrily past on the avenue, kept the cement of the path mostly clear, but leaves were lodged decoratively edgewise in the grass of its margin. Matthew had been hoping that he would be able to think about Leif while he biked—that he would be carried forward in his thoughts about him by the sensations of progress and perspective that came when one was moving quickly and unprotectedly—but the path wasn't level, and he had to study the seams of its cement panels, which the freezings and thawings of previous years had shoved into each other and out of alignment, plate-tectonically. At the end of each block, too, the path dipped into and out of a crossroad, and he had to keep a lookout for spasms of territoriality and resentment by drivers. He held his thoughts off.

In the library they came back to him. He sat in his usual carrel, a solitaire hidden from its peers by three rows of bookshelves that undergraduates no longer even went through the motions of consulting. He sat down in his customary, vaguely Danish-looking chair, took off his shoes, tucked his wind-chilled feet under him, and thought, *What have I got myself into?* He opened his book, and he opened his notebook, but they seemed to belong to a life he only faintly remembered. Did he really want a lover right now? How far had it gone? Was there already an expectation of fidelity? Did he want there to be? Was he proud of Leif, as a conquest?

He could start there. He thought he might be proud of the conquest, but he had no one to show Leif off to. He couldn't call his ex. There was no question that what was between them was over; they had never even attempted a nostalgic and fraternal session of sex by Skype. But they hadn't, on the other hand, reached the point of telling each other about new dates, and Matthew didn't think his ex was likely to want to hear that Matthew was dating a beautiful poet. A conjurer. A leader of men.

Matthew remembered having kissed the boy a few hours ago. He had sucked on his tongue. Sucked at the pleasure that was at the root of the world. God! It was so enjoyable to think about the strangeness of the fact of a new lover. It was like the ache in muscles the day after one has gone for a run for the first time in a long time. He remembered suddenly that Leif had written down for him Elspeth's address so that they could find each other there two nights from now. He took the slip out of his wallet. The paper was smooth and cream-colored; Leif had torn it from his little red poetry notebook. It wasn't even Leif's address; Matthew still didn't know Leif's address. But it was Leif's handwriting. A loosened version of architects' capitals. The strokes of the letters were as impersonal as spiders' legs. Matthew thought he saw that the impersonality was one of Leif's jokes, one of his masks. The paper had no aura other than a trace of the eel skin of Matthew's own wallet.

No sight line could fall on Matthew in the carrel where he was sitting, and experimentally he held the slip of paper over his book and notebook, as if his attention were a dog that could be trained by association and shifted. It didn't shift; he put the slip of paper away. He stared at his book and at the notes he had made from it almost a week before—

> *What, are they of so fatal a degree,*
> *That they cannot descend from that, and live?*
> *Unless they still be Kings can they not be?*

—and after half an hour he became aware that the sunlight was hitting the wall beyond the blinders of his carrel at a steeper angle. The morning was losing its subtlety and turning into mere day, and he was still in the same chair. He was nearly invisible on his own campus, now that he wasn't teaching and had lost his friends, and here in the city university's library he existed only liminally, as a body, and not at all as a person. It felt slightly unreal to be so full of Leif and of sex with Leif in such a place. Glass, pinewood louvers, and muted carpeting. He had grown up in educational institutions built in the forward-looking architectural style of the 1970s, or knockoffs thereof. Maybe this carpet hadn't been so muted when first installed. To still be sitting in a setting like this one past thirty, still technically a student . . . There were days when the academic way of life suited him, when, in fact, he took pride in his ability to accommodate himself to it. He went for weeks sometimes, for example, without reading the news, because what would the news be able to tell him about kingship in early modern Britain? He was setting himself outside the history of his own time in order to immerse himself in the history of Elizabeth I's, or Richard II's, or Charles I's, depending on the chapter he was working on, and it was the ferocity of his asceticism—this is where pride came in—that would win him a professorship someday. Probably not this year, though, since no department had replied to any of his applications.

There was a sort of historical jet lag in his topic, an inadvertent thematization of his own predicament. Sometimes he was almost guilty of trying to, say, explain Shakespeare by reference to the events of the Commonwealth, declared half a century later. But he saw the mistake and hoped that he would be credited with being too clever to make it unknowingly. He was careful to qualify his interpretations, and his advisers said not to worry. The more cynical one joked that anyway, in this job market, there was such a thing as too fine a specialization, chronologically speaking, and a little anachronism might be prudent.

At the moment prudence seemed to Matthew like something that he was probably only capable of arriving at accidentally. The sun was peering down from an even sharper height. It would be lunchtime at Occupy soon. It was also going to be lunchtime here, and he was starving. He stood up.

A peanut butter sandwich in hand, the arms of his shirt soaked from having biked so far, Matthew saw no sign of Leif but recognized Elspeth and her imperfectly bearded boyfriend at a folding table. "Is it like therapy?" they were being asked by a beautiful Mediterranean woman, about Matthew's age, in a stylish peacoat with comically large brass buttons. "It almost sounds like the sort of thing my therapist would be happy to hear I had joined."

"Kind of," said Elspeth.

"By which she means no," Raleigh glossed.

On the tabletop beside Raleigh and Elspeth stood an empty pizza box that had been opened up as a trestle, on the forward-facing white bottom of which the word SECRETS had been inked in ballpoint pen, each letter traced three times for visibility, and then encircled and cross-barred in red marker to symbolize negation.

"Are you recruiting?" Matthew asked.

"Would you care to join our working group, sir?" asked Raleigh.

"Go ahead and explain it to him," the woman in the peacoat told Raleigh and Elspeth. "That'll give me another chance."

"We're the Working Group for the Refinement of the Perception of Feelings," said Elspeth.

"WTFRPF," said Raleigh.

"Oh, maybe it's a joke," the woman said, aloud but as if commenting only to herself. She caught Matthew's eye. "I mean, their whole idea for the group could be a joke, couldn't it?" She spoke as if a joke would be as disappointing to her as an activity that her therapist would approve of.

Elspeth tried to explain. "The idea is what if people were to talk about their feelings and not be so careful to make sure that nothing happens on account of talking about them."

"You can't just leave out the part about how we read each other's minds," Raleigh protested.

"Sounds interesting," said Matthew, playing his role as shill.

"It does?" asked the woman. "I'm still quite confused."

"In fact I'll join," said Matthew.

"Just like that?" asked the woman.

"Actually, we're just pretending not to know each other," Matthew confessed, gesturing between himself and the young couple.

"Oh, I've been *deceived*, I see," she said.

"But the thing is," said Matthew, "we knew you'd see through us."

"You've lost me again."

"Because of our refinement of—what is it?"

"Refinement of the Perception of Feelings," Elspeth supplied.

"RPTGIF."

"Stop it, Raleigh," said Elspeth.

"Is that the official name now?" Matthew asked.

"I came up with it last night," Elspeth replied. "I think it's more precise."

"You're psychics or something," said the woman in the peacoat.

"Not me," said Raleigh. "I'm not any good at it."

"Our friend Leif is the only one who's *really* any good," said Elspeth.

"You know, this is pretty batty," said the woman.

"Oh, we know!" Raleigh agreed.

"What's it for, even, if it *is* real?" she asked. "I mean, it's a parlor trick, isn't it?" She included Matthew in her question. She had a grand manner, and one could see that in her mind it exempted her from any suspicion of rudeness. "Will telepathy replace the people's mic? It *would* be less roughhewn that way."

"One of the ideas is we'll use it to break crypto, actually," said Raleigh.

"Crypto?" the woman echoed. "That's like codes, right? Curiouser and curiouser." She looked at their pizza box indulgently. "I *so* want to be in on this." She sounded as if she were making an aside to a friend, though no friend of hers happened to be present.

"Crypto, really?" asked Matthew.

"That's why I'm supposed to work on the number cards," said Elspeth.

"Is this Leif's idea?"

"It's more that it's Raleigh's idea that it should be Leif's idea," Elspeth admitted.

"No, Leif's into it," Raleigh insisted. "And Chris is *really* into it."

"What 'crypto' will you break, exactly?" the woman asked. "My Gmail account?"

"Government secrets," said Raleigh. "Corporate misdoings."

"Drones and Bank of America and so on," the woman suggested.

"Exactly."

"And you'll do it with . . . mind waves."

"You make us sound crazy," said Raleigh, who didn't sound as if he minded.

"You're giving her the wrong impression," Elspeth objected. She tried once more to convey the idea: "It's about admitting that most of the time people are more aware than they'd like to let on of how other people are feeling. That's all. And that it hurts to be aware, if you can't talk about it."

"Fascinating," said the woman politely.

"You must have felt it sometimes," said Elspeth. "You came over to our table."

"And you're in on this, too?" the woman asked Matthew, appealing to him perhaps on the grounds that like her, he was a responsible age.

"I'm a fellow traveler."

"He hooked up with Leif," Raleigh revealed.

"Raleigh," Elspeth said reproachfully.

"And Leif is the swami or whatever," said the woman, arranging their story in her mind. "That makes you the groupie." She pointed a finger at Matthew.

"I'm a grad student in English, so . . ."

"So you're easy?" the woman finished for him. "Oh, I like you all so much, but you *are* crazy. Can I come to your meeting anyway? Even if I think so? Maybe I'll turn out to be psychic, too."

"You might be," said Raleigh.

"You all look so suspiciously sane, is the thing," the woman said. "Of course, I'm a poor judge."

"There seems to be a difference of opinion about what we're supposed to be believing in, exactly," noted Matthew.

"You should definitely come," Elspeth said, welcoming the woman. "It's at my apartment. The apartment I share with my roommates. They're not in it, by the way."

"He's not your roommate?" asked the woman, indicating Raleigh.

"He's my boyfriend," Elspeth explained.

"Oh, I see." She took down Elspeth's address and gave her name as Julia.

"What brings you to Occupy?" Raleigh asked as the dust stirred up by the beauty of their new recruit settled.

"The peanut butter," Matthew answered.

"Leif's not here."

"I know."

"Doing a background check?"

"I did do some googling," Matthew admitted. "I read a couple of his poems."

"There was a really great one in *Fence* last year," said Raleigh. "A longer one. You should check it out."

"Are you a poet, too?" Matthew asked.

"I only write code."

"Raleigh's a hacktivist," said Elspeth.

"No, I'm just a coder. I admire those guys, though. When they're not being complete assholes."

Now that the game of inducting Julia was over, the three of them were lapsing into politeness. Raleigh asked Matthew what he did for a living, and Matthew confessed he was in grad school.

"What's your dissertation about?" Raleigh asked.

"Oh god, really?"

Raleigh pointed to the emblem on the pizza box.

"There's an old legal term, 'reversion,'" Matthew began. "You possess something in reversion if another person has the use of it now but you'll get it after they die. Someone from another branch of your family may be living in a manor, say, and it will be yours if you manage to outlive them. Sometimes Shakespeare uses the word metaphorically, to mean anything in your future, anything you're looking forward to, but legally, technically, it's something you might not live long enough to put your hands on. My thesis is that in the poetry of the sixteenth and seventeenth centuries, the individual is no longer thinking of himself as the subject of a king but as someone who himself has a kingship in reversion. The interesting thing is it starts to happen quite early. Half a century before the demise of Charles I."

Elspeth asked, "Charles is the one who—?"

"They chopped off his head," Raleigh told her.

"That's what I was going to say."

"There's this fixation in the poetry on the metaphysics of kingship," Matthew continued. "On how kingship can be transferred and how it can be incorporated into a particular person and what sort of thing it really is, and the fixation has something to do with anxiety over who will succeed the virgin queen, and something to do with anxiety over how to think about the Host now that England is no longer Catholic—"

"Is this history or literature?" Raleigh interrupted.

"It's literature. I'm faking the history."

"Go on."

"It has something to do with succession and something to do with Communion wafers, but I think it has to be economic, too, because reversionary kingship is seeping in through the foundations of the self, the way economic alterations in structure do. It's a paradoxical state. It's something you've inherited, so it's from the past, but it's also something you don't enjoy yet, so it's in the future. It's a premonition, but a premonition of something that's your birthright."

"Do we have it today?" Elspeth asked.

Matthew demurred. "Representative democracy works a little differently. . . ."

"People don't really want to be king anymore," said Raleigh. "There aren't even any lunatics in the asylums who want to be Napoleon anymore."

"Maybe they want to be reversionary one-percenters," suggested Elspeth.

"One-percenters are too boring," Raleigh objected.

"They have no charismatic virtues," said Matthew.

"They have no charismatic *vices*," Raleigh corrected him. "They would be charming if they would only let us see them being greedy and trivial."

"I wouldn't find them charming," Elspeth said.

"Yes you would," Raleigh insisted. "They'd be like the millionaires in screwball comedies."

"So that's it, basically," Matthew concluded. "And then a chapter on Marlowe because, you know, I'm gay."

"Why Communion wafers?" asked Raleigh.

"It's complicated."

"I thought it might have to do with the 'Was Shakespeare Catholic?' thing."

"Yeah, no. I mean, maybe. But not in my dissertation."

"Huh."

"So is this what you think about all day?" asked Elspeth. "I have a friend who's writing a dissertation, and she says it's all she can think about."

"It should be," Matthew replied. It was supposed to be. His penance and his opportunity.

"I look forward to reading it," said Raleigh.

"Oh, me, too," said Matthew.

After such an exhibition, silence naturally followed. Matthew wished he had said nothing, as he always did after expounding. One's thoughts about one's dissertation were like a gall on a tree. A corky, distended mass, as large as a human head. That was the kind of revelation he felt he made of himself when he talked about it.

But Marlowe wasn't incidental, he silently amended. *Edward II* was the key to *Richard II*, as he would show if he ever got to that chapter.

The next day, at the library—one of the libraries on his own campus, this time—Matthew looked up the longer poem of Leif's that Raleigh had mentioned.

Line breaks and alignments seemed to be important structurally, and it was studded with so many patterns and eye rhymes that at first Matthew was under the panicky impression that the fact of the poem's visual orientation was as much sense as he was going to be able to make of it. After a stanza or two, though, he began to piece together a story.

The owners of a small-town motel, immigrants from the subcontinent, had set aside a garden for their employees, out of sight of the motel's swimming pool and parking lot. A hose from the pool's service shed led downhill to it. As a subject for a poem, a garden was an indulgence, the poet admitted. For a gay, urban-dwelling poet, it was even a little bit affected, as well as a bit too aspirationally upper middle class, the conventions and associations of pastoral being what they are. Locavorism, etc. The poet felt he had a right to the material anyway, because he really had worked in such a garden, with his mother, who really had worked in just such a motel as a cleaner, in the employ of a couple very much like the motel's owners in the poem. The poet had a Marxian right by labor, therefore, and a feudal one by descent. His relationship to the labor of gardening had been moody and authentic. He had resented having to weed, and he had exulted in the creation of a lumpy, engorged, celadon Hubbard squash. "Et in Arcadia teenager." He knew, thanks to the experience, that a corn plant's roots prog into the earth like the arced and stiffened fingers of a practitioner of yoga as she supports herself on them, and he thought he should be free to draw on the knowledge. Unfortunately, the touch of "nature," in such an image, always came off as precious; mortification rather than death fenced the lost garden.

Still, he wanted to be able to say that the scent of a plant was as strong in its stem and its leaves as in its fruit, even at the cost of sounding dandiacal. That particular garden was still his world, or rather, his memories of it were the components with which he still assembled the world. Through which he perceived it. "My vegetable empire." In that garden he had learned how to work and how to be alone.

The stagecoach-wheel-size chandeliers of the reading room were swaying slightly, almost imperceptibly, in the middle space of the great hall, Matthew saw when he looked up from the literary journal. This might be a real poem, Matthew thought, although he wanted so badly to believe that it was that he couldn't trust his judgment. He was becoming the sort of person who would think this was a real poem whether or not an earlier version of himself might have thought so. He remembered the boy's ghostly white body as it had appeared to him in the darkness of his bedroom. He was in danger of falling in love.

Matthew laid his jacket down on Elspeth's bed beside the slate gray toggle coat that was already dear to him. "Can I get on stack?" he heard Julia's voice asking, somewhat stagily, in the parlor.

"Do we have a stack?" he heard Raleigh ask, in turn.

"We probably should," said Elspeth. "Let me get paper." She was in search of some when she and Matthew crossed paths in the hallway a moment later. "Oh, hi," she said. They were too shy to greet each other any more demonstratively.

"Thanks for having me over."

"Of course. I mean, it's a working group meeting." She excused herself to continue her search.

In the parlor, Matthew found Leif rising from his chair to welcome him. He felt a twinge of almost pain in his chest at seeing Leif again and seeing how beautiful he was. Leif was wearing the shirt that he had been wearing the night they met, a red-and-white-plaid shirt with skinny arms that made him look even lankier than he was. It wasn't the kind of detail that Matthew usually noticed or remembered. *I haven't lost him yet*, Matthew heard himself think, as they kissed, and as Leif rested the palm of one hand almost forgetfully against him.

Chris, the green-eyed man who had helped fill the tanks at Occupy with hot and cold water, nodded at Matthew with an upward jut of his head and gave up his seat so that Matthew could sit next to Leif.

"You mind?" Chris said to Julia, taking the chair next to her. Against the sun-darkened skin of his face, the pink of his lips looked raw. He was holding a baseball cap with fingers that were knotty and looked ten years older than the rest of him. "You going to help us out?" he asked Julia sociably.

"I'm here to learn more about you," Julia replied. She looked at him with eyes open almost aggressively wide. She had nothing to hide; she had hidden everything already.

"Matthew's a new recruit, too," Raleigh said to Chris.

"I met Matthew at Occupy," said Chris.

"I'm not going to wear the T-shirt or anything," Matthew said.

"That's what we need," said Raleigh. "Can we have T-shirts, Leif?"

Elspeth returned, waving a yellow legal pad. "Should I be stack taker?" Nobody objected. "Everyone, everyone," she said, calling them to order. "It can just be all stack. Whatever comes up."

"Julia had her hand up," Leif said.

Raleigh made a trumpet out of the curled fingers of one hand and spoke through it in a self-consciously "loud" voice: "Welcome to the Working Group for the Refinement of the Perception of Feelings."

"I think Julia should go first," Leif said.

"You're sort of the leader," Raleigh protested.

"We're anarchists, remember?"

"Let her go first," Chris seconded.

"Me? Really?" Julia let a hand drop onto her chest. Her voice had a rich color, Matthew noticed. It wouldn't have been suitable to speak too hurriedly with it. "I wanted to ask Leif a question about his *power*."

It wasn't inaccurate to call Leif's gift a power; no one corrected her. But there was something off about it. Julia spoke, Matthew sensed, from what she understood to be a position of some kind. Maybe it was her voice itself that gave it to her. Really fine things are usually strong as well as elegant. "Can he do it through the TV?" she asked.

She couldn't help but be condescending, Matthew saw. He sort of liked her for it; it was her way of being authentic.

"Did I say the wrong thing?" she asked when no one responded.

"It's a point of information," said Elspeth. "It's a valid point of information."

"No, of course," said Leif. "I don't have a television, so I don't really know. But I think I have to be there in person."

"Why?" Matthew asked.

"I don't know. I don't know how it works. Maybe there's something I have to smell? That would be gross, wouldn't it."

"So we need to get ourselves in the same room with them, somehow," said Raleigh.

"With who?" Elspeth asked.

"With the people we want to crack."

"You're so dramatic," Leif said.

"We could get them to arrest us," Chris suggested. He was studying Leif.

"They're doing a lot of *that*, I hear," Julia said cheerfully.

"Can *you* read people through a TV?" Leif asked her.

"I don't get anything at all from people, not even in person," she said, a little gleefully, like someone turning her pockets inside out for a beggar.

"You came to us."

"Oh, when people lose their keys, I know where to find them. I see them, usually. Sitting in a little heap, the way keys do, wherever they are. But that's so *trivial*."

"You see what the person who lost the keys is showing you," Leif suggested.

"That could be," she said.

"I bet you could see other things."

"How scary!" she said brightly.

Leif seemed to consider.

"Is it scary, boss?" asked Chris.

Matthew abruptly remembered having been frightened by a dream that he had had the night before. He couldn't remember any details. Only the fact that there had been something menacing came back to him. The unspecific fact of the menace, now, functioned as a shield that protected him from the thing itself that had frightened him in his sleep.

"That's why I wanted for us to have a group," said Leif. "To talk about it."

"So this *is* a kind of therapy group," said Julia.

"It's whatever we want it to be."

For a few moments they seemed to listen to and focus on one another silently. Chris, Raleigh, Elspeth, Julia, Matthew, Leif. Brutal, clumsy, earnest, proud, sorrowful, troubling. It was awkward. For a few moments, they were so aware of one another, even those who were more or less strangers to each other, that no one knew what to say.

There was a loud crack.

"What was *that*?" asked Julia.

"Our brain waves in alignment," joked Raleigh.

Elspeth hopped out of her chair. "I think it came from the bookshelf." She removed a handful of anthologies and looked into the gap. "It was the veneer panel in back. I knew we nailed it on wrong."

"There was probably a fair amount of torque on it," said Raleigh. "The way the bookcase is leaning."

"Come on," said Chris.

"Come on what?" Raleigh replied.

"I, officially, don't believe in *this* kind of thing," said Leif.

"What do you mean, 'officially'?" asked Julia.

"Officially as in for the record."

"In other words, you do."

"Secretly everyone does."

"You're all north by northwest about this, aren't you," said Julia. "Except you," she added, turning to Chris. "You're north. In a way, you're the only one who takes it absolutely seriously."

"Oh, Chris, you're blushing," said Elspeth.

"I don't blush." The gold of his skin didn't completely hide it.

"Dinner," announced Matthew, a couple of nights later, in his apartment.

Leif, who was sitting on Matthew's folded-up futon, looked up from his laptop. They had agreed that the evening wouldn't be a date, so that they could spend in each other's company the time that they needed to devote to reading and writing. Matthew had cooked a simple meal, dal with wilted spinach and caramelized onions. After setting two bowls of it on the table, he untied his apron and went to take a piss.

He heard Leif knock. "I need to wash my hands," Leif explained through the door, which Matthew hadn't pulled all the way to.

"Come in."

"Oh, I have to pee, too, actually," said Leif.

Matthew made room for him, and Leif took out his long, thin cock, floppy like a new-landed fish. He was pee-shy, at first. "I always think of Stephen Dedalus and Leopold Bloom crossing streams," said Leif. "Is that hopeless?"

While Matthew was washing his hands, Leif put his hands into the sink, too, but it was an obstruction rather than a pleasure, and Leif apologized. "I was an only child, so I don't know how to share."

"You don't share. You struggle brutally for survival."

As they returned together to the table, Matthew briefly had the fantasy that the table had been set not by him but by people they couldn't see. They were happening upon the meal, in the course of a quest of some kind.

"How's your post going?" Matthew asked, once they sat down.

Raleigh had set up a blog for the working group, and Leif was trying to write something for it. "Did you ever see *Escape to Witch Mountain*? It's an old, very bad Disney movie. There's a little girl in it who can open locks with her mind, but only when it's morally right for her to do so. I want to say that we could have something like that for codebreaking. We could develop the ability to find out any secret that it's morally right for us to know."

"Why not secrets you shouldn't know?"

"This is humanities, not science. There isn't a button you push."

"What if you wrote it as a poem?" Matthew suggested. "Instead of a blog post."

"I'm writing a manifesto," Leif replied scornfully.

They gave their attention to eating. There were still questions that Matthew hadn't found a way to ask: If the world was ending, what was the point in Leif's giving so much of himself away to strangers? If it was possible to know people's hearts without words, why didn't Leif know Matthew's?

Leif set down his fork. "It's very secure here," he said, surveying Matthew's bookshelves. "It's very sturdy. Here in your life."

"I could tear it down," said Matthew. He felt a yen for a cigarette even though it had been more than a year since he had quit.

"Tear it down for me?"

"For me, too, maybe."

"Don't do that," said Leif. Studying his empty bowl, he added, "We probably shouldn't get too attached."

"No," agreed Matthew. "I just want to be able to fuck you now and then."

It wasn't exactly distrust between them. It was as if each of them were warning the other.

"What if you try to take what you want for yourself," Matthew suggested. He had decided that that was his own policy.

"I don't know how to want anything just for myself," Leif replied. "I always want it with someone."

"Just not with me."

"I don't want to hurt you," Leif said.

"Hurt me a little," Matthew said. "I bet you can't."

"Oh, I can."

"Come on, try." Matthew kneeled in front of Leif's chair and held down Leif's arms with his own.

The invitation led them to the futon, where their greed surprised them.

They showered afterward. They read for a while. When they went to sleep, they slept fitfully and without any pattern, because they were still struggling with each other over which way to face and how much to intertwine. How much to insist and how much to defer.

A little before one, Leif's phone gave the black-fly buzz that signaled its receipt of a text. They didn't get out of bed. A few minutes later, they ignored a second text, too. "You're blowing up," Matthew said, when a third one came in.

"It's happening," Leif said as he read. "The police are evicting everyone."

Matthew switched on his desk lamp and shielded his eyes from it. "Do you want to go?"

"We won't even be able to get close enough to see," Leif replied, still reading his small screen. "The police are using their clubs." Another text arrived. "Raleigh's going," he reported.

"Is Elspeth?"

"He didn't say. He's getting on his bike now."

"What about Chris?"

"He's two blocks south of it. The first text was from him."

Leif hunched over to write his friends back, which on his dumbphone sometimes required laborious repetition of the number keys to bring up the right letters. At the sink, Matthew poured two glasses of water. The edge of the circle of light cast by his desk lamp bisected Leif across his pale chest. The geometry of the scene suggested to Matthew that Leif would never be fully held by any claim of Matthew's. The stillness of the circle of light and the unsteady working of Leif's breath in his slender rib cage added to the impression.

"Do you have any earplugs?" asked Leif. "The police have bought some kind of new sound weapon with their 9/11 money."

"Are you going?"

"You don't have to go."

"I just didn't realize you were going."

"I want to see how far I can get."

Matthew took a bag of foam earplugs out of the top drawer of his desk. "This is so end times. A sound weapon."

"It's a war of the senses," Leif said. He stood up, pulled on his pants, and started buttoning his shirt. "It's a war over perceiving. Over what we're allowed to perceive, still. You don't have any swimming goggles, do you?"

"The strap broke last year," said Matthew. "I'll go, too."

"Why? It's not your thing."

"I won't get in your way," Matthew promised. "I'm going to go, okay?"

They walked their bikes down the stairwell of Matthew's building. Outside, by a trick of the light, the asphalt of the street looked wet even though it wasn't. They set off, Leif in the lead. The streets were mostly empty. It was quiet, and they were alone and unwatched. As the black-and-white city scrolled past, Matthew felt terribly free, as one does when one understands that one has lost touch with one's old life.

The city was like a sleeping dragon; they were coasting past it almost noiselessly, so as not to wake it up. The only sound was the creak of their pedals, echoing off the facades. As each streetlamp passed, the burnish of its reflected light rolled up alongside them on the asphalt, like a dolphin curious about a new boat in her waters, and then veered away.

It was so quiet that Matthew had the impression that he and Leif had survived something. They were touring the aftermath.

"Look," said Leif, pointing below them as they mounted the bridge. "They've shut the bridge to car traffic."

Two police cars, lights flashing, were slanted across the bridge's car lanes, and beyond the police cars, the gray pavement was empty.

After looking down, Matthew by reflex looked up, into the beautiful double rigging of the old bridge, which was unusual in that it was both a cable-stayed and a suspension bridge, doubly supported because its build-ers had meant for it to stand for all time. Cables that spread at an angle crossed cables that fell straight down, interlacing like fingers and creating diamonds that in their sequence of gradually varying dimensions seemed to be unfolding as Leif and Matthew rode past them.

They crossed the water; they descended into downtown. Tonight it didn't seem like misplaced prudence for them to lock up their bikes long before their destination, and while the chants and the sirens were still faint, they chose a No Parking sign on an empty street. As they threaded their locks and cables through their wheels, three curly-haired men with backpacks walked up with nervous speed.

"Any news?" asked one.

"We just got here," said Leif.

"We heard they have water cannons," said another.

The shapes of the men's noses didn't match; they weren't brothers. Leif told them the rumor he had heard about the sound weapon, and he gave them three pairs of Matthew's earplugs. "I don't know if they'll work," Leif cautioned.

"They might be handy in Central Booking, anyway."

"Don't they make you empty your pockets at Central Booking?" asked the third curly-haired man.

"I think they just take your belt and shoelaces," replied the first.

The men hurried on.

"I don't want to go to jail," said Matthew.

"Do you want to go home?"

"No, let's just not get arrested."

As they walked north, toward the site of the encampment, they began to notice small groups of others headed in the same direction. They passed a row of glossy white SUVs bearing medallions that identified them as the property of the Department of Homeland Security. The trucks were backed up diagonally onto the sidewalk, their engines idling. They were as yet unscratched by the city. Matthew wondered where the Department of Homeland Security was kept when there wasn't any civil unrest. Outside of airports, he had never seen any sign of it before.

"Raleigh says to go one block west," Leif said, reading his cell phone.

When they did, they found sidewalks that were at last a little populated. There was a chant—"Whose streets? Our streets"—which built for half a dozen iterations, but after a few more, the voices in it fell out of entrainment, and in the end only one persisted, almost scoldingly. It was the middle of the night, after all. At the next intersection, a file of police, in helmets and black plastic armor, stood abreast to block the way to the park that the occupiers no longer occupied. Behind the police was parked a paddy wagon, one of its back doors open, the corner of a bench inside it visible. From every officer's belt there dangled an insect-like furl of disposable plastic manacles. It was the multiplicity as much as the shape of them that suggested insects. Professional dog walkers sometimes carried a dispenser of baggies in the same place.

To pick up the shit that is us, Matthew thought.

"If you step into the street, you *will* be arrested," a policeman warned the crowd through a megaphone.

"What's that about?" Matthew asked.

"It's their rule," said Leif.

"If you don't color inside the lines, you go to jail? Don't we have a right of assembly?"

Leif didn't meet Matthew's eye, as if wary of Matthew's simple anger. He waved; he had spotted Raleigh, Elspeth, and Chris on the sidewalk opposite. Diana was with them. Matthew and Leif made their way to the crosswalk in order to join them safely.

"You made it," Raleigh said. He clapped a hand against one of Leif's. "Diana says the police are pulling everyone out of the park."

She gestured with her phone. "That's what I *hear*."

"We *will* arrest you if you are obstructing the flow of traffic," repeated the police officer with the megaphone.

"They keep saying that, and *they're* blocking a whole *street*," said Raleigh, and to Matthew it sounded reckless of Raleigh, under the circumstances, to give voice even to a mild statement of fact. No wonder Leif had been wary of Matthew's anger a few minutes earlier. There was risk in letting one's temperature get too high.

"I can't be here," said Diana. "I have a meeting with my adviser first thing in the morning."

"Oh, are you in grad school?" asked Matthew.

"Sociology."

"English," Matthew identified himself.

"Nice."

A new chant began and staggered across the sparse crowd. As it passed through their group, Raleigh and Chris seemed to compete in giving voice to it.

"This will make Occupy even bigger," said Raleigh, perhaps a little heady from the shouting. "The way the first arrests did. The way the pepper spray did."

His hopes hung in the air, unseconded.

"What if we walk down to the water," Leif suggested.

"Y'all are going to do your witchy thing, aren't you," said Diana. "I'll have to leave you to it." She gave out hugs.

"Peace," Chris told her, unselfconsciously.

Another chant started. "Are we really going to just walk away?" asked Raleigh.

"What're you gonna do, man," Chris replied.

Across the street, Matthew saw the three curly-haired men standing on the curb, glaring at five policemen who seemed to be daring them to step off it. As if to suggest an answer to Chris's not-quite-question, one of the curly-haired men did step off the curb, his jaw out, and the police at once rained down blows on him with their clubs, as if he were a nail that they were competing to hammer. As the man's friends grabbed at him ineffectually, the man crumpled to his knees, and the police bent him forward, twisted his arms behind him, and fastened his wrists. The police had done this many times before, Matthew saw, and the curly-haired man never had. They knew where to hit so that his body gave out quickly.

The police took the man's friends, too, for having reached out to him. "Let's go for a walk," Leif repeated.

"Tell us again about our great powers, Leif," Elspeth said, as they walked alongside a steel balustrade that edged the river, which was black and glittering.

"What do you want to hear?"

"How we're going to save the world."

There were no chants or sirens in the air anymore, just gray sighs from cars on a highway that they had had to cross to reach the water. The river itself was silent.

"We're going to save the world by being beautiful together," said Leif.

Matthew wanted to button Leif's coat for him. He himself had put on his wool hat and bike gloves. "Like in a Ryan McGinley photo shoot?" Matthew asked.

"Beautiful in our *souls*," Leif specified.

"You make it sound easy," said Raleigh.

"Easy as pie," said Leif.

The city's light fractured on the disturbed surface of the river, each of its thousand glancing reflections taking for a moment the spiculate shape of a skate's egg sac and then bouncing into a frame of open jawbones and then reverting to an egg sac again. CGI *avant la lettre*, thought Matthew.

"Tell us," Raleigh insisted.

"It'll be easy because of the meaning of life," Leif said, his voice cracking a little under the strain of finding a tone that acknowledged his grandiosity but did seek nonetheless to be a little bit believed. The meaning of a life wasn't assigned, he explained. Most people dodged the challenge by referring it to their children, still mute and unable to object, so that the question of this generation had to be answered by the next. If people began to recognize, however, that survival generally was in jeopardy, postponement became impossible. Through anticipating their children's deaths, parents became acutely aware again of their own, and once aware, became unable to shift their attention away. To survive their parents' distraction, some of the children became caretakers. They learned to solve problems that children shouldn't have to or even be able to solve, becoming so sensitive to the fears and needs of those around them that something in them was broken. An inner ear that in an ordinary childhood was trained on the child's inner self was turned away, in their case, to others. It was a sort of generational fail-safe mechanism. An injury became a gift. That is, the injured themselves became the gift, though they soon learned that they had to hide their nature in order to get through daily life.

"And you think that's us," Elspeth said, when Leif paused, his elaboration having reached a height that he didn't seem to know how to climb down from. "You think we're the caretakers, and you think we'll reform the political system."

"Oh, maybe," Leif said.

"Don't we save the world?"

"It might be more a matter of helping people become able to talk about the ending."

"That's so dark," said Raleigh.

In the absence of a moon, Matthew noticed that he seemed to have set himself the task of scanning the shadows beyond the radiance of the walkway's lamps. He could see best when the friends were between lamps, almost part of the dark themselves. The glare directly under a lamp slightly blinded one.

"Really, you think the world is ending?" asked Chris.

"I don't know. It looks like it."

"You have this gift, and you could use it."

"What's my gift?"

"You see things."

"I guess things."

"You see everything you were just talking about."

"I'm just making things up. I can't do anything about anything."

"Why do you say that?" asked Chris.

He asked it with a note of sorrow so real that Leif was unable to continue with his persiflage, if that's what it had been. They had just seen people like themselves being beaten. An experiment in optimism was coming to an end. It was cold. It was late. Matthew had briefly worried, when Leif had begun to talk, that the talk would feed the folie that Leif and his friends had been sharing, at a moment when it might have been natural, and as painless as it ever would be, for them to leave the folie behind. But his harboring of this worry, Matthew had to acknowledge, felt too much like siding with the forces that he had seen in action a few minutes ago, a few blocks away, and he found, to his surprise, that he not only felt no relief over the modesty of Leif's claim for his abilities but that he even shared Chris's disappointment: he, too, evidently, wanted to hear from Leif that soon there would be a better world, that Leif and his friends would be the cadres, that the poor would be fed without humiliation, that governments would invest in the health and well-being of citizens, that henceforth ingenuity would be directed into the creation of art, the discovery of new energy sources, and the preservation of the environment rather than into efforts to confuse consumers into making choices against their interests.

Matthew, too, was a utopian, hopelessly. Meaning, he was ungroundedly hopeful. Where was he? They had walked to the end of the city, to the tip where the ferries ran, though none were running now. There was so much he was going to have to give up on, Matthew realized, before he would be able to return to the life he had thought worth living.

The despair of that night turned out to be only momentary; the members of Leif's circle recovered their spirits surprisingly fast. There seemed to be something restorative, in fact, about the blow they had received. It might even have been the case that awareness of failure—the now demonstrated certainty of it—liberated their energies. If, in the end, their effort was going to be crushed, then they could cause no harm even if they were mistaken, and they might as well pour into their cause the selves that they now, definitively, didn't know what to do with. Matthew, as usual, held back; he limited himself to the role of fellow traveler. But he attended the meetings, because he couldn't bear to be away from Leif, and the meetings were held more and more often. The police reopened the once-occupied park, and though they strictly forbade any rebuilding of the occupiers' infrastructure, the place was more pleasant to visit than ever. The site of defeat felt strangely like one of victory. Did it cheer the occupiers to know that the powers that be had been afraid enough to insist on stopping them? They were free now to feel the approaching chill of winter as provocative rather than menacing; they weren't going to be sleeping in it. The members of Leif's working group returned to the park to recruit. They were now sans pizza box. Their recruiting stand could no longer consist of anything more than a few people standing together, in a configuration that they hoped would seem welcoming. No one took advantage of their welcome, however. Maybe they now seemed, despite their intentions, too much like a completed and therefore closed circle.

It hardly mattered. This smaller setback, too, seemed not to dismay but to enliven them. It reinforced the sense they had of being set apart, misunderstood by the blundering world, and they let the recruiting effort subside into a bit of a joke. Through a website, Raleigh had a T-shirt printed with the words GOVERNMENT TRANSPARENCY NOW in large type, and the words THROUGH ESP below, in smaller print. A second T-shirt read, more simply, OCCUPY TELEPATHY. A third: LOOK INTO MY EYES . . . YOU ARE GETTING SLEEPY, VERY SLEEPY . . . YOU KNOW YOU WANT TO JOIN THE WORKING GROUP FOR THE REFINEMENT OF THE PERCEPTION OF FEELINGS. Which was all fine if you were Raleigh, declared Julia, who claimed for a few days to be vexed at the others for not having texted her the night of the eviction and who made a show, accordingly, of her right to be free with criticism. But it wasn't fine if one wanted to be taken seriously, she continued, with her usual ruthless aplomb. She, for one, was an admirer of a design that

Elspeth had shared with her, a mandorla of a white dove flying and a white dolphin leaping, the arcs and shapes of their bodies mirroring each other across a choppy horizon that divided blue sky from green sea. A fin of the dolphin and a wing of the dove seemed, loosely, to correspond, though each animal remained distinctly itself—a remarkable achievement for someone who was no artist, as Julia bluntly put it. ("No, that's okay," said Elspeth, when the others nervously laughed at Julia's inadvertent cruelty. "I mean, I'm *not* an artist, she's right.") Julia decided to have T-shirts silk-screened with the design and with the discreet triliteral RPF, and she requested people's sizes. No self-serve website for Julia.

Only Raleigh wore Raleigh's T-shirts, but when the box of Julia's arrived, one afternoon at Elspeth's apartment, everyone tried on her shirts. Even Matthew was a good sport. "A little culty," was Raleigh's verdict, once they had donned their new uniforms. They stood in a circle, pulling forward the hems of the shirts and looking down at the colorful symbol upside-down on the fabric in front of them. The shirts rendered all their bodies shapeless in the same way.

"We could sell flowers at an airport," Matthew suggested.

"Why?" asked Elspeth.

"It's something cults used to do before 9/11."

"I'm glad you bought them for us," Elspeth said to Julia, as if afraid that Julia might take Matthew's joke in bad part.

"It's not very Occupy, though," Raleigh said.

"Why not?" Julia asked.

"It's kind of a commodification."

"It's just something to wear, Raleigh," Julia said. "And you started it. They *are* culty, but there's usually an effect of alienation, I think, when a number of people dress alike. Uniformity suggests ritual. Suggests the submerging of the individual in a higher cause."

"A warpath," said Raleigh. "A human sacrifice."

"But the blue is so soothing, isn't it?" Julia continued. "I was very particular with them about getting the blue right."

"And doves and dolphins are soothing," said Leif.

"That's why I drew them," Elspeth mildly insisted.

"Not to mention psychic," said Raleigh. "Everyone knows dolphins are psychic."

Matthew excused himself, and in the bedroom of one of Elspeth's roommates, he changed back into his own shirt. He folded the T-shirt carefully—the uniform that he had said he was never going to wear. So the campaign had colors now. He should have shown Leif the bearings of Richard II: a white hart, lodged, its front hooves delicately crossed, beneath a sky of starlike suns—the sign of a king who was to be unkinged. The numerousness of the suns undermined their celestial majesty, and so did the hart, because a hart implies hounds. A hart brings to mind the hunter who became, by love's enchantment, the hunted. White for purity. *Noli me tangere.*

Was Leif the hart, or was Matthew? The first to declare love makes the other responsible for reply—makes the other the caretaker, to use Leif's word—and Matthew didn't want to do that to Leif. He believed that much, at least: he believed that Leif needed to be spared a moral burden if there was any hope of his someday setting his feelings free. He wanted Leif that badly already: he wanted him with his feelings free. He had a suspicion, sometimes, that Leif continued to entangle his feelings in his folie in order to keep them from Matthew. The folie, in this understanding, was a kind of secondary enchantment, with the purpose of holding Matthew at bay, in counteraction to the first, the original charm of attraction cast by Leif's mere self.

"There's always one thing you can't see," Leif was saying, when Matthew returned to the parlor. "One kind of thing. It's because you can't see it that you became so good at seeing all the others."

Since the eviction, Leif seemed to hold forth more often about his theories. "What is the thing for you?" Matthew asked.

"He won't be able to say, probably," said Raleigh.

"A reader of people could get round his blind spot by dead reckoning, maybe," Leif speculated.

Matthew picked up the tarot deck and shuffled it.

"He could get round it the way an autistic person memorizes the rules that normals follow," Leif continued. "My blind spot is something about you, probably," he said to Matthew.

"You think so?" In Leif's inability to see was Matthew's safety. The convention of their talk was still that Leif was the innocent and Matthew the roué. *I'm going to be the Daisy to your Steerforth, aren't I,* was how Leif had put it at one point.

"And another thing," Leif continued. "It's no biggie to read someone you like. Skill is in reading someone antipathetic."

"That's like academia," said Matthew. "You don't win any points for paying attention to a text that's interesting."

"Are we supposed to be writing these down?" Raleigh asked.

"Have a little respect," Chris ordered sharply.

Raleigh paused before answering. "We're not a cult yet, Chris."

"Boys, boys," said Leif.

Julia interposed: "It would be skill, in other words, if Raleigh were to read Chris's mind at the moment."

"That's why gays are better at this sort of thing, I think," said Leif. "We aren't really capable of not imagining what the other person is thinking, even if we don't like him."

"That's racist," said Raleigh.

"It's not 'racist.' I think it's a survival thing."

"You know what I mean. But anyway, Chris and I love each other. We're just having a disagreement."

"I was just beating up on him a little," Chris confirmed.

"It's interesting that *he's* a writer." Julia made confidences in Matthew from time to time, with the air of having discovered a capacity for disloyalty in him. They were complicit, her manner implied, in the way of slummers who in the depths of the slums have recognized each other, seeing in each other the desire that isn't visible to the natives around them. "I should have expected it but didn't."

"You thought you would be the writer."

"Well, I did come downtown with that idea. And we can both be, can't we? All of us, even. But the truth is that I did think I would 'find' something. It sounds so awful, doesn't it, when I put it like that. What I find is that he's writing it himself."

"I don't think he writes poems about it. I wish he did."

"Because they would be so fascinating?"

"No," Matthew replied. "I mean, they would be, but what I think I hope is that if he did write poems about it, maybe less of it would need to actually happen."

"Oh, see, now you're problematizing my search for 'experience.'"

"Is Leif here?" Matthew called into Elspeth's apartment one afternoon, after he had failed to find Leif behind the counter at his café.

"He'll be here later," Elspeth's answer came down the hall. "He had a cough again."

Elspeth was sitting at the dining room table with, unexpectedly, Chris, the tarot deck between them. "I have to get as good at it as the rest of you guys," Chris explained, grinning at Matthew over his shoulder.

"*I'm* no good," Matthew said.

"Don't say that, man."

"You can stay if you don't transmit anything," Elspeth told Matthew.

Maybe she thought Matthew's presence could function as a sort of psychic Wi-Fi relay station. Matthew had his satchel with him, and he decided to sit in the parlor until Leif arrived. "Is Chris reading you or you him?"

"She can read me like I'm talking."

"He's trying to read me." She was keeping a tally of some kind on a scratch pad.

The weak-backed sofa protested as Matthew sat down. He set a book on his lap, and on the lumpy seat cushion beside him he set the corresponding notebook, half full of notes. It would be more efficient to take notes on a laptop, but he liked the sight of his own jittery handwriting, a record of his industriousness even if nothing more came of it.

He read a few lines of sixteenth-century poetry. They happened to belong to an ode to "solitariness," ambiguous in the usual way: solitude isn't worth having without the right person to share it with. In the next room, Elspeth drew three cards. Chris was sitting hunched forward in his chair, arms folded, elbows on knees, his bristly gold head angled at her fixedly. Like a raccoon or a small bear, fond of its keeper.

"Death?" Chris suggested.

"Do you see anything?" Elspeth asked. "Maybe close your eyes."

On the sofa Matthew decided to close his eyes, too.

"It's dark," Chris said.

"*How* is it dark."

There was silence as Chris struggled. It was dark as a symbol, Matthew thought, in his own darkness. The dark that he and Chris were looking at was the dark of eyes closed in a north-facing room in a cluttered apartment on a late fall afternoon—a mild and susceptible dark. It stood for another dark, by a sort of metonymy. One couldn't ever actually see this other dark, though one was going to be alone with it before too long. With it and in it. The world was ending, after all. One of the chosen cards was probably a one of swords, Matthew guessed. A threat or a distinction. A line drawn.

"Well, tell me what you mean by death," Elspeth coaxed.

"Maybe there's something I'm afraid to see."

Matthew opened his eyes. Chris's were still shut, and in looking at him, Matthew felt the mixture of envy and scorn that one feels when watching people with their eyes shut, as for example when they're praying.

"Is there an arrow?" Chris asked.

Elspeth looked again at the pictures on the cards. "No arrows."

"Oh, fuck it," said Chris, opening his eyes.

"No," said Elspeth pityingly.

"I suck."

"You don't let the images in."

"Death means change, doesn't it?" It sounded like something he had heard Leif or Elspeth say.

"It isn't usually death death. But I didn't have the death card out." She shuffled her hand into the deck without showing him what the cards had been.

Matthew realized that he had almost forgotten that straights have love-dramas of their own. Though it might be that an attention like Chris's was the one thing that in Elspeth's case, Elspeth couldn't see. "Where's Raleigh?" Matthew asked from the sofa.

"He took Julia to a spokes council," Elspeth answered. "She wanted to 'see.'"

So Elspeth had also noticed Julia's scare quotes. Unlike Matthew, Julia made no attempt to discard or naturalize her status as an interloper. "Where do you think her money comes from?" Matthew asked.

Elspeth looked startled. "She does have nice clothes, doesn't she."

"She has an office," Chris volunteered. Two blocks from her house, he reported. Chris worked for a moving company, and he said that she had asked him how much it would cost to have a few bookcases moved, along with the books they held. "You could do it with only one man, but you would need a truck," Chris said now, repeating the calculation he had made for her.

What came into Matthew's mind, and, he suspected, into Elspeth's and Chris's own, was that it might have been Chris's beauty and the angry heat that always seemed to be rising from him that had prompted Julia to consider hiring him. It would be hard for anyone who liked to sleep with men to look at Chris and not wish to see him put to work. It would have been indecent, though, to joke about Chris's beauty at the moment, or even to mention it, given the steadiness with which Chris was watching Elspeth.

Perhaps this is how it ends, Matthew thought. The occupation, no longer instantiated, would disperse, and the members of the littler groups that comprised it would break up into new pairings. Matthew was willing to assist in betrayal if unbinding the others would free Leif for him.

It had to end, after all; even the silence in the room now supported that conclusion. The silence was an example of the great flaw in Leif's scheme, which Leif himself, whenever he felt confident enough to tackle it, referred to as the Problem of Democracy and Feelings. Also known as the Problem of Secrets. If feelings could be made generally audible, was anyone safe? There were cruel people in the world, after all; in a state of perfect knowledge, not everyone would forbear to take advantage. And even between those who had power to harm but would do none, if you knew that I wanted to go to bed with you, and I knew that you didn't want to go to bed with me, would anything be gained by a license to say what we knew? What if people have come to prefer not speaking their intuitions, and even not knowing them, for a reason?

With more talk might come more understanding, Leif hoped. One might be able to learn to tolerate close handling of awarenesses that had previously seemed too painful, including even perhaps an awareness of not being loved where one badly wanted to be. That was Leif's hope, at any rate. Matthew wasn't sure that Leif had any experience of what such a disillusionment might feel like.

"Well, she isn't defined by her money, is she," Elspeth commented. "I think she's genuinely interested in what we're doing. It's too bad we didn't text her the other night."

"We had other things on our minds," Chris said.

A few steps over the threshold of Matthew's apartment, Leif halted for a moment, as if he were waiting, even after so many visits, for Matthew to renew the invitation to make himself at home. "I've been thinking of having an action."

"What kind?" Matthew asked.

"Like an Occupy action. I don't know. Chain ourselves to something. Hold a public séance." He studied Matthew for a response. When there wasn't one, he consolidated a few stacks of books in the windowsill and sat down beside them. "It's so hard to figure out what the action would be, though, that I wonder if it's a philosophical problem." He looked out the window, down into the street, where the brief day was folding itself up and taking itself away, an impatient employee.

Matthew switched on his desk lamp.

"Maybe the problem is," Leif continued, "that an action will always be an imposition of feelings rather than a perception of them. Even if you want the action to be about perceiving them."

"It can't express them?"

"To express them, it would have to come out of feelings that people were having in the moment, and you can't plan for those. So you can't plan that kind of action. It's the problem of monogamy, really. The problem of making promises about feelings."

"You don't think it's possible."

"Do you think it is?"

Their reflected selves were now floating beyond the window, in the dark, two stories above the level of the street. Escapees. Matthew went to make tea, and while the water came to a boil, he stood watching the kettle and tried to reason with himself. If he got out now, he would free himself of the need to make allowances. He would free himself of the need to be considerate. He could just say that he didn't think any of it was possible. And it wasn't possible. The trouble was that he wanted Leif anyway. They were probably going to have each other again tonight, though nothing was certain. He was looking forward to it. Not knowing for certain made him look forward to it even more. He had never been able to walk away from a hunt.

Afterward, as Matthew lay in bed next to Leif, having gotten what he wanted one more time, and feeling no freer, feeling in fact even more deeply held, he felt confronted by the realization that he didn't understand. *What if it's fatal*, he wondered, using a word he wished he hadn't thought of. The word, in this case, meant fated, he told himself.

He got out of bed quietly and sat naked at his desk, in the dark, the slats of the folding chair at first cold under his buttocks. He wanted Leif and he liked him, even though he thought Leif was a little grandiose at times and perhaps a bit crazy, but there was something uncanny and imperious about the way he wanted him. The wanting almost seemed to come from outside Matthew.

An axle creaked once in the chair beneath him, as if a cricket had found enough daring for one stridulation. Matthew held still; Leif didn't wake up. Had he wanted Leif to wake up? Had he twisted in his chair deliberately? Did he know anything about his own intentions anymore? He told himself that he was brave enough to be in love, if that's what this was. He wasn't the sort of person who needed to be in control for its own sake; he wasn't a tyrant or a prude or a stuffed shirt.

He looked at Leif. In the dark, Leif's features, just beyond the threshold of visibility, seemed to billow and alter, under the strain of Matthew's attempt to see them, until Leif coughed, in his sleep, and in the motion of the spasm became distinct to Matthew's sight: Leif's frame curled forward, and his arms shifted apart, like a dog acting out a dream.

Matthew was a little afraid of the warmth that he knew was in the bed with Leif now, mantling him. If Matthew joined it, it would keep Matthew from minding that he didn't understand. What had he given to Leif that he couldn't get back except by keeping him? If it were a tarot card, which card would it be? The Fool, the Lover, the Hermit?

He got back into bed and folded Leif in his arms. The Sun, he remembered, was the sign of sovereignty as well as the light to see it by.

2.

It had worked, Chris repeated to himself as he and Raleigh were shunted into a holding cell at Central Booking. There was a clang as the gate caught behind them, but Chris didn't really mind. A few hours ago, just before he was arrested, he had been able to see fear in a security official's eyes. Elspeth had seen it, too; Chris had shared a look with her when it had happened. Leif had done it.

The holding cell was capacious. Three of the walls were cement, painted lime green. *Which is the color of shoots*, Chris thought. *Of spring*, he silently joked.

In fact, flat light from fluorescents overhead denied any suggestion of a specific time of day, let alone season. A dull steel bench ran along the walls, and Raleigh pointed to an open stretch.

None of the men already sitting in the cell looked at them directly. They weren't being sullen, Chris knew. Only cautious. They were making an effort not to show too much or too little face.

"They didn't arrest the girls," Raleigh said, in a studiedly normal tone of voice.

"They weren't in the street," Chris said. He had a clear memory of where the girls had been standing when the police had unrolled their orange webbing.

"At least not while we were with them," Raleigh replied, staking his usual claim to know a little bit more and a little bit better. Chris didn't mind that, either. Especially not today, when the members of their working group at last knew what they were capable of. What Elspeth and Leif were capable of, at least. And maybe the new guy, Matthew, though who knew because he never fully put his shoulder to the wheel. Chris himself didn't have what they had, and that was yet another thing he didn't mind. He had been given instead an opportunity to fall in love. You can only fall in love with people who have a greatness or beauty you don't. You could say that what Chris himself had, instead of gifts like Leif's or Elspeth's, was the privilege of honesty. He saw how things were even when they didn't take a form presentable enough to talk about out loud. He saw, for example, that he couldn't help but love Elspeth and, in a different way, Leif.

And right now, he saw that what the other men in the cell were likely to resent about his comrade-in-arms Raleigh wasn't Raleigh's whiteness so much as his weakness. The way Raleigh nodded at one of their cellmates and then did a sort of air-drumming on one thigh. The weakness registered as a luxury that Raleigh's whiteness had purchased for him. He came across as someone who had never really had to put on armor.

"That's the phone," Raleigh said, noticing a brown landline mounted on a post in the center of the cell. "We should be careful because it'll be bugged. There was an article about it online a couple months ago. Do you want to call?"

"Go ahead."

"I should call Elspeth."

Raleigh said it as if he needed to call his mother. Chris watched him walk away. There wasn't going to be any need for Chris to point anything out. All he was going to have to do was wait for Elspeth to see for herself.

He arched his back and stretched his arms. It wasn't exactly a comfortable bench. He felt aware of the walls, the confinement. But he could pace if he had to, he told himself.

"Y'all aren't really in-here in here, are you," said a young black man in a mustard hoodie, not far away on the bench.

"What do you mean," Chris said.

"Or maybe you are. I wasn't trying to disrespect you."

"We were at an Occupy protest."

"I thought you might be in here for a school project, like." He looked away, as if to signal that he didn't need for Chris to respond.

"It was a protest against evictions," Chris said. "Against banks. We had a camp downtown, until a few weeks ago. It was political, but not like Republican or Democrat political."

"Hey," the man said, leaning slightly toward Chris and lowering his voice. "In here you maybe shouldn't tell nobody what you in for." Louder: "Know what I'm saying?"

"We were standing in the street."

"In here you might not know who you talking to."

Chris nodded. "My friend says the phone there is bugged."

"Not if you talking to your lawyer."

"They stop listening then?"

The man laughed and nodded. "Yeah, they stop listening then."

The man's name was Calvin. He lived on this side of the river, he said, but far uptown. His girlfriend was still in school and wanted to be a nurse, and if he was arraigned quickly, he might not have to tell her what had happened to him this morning.

"So the National Lawyers Guild is going to have someone upstairs for us," said Raleigh, returning.

"It's not going to be serious," Chris replied.

"Do you want to know or not?"

"Yeah, tell me."

Raleigh proceeded to tell him in detail exactly how it was going to turn out not to be serious.

An hour and a half later, a guard called Chris's name but not Raleigh's.

Raleigh came with Chris to the gate anyway. "You're not arraigning us at the same time?" Raleigh said. "We were arrested together."

"Get back," the guard ordered Raleigh. "Get back behind the line on the floor there. That's right." The guard opened the gate, cuffed Chris, snatched him out, and banged the gate shut. Chris didn't say anything, because he was still chewing the last mouthful of a peanut butter and jelly sandwich, which he had had to bolt. He nodded good-bye to Raleigh and to Calvin. After he swallowed, he became aware that he wished he was able to wipe the corners of his mouth.

The guard didn't make any small talk with Chris. The police lorded it over you when they had you, as if they thought it would make you forget about how free you were when they didn't.

The guard directed Chris into the elevator that had originally brought him and Raleigh down. Inside it, in the silence, Chris thought of the first trip he had taken to New Orleans after Katrina, while it had still been raining. Storming, really. He and a friend of his, an anarchist from Galveston, had gotten the idea that they were going to help. They had bought first aid kits, bottled water, and protein bars, and they had driven a loop around the city in order to approach it from the east, first by car, and then in a johnboat that they had liberated from its tie-up. There hadn't been any police in the area at the time. There hadn't been any authority at all. He and his friend had got close enough to see people standing on roofs but had turned back when a few rednecks in retreat had warned that they would have to be willing to shoot with live ammunition if they went any further. They hadn't quite believed the rednecks but hadn't had the courage to disbelieve them. Chris hadn't even owned a gun, at that point.

The water had been clear, at the place where they had made their decision. Dark green but clear. It should have been muddy from all the rain. The people standing on the roofs had kept waving, in the silence of distance, as Chris and his friend had wheeled their boat around.

"Get out," the guard said as the elevator door opened.

He made Chris walk ahead of him. On this floor the walls were white, with a soft, intermittent gray stripe at waist level where the bumpers of cleaning trolleys, pushed by inmates, had rubbed against them. Mounted on the wall, halfway down the corridor, was a board the size of a door—maybe it had actually been a door at some point—with laminated photos of the Fallen, in three rows. ALL GAVE SOME, read a motto along the bottom. SOME GAVE ALL. In addition to police, guards, and inmates on cleaning duty, a few men in suits were in the corridor, probably lawyers. Chris wasn't able to stop himself from feeling ashamed of being seen by them with his hands cuffed behind his back. He wished he could believe that he was feeling the shame of the men in suits rather than his own—their shame at their complicity, maybe—but he knew that he didn't have Elspeth's or Leif's susceptibility.

The guard opened a door. "Go on." Inside was a white room with chairs and a table. Set into the far wall was a window with mirrored glass. The guard uncuffed Chris and ordered him to sit. A viewer at the window would have a good vantage on him.

"I don't have a lawyer yet," said Chris.

"You don't need a lawyer for this." The guard left and shut the door.

Chris stood up, the way he did when left in an examining room to wait for a doctor. At least he was in his clothes and not in a backless surgical bib. The table and chairs were made out of a slightly wobbly plastic, like lawn furniture, so that they couldn't be made dangerous. Chris had visited a friend in a locked ward once, and in the bathroom, water had come out of a blunt hole in the ceramic of the sink rather than out of a faucet.

He leaned his head close to the mirrored glass and shaded his eyes against it, to break its reflectivity. Under a smoky green haze, two cops were watching him from closer than he had expected.

There was nothing on the walls of the interrogation room other than a few scuffs and a patch of puckering where moisture appeared to have gotten trapped under the paint. Chris sat down in the wrong chair.

His back was therefore to the door when it opened. "All right, boss?" asked the guard. He was talking to the security official frightened by Leif a few hours ago.

"No, don't get up," the security official said to Chris. "All right," he told the guard, who locked the two of them in the interrogation room alone.

Against the blankness of the room, it was hard to appraise the man's size. He was wearing a dark blue suit, probably the same one he had been wearing when Leif had spooked him, and it hid him, the way suits do. He wasn't losing his hair yet. Chris thought he remembered noticing that the man had been a little shorter than Leif.

The man patted the pockets of his suit coat until he confirmed by touch the presence of something he was looking for. "This isn't official," the man said. He was wearing a wedding ring. "I thought we might be able to help each other."

Chris waited a moment, and then, because he didn't want to be impolite before he had to be, he nodded.

"Was your friend looking for me?" the man asked. "The one who came after me."

"He didn't 'come after' you."

"I think we mean the same guy," the man said. "Your boyfriend."

Chris shook his head. "We're in a working group together."

"What's that." The man delivered his questions as orders rather than requests.

"It's an Occupy thing. Do I have to talk to you?"

"I asked to see you because I saw you'd helped out before." He studied

Chris's eyes; Chris didn't look away. "There are all these sharing things they've put up now, since 9/11. For the different agencies. So I can see this stuff now, whenever I'm working with the city." He took out of one of his suit coat pockets a pair of reading glasses and out of his breast pocket a sheet of paper folded vertically. He put the glasses on his nose and made a show of looking at the paper. "There was New Orleans, and it looks like, after that, there was *Toronto*." He said the word "Toronto" as if it were exotic.

A couple of weeks after the hurricane, Chris had returned to New Orleans alone and had joined a group of anarchists and socialists repairing houses and organizing food and medical care. The group had had to make its own decisions, and everyone by then had had guns. When the police returned, Chris, because he was not only white but from Texas, had been the one sent to warn the police that it would go better if they kept their distance for a little while longer. He had gotten to know a guy on the force, who had asked Chris to keep him up-to-date. The guy had said he thought it would help keep things calm, and it had, more or less.

Chris had kept the extent of the contact to himself.

"I could have asked your friends instead."

"Could have asked them what?"

"I could have asked them first about your talking with the department in New Orleans, but sometimes people get the wrong idea."

It wasn't smoothly done. Chris saw that the man didn't think it needed to be.

"And then what were you doing in Toronto," the man went on.

"Fighting neoliberalism," Chris answered.

The man smiled. "You talked to some interesting people."

Chris had gone for the G20 protests. One night, at a communal dinner, the host, as soon as he heard that Chris had volunteered in New Orleans, had wanted to talk to him about a sort of counter-NAFTA he was setting up. His group had come up with a new strategy with explosives, the host had said, not very quietly. Chris hadn't interrupted; he hadn't wanted to be rude. *Did he talk to you about it, too?* another guest had asked Chris, afterward, in the street. The man asking had offered Chris a cigarette, and in his question there had been the same note of complicity in hardheadedness that the cop in New Orleans had always used. That was how Chris had been able to tell. A little stupidly he had told the man, as he accepted his cigarette, that he saw through his cover. *Bright kid*, the man had replied. It had immediately been tacit between them that Chris wasn't going to give the man away. He had asked for Chris's name, and Chris, even more stupidly, had told him. He was only there to protest, he had said. He wasn't going to take part in the black bloc action. *Which one is that?* the man had asked. Chris realized he had said too much. When he didn't say any more, the man had advised him to keep in mind that a Canadian like their dinner host was a foreigner, and to collaborate with even a Canadian in an attack on an American target would count as treason as well as whatever specific crime was being committed.

He had left Chris to finish the cigarette alone.

Chris hadn't been sure that the man had been American because his accent had been hard to place, but evidently he had been. And evidently they always wrote it down whenever they talked to you.

"My name is Joe," the interrogator said. "Tell me what your working group is about."

"We just talk to people."

"Like me?" the interrogator asked. "Like the way your friend talked to me?"

The interrogator had been standing beside and slightly behind two cops, four or five hours before, and maybe it had been on account of his suit, a little nicer than a bureaucrat in law enforcement usually wears, that Leif had singled him out. Had called on him without his name, the way

Leif was able to. Chris had been standing in the road with Raleigh, waiting to be arrested for obstruction of the traffic that would, theoretically, have existed where they were standing if the police and protesters hadn't. Matthew and Leif had been on the sidewalk with the women because Matthew had said that he didn't want to be arrested. Leif had probably felt restless standing there on the sidelines and had started to banter with the man. Almost to flirt with him. *I bet your password has something to do with boots, doesn't it. You're showing it to me by thinking of it right now, you know. Oh my god, you're showing* them *to me. Boots twenty-four seven. Boots twenty-four seven Charlotte, or something like that. Is that it? Am I right?* At the guess, there had been a flare of anger in the man's eyes. *Heterosexual realness for the win!* Leif had crowed.

"There was more to it than talking," the interrogator said now.

"Do you think he read your mind?" Chris asked.

The man watched Chris for a moment, as if weighing whether Chris was trying to insult him. "What kind of research on me had your friend done?"

"I don't think he even knew your name."

"It's Joe."

"Yeah, you said."

"Can you tell me my last name?"

Chris wished he could, to fuck with him. "I'm not as good at it."

"You think he read my mind," the interrogator inferred. "You believe he can do that sort of thing." The man was making an effort not to sound incredulous.

He waited for Chris to speak, as if he was hoping that Chris would volunteer an explanation of his faith in the phenomenon if not an explanation of the phenomenon itself. To keep himself from talking, Chris studied the man. He had the average, undistinguished features of a local news weatherman, of someone you would pass in the drugstore without noticing. Of someone who had never expected to live in a world that needed much explanation and was a little resentful about the discovery that he did.

"He's a gay guy? Your leader?"

"You should ask him."

"Have you slept with him?"

Chris let the question go.

The man tried another angle. "Do you know much about the law? You didn't go to college."

"I went for a year."

"Your friends went all the way through, didn't they. But I wonder how much more they know. It's a funny part of the law. If I know your mother's maiden name, I usually don't even need your password, these days. If I know the name of your first pet or your kindergarten teacher." His tone became reflective. "And is it wrong to know that kind of thing about someone? I think it's something we're still figuring out, as a society. Where to draw the line."

"What are you figuring out? Why we're not supposed to know each other's secrets but you're allowed to?"

"There are controls on us," the man said. He had gone touchy, suddenly. "There are *ethics*." He had to live up to the authority he had over someone like Chris, and he felt that he did live up to it. "We're only trying to protect you, you know that, don't you," the man said. "Or do you not give a shit."

Chris gave a shit. That was his whole problem. For example, he was acutely aware right now, even though it wasn't in his interest to be, that the man was asking Chris to give him the benefit of the doubt. And a part of Chris, also against his interest, wanted to give it to him.

"I can't help you, man," Chris said.

"What does he want?"

The man still hadn't asked for Leif's name; probably he already knew it. "Peace and love," Chris answered. "What does anyone want."

The man pulled back from the table, looked at the ceiling, and made a sort of froglike face, as if he were judging Chris. He stood up, opened his wallet, hesitated, and then took out a business card. "If you want to get in touch . . ."

Chris stood, too. Maybe he was going to be able to go home now. He let the man hold the card out until the gesture became awkward. "No thanks," Chris said. "If we want to find you, we'll be able to."

It was a line that the man could have used on him. The man grimaced. "Are you *sure* your friends are looking out for you, 'Hyacinth'?" He said the flower name distinctly. He laid the card on the table before he left.

It wasn't until after Chris had pocketed the card that it occurred to him that the cops behind the mirrored window had watched him do so.

"Did you read him?" Raleigh asked, when they brought Chris back to the holding cell.

"I can't read people, Raleigh," he answered.

During Chris's absence, they had been joined by many more Occupiers, so many that it was easy to dodge Raleigh's curiosity.

In the afternoon, for a few minutes, while Raleigh was on the phone, Chris was able to talk to Calvin. "How do you know," Chris asked, "when somebody you're with is talking?"

"You got a bad feeling?"

"This guy upstairs called me a name I never heard before. It was super gay."

"Don't let them get to you, man."

"No, I mean, he made it sound like a name other people are calling me. That people I'm with are calling me behind my back." Chris looked at his hands. "We haven't done anything," he added, in frustration.

"They got all kinds of laws."

Chris doubted that they had laws for what he and his friends had been doing.

That night, as he lay under the unextinguished fluorescents, not far from Raleigh on the cement floor, which was cold, he mulled over the two pieces of evidence: The business card of Joseph P. Bresser, operational security consultant. The nickname Hyacinth. He would have told Raleigh about the business card if it hadn't been for the nickname. The nickname probably had something to do with his looks.

Matthew and Julia were the new additions to the group, the ones the rest knew the least about. They were a little older, and with age, one accumulated compromises, which made one vulnerable—fissures where the establishment's grappling hooks could catch.

Sometimes Chris wondered if it was really true that he couldn't read people. Maybe it was just that he thought it would be rude to, that it would be unfair to try to go behind another person's mask. He was willing to imagine undressing a woman. Was that different? He had undressed Julia in his mind, once he had become aware that she wanted him. He hadn't taken advantage because he hadn't been sure it would be possible in real life to fuck her hard enough to make himself actually present to her.

He was getting off track, but it seemed natural to consider the sexual side of people when trying to assess their capacity for betrayal.

Matthew seemed to want Chris, too. That was his m.o.; you were supposed to wonder. That was okay, fuck him. Matthew and Julia both had that go-for-broke attitude toward sex that people reach just as they're about to age out of their years of being attractive. Almost all the encouragement that they were likely to receive in the course of their lives for being selfish about sex had come to them recently.

At the moment they were still so confident that Bresser would probably only have been able to turn them if he had found something to frighten them with. Something to knock them off their footings.

Chris turned his head to look at Raleigh, whose footing had never been very stable. Raleigh had taken off his glasses, folding them into his shirt pocket, and under the livid glare of the cell's lighting, he seemed to be holding his eyes shut with an effort of will. Beneath his billy-goat-ish beard, his mouth was at work—chewing, or sucking—as he dreamed.

When Raleigh had first showed up in New Orleans on the socialists' doorstep, he had annoyed everyone, including Chris. He had introduced himself as a coder from Tulsa, as if people trying to repair a broken-down society needed a coder, and they had been able to tell from the way he had said it that he thought that as a coder he had been too good for Tulsa, and would probably have considered himself too good for New Orleans, too, if it hadn't become in its misery a worthy cause. He had worked hard, though, it turned out. That was the upside of Raleigh's constant need to prove himself. Chris had eventually even grown fond of Raleigh's geeky arrogance, once he got to know him. He had gradually become willing to overlook the air that all Raleigh's efforts had of being done for the sake of a résumé that he was drafting in his mind, an inventory of his virtues that would someday cause him to be well regarded by a higher class of people— the ones that the rest of the people in the New Orleans group had been in the habit of referring to, not really joking, as the enemy.

Raleigh had been too angular for the South. His personality made more sense at Occupy, with its bickering and rulemaking. In New Orleans, they had had to do a lot of what they needed to do without being seen to have planned for it and in some cases without spelling out the nature of what they were doing. Such as continuing to talk to a guy in the force without letting anyone else know you were still talking to him. The people in the movement had had to become *figures*, Chris had tried to explain once to Raleigh, but Raleigh had objected to the word. He had seemed to think that it would be enough for them to be themselves.

He had always been sort of an idiot.

The city kept them overnight. What Chris wanted to do after they got out was go home, take a shower, and lie in bed.

After a shower, he did lie in bed, alone. It was the middle of the afternoon. He didn't jack off. He studied his white ceiling and the white walls he hadn't decorated. He listened to semis trundling past on the four-lane avenue that was half a block away. From time to time, in the space above him in the room, phrases that he had heard spoken in the past twenty-four hours repeated themselves almost aloud. It was pleasant not to have to account for himself to Raleigh or a policeman or Calvin or anyone else.

He dozed. When he woke up, in the afternoon, it came to him that he had been strong, as a person, and that it would be reasonable for him to feel a certain amount of pride. He had passed through an ordeal. He had stood up, and he had been sent to jail for it, and he hadn't said anything.

The day began to die, and he got dressed and took the subway north to Elspeth's, where the working group was meeting.

A slightly odd thing happened when he arrived. Raleigh opened the door but remained on the spot, eyeing him and blocking his way. Chris's first interpretation was that Raleigh must want to establish that he was the one giving Chris permission to enter Elspeth's home—that he held a priority, on the site of Elspeth's apartment, that he wasn't willing to surrender. Chris looked politely away, to Elspeth's coat, hanging beside them in the entryway; the blue fingers of her wool gloves limply signaled from the pocket where they were trapped.

Chris's second thought, however, was that Raleigh had somehow learned of the invitation that Bresser had extended. A little steam cloud of indignation rose through him—Raleigh had no right to suspect him—and for a few moments, he couldn't speak.

"Hey," Raleigh at last said, saluting Chris with a backward nod of the head that acknowledged that he had had to be the first to speak and that he noticed such signs of relative rank. There was a nervous appeal in his eyes, and Chris came up with a third understanding of what Raleigh wanted: he wanted Chris to testify to the backbone that *Raleigh* had shown in jail.

"Hey," Chris replied. He put an arm over Raleigh's shoulders and hugged him from the side, and Raleigh laughed, pleased, as Chris pushed past him.

The rest of the group were in the parlor, too excited to take seats. Chris reminded himself: There had been a new recognition of Leif's power. And someone here had betrayed him.

He congratulated Leif.

"On what?" Leif asked. "You and Raleigh did the time."

"You read that man's password. That guy yesterday morning."

"I startled him, maybe."

"No, you read his password." He gave Bresser's business card to Leif. "He was so freaked out that he interrogated me about you at Central Booking."

Raleigh scurried around to look over Leif's shoulder. "What's this?"

"Let me see," said Julia. The others, too, crowded in.

The hand of Leif's that was holding the business card drooped, but no one dared to take the card from him. Instead, they all crouched in order to be able to keep looking at it.

"You did it," Chris told Leif. He and Leif were the only two in the room standing tall. He wanted Leif to realize what he had done. He wasn't making any claim on it for himself. He never wanted to, when he was with Leif, which, if you thought about it, was a remarkable feeling to have about someone.

Leif turned the card over; the back was blank. "You must hate this," he said to Matthew, who was sitting beside him. "You were hoping it would go away."

Matthew shrugged.

"Who is he?" Raleigh asked. "Why did he want to talk to you?"

"Who's Hyacinth?" Chris replied. He watched Raleigh's eyes.

"Hyacinth?"

"Who is he," Chris insisted.

Raleigh hesitated.

"Oh, *Christopher*," broke in Julia, in a deliberately plummy voice.

He turned on her. "Did you talk about me?"

The silence in the room was heavy. "Are you snitch-jacketing her?" Raleigh asked, his voice cracking.

The members of the working group were waiting for Chris's answer, but he felt as though he were holding not a grenade but only an antique colored-glass Christmas tree globe, too tightly.

"I did call you that a few times," Julia admitted, "but I never 'talked' to anyone." She adjusted her scarf, the way a bird rouses and then settles its feathers. "I think I called you Hyacinth out of fondness, really."

"It's from a Henry James novel," Raleigh explained, a little sullenly.

"You make it sound like you've read it," Julia said, amused.

Fuck them, Chris thought. As the wind rattled one of the parlor's window sashes, his mind left and went again to his memory of New Orleans. In the silence between when he and his friend had cut their engine and when they had restarted it, rain had sprinkled the flat green surface around them, harmlessly.

Raleigh started talking, about how everyone makes mistakes sometimes, and sometimes they hurt each other's feeling, but if everyone in the working group continued to stand together, as a working group, no one would be able to do anything to them, and no one would be able to stop them, because principles are more powerful and more important than individuals, and they could beat this guy, they could take him down, and as Chris listened, and realized that he didn't believe, and sensed that no one else really believed, either, he decided that he would be perfectly happy to let Raleigh shove himself into the danger that Raleigh was pretending not to see.

"I think Bresser had us under surveillance," Raleigh suggested. "I think that's how he knew about this nickname."

"You think he was watching us before Leif even saw him," Elspeth said.

"And we should doxx him," Raleigh proposed.

"Wouldn't that be dangerous?" Matthew asked. "He works for the government."

"No, he's a contractor," Raleigh said. "This isn't dot-gov or dot-mil," he said, tapping the email address on the business card.

"He'll have a new password by now," said Elspeth.

"Then Leif can read that one, too."

"I don't know if he can," said Leif.

"I bet you can."

Leif noticed Chris's silence. "You're doing your chthonic straight-boy thing."

"My what?"

"That's very close to a description of the character of Hyacinth, actually," Julia said.

"Let Raleigh doxx him if he wants to," Chris said. "Diversity of tactics."

"*You* don't want to?" Raleigh challenged him.

"Sure I want to," Chris lied. If Raleigh needed the spur of competition, Chris was willing to give it to him. He was willing to sit right next to him. He was willing to hold his fucking hand.

"You're going to break into this man's email?" asked Elspeth.

"Let's vote on it," Raleigh suggested.

"You don't vote on right or wrong," Elspeth said.

"Why not? This is America."

Instead of voting, however, they argued, for hours. During the argument, Chris wondered if it was right for him to be holding back some of his thoughts, but he didn't think he could accuse himself of bad faith, exactly. A doxxing was the sort of thing that deserved to happen to someone like Bresser, and it wasn't Chris who had planted the idea in Raleigh's mind. The mere sight of Bresser's card had seemed to place it there, and it was Julia who had seconded Raleigh's motion. She was rich; to her, it probably always felt natural to reach into what belonged to other people and take.

He didn't think they were likely to get caught. Every week he got spam from a friend whose email account had been hacked, and no one ever talked about catching the hackers or even trying to. If he thought, even secretly, that they weren't going to get away with it, he wouldn't be taking part himself. So that wasn't what he was holding back.

Bresser had said get in touch. Well, they were going to get in touch all right.

Still, he might have ended up saying something if the individual members of the working group hadn't, without his lifting a finger, taken the sides on the question that they did—Raleigh and Julia choosing to go after Bresser, Leif and Elspeth choosing not to. The ones Chris might have wished to protect were protecting themselves. Elspeth, in fact, became vehement. As a matter of ethics, she asserted, anarchists shouldn't do anything that they didn't want done to themselves, not even if it already had been done to them—and no one knew for sure, in this case, that it had been. It might just have been a coincidence, she argued, that Bresser had used the same nickname for Chris that Julia had. It was also possible that someone in the group had said the nickname aloud at Occupy one day and that it had been overheard by a plainclothes detective who had reported it to Bresser. Even if the nickname was upsetting (here Elspeth had glanced at Chris), the distress shouldn't become a pretext for retaliation. They should be modeling a community of trust.

He didn't let her know that he wanted to be able to agree with her; that much did go on his conscience. But it seemed to him that the only way he knew to get by in the world anymore was by drifting in it, like a spider hanging in the air from a silk that it has spun out of itself.

"He has to be monitoring us," Raleigh claimed, of Bresser.

"Then he's monitoring *this*," Elspeth pointed out, gesturing to the room that contained them and their conversation.

"No, I think he's monitoring our email, if anything," Raleigh said.

"So is he or isn't he, Raleigh."

"My guess is he's monitoring our email. I did call Chris 'Hyacinth' once in an email."

Chris didn't say anything. It was working so well to let them do the arguing, and he didn't want to seem to have been waiting for a confession from Raleigh. He didn't think that he had been waiting for one.

When Chris came back the next afternoon, when he knew Raleigh would be away at his IT job, it was for a second chance at being seen through.

It should have been easy for Elspeth to see through him. He had worked all morning at a move, from a basement to a second-floor apartment, sweating out the toxins and the obscurities in his system, drinking bottle after plastic bottle of spring water. At home afterward, he had showered and combed his hair, which was just beginning to be long enough to curl behind his ears. After so much exertion, he knew that he was fresh and that his mind was clear. It was the knotted-up part of Elspeth that was attached to Raleigh. The clear part, responding to Chris's clarity, should be able to see him.

As he rang her buzzer, he remembered that Raleigh and Julia had left the meeting together the night before, claiming they wanted to talk tactics, which they had said Elspeth wouldn't want to hear.

Elspeth flushed when she recognized Chris. He felt a little flutter of hope, even though he knew that her flush was probably because she still felt angry with him, or at best was embarrassed about having been so angry with him the night before. He wanted to imagine, instead, that she had hoped to see him and that her face was flushed because her wish had come true.

"I can't talk long," she warned. "I have a piece that I have to finish checking by tonight." Around her laptop on the dining room table, pages were fanned out like the spokes of a wheel. "Do you want some tea? I have chamomile."

"It doesn't make you go to sleep?"

"Not me. I'm too anxious."

"Sure, if you're making it."

"I'm always making it." She vanished into the kitchen.

There was a little elephant, knitted out of pink yarn, on the dining room table next to her work. With a finely sharpened pencil, in a tidy italic script, she had written notes in the margins of the article that she was fact-checking. Her letter shapes were quick and peppery.

Once she put the kettle on, she leaned against a jamb of the kitchen doorway, her slender arms folded. "I can't play cards today," she told him.

"I didn't think you'd be able to."

The furthest she would have been able to see, in any attempt that she might have been making to see into his motives, was to a detection that it was against his own better judgment that he had taken Raleigh's side the night before. Somewhat against his own nature, even. His choice might irritate her, but she wouldn't be able to see why he had made it.

"Are you mad at me?" he asked.

"It wouldn't matter if I were."

She could probably tell that he was hiding, but he had to hide at least a little if he was going to have any chance with her.

She turned away, to pour the boiling water. When she returned to the dining room, she was carrying two mugs. She set one down on the table in front of him. "It's hot," she told him. "The mug itself." Her fingers were so slender. How could she bear it if he couldn't? She took the seat where she had been working, and he sat down in a chair facing her on the same side of the table. She held her mug in two hands and tossed her hair out of her eyes.

Do you want me to ask them not to, he asked her, mentally, as she watched him. "Do you want me to ask them not to?" he repeated, aloud.

"Who—Raleigh? What makes you think he'd listen?" she said. She looked away.

He poked at the sachet in his mug with an index finger, and the hot water stung a little. He wiped the finger on his pants.

"Leif is afraid," she told him.

"Of what?"

"Because of the Hyacinth thing, he thinks maybe the government has caretakers on its side, too. People like us."

Chris frowned.

"It's possible," she said.

"You don't think Bresser's one," said Chris.

"I didn't get a good read on him."

"Well, he's not one," he said. "He's not at all like you and Leif."

"We don't know that every caretaker is going to be like us."

"Yes we do," he insisted. He hadn't wanted to hand Bresser the keys to his soul. Wanting to was how he recognized a caretaker.

They fell silent, and in the silence, after a while, his desire for her became so evident that it grew difficult for either of them to think of a natural-sounding way to talk about anything else. He was a beggar. He was begging for her love. She was able to see him, he knew. The rawness and the bloodiness of his heart were in front of her. The sky, seen through the warped old glass of the windows, was featureless.

"Could you do it?" he asked.

She stopped looking at him. "Raleigh thinks of me as a weapon, too, now."

He repented sharply. "I'll tell them not to do it," he volunteered.

"No, I don't want to owe anyone anything right now. Not even you."

It wasn't really him that she was angry at. That is, if she could see through him, it wasn't.

"I'm not afraid of being caught," Elspeth said.

"I know."

"In case you thought that was why. I thought the whole point was that we understood that we had been damaged by knowing other people's secrets. The whole point was that we had been hurt because we knew other people's secrets without having asked to know them and without wanting to know them."

He sat still. It would have been presumptuous to try to take her in his arms.

"And now Raleigh and Julia say they want to go looking for secrets," she continued.

There's a sweet pain in sitting next to someone who is tacitly forbidding you to speak. It occurred to Chris that under a strong impulse he was at last experiencing something like the intuition that was constant for Elspeth and Leif. This must be close to what the burden felt like that was always pressing on them.

Before he found the courage to speak, however, the silence was interrupted by the scrape of Raleigh's keys in the door.

"Hello?" they heard Raleigh say.

"We're in here," said Elspeth patiently.

"Oh, hi, Chris," Raleigh said as he came around the corner, without disguising his disappointment. Raleigh had passed beyond the wish for Chris's support that he had been feeling the day before. He had a new ally now.

"Perfect timing," Julia greeted Chris.

They had converged outside the not-quite-converted warehouse where Raleigh lived, which was a couple of subway stops beyond the neighborhood where Raleigh would probably have preferred to live if he could have afforded to. Across the street, there was a chicken processor, as windowless as a telephone company building, and at the end of the block there was a cement yard. Under the quivering sodium of the streetlamps, the asphalt was swirled with gray where workers had hosed off the troughs and undercarriages of the cement trucks, diluting the powder and dispersing it until the particles were no longer in any danger of consolidation.

When the buzzer sounded, Chris opened the door and held it for Julia. Was she pretending for his benefit? Had she left Raleigh's apartment a few minutes earlier so that Chris could see her arriving? She smiled at him like a salesperson. If she was concerned about Chris's impression of her, it didn't push her as far as conversation with him.

He followed her down a blind, irregular white corridor. He remembered it from a party that Raleigh had invited him to, a week after they had run into each other at Occupy. When they had first seen each other, they had embraced. It had been four years, after all. It had been hard not to love everybody you met at Occupy in the early days, and if it was an old friend . . .

The corridor zigzagged between apartments that had been partitioned out of what had once been a factory floor. At each threshold, a family of boots and shoes waited.

Chris was pretending at least as much as Julia was. He was pretending that he wanted to help carry out something he in fact didn't think they would be able to pull off. He was here to witness the vindication of an idea that Leif had presented in one of his blog posts, namely, that the capacity that interested them either was, or was inextricable from, a supersensitive variety of tact, and couldn't be used to open any door that it wouldn't be appropriate to open. Chris reasoned that it was only because Raleigh and Julia lacked the capacity that they were willing to try to open the door in this case. A curiosity like theirs was bound to be harmless. Almost by definition.

If there was any danger tonight, it was probably in Chris himself. Reading people had something to do with playing oneself false in order to accommodate the wishes of others, and he seemed to be doing more and more of that lately.

Behind the apartment door, a song was blaring. When Julia's knock went unregarded, Chris stepped in front of her and pounded with the butt of his fist. "It's open," they heard Raleigh yell. The music was extinguished. Julia opened the door on Raleigh walking toward them. "Hey," Raleigh said. He seemed wary.

"Hello," Julia said, mostly to the high, empty space of the apartment, which she made a show of noticing, as she walked past Raleigh.

Raleigh lived with two roommates, posers like him. Since the apartment had few interior walls, the men used their possessions to establish individual zones for themselves. A metal rack that held LPs staked a claim in one corner; a garment rack on wheels marked turf in another. Worn magazines were stacked high on a desk, and when Chris got close, he saw that they were gay porn, decades old. The openness of their placement seemed to be part of the room's sparring.

"Is this Debbie Harry?" Julia asked, about one of an array of what looked like Polaroids taped to the wall outside the bathroom.

"Those are Warhols, actually," said Raleigh. "Philip's gallery had a set of them in, and he stayed late one night and made color xeroxes."

"Huh."

"He gets away with murder."

"Is it murder to make color xeroxes?" Julia wondered. "By the way, this *is* Debbie Harry."

"Drinks?" Raleigh asked. He listed brands of liquor.

Chris didn't know what any of them tasted like and asked for a beer.

"Take one of Jeremy's," Raleigh said. "He owes me."

Beer, condiments, and a pizza box were all the fridge contained.

"Bachelorville," Julia said. She took a beer, too.

The apartment was a profane place, Chris felt. Not like Elspeth's. Everything in it seemed to be trying to make a statement. There was a machine that attached to an electric saw and vacuumed up sawdust while the saw was in operation. There was a plastic chair in the form of a smiling ladybug, probably hauled in off the street. The atmosphere in a room like this could never be subtle. The night of Raleigh's party, several women and one man had come on to Chris. It had only been because of Occupy that someone like him had even been visible to them.

The gift could never be used here because the gift was like faith. If it hadn't been given to you, the most you could feel was envy, and it would be a strange kind of envy, since it would be of something you couldn't even honestly say you believed in. A kind of longing. But here the three of them were.

"So are we doing this?" asked Raleigh.

"Didn't you use to not believe in it?" asked Julia. She had found a non-pornographic magazine and was leafing through it.

"I don't think it's what Leif thinks it is. I think it's probably unconscious pattern recognition." Raleigh perched on a stool at a high island table in the kitchen and flipped open a scuffed blue-and-gray laptop. Three heavy thesis clips held shut one of its edges. "Like maybe the cells of the brain that are supposed to solve the Fourier transforms in sound start to work on decryption for some reason."

"You're such a nerd," Julia said.

The mild neg seemed to please him. "I'm just going to set up a proxy before we start so we're not totally out in the open."

Julia placed a stool so that she would be able to watch Raleigh's screen over his right shoulder. "Who's going to do the mind reading?" she asked. "I mean, with the three of us."

"We're not so bad at it," Raleigh said.

"We are, actually," she insisted.

Raleigh snorted in what might have been agreement.

Chris took up a position at the end of the island table, where he could see Raleigh's and Julia's faces but not the screen. He didn't want to get any closer.

"Cybercrimes aren't that riveting to watch, are they," Julia observed, with a glance at Chris.

"We're not the ones committing the real crimes," said Raleigh.

When the doorbell sounded, however, they froze. "Shit," said Raleigh. He hurriedly set about shutting down the machine. "Chris, could you see who it is? The middle button on the intercom beside the door here. Only the middle button. Don't press anything else yet."

When Chris pressed it, a small monitor flickered into life, revealing Leif, in pixelated chiaroscuro, captured by a fish-eye lens downstairs on the building's stoop. Through the monitor, Chris watched as Leif, unaware that he was being watched, reached toward the fish-eye lens to ring the doorbell a second time.

Unprepared for the bell, the other two in the room with Chris were again shaken by it.

"It's Leif," Chris told them.

"Is he alone?"

"Yes."

"Then let him in."

"I already did."

Raleigh shoved his laptop shut. "This stupid fucking thing." He padded over to the apartment door, opened it, and left it ajar.

In the monitor, watched without his knowledge, Leif had seemed ordinary.

"Goodness," said Julia, recovering. "Is there nothing to mix with that vodka you were telling us about?"

"Not really."

She looked in the refrigerator herself. "Ketchup."

"Knock knock," Leif said, as he let himself in.

"What a lovely surprise," said Julia, as if welcoming a visitor to a country house.

Leif's eyes were glittering. "Have you started yet?" he asked.

It had been a mistake for Chris to expect that Leif would refuse to participate. It had been a mistake to count on that.

"So you changed your mind," said Raleigh.

"I broke up with Matthew."

"You did?"

"I don't know. Maybe. I wanted to be here if you were going to do it." He was on edge.

"Awesome," said Raleigh.

Maybe the gift was as amoral as the five conventional senses.

"You know what this is going to be?" Raleigh continued. "This is going to be justice." He took up his place at his laptop again.

"'Justice,' really?" said Julia doubtfully, as she reclaimed the seat to his right. "We're just taking a look. We're not doing anything, really."

"Did you read Bresser's website?" asked Raleigh. "He runs a private company that does government surveillance."

Chris wasn't going to be able to protect Leif. But maybe Leif didn't need protection. Maybe they would get away with what they were about to do. Chris scraped a thumbnail against the label of his beer.

"And then also, I thought, *If Chris is going to be here . . .*," said Leif.

"What do you mean?"

"You're a rock," said Leif. He put a hand on Chris's shoulder as he crossed behind him, to stand on Raleigh's left. Chris looked away and let Leif think he was looking away out of bashfulness.

Raleigh booted up his laptop again. "Let's hope Bresser doesn't have two-factor authentication."

"So let's do it," said Chris impatiently.

"Hold on," said Raleigh. "I have a little script I need to launch first."

The group fell silent. Chris watched the faces of the three others as they studied the screen that they were going to try to enter. A wavering light dusted Raleigh's fingers as he typed. Inside the machine, the hard drive clicked and burred. A fan switched on and began to whine.

"I didn't even know you could do that with this kind of computer," Julia commented.

"Do what?" asked Raleigh. "Unix?"

"I didn't know you could just enter text like that. Is this 'code'?"

"Oh, you mean command-line mode."

"'Command line,'" she echoed. "That sounds so *executive*."

Leif pointed at the screen. "Here?"

"Not yet," said Raleigh. "Let me do one more thing first."

If they were thinking about Chris at all, they were probably imagining that he wasn't looking because he was too stupid to understand what was happening on-screen.

"What?" Leif asked Chris, as if he had heard Chris's thoughts.

Chris shrugged.

"I'm not always everything everyone thinks I am," Leif said.

"I know," Chris said.

"Here we are," Raleigh announced.

"This is it?" asked Julia.

Leif closed his eyes. Was he going to be able to reach Bresser? Wouldn't his mind be too full of the fight that he had just had with Matthew? Of the excitement of wrongdoing that was sparking between Raleigh and Julia, beside him? Of the disappointment that Chris felt? Unseeing, Leif raised his hands in front of him and held them there, without touching them together, as if something invisible was being woven between them.

3.

Why is she pounding on our door? Elspeth wondered, from inside what must have been a dream, as the pounding woke her up. In the dream, as in real life, she had been in bed with Raleigh. But in real life Julia wouldn't pound like that.

"Raleigh," Elspeth said. He was still sleeping. A margin of rumpled bedclothes ran between the two of them. They had had an argument about of all things sex after Raleigh had come in the night before. "Raleigh, who do you think it is?" The clock told her that it was almost eight thirty. She didn't like the idea of being caught by a stranger in her T-shirt and underwear so late on a weekday morning.

"Who?"

She put on yesterday's jeans and a sweatshirt. "At the door." She stepped into her slippers and tugged them on as she walked. "Just a minute," she called out.

Her landlord had been supposed to send a repairman to look at the radiator in the dining room, which leaked, but she had asked for the repair two months ago, and she had given up expecting it. She had gotten used to the leak, which was a slow one. In the early morning and at bedtime, a few drops of water trickled out, and a ramekin of hers was under the grille now, to catch the drops. All she had to do was try to remember to empty the ramekin every few days.

Under the pounding, the edges of the door were shuddering. In her heart, she knew by now who it was, but there wasn't anything she could do about it. Would they want her, too, or only Raleigh? "Just a minute," she repeated. She threw the deadbolt.

"Morning," said one of two policemen in uniform. A third man, not in uniform, stood behind them; under a winter coat he was wearing the gray smock of a technician. "We have a warrant for the arrest of a Mr. Raleigh Evans for fraudulent access to a protected computer, and we have a warrant for all the internet-enabled equipment in this apartment," the first policeman continued. He stepped into the corridor and surveyed the shut doors of the three bedrooms.

"He's still in bed," said Elspeth.

The cop followed her eyes as they singled out the bedroom door that was hers. "Anyone else here this morning?" he asked, lowering his voice as if he were concerned about waking people up.

She shook her head.

"Is that a no, ma'am?"

"Yes, no. No one but us."

"Do you know whether Mr. Evans is armed."

"No, of course he isn't."

The cop quickly opened the two doors of her roommates' two empty bedrooms and left them open. Then he nodded his head sideways toward Elspeth's door. The second uniformed cop took the signal and stepped past Elspeth. He had a raised gun.

"We're gonna need all your computers and all your phones," said the first cop, placing himself between Elspeth and her bedroom as the second cop turned the knob with the hand not holding a gun.

As the cops walked through the socially defined barriers within the apartment, they seemed to topple them out of existence.

"Raleigh Evans? Rise and shine," Elspeth heard the second cop say. "You're under arrest, Mr. Evans, for fraudulent access to a protected computer."

"Who are you?" Elspeth asked the first cop.

"Seventy-second Precinct, ma'am. Are you sure there's no one else in the apartment with us? Anyone I don't know about?"

"I don't—," she began. "Raleigh—," she began again.

"I need you to stay where you are, ma'am, and I need you to remain calm. Take a breath. One breath at a time."

The cop was about thirty. His badge read DILEO. His chin was shadowy with a beard even though he had shaved. From overeating, it was beginning to swim in his face. She wasn't able to read him. His true self was hidden like the soft body of a beetle inside its chitin.

"I don't consent to this search," she said, remembering a piece of advice from an Occupy workshop.

"We don't need you to, ma'am. We have all the warrants we need."

She heard the second cop give Raleigh permission to put on pants and a shirt so long as the cop was able to check them first. They were going to take Raleigh away in a minute, she realized.

Her phone was in a pocket of her jeans, and she took it out. "I'm going to record you," she announced, holding it up. Her hands were trembling.

"Can't let you do that," said Officer Dileo.

"I have the right to record you."

"Not with that phone. The judge wants that phone."

The man in the smock spoke up. "We're responsible for preserving the integrity of the evidence, ma'am."

She made a conscious effort not to jerk her hands away as Dileo took the phone out of them. "What about the integrity of people," she said. *What a weak retort*, she admitted to herself, silently.

The technician slid it into a dark gray bag.

"I *need* it," she said a moment later, as she thought ahead to the next few hours. "I don't have a landline."

"You can take that up with the phone company," Dileo said.

"Are you laughing at me?"

"No, ma'am," said Dileo, with a glance at the man in the smock.

"I'm going to need a lawyer, Elspeth," came Raleigh's voice.

"You dressed, then, sir?" said the second policeman. Elspeth heard the click of handcuffs closing on Raleigh.

"Is that necessary?" she asked. No one answered her.

"Okay, John," Dileo said, nodding to the man in the smock, who now slipped into the bedroom, too.

"You all right here?" the second cop asked the first, as he pushed Raleigh to the bedroom door. Raleigh was wearing his glasses instead of his contacts, and the lenses were filthy. "I'll take him down to the car."

"Good-bye," Raleigh told Elspeth, more as if he were quoting a valediction than saying one. His hands were cuffed behind his back, and the second cop pushed him forward by lifting the cuffs, so he wasn't able to stop when he came abreast of her. It didn't seem right to touch him.

"Hold on," said the technician, emerging from the bedroom. He had found Raleigh's laptop and was holding it open on one palm, waiter style. "Password?"

"Whippoorwill. Two *p*'s, two *o*'s."

"Raleigh," said Elspeth. Why was he giving them that.

"What? We didn't do anything. Everything we downloaded was about us. If you had looked—"

"You don't have a lawyer yet," she reminded him.

"They're not recording."

"They're remembering."

"Are there different passwords on any of these partitions?" the technician asked, tracing on the mousepad with the index finger of his free hand.

Helpful again, Raleigh shook his head. His job, after all, consisted of answering questions that people asked about computers.

"All right, then," the second cop said, and pushed Raleigh out the apartment's front door.

Officer Dileo told Elspeth that her cell phone would no doubt be returned to her in a day or so, and it wasn't until after he had left with not only Raleigh's phone and hers but also their laptops, her router, and the laptops of both her roommates that it occurred to her that he had almost certainly been lying, in order to make her more amenable to surrendering them.

Without the internet and without her cell phone—without any way to communicate that did not begin with walking downstairs and out of the building—it felt very quiet in the apartment. Would it be heartless to take a shower? For the moment what she felt most urgently was that she was unsupervised.

She undressed and stepped into the apartment's old tub and let the water run over her. In old stop-motion animations, water was sometimes represented by crinkled strips of aluminum foil, but when it ran over your skin maybe it looked more like cling wrap. Through the moving film of it she inspected herself for signs of age that hadn't yet come, playing for consolation a familiar game against herself.

It was a relief to her that her latest fact-checking assignment was safely finished, she thought, as she dried herself in a yellow towel. She had to find a lawyer for Raleigh. She didn't want to fail him, whether or not she and he were going to stay together. She also had to find a new phone for herself before her mother tried to call. What a nerd she was, to be relieved about having finished her fact-checking. But it was harmless that she was a nerd. It wasn't because of that that she and Raleigh were going to break up, if in fact they were going to.

The wife in the couple who lived across the landing was a stay-at-home mom, and after getting dressed, Elspeth knocked on her door. She looked down at the gray house slippers that she had put on over her socks, wondering if they were respectful enough. The woman's baby was a girl, she reminded herself. She didn't think she'd ever been told its name.

The door of her own apartment was ajar, she noticed. She stepped back over and pulled the door to. In case the police came back.

She should probably lie about why she needed to borrow a phone. She heard a soft thunk, as an appliance of some kind inside her neighbor's apartment reached the end of one of its cycles. Maybe no one was home.

"Who is it, please?" came a small, brittle voice, very near. The woman must have been studying Elspeth through the peephole.

"It's your neighbor. I'm your neighbor," Elspeth said. "I wonder if I could borrow your phone? I can't find mine." She was a terrible liar.

"I could call it for you," the woman offered, not opening her door.

"I think it's dead?" Elspeth said. "And the thing is, I need to call a friend."

The woman opened the door. She had a triangular face and a small mouth. She was holding her baby and joggling it.

"I hope I didn't wake her up," Elspeth said.

The woman frowned a no. "Come in." She padded down a dim corridor, a mirror image of the one in Elspeth's apartment. The floor of the woman's kitchen had brick-colored tiles where Elspeth's had linoleum. The woman nodded at a phone on the wall beside her refrigerator and sat down at her dining table to watch.

Fortunately Elspeth knew Leif's number by heart. The call went to voicemail, however. She tried Raleigh's even though she knew there would be no answer; there was no answer. She tried Leif's again, and again the call went to voicemail.

She was aware, as she listened to Leif's voice inviting her to leave a message, that she was losing time.

"Not picking up?" the woman asked.

"Let me try one more time." She didn't know what else to do; she didn't know anyone else's number by heart. If she went to the jail by herself, without a phone, she might wait there all day in the wrong place without knowing any better.

With a look of alarm, the woman abruptly rose and stalked out of the room, leaving Elspeth momentarily alone. "There's someone at your door," she said when she returned.

"*My* door?" asked Elspeth. Was it the police again?

"It's a man," the woman said. "Are you in trouble?"

"No," Elspeth said. "No," she repeated, trying to sound more convincing.

The man knocking muffled knocks on Elspeth's door, with a fist that was clutching a wool cap, was Matthew. He turned around and showed her the thick but even features of his face. She was proud of always being polite with Leif's lovers. He didn't seem surprised that she hadn't been in her own apartment.

"This is my neighbor," Elspeth said, gesturing to the woman on the threshold behind her. She still didn't know the woman's name. "I was just trying to call Leif," Elspeth explained to Matthew.

"They took him."

"But I didn't think he—"

"He changed his mind."

"Do you still need my phone?" Elspeth's neighbor asked.

"Oh, thank you," said Elspeth. "I guess not. Thank you so much."

"Wait," Matthew said, but the woman shut her door, and bolted it. "They took my phone, too."

"She has a baby," Elspeth said. "Let me put on some shoes."

She should wear her sneakers, she decided, trying to think ahead. Matthew followed her into the apartment. She had never been alone with him before. It was like being followed by a pet bear; there was a reason they used that word.

On the sofa in the parlor, she laced the sneakers up. The tarot deck waited primly on the coffee table for a reading that might never happen again. They had probably arrested Chris too. It was too bad that he had been mixed up in this. It was especially wrong to keep someone like him in jail, but then he was the sort of person who usually got put in jail. A person who mostly knew himself through action.

That was her mistake, she thought, catching herself. Thinking that men wanted her to help them understand themselves.

"Did they arrest Julia?" she asked.

"I don't know. Should we go to the courthouse? It isn't the same one as before."

Elspeth took out the slip of paper where Officer Dileo had written down the address. It was on this side of the river this time. "What did they do, do you know?"

"Downloaded something," Matthew said.

"Raleigh said it was about us."

"Well, it's gone now."

Every night, a script on Raleigh's laptop backed up the contents of his hard drive to the cloud. He had set the script up on Elspeth's computer, too, and they shared a password because Raleigh had bought the family rate. So the file probably wasn't gone; there was almost certainly a copy in the cloud. Elspeth found that she didn't want to tell Matthew about this backup, though. She felt possessive, the way mourners sometimes do. Anyway, the copy virtually didn't exist so long as she was the only one who knew that it existed.

"I should call Raleigh's parents at some point," she said. "I guess from a pay phone? I could call Leif's mother for you, too, if you want."

"I can call her," said Matthew. "If you have her number," he added.

There was a knock on the front door by an unfamiliar hand. Elspeth thought, as she walked toward it, that she wasn't going to be able to resist this kind of summons anymore. She had lost any chance of acting on her own volition for the foreseeable future. Every step she took was going to be fated.

It was only her mouse-faced neighbor again. The baby, still in the woman's arms, glared at Elspeth sleeplessly. "It's on TV," the woman said. "There's a story about your friend."

"What's on TV?"

"You're in Occupy or something, they're saying," the woman explained.

Elspeth retreated to her dining room, neighbor and baby following, and turned on the little TV on the sideboard.

"It's channel ten twenty-six," the neighbor said.

"We don't have cable."

"Can you get the local news?"

The burble of daytime television suddenly coated the room. Elspeth picked up the remote and made the machine chunk from channel to channel, each one angry and total.

OCCUPY HACKS HOMELAND SECURITY, read a headline on the screen.

"Wait," said Matthew.

"—tell us what that means exactly, Jim, a 'protected computer,'" said a blond woman in a navy blazer. "It's a little confusing."

"It sure is, Vera," said an expert standing in front of a scrim. "'Protected computer' is a legal term. It means, 'protected by this law.' By the CFAA. It doesn't mean anyone has necessarily *done* anything to protect or guard the computer in question."

"What's going on?" asked Elspeth.

Matthew read the crawl aloud: "'Four arrested for breaching computer of city police/DHS contractor.'"

"For those just joining us, a breaking story this morning. We don't as yet know their names, but a short while ago our camera team was able to film one suspect as he arrived downtown for processing."

Elspeth could see even through the television that Raleigh had decided that as a matter of principle he wasn't going to hide his face because he shouldn't need to. His exposed face was stiff with the effort of not looking at the prongs of the camera lenses aimed at him. There were calls for him to say a word or two, and though the calls were faint in the soundtrack, they were probably harsh in real life.

It was unfair of Elspeth to feel angry at Raleigh for relaying to her the pain that he was in.

"Where will we go if they come here?" she asked Matthew.

"They did come here," said her neighbor.

"I mean the newspeople."

The woman's baby squirmed impatiently, and the woman expertly rotated it so that its flailing limbs could grab only air. "I don't want them here," she told Elspeth.

"No, of course not," Elspeth agreed.

The woman said she needed to take her daughter back into her apartment. "Good luck," the woman added at the last minute, as if deciding that her curiosity had in the end committed her to Elspeth's side.

"Can I turn it off?" Elspeth asked Matthew.

"Please," Matthew said.

Being instantly deprived of the television's sounds and images, even though she hated them, felt to Elspeth like an amputation. She laid her palms over her eyes.

"Latte," Greg, one of Leif's fellow baristas, said to Elspeth, predictively, from his station behind the counter, when he saw Elspeth walk into the café with Matthew.

"No, I—," Elspeth began. But she changed her mind: "Well, to go, maybe. Did Leif call?"

Greg shook his head. He was a short, heavy, quiet man, with a wispy beard. He was already balding even though he was Leif and Elspeth's age, but his baldness, even from under the cyclist's cap that he always wore in the café, made him look younger, not older. "You?" he asked Matthew, as he began, on Elspeth's behalf, the rhythms of his practiced routine at the espresso maker.

"He wouldn't have been calling from his own number," Elspeth said.

Greg met Elspeth's eyes again. "I'll check," he said. She knew he would never tell her that he thought she was pretty, so she always wanted to be considerate with him, but not in a way that might make it seem as if she were making an effort to be considerate. He took the café's cordless phone from its charging stand and paged through its small screen. "There *is* a message," he said. He listened to a few seconds, while staring at the middle distance. "It's actually for you," he told Elspeth, pressing a button in the phone to replay it.

"Greg, is it your shift today, or Juniper's? This is Leif. . . ." The recorded Leif seemed to forget for a moment what he wanted to say. People were talking in the background. "Listen, if my friend Elspeth comes by, could you give her a message? Tell her to call Raleigh's parents. Call her boyfriend's parents. And also I guess tell her we're fine? Raleigh is all figured out. Her boyfriend. We haven't figured me out, but that's okay. I'm just going to sit here for a while." The recorded Leif laughed. "There's not any rush." Leif's voice was too fast. He didn't sound like himself. "So, to call Raleigh's parents. That's the message." Then, as if to himself: "What a—." And the message ended. *To replay this message, press one. To save, press—*

Elspeth handed the phone back to Greg. "It's from Leif," she told Matthew.

"Can I listen?" he asked.

Leif shouldn't be in there. He had recently been claiming that he was learning how to understand what he sensed, how to place it even while he was in the middle of hearing it, but sometimes it was hard to tell whether a voice was coming from inside or outside, especially if you and other people were contained together in a bounded space. In an elevator, for example. Or in a subway car. When she and Leif were in college, the tram that had run through their urban campus had begun its journeys underground, and it had always been a relief to both of them, and they had used to comment on it, when the tram had emerged into the light and air, like spring parting from winter, and the attentions boxed up in the car with them had become free to scatter out the windows into the surrounding city.

"Can we call him back?" Matthew asked.

Greg found a number in the phone, and Elspeth tried it, but it connected only to an error message.

"You don't want to call anyone else?" Greg offered. He pointed at Matthew: "You want anything, while I'm making the latte?"

Matthew checked his wallet and then asked for one of the hard-boiled eggs perched in a small steel tree beside the cash register.

"I'd have to call Information," Elspeth said.

Greg shrugged.

"It was the police who took our phones," she disclosed to him. Someone at a table looked up from his book.

Greg handed Matthew a saucer and then an egg. "Seventy-five cents."

"That's all?" asked Matthew.

"It's an egg," Greg said. "You could also use my phone," he suggested to Elspeth. He dug it out of his pocket and wiped it off on the forearm of his shirt. It was a couple of models old, and the glass was crazed in one corner. A pudgy, grizzled black Lab was the wallpaper.

She shook her head. She couldn't do it to him.

Matthew understood. "Fuck," he said.

"Or am I being paranoid?" Elspeth asked him.

"I don't know. I kind of don't think so."

"Here," Greg said, taking the café's cordless phone from its cradle and holding it out to her again. "What are they gonna do. I could have let anyone borrow it."

She left Matthew to his egg and stepped out the front door.

The café was in a brick building from the late nineteenth century, at the intersection of a street and an avenue. At the entrance, a shallow triangular porch had been carved out of the ground floor, exposing a thin, cast-iron column that supported the corner of the building. Elspeth sat down on a bench whose paint was molting. A shadow ran away from the column in a sharp stripe.

It was a quarter past ten, and she was still in her own neighborhood. At least it would be an hour earlier in Oklahoma. The bars on the phone's screen were steady. She asked Information for the number of Raleigh's mother.

Raleigh's father answered. Maybe Raleigh's mother wasn't listed? Twenty years ago, a newly divorced woman in Oklahoma might not have wanted to list her landline under her own name. It was like doing archaeology, having to make one's way through the pre–cell phone system.

"How is he?" Raleigh's father asked. He had a dry, curling voice.

"I'm not downtown yet."

"Ohh," piped the voice.

"We don't have our phones. They took our phones. I just got the message to call you."

"He's on TV," Raleigh's father told her.

"I saw a little of it."

"I imagine he wants to say why he did it, but his mother is talking about a lawyer."

"Did she find one?"

"I imagine he wants to blow the whistle. That's why he did this, isn't it?"

"I don't know."

A woman's voice in the background murmured, and Raleigh's mother took the phone.

"I *thought* this was your number," said Elspeth.

"How is my son?" It was like a line in a play.

"I haven't talked to him yet. They took my phone."

"Your phone?"

"We can't talk to him unless he calls us, and they took our phones."

"Even if you go? To where he is?"

"That's how it was last time. Remember? There's no way to see him."

"Oh," she said. "I was sure you saw him last time."

"Not until they brought him to the courtroom."

"So you did see him."

"When they arraigned him."

"Sweetheart, I think somebody needs to be there."

"We got a message to call you? You found a lawyer?"

"We did. You know, Raleigh said he thought you were probably going to have to get a separate lawyer for yourself."

The fingers of Elspeth's that were holding the phone were aglow with cold. She switched to her other hand.

"I don't know why he would say that," Raleigh's mother continued.

"Maybe it would be safer that way," Elspeth suggested.

"Maybe so, dear."

"Could I get his lawyer's phone number, anyway?"

"His roommate Jeremy found the lawyer. He's a professor. Isn't that lucky?"

"The lawyer is a professor?"

"From Jeremy's college."

"Do you have Jeremy's number? I don't even have that."

"I wrote it down. Raleigh had me call Jeremy's workshop, and then Jeremy called me back. His workshop is called a gym, apparently. Did you ever hear?"

"It's a thing," Elspeth said.

She blew on her fingers while she waited for Kimberly Evans to find the piece of paper where she had written down Jeremy's number.

"Who is Julia Di Matteo?" Raleigh's mother asked, when she returned to the phone.

"She's a friend of ours. A new friend. She's in our group."

"Her lawyer is already on television," she told Elspeth. "I think you need to go there, sweetheart."

"Did they say what *his* name was? The name of Julia's lawyer?"

"Jim, what does it say? Can you read it? Kenneth something. Did you see it, Jim?"

"That's okay," said Elspeth.

"We missed it. I'm so sorry. We weren't thinking."

"You were thinking great."

"He was just saying no comment, the way lawyers do. He seems to be there at the courthouse."

"Did you . . . ?" Elspeth began, but faltered. These weren't even her parents, but it was still hard to ask. She began again: "Did the lawyer say anything about bail?"

"The lawyer," Kim repeated. "Do you mean Jeremy's lawyer? But we haven't talked to him yet. We didn't need bail last time."

"Occupy was just a protest."

"Well, what did Raleigh do? Do you know what he did?"

"I wasn't there."

"You let him go by himself?"

Elspeth didn't say anything.

"It's not right between the two of you, is it," said Raleigh's mother.

Elspeth remained silent.

"I shouldn't say that. I'm sorry."

"It's okay," Elspeth told her.

"It's just that I don't know what my son did."

Elspeth let Raleigh's mother enjoy for a minute the sorrow that it seemed to console her to feel, and then Elspeth excused herself from the phone.

At the foot of the courthouse stairs, Elspeth said an interim good-bye to Matthew, who had decided to buy a new cell phone and try to port his old number to it. Nearby, white vans from several television stations were parked illegally, their doors thrown open, the mouthless gray flowers of their transmitters raised high on tall white metal arms. Elspeth tried to pretend that she didn't care that Matthew was leaving.

"I'll be quick," he said, as he walked away.

She headed up the weathered stone stairs alone, at a deliberate pace, tightening around her shoulder the strap of her purse. Jeremy had promised to come to the courthouse as soon as he could, and Diana was bound to come once she picked up the message they had left with her department's secretary.

There was still no lawyer for Raleigh. Raleigh's parents and Leif had been mistaken about that. All Jeremy had been able to do so far was leave a message with an old comp-sci professor of his, who had been in the habit of boasting, in his lectures, about a friend at the law school who was making a name for himself by writing about ethics on the internet. Jeremy thought the law professor might want to take Raleigh on pro bono, but not even the comp-sci professor had called back yet. As for Julia's lawyer, Greg had found his name and number by googling, but he had been out when they called, and they hadn't been able to give his receptionist a number where they could be reached.

She and Matthew had come to the courthouse even though they hadn't really solved anything. Even though they lacked the means of solving anything. They had come at Elspeth's insistence, because she had felt guilty about her shower, guilty about her latte, guilty about not knowing what to do. Any more delay had seemed unbearable. But now, as she came close enough to the courthouse to see which of the gray arches was for entrance rather than merely for display, she realized that she had come too soon. She had distrusted her instincts. She was going to fail.

Well, maybe. As she fell into line for the metal detector, however, her mind switchbacked on her yet again, and she realized that you could never be ready for a place like this, not with all the cell phones and all the lawyers in the world. It would never be any easier, whether sooner or later. She set her purse in a beige tray, conscious of having no phone to set beside it. Let alone a gun. A group of court police officers, conspicuously armed, were joking with one another behind a row of framed rectangles of lightly smoked plexiglas. One of them motioned impatiently for her to step through the gray portal, whose signal light had blinked to green without her noticing it. "Come on, miss." After she passed through, she stood stupidly still for a minute, not knowing where to go, until she noticed that the tray carrying her purse was being buffeted by later trays at the end of the conveyor belt.

The building had a grand interior. Its marble floors had been polished by the traffic of a century of citizens. In a central hall, under a vaulted dome, a processional staircase broke like a wave into smaller flights before it reached the ground, though almost no one was walking up or down its steps. There was probably a dismal, overburdened elevator tucked away in a corner.

From an archway, a male and a female police officer studied Elspeth without interrupting a conversation that they were having. It was hard to be observed. Once, on the street, a homeless woman had flinched under

Elspeth's glance, as sensitive to observation as Elspeth herself, and had recovered by asking for the time. The question put them on an equal footing; everyone is subject to time.

Elspeth caught the female police officer's eye. "How do you find out when someone is going to see a judge?"

"When was the individual arrested?"

"This morning."

"But what time this morning?"

"About eight thirty."

"They're probably still in the bull pen, but the arraignment clerk will know. Room two nineteen."

"Is that the second floor?"

"Yes, ma'am. Go right when you come out the elevator."

There was still about $1,700 of unused credit on Elspeth's credit card. It might be enough to pay one person's bail. She hoped she wouldn't have to choose.

She took a staircase in a corner of the building, despite a guard who offered to direct her to an elevator. It was a prettier building, with its facings of glittering, colored rock, than the one that Chris and Raleigh had passed through after the Occupy protest, but somehow the prettiness made it more sad. The prettiness and the solidity. *We have a customary way of seeing people,* the rock seemed to say. *We have seen people of your type before.*

A couple of dozen people were waiting in the corridor outside room 219, and as Elspeth sidled through the crowd, she felt herself touched by their awareness of her, by their appraisal. There was something wrong, she heard them all but say.

Of course there was. Most of them were here to rescue a loved one.

"Is there a line?" she asked a Latina woman.

"No line," the woman said, smiling. She pointed to the office's open door, and Elspeth noticed a sheet of paper taped to it. "Please, lady." The woman gestured toward the sheet of paper.

Beside a column of names, the sheet listed courtrooms and times. Elspeth's friends were not on the list yet.

A cell phone behind Elspeth chirped. "Can I call you back, Dan?" asked a tall woman with her hair pulled back in a scrunchie, in a quiet but public voice. The woman silenced her phone but did not put it away. Elspeth had the impression that the woman was focused on Elspeth even though the woman was not looking at her.

The woman was a reporter, Elspeth realized.

Elspeth walked into the clerk's office. At a tall wooden counter, like a library service desk, she waited to be noticed by two women seated just beyond it. The women were talking about a birthday cake that one of them had ordered for her daughter. It had been ordered on a Tuesday and then was ready for pickup on Thursday. The decorations had been lovely, the frosting and everything. A computer screen faced Elspeth, and Elspeth could see that one of the women was inputting data into a spreadsheet as she and her friend talked.

"Be with you in a minute, miss."

Silently several people from the corridor slipped into the office and assembled along the wall behind Elspeth. She felt that if she were to stamp a foot they would flutter away and then edge silently close to her again. She wished she could laugh. Every so often a fact-checker at her magazine was able to win permission to write and publish a short piece. If it hadn't been her that this was happening to, maybe this could have been her chance.

The woman inputting data at last came to the counter. "Can I help you, miss?"

"What if a person's name isn't on the list on your door?" she asked in a soft voice.

"What's the arrest number?"

"Oh. Where would I find that?"

"Name?" the woman asked. Her tone was brusque, to offset the favor she was granting.

"There are a few names? Can I write them down for you?"

The woman looked at Elspeth over her glasses. She didn't say yes or no, and as Elspeth looked around for something to write on and write with, the woman walked away, and Elspeth's heart sank. The woman came back, however, with a ballpoint pen and a blank form.

"Where should I write the names?"

"Tchh. Anywhere, dear."

Elspeth wrote Raleigh's, Leif's, Chris's, and Julia's names across the top.

"Are you family?" the clerk asked, as she took the piece of paper and studied it. When the paper began to tremble in her hands, the clerk folded it in order to disguise her tremor.

"I'm a friend. I'm pretty sure Julia's the only one who has family in the city."

Muttering broke out behind Elspeth.

The clerk surveyed the reporters. "You have no business being in this office unless you have business in this office," she declared.

No one stirred.

"Do you have business in this office?" the clerk asked, singling out a man with a steno pad. "If you can't answer me, you better step outside, young man. Yes, you." She glared at him until, reluctantly, he left the room.

She didn't soften the sternness of her look as she returned her attention to Elspeth. "They're here, miss," she said, of Elspeth's friends. "They're all here. Do they have legal representation?"

"I think Julia does."

"They need representation, miss."

"I know."

The clerk explained that if Elspeth's friends couldn't afford representation, the state would provide it. Elspeth's friends could call the public defender's office from the phone in the holding area. She wrote down for Elspeth the common three-digit phone number for all city services.

The audience was over. "Can I see them?" Elspeth asked. "Can I see my friends?"

The clerk paused in her return to her desk. "Are any of them . . . injured?"

"No," Elspeth admitted.

"You'd have to ask the district attorney." She was washing her hands of Elspeth. "Room two-oh-four." She exchanged a glance with her colleague, as she took her chair, and the two of them palpably began to wait for Elspeth to leave.

"Could I ask you—," the man with the steno pad began, putting himself in Elspeth's way.

She twisted past him and then sped up, with sliding steps. She felt the herd turn and follow her.

"Are you a member of the cell?"

"What were you after?"

"Do you want to overthrow the government?"

She hated the reporters for wanting to know about her friends now instead of a week ago. For rewarding catastrophe with attention instead of rewarding an effort at change.

"Do you know Leaf?"

"What was your official role in Occupy, personally?"

"Do you have a website?

She thought of the television footage of Raleigh bequilled with their questions, keeping himself visible but not answering. He hadn't been willing to tell her, last night, why he had touched her so clumsily when he came to bed. He hadn't been willing to say what his hands hadn't been able to keep from saying. She wondered if the two of them would ever put their hands on each other again.

But she wasn't as defenseless as he was. "*I'm* not in handcuffs," she said, rounding on the reporters as they caught up to her. The sentence had come out as a non sequitur. As if to explain it, she slapped the steno pad out of the hands of the man who had been browbeaten out of the arraignment clerk's office and was at the head of the pack. It skidded across the marble floor.

The reporters were startled.

"Leave me the fuck alone!" she shouted, a little louder than she had meant to. "I'm just a *person*."

As she walked away, she felt, despite herself, a sense of loss as the pedicels of their attention detached and retracted. They would have let her feel human if she had been willing to give them the information they wanted.

Two-oh-four, she thought, suppressing herself, focusing. Was it stupid to go to the district attorney's office? She kept walking while she thought about it. She would look at the room. She would at least look at it.

She was holding the world together by going over the pieces in her mind, like a dog licking a wound to will it to close. Some veins in the marble were the dark, translucent green of the crepe-like seaweed that clung at water level to the city's older piers.

Just as she came to the district attorney's office, a man in a suit but no tie walked out of it. His features were at first disorganized, but when he caught sight of her, they drew together into an expression. He had recognized her. It was Bresser. She could tell that he wanted his face to be neutral, but he was looking at her with anticipation despite himself. He might even have been looking at her with an expectation that he would be congratulated. Was that possible? She must be overreading. She knew that she was pushing to the limit her ability to perceive.

"So you're a fan of Henry James," she said.

He gave a half chuckle, meaninglessly. "You mean the hacker?" He was the kind of boy who thought that if he pretended to know a secret, the other boys on the playground would let him in.

"Excuse me," he said, and walked importantly away. He had remembered who he was.

Elspeth wasn't in any such danger. Where she was standing, the marble corridor was open on one side to the central hall below, and she drifted to the broad balustrade that looked out into the hall. The stone of the balustrade was cold to the touch. In the quadrangle below, there was no sign of Diana, Matthew, or Jeremy.

There was only a television reporter in a vest and skirt, shaking her hair clear of her headset. The reporter laid the headset neatly on the floor beside her. She put an earpiece in her left ear. Her camera stood a few feet from her, independent, on an unfolded tripod. Her right hand held a microphone; her left hand, a small panel. From the skylight there fell soft and vague illumination, and a lamp on the prow of the camera gleamed at her, a guiding star, further smoothing her features. "Good morning," the reporter began. But either she hadn't been ready to continue or she hadn't liked the way her first words sounded, and with her panel she clicked the gleaming light off. She looked down, looked up, hunched her shoulders, squared them, looked straight ahead, clicked the light back on, dropped the hand that held the control panel below the frame of what the camera was recording, and began again. "Good morning," she resumed. "I'm on location at Central Booking, where authorities have not yet released the names of the four Occupy activists accused of breaking into a computer associated with the work of the city police and through them with that of the Department of Homeland Security. We were able to broadcast footage of one of the suspects earlier this morning, however, and several users of social media are now saying online that they recognize the individual and that he was known to be involved in a group that claimed—and this is a little unusual—that claimed to be able to uncover government secrets through ESP. That's right—extrasensory perception. A photo currently being shared online shows the individual wearing a T-shirt that says—I hope you're able to share the photo with our viewers, John, because in it you can read the motto pretty clearly—'Government Transparency Now through ESP.' We're not sure what to make of it, and authorities have not confirmed the identification, but if it turns out to be the same individual, and it looks to me like it is, then this raises some very interesting questions. John?"

Very interesting, indeed, thank you . . . A dew of fear had condensed under Elspeth's palms, while she listened. She had told the reporters that she was a person, but they wouldn't believe her now. A fool was not a person, for them.

"I'm sorry," said a woman's voice. It was the tall woman with her hair in a scrunchie. She had also been watching the reporter make her video. She was standing at a careful distance from Elspeth. Her face was angular but well composed. "They'll say anything until they get the story. I know you don't want to talk right now, but you might at some point, and I'd like to give you my card, if that's all right."

"I'm never going to want to talk," said Elspeth, but she accepted the card. She wanted to tell the woman—to warn her—that everything the TV reporter had broadcast was true.

"That's all right," the woman replied cheerfully. She was only doing her job. Often, by the time you meet someone, both they and you have already made all the decisions that will determine the encounter between the two of you, and the only freedom that remains to either of you is whether to be pleasant.

For politeness's sake, Elspeth thanked the woman for her card and then looked back out over the balustrade to signal that the conversation was over.

When Elspeth turned to make sure that the woman was gone, she saw a cluster of other reporters studying her and murmuring. Noticing her glance, they approached.

"I don't want to talk to you." She fumblingly pulled up the hood of her coat and walked to the stairwell.

On the ground floor, she leaned against a pillar in an archway, hiding herself as deep as possible in her hood, and watched who was entering the building. She decided to wait here for her friends. Of course she was hidden no better than a horse is hidden by its blinders. Soon she was aware that the reporters were standing a few yards behind her, to her right. She could sense their presence even without turning to look, the way one used to be able to hear the high, tinnient whine of a non-flat-screen television even if its sound was off.

She didn't draw back her hood until Diana walked through the metal detector.

"Baby," Diana said, embracing her.

"I shouldn't be touching you," said Elspeth.

"What do you mean?"

"The reporters will try to talk to you now."

"What reporters?" Diana asked.

The palm of Diana's hand felt very sweet and soft to Elspeth as she held it. It had in it all the humanity that Elspeth had been longing for and that she had been afraid she might have to ask the reporters to give to her.

"Oh, I see," Diana said.

"They're horrible," said Elspeth.

"Oh, baby." She let Elspeth cry a little. "This is hard. Of course it's hard. It's much harder than before, isn't it." Even through her tears Elspeth was aware of Diana learning that she couldn't look toward the reporters except at the risk of compromising the reprieve that Elspeth's outburst of emotion was winning from them.

"I need to wait here for Matthew and Jeremy," Elspeth said.

"That's okay."

"I'm going to need to use your phone. I still haven't talked to anyone. Not to Leif, not to Chris, not to Raleigh."

"That's okay."

"I thought Raleigh had a lawyer, but now I don't think any of them do except Julia."

"I took the liberty of calling a lawyer I know through Occupy. I hope that's all right."

"That's wonderful."

"He's a little head-in-the-clouds," Diana said. "He's a little true-believer. But he's willing to jump right in."

"Is he on his way?"

"He will be if I call him."

"Who's he for?"

"I was thinking Leif?"

"Oh yes, that makes sense."

"Didn't you say Raleigh had a lawyer? But we can give him to Raleigh instead if you want." Diana took out her phone, scrolled to the number, and tapped it. "This guy gave us a lot of good advice about the Kitchen. Right now he's representing a couple of people against the city. He doesn't work for free, but we'll find the money somewhere."

The phone was already ringing; the money was already being spent. "We'll find the money," Elspeth echoed, remembering that if her mother had tried to reach her this morning, she wouldn't have been able to.

"I'll give him my credit card for today," said Diana. "Let's just get him here."

"You're a graduate student."

"But for a graduate student I have really good credit." She put a finger in her phoneless ear. "Michael? I'm at the courthouse now."

"We should give him to Leif," Elspeth said softly, but Diana was already negotiating, and Elspeth couldn't tell whether Diana had heard her. Elspeth resumed watching visitors to the courthouse unshoulder their backpacks and empty their pockets.

"He'll be here in an hour," Diana said, once the call was finished.

"You know how Leif can sometimes tell what someone is thinking?" Elspeth asked, almost in a whisper.

Diana double-checked that she had hung up her phone. "I know he's a sweet kid," she replied quietly.

"They know about it."

Diana nodded and looked away.

"Someone gave the reporters a photo of one of Raleigh's T-shirts," Elspeth continued.

"I thought the T-shirts were a joke."

"It was something we were working on," said Elspeth. She was ashamed to be talking about it. She wanted to tell Diana that it was from the same part of Leif that made him a poet, but she couldn't. Instead, she said, "It's how they broke in."

"You shouldn't tell me about it. You shouldn't tell me or anyone anything about what they're charged with."

Elspeth nodded. She watched Diana try to think of something to say that wouldn't hurt Elspeth's feelings. By talking about it when Diana didn't want to hear, it was as if Elspeth had tried to pull Diana underwater with her.

"Look, there's Matthew," Elspeth said, noticing Leif's boyfriend as he took a place in line for the metal detector. "And there's Jeremy, too." The men were standing one in front of the other but didn't realize it because they had never met before. Straight Jeremy in his pretty golden beard and gay Matthew in his muddy black one.

After the security check, Jeremy crossed in front of Matthew, cutting him off. Yellow, pollen-like sawdust had been sifted in a neat parallelogram onto the stomach of his work shirt. "So the good news is Felix Penny says he'll represent Raleigh for today. And for the duration, if he likes the case. The bad news is he won't do it pro bono."

"Have you talked to Leif or Raleigh?" Elspeth asked Matthew, instead of responding to Jeremy's news.

Matthew nodded. She saw that he was bewildered, as she was, by the surrender that they were going to have to make not just to Diana and Jeremy but to strangers chosen by Diana and Jeremy. She and Matthew weren't the sort who knew how to cold-bloodedly do what needed to be done. "Matthew," he identified himself, not quite apologetically, to Jeremy.

"Hey. I just put your number in my phone," Jeremy replied.

"Felix Penny is sort of famous, isn't he," said Diana. She waved to Matthew.

"He had a book about privacy last year," said Jeremy. "Raleigh's calling his parents right now to see if they can afford him."

"And Diana found a lawyer for Leif," Elspeth told the men.

"His name is Michael Gauden," said Diana.

Merely to the names Elspeth was already beginning to feel that they had responsibilities. That for the lawyers' sakes, there were selves that they were going to have to be careful from now on to be. "We're going to have so many lawyers," she said.

"I don't think this would be a good time to cheap out," Jeremy said.

As if expense were what made her anxious. As if it would be willful of her if it were. "How are they all doing?" she asked Matthew.

"Chris isn't sitting with them."

He was blaming himself, Elspeth thought.

"Your friend Chris went upstairs," Jeremy said. "Even though Raleigh told him not to."

"Did he have any choice?" Diana asked.

"You can always tell them you want to talk to your lawyer first," said Jeremy.

"But he doesn't have a lawyer yet," said Elspeth. "Is Leif all right?"

"He's a little . . ." Matthew raised his hands but didn't know what gesture to make.

"How's Julia?" Elspeth asked, making an effort to be fair.

Neither Jeremy nor Matthew answered.

"She'll be by herself, on the women's side," Diana suggested.

"Oh, that's right," said Elspeth.

"Can we talk about bail?" Jeremy asked. His impatience, she foresaw, was going to be one of the instruments working to conform their irregular selves.

They hadn't been paying attention to the reporters.

"How many of you have ESP?"

"Can you tell me what color I'm thinking of right now?"

"Were you acting on instructions from the spokes council?"

Elspeth muttered, "We didn't even go to Occupy that much."

"Don't, honey," Diana cautioned her.

"Could you repeat that? I didn't catch that."

A reporter swung a microphone from one friend's mouth to another's, tracing in the air a map of his fluctuating hope. The friends were backed up against the pillar that Elspeth had chosen half an hour ago to lean against.

"Go on, shoo," Diana said, not quite in earnest.

"Shoo yourself," a reporter in back answered her.

A wider crescent was gathering, drawn by the burnt-match smell of conflict.

In a loud monotone Jeremy declared that they had no comment.

"When are you going to leak the files?"

"What are you going to do to protect the privacy of government officials named in the files?"

"How many networks have you broken into using ESP?"

Under his breath Jeremy asked, "What is this ESP horseshit?"

While alone Elspeth had felt powerless, but in the company of her friends, she no longer quite believed in the reporters' capacity to pen her in. Now that her side had cell phones, she didn't need to keep standing where she was. Raleigh and Leif were sure to call Matthew's new phone in a minute. She was going to ask to talk to Chris, too. She was going to figure it all out.

Across the vestibule she recognized the leonine white hair of Julia's lawyer.

"Sir! Sir!" she cried.

"Elspeth!" Jeremy shouted, as she darted away.

The reporters, too, pivoted.

The lawyer was even taller than the headshot in Greg's phone had led Elspeth to expect. "You're Julia's lawyer," she accosted him.

He looked at the parade raggedly trailing her, and his eyes seemed to make a calculation. "I didn't catch your name, sweetheart." He extended his hand.

"Elspeth Farrell."

"Kenneth Montague," he told her. He took his time shaking her hand, as if no one were closing in on them. As if they were alone. "Pleased to meet you." He studied her eyes. "Hey," he then said, looking up, as if he were only just now noticing her pursuers. "Hey, I already talked to you assholes. And that's not on the record, by the way, my calling you assholes, because you know I love you guys. Officially. Nah, just kidding. Of course I love you guys. But seriously, we're trying to have a confidential conversation here, so back the fuck off. I don't mean to use language, but could you give us a little space? I'll have more for you later. I always do, don't I? You know I do. Thank you. I love you guys." He showily winked. And then took Elspeth under one of his wings and turned.

She stopped him. "These are my friends."

"Which ones, sweetheart?" he asked.

"These three."

"One, two, three, then," Montague said, and returned to motion. "It's rude to count, I know," he apologized over his shoulder, "but I have to make sure we're not bringing any fucking *journalists* with us. Mind if we talk outside? For just a minute. On the steps? They won't go outside; it's too cold for them. The dirty so-and-so's, as my mother used to say. I hope you don't mind, I happen to be on my way to get a sandwich."

The police didn't search you as you left the building, and in a moment they were standing in the midday sun of late November.

"So how can I help you?" Montague asked. He looked almost through them when he looked, but his eyes, though hooded, were incapable of hiding. That was why he talked the way he did.

"Why can't you just represent everybody?" Elspeth asked.

"That's a tall order," Montague replied, as if she were joking.

"Wait a minute, Elspeth," said Jeremy.

"I know you found someone," she told Jeremy, "but he's not here yet."

"Who'd ya find?" Montague asked. "If you don't mind my asking."

"Felix Penny," Jeremy said, as if the name itself were a more precious coin.

"Don't know him," said Montague affably. "He a trial lawyer?"

"He's a law professor," said Jeremy. "He writes about computer ethics."

"Computers. That'll be useful. You got somebody on the way, then."

"Two lawyers on the way, actually," said Diana.

"Oh yeah? Who else? Out of curiosity."

"Michael Gauden?" said Diana.

The lawyer nodded.

"Do you know him?" Elspeth asked.

"He's a young guy, isn't he?"

Diana defended him: "I think he's been in practice for several years."

"He'll be great. I'm sure both of them will be."

"But we don't have a lawyer for Chris," said Elspeth.

Montague gave her friends an opportunity to respond to her, but they didn't take it.

"Could you help him?" Elspeth asked.

Montague looked at her almost tenderly. "I can't, sweetheart. I can't. I told the Di Matteos that I would represent their daughter, and I can't do anything to dilute that."

"What do you mean, 'dilute'?"

"I can't represent a person unless I can promise her my first loyalty, and in this case, I've already given it to Julia. That's me. That's who I am. But even if I wanted to try to split my loyalty—even if I were *willing* to do that—this judge would never waive the conflict."

"You know who the judge is going to be?" asked Matthew.

"This one's sharp, isn't he. It's the quiet ones you have to watch out for. I know who the judge usually is when this kind of case happens at this time of day on this day of the week, but no, I don't know for certain who the judge will be. But it doesn't matter. None of the judges here want to bother with a conflict."

"Where would the conflict be?" Elspeth asked.

"Conflict of interest," said Montague. "Between the accused."

"But they're all accused of the same thing."

"Well, as your friend here will probably tell you"—Montague glanced at Matthew—"we won't know for sure what your friends are accused of until the grand jury issues its indictments, and that may not be for a little while. A lot can happen between now and then."

"I don't understand."

"What don't you understand, sweetheart?"

"Why would they be in conflict? They're all together."

"But they might not stay together," Montague softly said. "They might choose different defense strategies."

"What difference would that make?" she persisted. But it was beginning to dawn on her.

"The strategies might not be compatible."

"How could that happen if everyone tells the truth?"

"Elspeth," Matthew cautioned her.

"It's better if everyone has his own lawyer," said Montague. "Trust me. It's always better."

He meant, she realized, that one of the accused might decide to testify against the others. "It's better for criminals, maybe," she said. She turned away.

"I'm sorry," Montague said.

She didn't reply. She needed, at the moment, to be unfair to him.

"How much do you think bail will be?" Matthew asked.

"Hard to say, with all the excitement."

"You mean it could be high? What if we can't find the money right away?"

"You know the island the city ships people to? Technically it won't affect the case, but can I be honest with you? You don't want your friends to go there. It's not a nice place. It's not a happy place. I'm saying this because people like you—no offense—it's because your lives are blessed, and I mean that—people like you don't know how bad it is. People like you may think you have an idea, but you don't have an idea."

"Thank you," said Matthew.

"And I shouldn't say this, either," Montague continued, "but when you're looking for someone for your friend, ask for someone with federal trial experience. Don't get hung up on it, but: if you can."

"Federal trial experience," Matthew repeated.

"You didn't hear it from me, but the word is there are going to be federal charges."

Matthew nodded.

"Good luck." He shook all their hands and clasped Elspeth's.

"What does that mean?" Matthew asked, after he was gone.

"Fuck," said Jeremy.

Matthew's phone rang. "It's jail," he said, and handed the phone to Elspeth.

"Hello?" Elspeth said.

"Hey."

"Raleigh? Are you all right?"

"I'm fine."

"Are Leif and Chris all right?"

"They're having a little trouble, but they're all right."

"What do you mean, trouble?"

"Leif is, one minute he says it's all his fault, and five minutes later it's ridiculous that he can't just walk out of here."

"It *is* ridiculous."

"You know they listen to these calls."

"He's so innocent he wouldn't even know *how* to do anything wrong, assholes," she said to the listeners.

"Assholes," Raleigh echoed admiringly.

"I'm sorry."

"Don't apologize to me," he told her. There was a simulation of no more than camaraderie between them, and she couldn't tell if they were faking the camaraderie for the benefit of eavesdroppers or out of some idea of not, for the moment at least, disappointing each other. Of not reckoning with too many big questions at once.

"How's Chris?" she asked.

"I wouldn't worry too much about him."

"He's okay?"

"I don't think he's worrying about us."

"Jeremy said he's not sitting with you."

"He went upstairs after I told him not to, and when he came back and I asked what he told them, he said, 'Do you think I'm stupid?' And I said, 'That's what you told them?' And he said, 'No, that's what I'm telling you.'"

"He's mad."

"But why's he mad at me?"

It was a boy thing of some kind. "Can I talk to Leif?"

"Sure. Yeah. Let me get Leif."

She pictured the handset of the jail telephone left to hang alone upside down from its cable, swaying. She remembered Leif sitting on a window-sill in her dining room at a party in the spring, wearing what he called a peasant frock, of blue-and-white gingham, and kicking his crossed legs while he smoked.

Raleigh returned. "Do you know how Julia's doing?" he asked.

"We talked to her lawyer."

"Did he say how she's doing?"

"No." It embarrassed her that it hadn't occurred to her to ask.

"She's by herself," he said.

"I know. It must be awful."

"Did you get my messages, by the way?"

"I still don't have a phone."

"You can call your messages even if you don't have your phone."

"You can?"

"Forget it," he said. "It would have saved some time."

"I'm sorry."

"No, it's fine." He was holding his breath; he was keeping even that back from her. "I miss you," he unexpectedly said.

Did he want her back? It startled her to realize that she already thought of him as gone. Or of herself as gone.

"Are you going to say anything?" he asked.

"I miss you, too," she said clumsily.

"I'm in jail, Elspeth."

"I know."

He passed the phone to Leif.

"Elspeth?" Leif's voice seemed very bright, after Raleigh's caution. "I'm going to have to become a celebrity."

"That's great."

"No it isn't." He laughed as if he had meant for her to misunderstand. "I mean become a celebrity the way John Clare became Byron." She and Leif had decided, one afternoon, that the impoverished poet of birds' nests and unfenced meadows must have been one of their kind and that it must have been partly under the strain of failing to understand his gift that he had begun to confuse himself with his more famous, more wealthy, and more libertine rival. His greedier rival.

"No, don't do that," she said. "Stay yourself."

Greed for life being a sign of sturdiness.

"I'd only do it consciously," he said.

"You'll be out soon."

"FYI, I won't come back, once I get out. I just won't."

"You won't have to. It's just till they set bail. They'll set it tomorrow at the latest but probably by the end of the day today."

"I'm having these *thoughts*. I'm going to have to write a poem, I'm having so many of them."

"What kind of thoughts?"

"Thoughts about thoughts. I was thinking that everything a person says is really a synecdoche, for one thing. There! 'For one thing,' for one thing. A part for the whole. And often an atypical, misrepresentative part."

"You mean sometimes people don't tell the truth."

"I mean they can't tell it. If only because you can't say everything. If only because you can only say one thing at a time."

"That's interesting."

"No. It's just a way for me not to think about this. This place that I'm in. I'm gesturing toward it, but you can't see."

"Do you have something to focus on? Can you focus on Raleigh?"

"No." He laughed, but it was a forced-sounding laugh, and it irritated her instead of stirring her pity. He wasn't taking care of himself. "What's funny," he continued, "is there are all these not-stories down here, in addition to the stories. These sort of snowclones that aren't anybody's experience but that we all feel they want us to fit ourselves into. They're so ludicrous. How bad we are, for example. How weak we are. How good the king is to be willing to pardon us if we confess our sins. The not-stories are all so weepy. They're not dangerous because we hold them at bay. We spangle them with little particles of hate. With little pearlescent antibodies of hate."

"Up here there's this pretty marble on the walls, and I've been focusing on it sometimes."

"We just have cinder blocks."

"It won't be too much longer," she assured him.

"I don't think I can be a cinder block right now."

He had looked very pretty, when he had showed up for her party in his peasant frock. He hadn't looked like a man passing but like a girl too young to need makeup.

"I'm so sorry, Elspeth," he said.

"You haven't done anything."

"I don't think I have, but then sometimes I think maybe I have."

"Don't say that. I mean, don't say that, but also I mean this phone is bugged."

"I don't care. I'm so sorry. I'm so ridiculously sorry. I'm sorry even for the versions of the story that aren't true. I'm synoptically sorry."

It was too much, and she felt another twinge of irritation. As well as another twinge of self-reproach at the injustice of her irritation.

"Talk about something else. Talk about your idea for a poem again."

"I *am* talking about it."

4.

From across the courtroom Julia's mother and then father met her gaze, smiled, and tentatively waved. For once her mother had taken off her reading glasses altogether—she must have put them in her purse—instead of parking them up in her hair like the goggles of a speedster who had just stepped away from the racetrack. Her mother had such lovely, thick hair. She left it silver.

It was a pleasant enough courtroom. The little banisters that fenced off the chancel or whatever it was called were a honey-colored wood. The room didn't smell, and though it was vile to notice smells, the fact is the smells hadn't been too good up to now and the not-too-goodness had been a pretty salient aspect of the setting. The ceiling in the courtroom was too high for anyone to scratch into it, or pick at it, or smear it with the brown, dried, brittle-looking, fingerpainted swirls that Julia, downstairs, had at first feared were feces but eventually pieced together must be peanut butter, scooped out of the insides of the provided sandwiches. Which was resourceful.

There was solemn coughing. A lamp or a glare from a window had caught in her father's eyes, and the reflection glittered there almost uncannily, in a way she had never seen in real life before, though she had seen it in animated movies.

Her lawyer, Kenneth, was clasping his hands over his crotch, in the style of a pallbearer or a groomsman. She imitated him. Under the circumstances there wasn't much else one could do in the way of making oneself look presentable.

"Julia Di Matteo?" said, in an almost conversational tone, a young black woman who had been standing silently next to the defense's table since before Julia had been brought into the courtroom.

"March fifth, nineteen eighty-five," Julia supplied.

The woman smiled, and Julia felt stupid for being all promptness and compliance.

"Docket thirty-six five twenty-seven," the woman said, in a voice that was now one of proclamation. "The People against Julia Di Matteo."

What a horrible thing to say.

"Consent to waive the reading, counsel?" asked the judge, who, at his remote desk, had flipped open a manila folder.

"So waived," said Kenneth.

"Your Honor, a few notices, if I may," said a tall man with a politician's pompadour, who made no eye contact with Kenneth or Julia or even the judge before speaking. He was standing at what had to be the district attorney's table, since its placement mirrored that of hers and Kenneth's. "Hereby give notice that our office will be presenting the case of *People versus Julia Di Matteo* to a grand jury." He went on to give several more notices, droningly, rocking on the balls of his feet as he did so.

The judge registered his words with irritated glances. After the man finished, there was silence for a few moments as the judge flicked through papers in the folder before him.

"You have a proposal?" the judge prompted.

"Computer trespass and criminal possession are Class E felonies, Your Honor," resumed the man with the pompadour, "and the accused and her co-conspirators had reason to know they were breaking into the network of a contractor working with the city police and through the police the Department of Homeland Security. These are serious charges, Your Honor, and we don't currently know the modality of the break-in or who else might be involved. Because we believe that through her family the accused has access to considerable resources, we're asking for bail of one hundred thousand over twenty-five thousand, with a ban on all internet and computer activity."

"Counsel?" the judge said to Julia's lawyer.

"Your Honor," said Kenneth, "we will be contesting all these charges, as you are aware, and not even my colleague here has suggested that there was any vandalism or any intent of personal gain. My client was born and raised in the city and owns an apartment here, which is her primary residence. Her parents, who are present in the courtroom, also live in the city. Her father is a respected member of the investment community, a position that my colleague makes allusion to, and her mother works here as a college professor of, I believe, art history. My client told me, just now, that last year she performed her civic duty in this very court system as a juror. She belongs to this community, Your Honor, and we ask that she be released on her own recognizance."

Looking down at his papers, still rocking on his feet, the man from the district attorney's office shook his head and silently, admiringly mouthed the words *civic duty.*

"Bail is set at five thousand over fifteen hundred," pronounced the judge, "with an absolute ban on all computer and internet activity. Counsel will explain the ban to the accused carefully. I don't want her saying she didn't know her phone was a computer when we have to put her back in jail."

Kenneth spoke again: "Your Honor, my client's father would now like to post bail on her behalf."

"He may approach the clerk."

Julia's father put a palm up like a schoolboy and left his seat in the gallery.

Kenneth had told her only a few minutes ago, in the waiting cell, that the judge was likely to forbid her to use the internet, and she still had a little trouble believing in the condition. How would anyone know if she read the newspaper later tonight on her mother's tablet? Of course her mother would feel obliged for Julia's sake to keep the tablet away from her, and at the moment she hardly wanted to worry her mother further or force her mother into the position of having to try to deny her something in order to protect her.

"I wonder, ma'am," Kenneth said to the woman who had read the docket number at the start of proceedings, "whether, as a courtesy, the officers of the court would be willing to provide for a private egress."

"But, Kenneth—," Julia interrupted.

"Julia?" he responded. To the woman beside them: "One moment, ma'am. My apologies."

"I want to see the others. They're ahead of me, aren't they? They're probably just outside. I want to see them just for a minute."

"I don't think they'll still be outside, sweetheart. Because of the press."

"Oh, the press is just *writers*."

"It's your decision."

"Then I think that's what I want."

"It looks like we'll make our way out of the building on our own steam, ma'am," Kenneth said to the judicial officer. "But thank you for your consideration."

The clerk finished a third counting of Julia's father's hundred-dollar bills.

"Adjourned to Part F," the judge declared, and rapped his gavel.

"That's it?" Julia asked.

"Oh, I know," Julia said, when Kenneth reminded her not to speak to the reporters. She embraced her parents. "Momma, I want to go home with you and Daddy. I don't know if I'm going to spend the night, but I want to go home with you for now, anyway."

"We can order Szechuan."

"No, something with vegetables."

"We can get Szechuan with vegetables."

"I want vegetables that look like vegetables. My god, I've been dreaming of vegetables."

"Julia," interrupted Kenneth, "you and I need to have a little more conversation, so if you don't mind, I'll ride uptown with you. Can I call you a taxi?"

"Daddy can call one."

"No, I got it. I got someone I work with."

"Oh, that's lovely. Momma, I just want to see my friends first, on the way out. *Really* quickly."

Her mother looked to Kenneth, but he was talking to his driver. "I'll just tell Eileen that we're ordering food and to go ahead and feed Robbie," her mother said, taking out her phone. "I haven't told Robbie anything yet."

"There's plenty of time," said Julia.

"They may need the courtroom for another hearing," said her father, who had been monitoring the looks that they were getting from the bailiff.

Julia was aware, as she neared the door, that a file of people were now glancing up from their phones at her, despite being still so intent on their texting that they occasionally wrong-footed themselves. She wasn't going to be afraid of them. She needed to see Raleigh, if only to find out what she was feeling for him, which seemed to have hidden. Of course she wanted to see the others, too.

"Kenneth, you're coming with us, aren't you?" she asked.

"I'm right here."

She pushed her way into the gloomy marble corridor. Greenish stones like these were known as verd antique, she remembered. Men and women crowded near the doorway looked at her at first unseeingly and then with something like alarm. "Julia," one said, holding out his cell phone. "Julia Di Matteo," said another, making the same gesture.

How unpleasant to be beckoned as if one were a dog.

"Kenneth, you'll stick with my mother and father, won't you?" she asked.

She shoved firmly, and once she had broken through the crust of reporters, she wheeled around, scanning for her comrades. The reporters watched her, appalled; they hadn't expected a person in her position to run their gauntlet. She hesitated, in their presence, to call out her friends' names. Where *were* they? She had been looking forward to telling them the whole story, starting with the way the police had woken her up—by calling her landline and ringing her doorbell at the same time. It had been unnerving.

She made a little dash down the length of the corridor. The pattering on marble of the reporters' footsteps behind her—as they hurried to narrow the gap she had briefly put between herself and them—sounded like soft, reluctant applause.

They must not have waited. Maybe they had wanted to but hadn't been able to.

"Were the others in the same courtroom?" she asked the nearest reporter.

"Did you have an arrangement to meet them?"

"Oh, you're no help, are you," Julia said. She had the mad idea of trying to picture where her friends had gone as if they were a misplaced set of keys. But she knew without any conjuring that of course they had returned to their homes on the far side of the river. She hadn't been aware until this moment of how much strength she had been borrowing from the idea of her solidarity with them and theirs with her.

"Julia," appealed one of the journalists.

"Julia," appealed another.

The reporters were typing into their phones notes about the look of dismay on her face. It was a strange way for a person to make a living.

"We just push on ahead, sweetheart," said Kenneth.

"Oh, I'm fine," she reassured him. She smiled for her parents and took her mother's arm.

It was a luxury, in a city so crowded and expensive, for one's parents to have preserved a shrine to oneself, even a slightly stripped-down one, and Julia sat on the limp, quilt-covered bed in her lamplit childhood bedroom with appropriate gratitude. Appropriate and familiar. On top of a lime green dresser stood a bowl full of spools of ribbon. The room was now usually vacant and therefore private, and on that account her mother found it to be a convenient place to wrap presents. Beside the bowl of ribbons was a wooden carrousel, painted in candy colors, which played a folk tune when wound up. It was too babyish and too girly for Robbie, and it should have gone to Goodwill long ago, but perhaps it had become a sentimental favorite of her mother's. Still hanging on the wall was Julia's poster from when she was in high school of poker-playing puppies. Such an excellent poster, and it wasn't just out of loyalty to her younger self that she thought so.

"How long are you staying?" asked apple-faced Robbie, at the threshold.

"Just to say hi."

"How was your day?" he asked.

"It was so busy! I haven't been able to take a shower yet, can you believe?"

"Are you stinky?" he whispered.

"I think I am."

"Momma will let you take a shower here," he said with confidence.

"She might even *make* me take one."

"But you wouldn't mind," he inferred.

"I wouldn't mind," she agreed. "And what did you do today?"

"I had class," he said almost wearily.

"Which one?"

He sighed. "Nutrition." He would probably never live alone, but their parents wanted him to know how to. He was only twenty, but his hair was already thinning, and the lenses of his glasses were as thick as ice cubes.

"Did you like it?"

"Yes," he said flatly.

"Are Agnes and Charlie still in your class?"

"Agnes is," he said. "Do you want to play Life?"

"I can't tonight, honey. I'm sorry."

"Okay," he accepted.

"I need to go ahead and take a shower."

"Okay." He shuffled out of the room.

Was there ever anyone so heartless, Julia wondered of herself. But Raleigh didn't have the number here.

There were three space heaters, girdled by their power cords, in the closet of the bedroom, and after her shower, over dinner (undistinguished Middle Eastern, in the end), Julia asked if she could take one back with her.

"Is there anything else you need? Don't we still have those little phones we bought for Spain? That's the kind Kenneth wants you to use, isn't it?"

"We threw them away, remember? While we were still in Barcelona."

"How wasteful."

"It was very one-percent of us."

The glass of the little kitchen television remained dark. Julia knew her parents were refraining from turning it on out of a wish to protect her, and out of a wish to protect them, she refrained from saying that in fact she wasn't so fragile. Of course they would watch it later, in their bedroom, after she had left. And she would watch it in her bedroom, twenty blocks uptown.

"I'm going, after dinner," she told them.

"You know they're still downstairs," her father said.

"Are they? But the little alleys in back are connected, Daddy. If I go out that way, I can come out to the street two whole buildings down."

"Through the basement?"

"Behind the basement. The alleys connect in back."

And that was how she left, after hugging Robbie, who was more solid, in an embrace, than other people. More surely rooted. Edgar, their doorman, took her down in the elevator. She pushed all her hair up under her hat. After Edgar threw the bolt that deactivated the alarm on the rear door, she walked the length of two shallow, unwelcoming cement yards, climbed a fence with the help of two giant tractor tires that had been chained to it years ago by the neighbor's super, for what purpose no one had ever been able to discover, and from the third yard took an underpass, through which that building's porters carted out the weekly garbage and recycling. The underpass was lit by only one bulb, weak and jaundiced, and she opened and shut behind her the steel-grate door at the end of it, with two hands, so gently that there was no clang. Only a clean, pleasant snick. Without looking back to where the reporters would be, she walked briskly toward the lights of the avenue, at the end of the block. No footsteps followed her.

At the corner, a taxi slowed, and she got in with a nod, without speaking. Only once she had clapped the door shut did she give her apartment's address.

"Straight ahead for eighteen blocks is all, really," she told the driver, the space heater lolling on the seat beside her, in a brown paper grocery bag that her mother had insisted on fetching from the kitchen utility closet.

She had got away. She was herself still.

How strange, she thought as she noticed her relief, to worry not that one might cease to be but that one might be overwritten. Scripted by other parties.

She wished she could take notes. She was so certain that Kenneth would discourage her that she hadn't bothered to ask for permission, but she knew she was going to write about this someday, when it was all over. And she would want then to be able to remember not just her perceptions but the textures of her perceptions. Including the taut helplessness of not being able to write anything down while it was all happening. She would have to register as much as she could on her memory. On her self, as it were. The way one writes a phone number on one's hand.

"Halfway down the block, on the left, where those forsaken-looking people are standing," she told the driver. This time there was no dodging them. The meter chittered out a receipt as the taxi coasted to a stop.

The reporters began to try to talk through the closed window.

"Is this all right, ma'am?" the driver asked. He had a desi accent.

"No, but they can't hurt me."

He opened his window. "Get away. Go," he said chivalrously, but the reporters only massed at the opening he offered them, and he had to raise the glass of his window again. He shook his head. "Are you famous, ma'am?"

"Tonight I seem to be."

"And what is your name, may I ask?"

"I'm sorry."

"It's all right," he said, with a little wave. "You are perhaps an actress?"

"I'm a writer."

"A famous writer," he said with satisfaction.

"Hardly."

"Good night, ma'am," he said, as he handed her the change. "But tell me your book, and I will buy it."

"I wish I had a book."

While she was climbing her stoop, she didn't reply to the reporters, but once inside, she said quietly, through the glass, "You should get some sleep; it's quite late." They probably didn't hear her over their own talking.

While still on the threshold, she heard her landline ringing, and she left her keys dangling in the lock to answer it.

A strange man asked for her.

"How did you get this number?" she asked.

"From Information."

"It's not in Information. I pay an extra dollar and forty-five cents every month not to be listed. *And* I'm in the Do Not Call registry." She hung up. "Jesus," she said, allowing herself, now that she was in private at last, a note of exasperation.

She dropped the space heater onto the sofa and tossed down beside it the mail that she had carried upstairs pinned under her elbow. She shut and locked the door. She flicked off the overhead light that she had flicked on when she had hurriedly entered, and she fumbled at the switch of the lamp beside her sofa, which gave a gentler light.

There, she thought.

In the kitchen, by the light of the open refrigerator, she made herself a vodka tonic. She stirred it with a spoon; she tasted the spoon. Returning to the sofa, she took pleasure in its being such a nice sofa, in its charcoal, minimalist way. Even tonight she was not sorry she had chosen not to have a cat, because thanks to the catlessness of her apartment, the sofa was still a nice sofa, two and a half years later. She sipped; she picked through the mail. There was a handwritten note from a woman she had known a little in college. The girl was producing a documentary; you could donate online.

The door buzzed. At the intercom she hesitated but then, pressing Talk, asked, "Who is it?"

"It's me." It was Raleigh.

She scrambled down the upper flight of stairs, but at the landing, as she turned, she slowed. She wasn't going to let him in if the reporters were still there. She didn't want it to be a matter of public record. She loped down the lower flight of stairs more cautiously, in a syncopated two-step, knowing that on the lower flight she was visible from the sidewalk.

But the reporters were gone. She looked past Raleigh, up the street and down the street, to be sure.

"They left," Raleigh said. "It's completely safe."

"Just come in," she replied impatiently.

"I waited for them to leave."

Men were always more boyish when you had them on your hands than when you imagined them.

"Would you like a drink?" she asked as they walked upstairs. She sounded like her father, she thought. She sounded public. She hadn't known whether they were going to do this again. She hadn't known whether she wanted to. In her apartment, once she turned the deadbolt, she left him in the living room and slipped into the bedroom for a moment, to look down at the street again from behind the curtains. They really did seem to have been left alone.

"It's *okay*," Raleigh said when she returned. He seemed to be insisting that she agree with him.

"There's so much going on," she said noncommittally.

They hadn't touched yet.

"You didn't wait," she said, when she gave him his drink.

"For what?"

"At the courthouse."

"You wanted me to wait?"

"Oh, I don't know," she said.

"Julia."

"What? Don't tell me to be reasonable."

She rocked her glass in an attempt to make the ice cubes in it clink, but they would only swivel. She wanted to pick at them with a finger, but that would be unladylike. When they had first kissed, two weeks ago, on the very sofa where he was now sitting, he had said afterward, almost angrily, *God I wish I hadn't done that*. And she had replied, with asperity, *You weren't the only one doing it*.

"We could go to that horrible diner," he suggested.

"It's a nice diner. It's only the food that's horrible," she said. "But we should stay here." Which more or less sentenced them, but not yet, she told herself. Not just yet.

As if there had been a gentle tug, the blinds of sleep scrolled up and let in her senses, even though it wasn't light yet. Raleigh's warmth beside her under the sheets was sweet, and she was aware of wanting, dangerously, to hold on to the sweetness. To have a younger man as a lover in late fall, and maybe early winter. Would it last that long? It was sweet now, whether or not it was going to last. The smell of his anxiety had softened over the course of the night to something like nutmeg.

This much, even unto staying the night, hadn't happened before. It might not happen again.

He curled inward as he stretched. "You can't have this, in jail," he said.

"Sex?"

"Just, lying in bed with someone." He brushed his knuckles across one of her breasts.

"Raleigh," she said.

"We're in so much trouble, aren't we."

Would she put a scene like this in, or would it seem like too much? "We're hardly Bonnie and Clyde," she said. She got up.

"Where are you going?"

She slipped into her robe and peered down at the street. "They're already here," she said. "One of them, anyway." A woman in terrible clothes.

"I can't be here," he announced.

She let the corner of the curtain fall.

"Where are you going?" he asked again. "Why are we getting up?"

"To make coffee."

"Come back," he said.

"But you can't be here."

"Oh, don't be like that."

She sat on the bed but didn't get into it again.

"You know what I mean," he said. He began to stroke her.

"Let me go ahead and make coffee," she told him.

She took the good beans out of the freezer and milled a handful in her little spice grinder. She filled the kettle and put it on to boil. She wondered if everything was going to be different now. Maybe she wouldn't have time anymore to wonder how a day was going to pass and also whether it was passing too quickly. Whether she was putting up enough resistance to its passing. From now on, after all, there was going to be a lot to keep track of. She was going to have the inside story, when she finally wrote it, unlike the importuners downstairs.

"What if I offered to give her a quote," she suggested, when Raleigh, in underwear and a T-shirt, joined her in the kitchen. "In order to lead her away, so you could make a run for it."

"I doubt your lawyer would be crazy about that idea."

"Kenneth is a teddy bear. Don't you have to get to work?"

"Why? So they can fire me?"

"Why would they do that? Do you want anything in it?" she asked as she poured.

"Black is fine."

"You're still innocent."

"I can't do tech support if I'm not allowed to touch computers. But I do want to go in, actually. I want to hear how they put it. I want to be there when somebody has to try to figure out how to say it."

"If I gave her a quote, I wouldn't say anything, really," Julia reassured him. "I would just lead her on."

"Do you know about the mosaic theory?"

"I think so."

"What is it?" he catechized her.

"Oh, I don't know, Raleigh."

"It's the idea that you shouldn't reveal even a little detail that seems unimportant, because if there's someone on the other end collecting all the little details and fitting them together, the mosaic he assembles could give the whole picture away."

It must be very terrible, if he felt compelled to hector her about it.

"Felix doesn't even want me talking to anyone from the working group anymore," he added.

She didn't give him a reaction. And all this time she had been afraid that she would lose him because of Elspeth.

"Had you heard of Felix before this week?" Raleigh continued. "He wrote that op-ed a couple of months ago, about end-user agreements."

"Was it good?"

"He's got a book coming out in May. *Seeing Through Internet Privacy.*"

"That's so great for you," she said, smiling. She was going to hold on in her own way even if she lost him. She was going to learn everything about him—about all of them—and then she was going to write her account. She was even willing to read this vile Felix's book if she had to.

While he was showering she put out bowls, spoons, cereal, milk, and raspberries. She rinsed the raspberries without taking them out of their plastic clamshell. They didn't keep.

"You don't have cable, do you?" Raleigh asked as he sat on one of the barstools at her kitchen counter. Like hay, his hair was darker when damp. He was apparently one of these men who don't even need to comb their hair, let alone brush it.

"I do."

"I wonder what they're saying on TV now."

"It's okay, right?" she asked as she tapped the On button of her remote. "My TV isn't secretly a computer?"

"I don't know."

"I don't think it is. How horrible would it be if one were sent back to jail because one hadn't appreciated all the functionalities of one's cable service."

With a jagged advent there issued from the television labored, modulated shouting. A number of people had allegedly been killed by an American drone on the other side of the world.

"We're not the news anymore," Julia said.

"That was fast."

She tried another channel. "Oh, wait, here we are," she said.

"'I know you know I know you know I know your password,'" a news announcer read aloud. A chyron displayed this text, over a blue background, as the announcer was reading.

"And this is from @OccupyESP, which seems to be a parody account," reported the announcer's co-host. "At this point we don't know who, if anyone, is authorized to speak for the group, and an account like this is pretty much all we have to go on. Is that right, Jason?"

"They can't decide if we're a joke or if we're terrorists," said Raleigh.

"That's not us, is it?" asked Julia.

"Who would it be? Jeremy's not that funny. I mean, that's not funny, but Jeremy's not even that not-funny."

"They're usually little aspiring TV writers, aren't they?" Julia commented. "The people who do these accounts. Who pretend to be the weasel escaped from the zoo or whatever."

"'Yeah, we read your mind,'" read the announcer. "'Sea salt and vinegar, amirite?'"

"This is like the CIA's Twitter account," said Raleigh. "A little 'irony,' a little shit-eating knowingness."

"This doesn't count as being online, does it? If we see social-media messages on TV?"

"Elspeth is going to hate this. She got so mad about my T-shirts."

"But she liked mine, didn't she?" Julia asked. "I mean, they were essentially hers."

"Everybody liked your T-shirts," he reassured her, though they both knew that nobody would ever wear one again.

On another channel, a man in a red tie said, "Kind of a misconception, to say we were hacked, and I want to get out in front of that."

"Is that Bresser?" Julia asked, just as CEO, BRESSER OPERATIONAL SECURITY unfurled on the screen.

"The truth is, we were tracking them before they were aware of us," Bresser said.

"What do you mean, *tracking*?" asked the interviewer.

"I can't say too much because it's something we've been coordinating with the authorities, but what I can say, I think, is that we're a private company, and this has actually been a kind of proof of concept for us."

"This has been a good outcome for you? To be a security company hacked by Occupy?"

"There's a lot of data out there about people, public data, and what our company has is a new way of looking at it. A new way of putting it together."

"How does it work, Joe?"

"You know, okay, if you have a big enough database of, say, the English language and the Spanish language, you no longer need anyone to tell you that *five* is the same as *cinco*. You can just tell the AI to look at the way *five* relates to all the other words in English, and then at the way *cinco* relates to all the other words in Spanish, and the AI will see that the patterns have the same shape. They match. They're what we call homologies, and what we're doing at Bresser is we train the AI to look for these homologies."

"In order to find people?" the interviewer prompted.

"I shouldn't say any more because we're a business and I don't want to give away the company store. But the other thing I wanted to get out in front of, in this conversation, is the idea that these young people are psychics, or whatever they want to call it. There's no such thing. They're hackers, and the other thing is a smoke screen. There are things they knew . . ." He trailed off.

"Things about you?" asked the interviewer.

"They were watching us the way we were watching them. That's all it is. And they're in jail now."

The interviewer thanked Bresser for speaking with her and swiveled to face a camera at a new angle. Julia clicked her off.

"They were waiting for us?" Julia asked.

The blank screen was still holding Raleigh's gaze. "I don't know. He's selling his product." He looked away from the TV. "Our names were on some of the folders we downloaded."

"What was inside?"

"The files wouldn't open. I was going to try to figure out the file extensions the next morning. Yesterday morning."

"We don't even know what we did, do we," Julia said.

"Was I a sucker to believe in this shit?" Raleigh asked.

She put their dishes in the sink and ran a little water into them. She didn't like to leave dirty dishes for her cleaning lady, but she could, when she needed to. She made a mental note to remember to lay out the woman's cash.

From the bedroom window Raleigh and Julia watched the reporter below as she snapped and fluttered the pages of what was probably that morning's edition of her newspaper.

Ten minutes later, when Julia, strategically alone, opened the front door of the building, she saw that the woman had stowed the newspaper, folded, in a pocket of her backpack. The capitals on the front page were inches high.

"What's the headline?" Julia asked, from the top of the stoop.

The woman hesitated. "We don't write the heds." She was wearing a fake-leather skirt trussed on one side with what looked like rope. The cuffs of her blouse peeking out of her coat sleeves seemed to be ruffled.

"Who writes them?"

"The editors." Keeping her eyes on Julia, the woman unshipped her copy of the paper. FREAKS AND GEEKS. The woman was chewing gum, Julia noticed.

"I liked that show, anyway," it occurred to Julia to say. She restrained herself from glancing up to where Raleigh would be monitoring her progress. "Well, heading to the bus," Julia said.

"Where did you grow up?" the woman asked.

"Oh, it's not interesting."

"In the city?"

Julia laughed, slightly, at the incivility of the woman's persistence. As Julia began to walk down the street, the woman fell into step beside her. The decoy at least was working.

"I want to know," the woman continued.

"It's your job."

"No, this is an interesting story for me."

Julia laughed again. It was always pleasant to be flattered, even if one had the good fortune—or was it misfortune—to see through it. She took a deep breath of the November morning, and the air was cold enough and dry enough to have a menacing, almost diagnostic sharpness. The chill traced an outline of the air's passage into her.

The reporter was holding a digital recorder halfheartedly extended between them. Its red LED pulsed silently. An invitation, a hazard. With the arrest, the authority that the group had given to Leif had been interrupted, and everyone in the group was free to have a voice of her own now.

"But you went to school in the city?" the reporter tried again.

"No one cares!" Julia said cheerfully.

The arm holding the recorder drooped. "Do you not want to talk because you think we don't believe you?"

"Oh, I was never any good at it," Julia said.

"But I can tell you have it a little."

"Are you telling me that you have it?" *How did we get here,* Julia silently regretted.

"I know when I know something."

"What are we even talking about?" Julia asked. "I need to catch the bus, you know."

They had reached the avenue, though Julia's only real idea about the bus was that she would be able to look out the window.

"I read some of your friends' posts," the reporter said.

She wanted to hear the good news, Julia realized. She wanted to hear from the lips of one of the apostles that it would be all right if she let herself have feelings about everything she knew without being supposed to know.

"A week ago I could have talked to you," Julia said.

"I know," the woman replied. She shifted her backpack to her other shoulder. "Do you have any comment about Christopher Finn? He was released on his own recognizance."

It was a relief, probably to both of them, that the reporter had returned to her adversarial role. "Do you have his address?" Julia asked.

"Me?"

"You have all our addresses, don't you?"

In the end the reporter even mapped a route to the address on her phone. It didn't make any sense to take a bus, Julia saw. She walked to the subway.

A plastic potato chip bag that had been pulled into wiggly flaps—its delicate, oily inner pocket exposed—was drifting down the subway steps as Julia marched up them.

She emerged onto a treeless avenue. Sun-faded stuffed animals were wired to the metal frame of a drugstore's raised security grille. A trestle sign promised a sale. Two blocks away, an expressway was whining in its artificial canyon. Years of exhaust soot, cast off by the expressway, stippled the ledges and crevices of the drugstore and neighboring buildings. The soot had aged the facades the way a flashlight pointed upward at a raking angle appears to age a young person's face.

Julia had decided to interview Chris. He was the member of the working group she knew the least about. There was something arbitrary about assigning herself the task, but she would never do any of the research she needed to do unless she made an effort to will herself to.

Chris's street was slightly less grim than the avenue that led to it, the usual ratio between streets and avenues. At the edge of the sidewalk stood a row of brick tenements, their shoulders hunched. Surprisingly, the bricks were umber rather than the garish coral that were what one mostly saw through a taxi's window on the way to the airport. Julia checked building numbers as she walked, but because three unremarkable-looking people were waiting halfway down the block, she knew which building it would turn out to be.

"We don't know how late he sleeps," one of the reporters said, as Julia pulled open the outer door.

"That's very thoughtful of you," she replied, and let the door shut behind her.

The reporter tugged it open again. "We had agreed to wait until nine or until he came down himself."

"I'm a friend," she said, into the glass of the inner door.

"Who?" he asked.

"Even if you ask nicely, I don't think I'd like to say."

A door slammed upstairs.

"What do his tattoos mean?" the reporter blurted.

"Does Chris even have—?"

"I mean Leif Saunderson," the reporter interrupted. "What do his tattoos mean?"

"I never thought about it."

As Chris approached the door, in his heavy male way, a glow of anger reddening the dark-honey bur of his skull, the reporter withdrew.

Chris opened the door at first only enough to talk. "Who sent you?"

"It was my own idea."

He eyed the reporters beyond her. She remembered how badly she had wanted to see Raleigh after her arraignment. She had had the primitive fear then that while locked away from her he might have changed. That the fairies might have switched him. They had switched Chris, she saw.

He opened the door a little further. "I have to leave for a job in a few minutes."

"I just wanted to say hi."

He trudged up the stairs. His T-shirt hugged his skin, and under his broad shoulders, his narrow back had a snakelike compactness. The linoleum on his landing, she saw when they reached it, was that wretched, ancient, common pattern, the one that looks like a cross-section of gray-pink pavlova, the color of hamburger meat just slightly cooked. The pattern was scumbled by heavy wear. Chris picked his way past a basketball, a heap of cleats, spattered cans of paint, a full trash bag, and a bicycle. She could smell that he had just showered.

"Sorry," he said, unemphatically, of the debris. He unlocked the door at the end of the landing. There wasn't room for her to step past him, so he stepped inside first and yanked a ceiling light's beaded chain.

Nothing in the tiny room stood independent from anything else. Flush in a corner against two walls was a twin bed, which touched a dresser, which in turn touched a small desk. The chair that belonged to the desk was backed up against the doors of a wardrobe.

A plain navy blue quilt had been pulled square with the corners of the bed that it covered. Its fabric had begun to pill. Had it been worn rough by Chris's unshaven chin? By time, merely? Julia imagined that if she were to lie down on the quilt, it would powder her throat with house dust, but she didn't know, journalistically speaking, whether she could write about what she imagined unless she actually did lie down on it.

"I've never been out here," she said.

"What do you want?"

"To see how you're doing?"

To imagine that one was going to write about the same moments that one was living through—it was like treading water. One made flurrying gestures, but with one's mind, and kept an inch or two above the surface.

"And no one sent you."

"I don't think anyone's in a position to 'send' anyone anymore," she told him. She couldn't help delivering her lines as if she were on a larger, brighter stage than Chris's bedroom afforded. She leaned over Chris's desk toward the one narrow window, in part because to peer out the window was to not be studying Chris's bedroom, which it would have been tactless to seem too observant of.

"You're just here for yourself," he said.

"I have this idea, Chris. I know it's a little . . ." She had the gingerly feeling that artists have when they first mention to another person a new work they hope to begin. "I'm going to write a book about all this. Someday. About what's happening to us. It's a project, I guess. Maybe it's just a way for me to, you know, process all of this."

"Are you fucking kidding me?"

She was so startled that she almost laughed. "Yes." She shut her mouth, which she realized was hanging open. "I mean, no. I don't know. How is it for you?" she asked vaguely. "All of this?"

"Do you know how I got out?"

For a wild moment she thought he was going to tell her he had made a jailbreak. "Didn't the judge . . . ?" she began, but she faltered.

"None of you threw me a line."

Neither for Chris nor for any of the others would there have been a father who knew at once the name of the attorney he wanted for the case.

"I watched Raleigh on the phone," Chris continued. "I watched Leif on the phone."

"Chris," she said pityingly.

"Chris what?"

"You had to get on the phone yourself."

"You think I don't know that none of you wanted to talk to me?"

"But I thought you weren't able to . . . ," she began, but she couldn't bring herself to say it. What she couldn't now bring herself to say had been the ground that they had met on. It had all been nonsense, of course. She hadn't ever thought that any of them did have it, not really. Now that she acknowledged her disbelief, she saw that there had never been a ground for them to meet on where they could in fact have met. They had never really met. Her inability to say flatly now what she and Chris were talking about meant that they had never even really spoken. It had all been a misunderstanding. But did he have to be so horrible about it?

So horrible and so magnificent. Because, look at him. His face was like a war mask, of chased gold. She folded her hands.

"You're such a fucking idiot," he said, shaking his head—a little showily, she thought. "You don't even know what I'm saying."

It stung, but this was experience; she had wanted experience. "Then tell me what you're saying."

"I'm cooperating with the prosecution," he told her. "You shouldn't even be talking to me."

"Oh, Chris." She realized, as she waited for him to say more, that she wanted to hear that it hadn't been her fault. Which was stupid of her.

"At least the people on the other side know what they're talking about," he said, speaking softly because, she sensed, his voice was in danger of breaking. "At least they know where they are.

"You haven't talked to Elspeth?" he added, still more quietly.

She shook her head.

"I have to go," he said. "I'm gonna be late."

Chris's apartment was far enough from the center of the city that on the subway going back Julia was able to find a seat. From station to station, the car filled up with commuters—underslept, vaguely put upon, purposive. They assembled in a silent forest around her, unspeaking because they were nursing for as long as they could the privacy they were soon going to have to surrender when they began their workdays. Their presence was required somewhere, unlike hers.

Talking to whom she shouldn't was what she had most wanted to save. Once she confessed to Kenneth, there would be a long, boring conversation in which she would be gently guided. There would be an appeal to the pride she took in being sensible. But what if she didn't want to be sensible anymore? What if she understood that this was her last chance?

The postman always came early to her parents' apartment, and Julia carried the mail upstairs. "Is somebody getting married?" her mother asked, as Julia took out of the pile a heavy cream envelope, hand-addressed to herself.

"I don't know, Momma. I haven't opened it yet. Is there any grapefruit?"

"I didn't think it was in season yet, so I didn't get any. I could make you an egg, or maybe Robbie would let you have some of his cream of wheat?"

"No," said Robbie.

"Do you want an egg?" asked her mother.

"I need the cream of wheat," Robbie explained.

"I understand, sweetie," Julia reassured him.

"Will you play Life with me?"

"Oh, I can't today. Isn't Thanksgiving coming up? Maybe we can play on Thanksgiving."

"It's in two days," said Robbie.

"Is it really? I'd forgotten all about it."

"How can you forget about Thanksgiving?" he asked skeptically, as if he suspected that she might be making a joke.

"I've just been losing track of things lately," she apologized. She resheathed the invitation. "It's a dinner slash fund-raiser," she told her mother. "For a friend's art space slash gallery." Rich people were so continually asking one another for money. Maybe it was to distinguish themselves from people who would be ashamed to ask for it. From people who lived in rooms so small that all the furniture touched.

5.

"And the name of your first pet," the salesman prompted.

"I said I had a pet?" Raleigh replied.

"Looks like it."

Raleigh tried to guess what he had been thinking of. "I had a guinea pig named Skywalker for about five minutes."

"Awesome name."

"It disappeared a week after we got it. My mother told me it died, but I'm pretty sure she took it back to the store."

The salesman typed and then waited for the system to respond. "'Skywalker' works."

"Are we all set?"

"Almost." The salesman, reading instructions off his screen, began to punch activation codes into the new phone that Raleigh was purchasing. "It may be an hour or two before the new SIM populates in all the databases."

"What happens to the old phone?"

"You won't be able to make calls on it anymore. You said you lost it?"

"Will it be erased?"

"I don't know, but you don't have it anymore, right? So . . . whoa, you're already getting a call."

"I am?"

"Yeah, you're live already. I have to finish one more thing, though."

"Who's calling?"

"Uh, nine-one-eight . . . ?"

"My mother," Raleigh guessed.

"Maybe she's sorry about Skywalker, man," the salesman risked.

"I should talk to her," Raleigh said.

He stepped with the phone into the dead space between the store's plate-glass window and a rank of pedestals for sample phones.

"They gave you your phone back!" his mother exclaimed.

"I got a new one," he said. The sun even through the window was hot on his face. "They can transfer the number, when you get a new phone."

"Will that interfere?"

"With what?"

"With the investigation."

"That's not my problem, Mom."

"But if they think you're interfering, Raleigh."

"Felix said to do it."

"Oh. Well, you didn't tell me that Felix said to do it."

"What's up, Mom."

"Nothing. I just wanted to know how you're doing."

"I'm fine. I'm on my way to see Elspeth."

"Did she get home safe?"

"Last night? I guess so."

"Are her parents there?"

"Her parents?"

"I thought they might have flown in for Thanksgiving."

"I forgot it's going to be Thanksgiving."

"They must be worried about her."

"I guess Jeremy and Philip usually cook a turkey," said Raleigh, thinking out loud.

"Oh, I see."

"Mom, I can't come to Oklahoma right now."

"Oh, I know. I understand." She paused to blow her nose. "You're handling this so well."

"It's going to be fine. It's mostly for show, I think, what the government's doing. Security theater."

"Honey, I don't think you should talk about it on the phone. What if they're listening? They're saying that they've been listening to you all along."

"Who's saying? On TV?"

"They're saying that that's what you're fighting, really. I don't think I realized that." There was a tremble in her voice. "That that's what you're fighting."

She wanted to be reassured. "I'm not going to do anything stupid, Mom," he said.

"Your father says that you're taking a stand. You know you can always come home, if you think you're going to be lonely."

"Thanks, Mom. I know."

"For the holiday, I mean."

"I know what you mean."

"I'm so proud of you."

"Okay," he said blankly.

She hung up. "Mom?" He looked down at the shiny keypad to find the End button, but he saw that the phone already knew that the call was over.

"Do you need the receipt?" the salesman asked.

Elspeth opened her door.

It was only now that he was sleeping with someone else that he could see clearly not only her beauty but the kind of beauty it was: plain and unadorned, like the heroine of one of those books about frontier life that girls read in elementary school.

"Where are your keys?" she asked.

"I still have them, but I didn't think I should surprise you."

She looked away. He followed her down the corridor.

"After all the surprises yesterday," he explained.

On the dining room table, five tarot cards lay faceup in the pattern that dots have on the five side of a die.

"Were you doing a reading?" he asked. He knew the cards were only bright colors printed on heavy paper. One of the ones she had out was Death, who always looked to him more like a skinned raccoon than a person. Death was upside-down, flipping the figure's black garden of severed hands and heads into a night sky where the hands and heads were constellations.

One by one the cards quilped as Elspeth returned them to the bottom of the deck. "I guess," she said.

"They should have taken this deck when they confiscated the rest of our communication technology."

Elspeth smiled politely.

"Did you meet someone?" she asked abruptly.

"Where—in jail?" It was a gamble, but he had the impression that she was moderating her scrutiny of him, maybe out of tact, maybe because she didn't really want to know. "No," he lied, more boldly. It wasn't why they were breaking up, after all. Still, his heart raced with the excitement of lying. He thought it would be a tell if he looked away, so he didn't. But maybe it was a tell that he didn't.

"I'm sorry I was so useless yesterday," she said. "I don't know all the things you know. The technical things."

"It doesn't matter."

"You were mad at me."

"I was in jail."

"And now you want to be free," she said.

He didn't answer.

"Everyone should always be free," she continued. "We can be grown-ups about it."

He nodded.

"It's almost like I'm breaking up with you," she observed.

"It's a little of both," he conceded.

"Would you mind holding me?" she asked. "For old times' sake. Just for a minute."

Her small bones, loose in the small satchel of her body, felt familiar, but there was nothing that was sharply especially for him in the touch between the two of them. He was doing her a favor; it didn't feel like any more than that. Altruism wasn't love, he noticed.

"I'll miss you," she said, as she pulled away.

"I'll miss you, too," he lied.

"We'll still see each other, but I won't be the same," she told him.

"Be however you want to be."

"No, I can't do that. But I won't forget you."

Her words were so peremptory that he almost had second thoughts.

She excused herself.

In the alcove of the dining room where a dumbwaiter had once come through, Elspeth's dictionary, style manual, and gazetteer were neatly arrayed. The pink yarn elephant that he had given her one year for her birthday was perched on top of the reference books, and her pencils lay beside them, aligned according to the crimped green metal bands that fastened the erasers to the stems.

He shouted down the hallway. "I should go."

"You don't have to go," she called back. "Unless you want to."

She had cried, but she had washed her face. She knew better than to show it if she was the loser. Was he the loser, then? It wasn't something he should be wondering in her presence, but her mind was probably too clouded with emotions to be able to sense it.

She had guessed right, of course; he had met someone in jail. He and Julia had become cellmates there, in a way, and were aware now, even on the outside, that they might have to go back, aware as ordinary people weren't that the context for their lives was provisional.

"Has anyone told you yet what they're saying about you?" Elspeth asked.

"About me?"

"About all of you. You're the Telepathy Four. 'Free the Telepathy Four.' You're heroes online. 'Revolutionaries.' Diana was here till late last night, and we were reading on her phone."

"We didn't seem like heroes on TV this morning."

"It's different online. They think we knew Bresser was spying on us."

"You and Leif might have sensed it," Raleigh said. "When Leif read his password that first time, when Chris and I were arrested for standing in the street, Leif might have been picking up a signal."

"No, be honest. We didn't know anything until Bresser told Chris that somebody was calling him Hyacinth, and even then we only suspected. Online they think we knew-knew. They think we knew and were taking revenge, which they like because they hate Bresser. He keeps trying to talk to them. I think they hate him more *because* he keeps trying to talk to them."

"They're on our side," Raleigh said.

"For now."

"That matters, Elspeth. We need that." The internet was still a force that hadn't been understood. The only thing anyone knew for certain about it was that it was always on the side that didn't lose. "The police haven't seized our domain name, have they?"

"You mean our website? Can they do that?"

"Yeah, Elspeth, they can do that."

"What? I don't know these things."

He wished he could see for himself the searches for their working group by the searchers who didn't know its name, the comments by readers exchanging heated speculations about the motives of the group's members, the name-calling, the praise, the stuttered exclamations—all the electronic correlates of attention, which, unable to see, he imagined as a white network, floating distinct from the world, like light that had been abruptly disembodied somehow from the knotted sheaf of fiber-optic cables in which it had been coursing and pulsing.

"You have to take care of it because I can't take care of it anymore," he said. "It could change everything."

"Oh, Raleigh."

"What?" he asked.

A phone burred against the table. It was a throwaway candy-bar phone. The ringtone was primitive. "It's my mother," Elspeth said, to excuse herself, as she picked it up.

She turned her head away. "I'm okay. I slept okay," she said into the phone.

She rose, walked into the parlor, and stood at a window.

"We watched a DVD for a while and then she went home."

He hadn't realized that Diana had brought Elspeth back from the courthouse.

"He's here now," Elspeth said. "He's fine."

". . ."

"I haven't asked him yet."

". . ."

"This afternoon."

". . ."

"I hope so."

The staccato lines resonated through the twinned rooms. It occurred to Raleigh that if he went into the kitchen, he would be able to give Elspeth some privacy, but he didn't go.

"I hope it's not too expensive."

". . ."

"I wish you could. Bye, Mom." She depressed a button on the device, effortfully because it was still new to her.

"Is she worried about how much your lawyer is going to cost?" he asked.

"She's having somebody come today to look at the retaining wall. The basement keeps flooding."

She set down the phone and shoved it a little away from her. She had never really liked even her old phone, he knew, on account of the interruptions it made, and this one was uglier and even louder.

"I should get ready to visit my lawyer," she said.

"Is he anyone?"

"She. A friend of my mother's recommended her. She's somebody's daughter."

"What were you about to say before?" Raleigh asked. "When your mother called."

She hesitated. "It doesn't matter," she finally said.

Her thoughts weren't his to know anymore. Because he lacked any aptitude for intuiting them, discretion on her part protected her like a wall, high and featureless. He was less because of it.

"No, you were going to say something."

"No, I wasn't."

She had been going to say something about the two of them, he realized, but now she would never do that again.

He waited, but she waited him out.

"Oh fuck," said Raleigh, half aloud.

Three television vans were besieging the café where Leif worked. One was parked with its two left wheels up in the middle of the sidewalk. The van's sliding door was open, and as Raleigh edged past it, the skirt of his coat swirled a short arc into and out of its amber interior, where banks of heavy equipment were blinking silently, protected by nothing but the forbidding importance of being useful to television.

"Hey," a man said, and Raleigh was startled, as if the man had been able to detect in the incursion of Raleigh's coat a wish on Raleigh's part to commit sabotage. The man was wearing a baseball cap and holding a cigarette between fingers in fingertipless gloves. "Do you know him? Do you know what his tattoo means? Aren't you—?"

Raleigh went inside before the man could remember Raleigh's name.

Inside, it was standing room only. A few tables were held by regulars, and the floor around them was empty, as if the other tables and chairs, unanchored, had been carried away by a flood.

They had washed up on the shores of three islands of television people. At the center of each stood a reporter, almost clownishly well groomed. Other crew members, comparatively gray, were wearing hats, coats, and headsets in case they might need to rush outside. Next to their coffees lay their cameras, like derringers set down by tippling cowboys in a movie-set saloon.

Raleigh caught Greg's eye. "Hey, man," Raleigh said. He waited for Greg to serve a mint tea to the customer in front of him. "Matthew said Leif was here?"

"Down below. We used up all the Ecuadorean and he's getting another sack."

"These guys are buying coffee?"

"Anyone who wants to stay has to buy one coffee an hour. New rule."

A camera somewhere in the room softly wheezed twice.

"Excuse me?" Greg said. "No photography on the premises today."

"Sorry."

"You need to take the camera off and leave it on the table if you want to stay," Greg ordered. He watched until the man sullenly unlooped the camera from his neck.

"You're *good*," Raleigh said.

"You want anything?"

"A latte, maybe?"

"Coming up. Do you want a peanut butter cookie? On the house. They sent us too many."

"Sweet."

"Literally," Greg said. With tongs, he put a cookie onto a small plate for Raleigh. He surveyed the mostly silent, mostly still crowd before turning his back on them to make the coffee.

Eyes in the crowd shifted hungrily to Raleigh as soon as Greg couldn't see them.

A reporter, a woman in royal blue, leaned her head into a colleague's whisper. "Raleigh Evans?" she then said. She picked her high-heeled steps carefully as she crossed the room to reach him. "What's it like to work with Felix Penny? You've been a fan of his for a while now, haven't you? How exciting is that."

Greg turned and frowned, but he was pinned in place by the need to hold the milk, in its small steel tankard, around the spout that was noisily frothing it.

"I'm just here to meet a friend," said Raleigh.

"I won't take any of your time."

"He said no," Greg told her.

She didn't look at Greg. "If you and I could step outside for just two seconds . . . ," she suggested.

"Not today, thanks," said Raleigh.

"Well, think about it. I'll be right over here. I've been really looking forward to getting to talk with you." She turned to Greg. "Could I get one of those peanut butter cookies, too? They sound so good." She left a five on the counter and stalked back to her team, turning herself off as she walked.

Standing at the counter, Raleigh broke his cookie along a chord, broke a tip off the broken-off segment, and popped the tip into his mouth.

Outside, something creaked, and the café fell silent. The hush came on so quickly and was so absolute that one of the regulars, who had been lost in his book, looked up. Everyone in the café listened as one panel of the basement's metal door fell to, with a clank. Then, more softly, the other panel was also lowered into place. The arm of a lock rattled as it was threaded through the eyes of the door's handles.

Undisguisedly everyone watched the entrance.

"The Ecuadoran was under a whole dogpile of Brazilians," Leif said, when he appeared. He was hugging a dark plastic sack of coffee beans. He was wearing only a T-shirt and jeans, despite the cold, and his face was nearly as pale as the triangle of sky visible through the door behind him.

"Hey, it's *Raleigh*," Leif called out, when he saw him, and to Raleigh it almost felt for a moment like being greeted from the stage at a concert. A new interest in Raleigh rippled across the room.

In his excitement Leif coughed, gutturally, angrily, for almost a full minute.

"What are you doing here, man?" Raleigh asked, when the cough died down.

"Working."

"Why?" Raleigh asked, laughing at the assholishness of his own question.

Leif ducked under the counter with the sack of coffee and surfaced again behind it. "I don't know. I wanted to still have a life."

"You could have called me," Raleigh said. He came up to the counter so they wouldn't be too much overheard. "There's supposed to be a new ramp down near the canal I want to check out."

"I can write poems here sometimes, when it's slow."

"Are you writing one? Should I leave you alone?"

"No. It turns out it's not slow today. Greg is making them order all these coffees."

Greg, at that moment presenting Raleigh with his latte, let his head drop as if under the burden of the reproach.

"How's Elspeth?" Leif asked.

"We broke up."

"When?"

"Just now."

"Maybe you didn't really break up."

"No, we broke up," Raleigh insisted.

Raleigh glanced at Greg and saw that Greg had buckled his lips in a sympathetic grimace.

"It's okay," Raleigh told Greg.

There was a sink at the back of the baristas' work space, with a little dishwasher beside it, and Leif began rinsing cups and saucers that were stacked in the sink and loading them quietly into the dishwasher. "I should have gone to see her this morning," Leif said.

"Did you and Matthew break up?" Raleigh asked.

"No," Leif replied. He stopped rinsing for a moment but left the water running. "No no no no no."

"It's all right," Raleigh reassured him.

Leif resumed rinsing. "It's not all right."

"It is," Raleigh said. He watched Leif's eyes, but Leif wasn't crying. The counter was between them, and Raleigh didn't want to do anything that the television people wouldn't be able to resist photographing.

"We're torturing them, aren't we," Leif said of the television crews.

"*We're talking about his tattoo,*" Raleigh announced, in a loud voice.

Leif shook his head and coughed again.

"They're so into your tattoo," Raleigh commented.

"It's a nice tattoo," Leif said, with pretend pretend-modesty. He added, in a voice whose volume briefly matched that of Raleigh's announcement, "*It illustrates an Andrew Marvell poem.*"

There was murmuring.

"I'm actually writing a poem about it," Leif continued, more quietly. "About Marvell's trees. You know how there weren't any trees at Occupy?"

"There were trees."

"I'm trying to tell you about my poem."

"I know, but there were trees at Occupy. Remember that tree that the Media Working Group tied a corner of their tent to, and the cops made them untie it? Before the cops gave up on tents?"

"That doesn't count. That wasn't a real tree."

"Okay," said Raleigh, who knew about himself that he was capable of being a dick sometimes about what was a fact and what wasn't.

"I'm serious. That wasn't a real tree."

"It wasn't an *artificial* tree."

"They probably had to build a special container for its roots or something. It was like an office tree that happened to be outside."

"Okay. If you want."

"Just let me have this."

"I said okay," Raleigh repeated.

"Instead of trees there was *this.*" Leif thumbed a circle in the air.

"'This' what?"

"The people watching. The police, the journalists, bystanders. A paradise is a garden, and there have to be trees. 'This yet green, yet growing ark.'"

"You think Occupy needed the police?" Raleigh asked. "You think we wanted the police?"

"Don't get hung up on the police, per se. There aren't borders anywhere anymore, is what I'm saying. 'This' is how we make borders now—with the *way* people are looking. With the direction they're looking, and with the looking itself."

Raleigh wondered why and how it was that Leif always managed to put himself in the wrong with every group that he was part of and yet remain liked by it. It was his version of negative capability, maybe. Raleigh used to wonder if he should be writing down what Leif was saying when he talked like this, so that there would be a record when one day Leif became famous. Now Leif was famous, and if Leif were to speak up just a little, the world was ready not only to record but also to transmit everything he said. In the end it wasn't as a poet, though, that he had become famous.

"I thought the reason you liked that poem was because it was about being alone," Raleigh said.

"There have to be trees if you want to be alone. There has to be something alive that is protecting you but isn't watching you."

"So are we in 'paradise' now? If paradise is a ring of 'trees'?" Raleigh asked, looking back at the journalists.

"No," Leif said, annoyed that he wasn't being understood. "We weren't in paradise then, either."

Leif didn't want to leave, so he and Raleigh kept talking where they stood, leaning toward each other across the counter. Greg patrolled the café, retrieving an empty coffee cup here, wiping down a tabletop there.

Their talk was interrupted every so often by Leif's cough, which his night in jail seemed to have brought back. He was having trouble sleeping. Maybe it was the steroid they had put him back on. He wondered if it was making him a little manic. He kept coming up with ideas for poems, faster than he could come up with the words for them. But maybe he was just trying not to think about what he had done to his friends.

One idea, for example, was that all of Marvell's poems were really a single poem. There was only one garden, protected by only one wall of trees. There was only one beloved, who was either a little girl or a woman who wasn't quite ready to be in love. Or maybe it was the poet himself who wasn't quite ready—or who was, if he was honest with himself, a little girl. He would rather stay in the garden, was what he kept finding different ways of saying, because everything outside had been built on a foundation under one corner of which a severed head has been rolled. Everything outside stood upright only because the forces striving on either side to topple it happened to be in matched opposition, "fastening the contignation which they thwart," as Marvell put it.

Another idea was about a rule the British navy had in the eighteenth century requiring warships to stay in line while fighting. It made maneuvering clumsier than it had to be, but it also made it easier to spot any captain hanging back to save his own neck. Leif thought that today the authorities did the same thing with information. A government employee pretended not to know the contents of State Department cables released by Wikileaks—he stayed in line. Half a dozen newspapers ran articles about a conference call that all of them had had with the same government official, and none of the newspapers named the official—they stayed in line.

His talk seemed to get faster the longer he kept talking. "Maybe you are a little manic," Raleigh said.

"Just listen. Then there's confusion. The ostensibly democratic confusion of the internet." The energy in his voice—the speed and the note of panic in it—was running a current between the two of them. As if instead of Leif's ring of trees there were for the moment an electric fence. "A true statement can be reliably distinguished from a false one only by someone knowledgeable about the subject matter, and since no one can become knowledgeable about more than two or three fields, everyone who wants to understand the world has to depend on experts. The internet makes it easy for everyone everywhere to say anything, which is too many people to control, but because it's hard to become an expert, there are only ever a limited number of them, which makes them easier to control. Experts can't function as experts unless they can speak under their own names. A name is just a shortcut, but without it, you have to become an expert yourself every time you want to know whether someone claiming to be an expert really is. So if the authorities can keep a few experts in line and discredit the rest with witch hunts or personal attacks, information becomes indistinguishable from misinformation. Telling them apart becomes too much work. It doesn't matter if the secrets get told because almost no one can recognize them.

"Which leads me to my fourth idea, which is that a person who still does tell the truth, when there's so little point, is probably going to have something wrong with him. Because it's such a stupid thing to do. He's going to be damaged somehow. Not an insider, because an insider knows better. And not an outsider, either, because that takes a kind of strength that's too easy to recognize. No one on the inside would make the mistake of giving an outsider a secret. It's always going to be someone awkward, not quite realized, not fully assembled. A little broken. Someone easy to ignore, without anyone even making a conscious decision to ignore him. A throwaway person."

"You should write all this down," said Raleigh.

"The point is they're not going to listen to us even if we're not wrong."

The room was silent when the murmur of Leif's talk stopped. Some of the television crew members were still watching Leif and Raleigh, fixedly. Leif should add a theory about how sometimes you couldn't tell somebody something because they wanted to know it for the wrong reason. Unfortunately, once Leif was convicted, no reporter was ever going to seek him out for his ideas again. It probably wasn't his ideas that they wanted even now.

"But *you* got through," Raleigh said. "And you weren't supposed to be able to. There has to be something to it."

"To what?"

"To whatever we're calling it. The refinement of the perception of feelings."

Leif seemed not to want to join Raleigh in the acknowledgment.

"You know they're on our side online?" Raleigh continued. "That's what Elspeth told me."

"Are they?" Leif asked. He looked from Raleigh to the television crew members as if it hadn't occurred to him that any of them might harbor goodwill.

Raleigh wondered, while Leif looked, why Leif thought of himself as broken. Thought of all of them as broken.

"It's because they know we won't make it," Leif said, after having studied the ring of watchers for a little while. "If they're on our side, it's because that way there will be more pathos for them to feel when we go down."

After Raleigh left, it occurred to him that Elspeth would have wanted him to ask whether Leif had spoken with his mother yet and whether he liked his lawyer and how things were with Matthew more specifically. But he wasn't going back to Elspeth's. He was just taking the subway home.

There hadn't been a subway running between Elspeth's apartment and his when they had started dating. Later, during a yearlong spate of construction, the authorities had rerouted a line so that it did run between them. It turned out that there was an appetite for travel between Elspeth's establishment neighborhood and Raleigh's edgy one, and the authorities had recently decided to continue the connection indefinitely. But Raleigh might not ever make the trip again. Unless he came back now and then to see Leif at his café.

He walked along the platform to the position where his staircase would be waiting when he exited at his station.

A train rumbled in—one of the boxy, rattly older trains. The breeze that it forced into the station brushed Raleigh, and then the air grew still. It was the middle of the day on a weekday, and there were plenty of seats. The other passengers looked quiet. People who rode the subway at this hour usually were. The elderly. The unemployed. People who had gotten themselves excused from their jobs for an hour or two in order to respond to death, illness, or some lesser misfortune.

Raleigh wished he had asked Leif what they were going to do, but maybe they had both sensed that the topic hadn't been safe to talk about.

He shut his eyes. He hadn't slept that much the night before; he and Julia had tossed and turned. Between stations, rocked by the train, he dropped briefly into sleep. At the next station he opened his eyes and without focusing on anything in particular watched the doors scroll open, stand empty, and scroll shut. He let his eyes close again, and as the train was urged forward by its engines, he fell asleep more deeply.

He dreamt that he was in the emergency room at the end of Elspeth's block. He had been injured, but the injury had happened in another time-line, and no one could see it yet in this one. It was only just starting to cross over. It was like an exposure on undeveloped film. Greg was at the triage desk, pretending to be a doctor. He was addicted to a drug that he could get at the ER; that was why he was pretending. A trapdoor to the cellar was propped open behind him. The drug was inside, under green shadows. It was just mint tea, Greg said. Did Raleigh want any? But they had only given Raleigh aspirin last time Raleigh protested.

"We weren't in paradise then," Greg said.

Raleigh tore himself awake.

He was aware of stiffness in his lips, as if in his dream he had been trying to speak but hadn't been able to. He rubbed his mouth.

The subway car shuddered and clacked as it continued to carry him. In its yellow light, the triage desk, the figure who must have been Greg, and the trapdoor began to lose their substance.

He had slept through a few stops, but he hadn't missed the one nearest his apartment. In real life he had never been to that emergency room.

The fear he had felt in his dream, strangely, didn't go away. At first he couldn't figure out why. In his dream, the fear had had something to do with a shadow that was still developing.

Suddenly he remembered: he had been charged with a crime. In waking life. He felt himself blush. Whenever he woke up now he was going to have to remember.

When Raleigh opened the door to his apartment, he saw Jeremy sitting at the island table in the kitchen, tapping the keyboard of his laptop with one hand while the other hand played with his beard. His golden young-patriarch's beard. It took a moment for him to look up and greet Raleigh; he must have been trying to finish a thought. "Where've you been?" he asked.

"Out."

Jeremy's attention dropped back to whatever he was writing. He was drinking a mug of herbal tea with a pungent, grandmotherly smell.

It was late afternoon, and Raleigh still hadn't eaten. In the refrigerator there was only the same white pizza box that had been there since Sunday. "This is a week old."

"Go get something, then," Jeremy replied.

"Can I have some of this soda?"

"It's not mine."

"Where's Philip?"

"He's trying to score with a reporter."

Raleigh took the soda. "That's so wrong."

"They're just people."

"Who, gays?"

Jeremy sat back from the table. "Reporters. Reporters are just people."

Raleigh took a swig. "Does that mean you're talking to them?"

"I'm not *not* talking to them."

"Why?" Raleigh asked.

"Because you and your friends are going to be on trial and I imagine you're going to want to keep the public on your side."

Raleigh took another swig, a longer one. The soda sloshed and fizzed noisily. "I really appreciate what you're doing."

"You're such an asshole."

"I'm serious," Raleigh said. Then he belched, with mildly ironized shamelessness.

"I'm putting up a website for you," Jeremy said.

"For me or for all of us?"

"All of you." He twiddled a pencil stub. "I can't interview you directly, but your lawyers can tell me things sometimes."

"I'll ask Felix."

"He wanted you to go in and see him today."

"He did?"

"He called this morning."

Raleigh checked the clock on the stove. "Fuck."

"And your mother called last night. I told her you were at Elspeth's."

"I wasn't at Elspeth's."

"Well, I didn't know that, man."

It was probably all right. If Elspeth and his mother had compared notes, one of them would have said something to him this morning, so they must not have.

"I'm thinking we could sell those T-shirts," Jeremy suggested.

"My T-shirts?"

"Didn't Elspeth make some?"

"That was actually Julia. You should talk to her about it."

Jeremy added an item to a to-do list. It was strange to see him taking note of something Raleigh said. Raleigh was pretty sure he had never done it before.

"You could post one of Leif's poems," said Raleigh. "He's working on one right now that's going to be great. It's going to synthesize a lot of what's going on."

"My idea is the website will be more about advocacy."

"Well, he's probably going to want to send it somewhere like *n+1*, anyway."

"Does *n+1* print poetry?" Jeremy asked.

Jeremy's phone whirred on the tabletop, like an insect against glass. "Oklahoma," Jeremy said. He unlocked the phone and handed it to Raleigh.

"Dad, you can call my old number now," Raleigh said as he walked to the loft's front windows. "Didn't Mom tell you?" The windows went down almost to the floor, and you could look down through them at the tops of the heads of pedestrians. At their tonsures.

"Did she?" his father wondered.

"What's up?"

"Oh, nothing." He never liked to rush into a conversation.

"Is everything all right?" Raleigh asked.

"You know, I've been thinking, as I've been watching this . . . I've been watching all day." He preferred to back into his ideas, as cautiously as if he were parallel-parking.

"Thinking what, Dad?"

"Do you think it's accurate, the way they're talking about it? They're talking about it as a privacy issue."

"I haven't been watching."

"Because it occurred to me that it could be secrets, that's the other way of looking at it. It could be that your group doesn't want the government to have secrets."

"The idea of the group was honesty."

"See? See?" his father said. "But the media make it about themselves. About their concerns."

"I think the media worry about secrets, too, Dad."

"If you were to give an interview . . ."

"I don't think Felix would want me to do that."

"Well, he's a lawyer, isn't he. You know, it's overwhelming, if you're watching, and I've been watching since yesterday. They show your picture over and over, but we never hear you say anything."

"I think I should listen to Felix."

"But if this is *bigger* than that . . . ," his father hinted.

A placard near the ceiling listed salads and sandwiches. He had brought Elspeth here once, before they had figured out that they liked her neighborhood better, and she had ordered the barley and arugula.

"You go ahead," he told the woman behind him in line.

"Oh," she said. She seemed embarrassed by his offer.

When he tried again to read the placard, he became aware that he was doing so self-consciously. A woman ahead of him in line was eyeing him sideways while playing with the lapels of her boyfriend's coat. A man in glasses, waiting for his meal, had shifted to get a better view of Raleigh's face. The reporters in Leif's café had known who Raleigh was, of course, but because it had been their job to know and because Leif had been their primary interest, Raleigh had been somewhat shielded from the uncanniness of this kind of attention.

It was like moving in a field of static. Was there anything he could get out of it? Maybe the number of the girl he had just let skip his place in line?

A man with curly hair held up a cell phone and took Raleigh's picture.

"What the fuck," Raleigh said, with sudden rage. Everyone in this part of the city was supposed to be too cool to be obvious. Everyone in the *city* was supposed to be too cool.

The man glanced at Raleigh and then back at his phone.

"Seriously, what the fuck," Raleigh said.

The man pocketed his phone and blinked.

"Dude, you could be a little more gracious," said the man whose girlfriend had been playing with his lapels.

"Are you talking to me or him?" Raleigh asked.

The man with the girlfriend shook his head and faced forward.

When Raleigh's turn came, he gave his order in the same public tone of voice in which he had challenged the man who had photographed him.

At a shallow counter where you could eat standing up if you had nowhere to go, he unlocked his phone. Julia at least was an adult. "Should I come over?" he asked when she picked up. Let them wonder.

"Do you want to? Actually, there's something I need to tell you."

"Can you just tell me now?"

"Aren't they listening?"

"Who?" he asked.

"The people who took our phones. The people who have our phones."

"So it isn't about us."

"*This* thing isn't," she answered.

"But another thing is?"

"I haven't made up my mind."

"Is it a good thing or a bad thing?" he asked.

"About us? I think it's bad."

"You're so brutal."

"Not because I mean to be," she said. The nice thing about cheating was that there were no shoulds, at least between the two doing the cheating. There were only feelings, so everyone had to be lighthearted about them.

He remembered, though, that officially he wasn't cheating anymore. "I have something to tell you, too," he said.

"Raleigh?" said the counter guy. Raleigh's sandwich was ready. He found that as long as he stayed on the phone, he didn't care that much about the staring at him.

On Julia's block, a couple of buildings in from the corner, there was a ledge that had caught Raleigh's eye—a lip of concrete around a flight of stairs down to a basement dry cleaner's. From the sidewalk to the ledge was a little high, but high in an interesting way, as Leif liked to say. Of course, the drop on the inside of the lip was even steeper.

It was hard to find a good spot in the city that hadn't already been skated to death, and Raleigh was always on the lookout. He hadn't seen videos of anyone skating this one. You'd have to wait until after business hours, though, if you didn't want to deal with people from the dry cleaner's yelling. He didn't use to worry about that. He used to carry his board with him more, too.

That was how it happened: gradually and then all at once.

He rang Julia's buzzer. He looked through the glass of her front door at the green carpet accordioned over the treads and risers of the stairs and at the squat and dowdy newel, like the rook in an old chess set. It would only be poetic justice if Julia broke up with him now that he had broken up with Elspeth. She owed him at least a mercy fuck if she did, though.

As she came downstairs, his first sight was of her feet, in socks, and he suddenly remembered the way she had given herself to him the night before, and he wanted her again. It was a class thing, maybe. People of her class, when they fucked, fucked absolutely.

He was so stupid about her.

"Did you grow up with horses?" he asked, when she opened the door.

"In the city?" she asked. "I mean, I know how to ride."

"Yeah, that's what I mean."

"But that's like knowing how to swim," she protested.

"No it's not."

Even while walking up a flight of stairs she seemed to be thinking about her posture.

"So what did you want to tell me?" he asked.

"Wait till we get inside. I can put on music."

"I don't need music."

"Don't we need it in case we're bugged?"

"I don't think they can bug us after we've been arrested."

Inside the apartment she stopped beside the door.

"What?" he asked.

"I just wanted to say hello."

Usually she held him off for a while, but she played these games.

"I do have a few things to tell you," she said, after a minute.

She took ice cubes and vodka out of her freezer. It always felt as if they were getting away with something. Or as if they were forcing a mechanism that it wouldn't be possible to force for very much longer.

She poured drinks.

"Are you breaking up with me?" he asked.

"Is there a going out that would need to be broken up?"

"We're seeing each other."

"I don't remember saying that."

"It's what we've been doing."

"Oh, *facts*," she said dismissively.

They sat in opposite corners of the same sofa. She slipped a foot out of its shoe and stretched it toward him.

"What I wanted to tell you—well, it's one of the things I wanted to tell you—is that I'm writing about this."

"About us?"

"Oh, I hadn't thought about us." She looked at the ceiling. "You know, if 'us' comes into it, I might *change* 'us' a little. I might . . . *time-shift* 'us.'"

"Then what are you writing about?"

"All of it," she answered.

"Does your lawyer know?"

"I'm not writing about it *now*," she said. "I'm making a point of *knowing* about it now, for the sake of writing," she continued. "Of experiencing as much of it as I can. Does that sound crazy?"

"I broke up with Elspeth this morning," he volunteered.

"Why?"

"'Why?'?"

"Yes," she said. "No." She retracted her foot.

"I can't say to her that I love her anymore." His voice sounded more vulnerable than he had expected it to.

"How sad," she said with polite pity.

"What was it you wanted to tell me?" he asked.

"I visited Chris." Her ice cubes had melted into the grooves of her glass, and she shook the glass to swing the cubes around, loop the loop. "He said he's working for the police or whoever it is."

"Did he say anything else?" Raleigh asked.

"You knew?" she asked.

"It doesn't surprise me."

"In other words, you didn't know. You shouldn't pretend to know if you don't know."

"I wasn't pretending anything."

"Are you mad about something?" she asked. "I said it was sad," she continued, going back to the subject of Elspeth. "My Wellbutrin seems to be getting in the way of this vodka. Do you want a refill?"

The freezer door thunked. "Did you see Leif's lawyer on TV?" she called to him. "He gave—I guess it was a press conference. It's so stupid that we can't go on the internet. But they might still be recycling it on TV, if you want me to try to find it."

"What did he say?"

"It was very sweet, really. He thinks there's a right to play. He was just maybe a little too optimistic, for a lawyer."

"To play?"

"The way children do. As part of our common human inheritance."

"Oh no."

"A right to learn about the world by not taking it seriously. What? I think it's really sweet."

"Diana found him, didn't she. He's an Occupy guy."

"He's blond, and he has these cheekbones. As if he spends most of his day talking to elves or something. Although he's not talking to any now. Whenever they run the clip on TV, they cut to the DA saying in a deep voice that there's no right to play with the safety and privacy of others."

"Fuck."

"Oh, it's not that bad. He says it's because of Occupy. The elf says. Even just six months ago we might not have been able to see that we have a right to play. We're living at a historical advent."

"Is Diana a lesbian?" Raleigh asked.

"Diana?"

"Jeremy said something about it as if everybody knew."

"She seems so nice," Julia commented.

"She's great."

"Are you afraid she's making a move on Elspeth?"

"No. Jesus."

"You could have feelings about it," said Julia.

"That's not why I asked."

"Maybe you have feelings, though."

"I don't have feelings."

Maybe he and Julia were beginning to drift apart. Like boats that by virtue of being just a few feet away from each other are subject to slightly different currents and breezes. He reminded himself that even if he was admitting to himself that he was still in love with Elspeth, he might still want to spend the night with Julia. He might for that reason want to spend it with her all the more.

"Your friend Jeremy called," Julia said. "The Committee to Save the Telepathy Four wants to sell my T-shirts."

"Is that what he's calling it?"

"It sounds very superhero, doesn't it."

"We were a working group, not a committee," Raleigh objected.

"That moment may have passed."

"It's getting colder now, but Occupy will come back."

"Colder?" She was puzzled. "Oh, you mean colder for people who want to sleep outside."

"It's going to come back in the spring," he insisted.

The law school was in a white high-rise. Raleigh expected there to be a rampart-like desk in the lobby where he would have to present his driver's license, but there were only students, streaming across an empty, speckled-marble floor, untalkative perhaps because it was morning.

The absence of a desk didn't put Raleigh at ease. The authority that would have belonged to it devolved to the students, who weren't paying any attention to him. They were dressed like students anywhere; they weren't wearing suits, as Raleigh realized he had more than half expected them to. They were only a little younger than he was. Probably they weren't any smarter, but in a few years they would be making serious money, from positions inside the machine. He was inside a machine, too, when he went to his job, but he tried also to be outside it. Tried a little too hard, maybe.

In the elevator, which his fellow passengers rode in silence, Raleigh wondered why Matthew had chosen graduate school in English literature instead of law. It was probably the sort of mistake that someone gay was more likely to make—pursuing the aura left behind by power instead of power itself.

He himself didn't envy the law students, he was pretty sure. He was part of a cause, and none of them was ever likely to be. At the courthouse, the day before yesterday, Felix had said he was excited about the case. It raised important First Amendment issues.

The carpeting on the fourteenth floor muffled the chime of the departing elevator. Along a corridor, tall oak doors, flanked by columnar panes of frosted green glass, marked off each office. In the tech support department where Raleigh worked, no one had a private or even a designated work space anymore—you checked out a desk for the day only—but disruption didn't seem to have stripped any perquisites from law professors yet. On a bench, a few students were reading, pens in hand, while they waited. One looked up at Raleigh and grimaced not because she recognized him but because she didn't.

When he had stopped in at his job to explain the restrictions the judge had imposed, a co-worker had been sitting at the desk where Raleigh usually sat, which had a direct sight line to a window. By next week he would have lost dibs on it.

Taped to the lawyer's door was his most recent op-ed. The column of text was punctuated by a small black-and-white square photo of the lawyer's distinctive curly hair and heavy-frame glasses.

"It's open," Raleigh heard Felix call, from deeper inside the office than Raleigh had guessed that it extended.

The distinctive curls and glasses rose to greet him. Famous people had to continue to be who they were. The constraint was one reason they were so widely trusted and liked.

Raleigh's eye picked out a dozen identical bright spines on a bookshelf—copies of Felix's book. Nearby, in twos and threes, were the Italian, French, and German editions. On a credenza sat a boxy plexiglas-and-aluminum apparatus, which Raleigh recognized as a device for digitizing ink-on-paper books. It didn't look as if it had ever been used, but maybe you wouldn't be able to tell.

"Sorry I didn't get your message in time yesterday," Raleigh said.

Felix waved off the apology.

"Yesterday morning I ported my old number to a new phone, and I think maybe I thought—"

"Do I have that number?" the law professor interrupted. He looked into his phone. "I have a number for Jeremy and a number for your mother and a number for someone named Elspeth."

"I'm probably not going to be at Elspeth's much anymore."

Felix nodded, deleting her number.

"We're maybe not a couple anymore," Raleigh explained.

"A trial can put a lot of stress on a relationship," Felix said. He paused in case Raleigh was going to say more. "Listen, thanks for coming in. I wanted to talk with you a little about where my thinking is on the case and where I see us going with it."

The lawyer got up again to close and lock the door. They were protected by attorney-client privilege now, Raleigh suspected. He needed to pee, but he had just got there.

"The law that you're accused of breaking covers access to computers," the lawyer continued, as he returned to his desk, "and I'd like to argue that that's what this case is about. There's a lot of talk right now about what you and your friends may have *thought* you were doing, but in this particular case I think your thoughts matter much less to the law than what you actually *were* doing. Your thoughts would really only be relevant if we were going to try to prove your motives—which, by the way, I see as an intention to carry out a kind of protest, and I think we should accept and even embrace the link that social media and the press have been making between your group and the Occupy movement more generally."

Felix had already taken a kind of left turn in what he was saying, which Raleigh hadn't quite followed, but Felix would probably come back to the main road before long, and Raleigh would be able to catch up then. He shouldn't slow Felix down with his not understanding any more than he should slow him down with his having to pee or with his no longer having the same girlfriend.

"Your state of mind would really only be a useful defense if we were going to argue that you were influenced. Influence *has* crossed my mind. I do worry about it. I'd probably worry more if you were to, say, insist on holding on to a particular construction of what you were doing. Because that would be a sign, wouldn't it? If you were so attached to an unusual construction that had been put on things that you were willing to compromise your defense."

"An unusual construction," Raleigh murmured, as if he understood.

"Am I missing something? Did you give your friend money, for instance?"

"Who? Elspeth?"

"Leif Saunderson. Did he take part of your paycheck every two weeks, did you pay his rent for him, anything like that."

"Leif would never ask for money."

"Because he doesn't need it? Because he's above money?"

"He has a job."

"Did he ever ask you not to communicate with a friend or a family member?"

"No," said Raleigh.

"Yeah, see, it's something to think about, but I don't think there's anything there. And so we can just set your friends to one side, as far as I'm concerned, and say, 'This is a story about the internet and whether you can make a protest on the internet.' And the person at the center of the story, if we tell it this way, is you, which has some risks but gives us a little more control. You were the one with the computer skills to do what you did."

It would be almost rude at this point to say that he had to pee, because it would suggest that he hadn't been giving Felix his full attention. "But we didn't . . . ," Raleigh began. He uncrossed his legs, which helped. "I didn't . . ."

"Go on," Felix prompted. He was always very amiable, Raleigh noticed, even if he knew you were about to contradict him.

"I didn't do anything that required any special skills," said Raleigh.

"It may not have seemed extraordinary to someone with your experience, but . . . Listen. The rules for discovery in this state are tremendously unfair to defendants, so if they were making a log or record on the server side or if they were able to extract one from your laptop, I may not be able to get copies of that until literally the last minute. Until literally the day of. So it might be a surprise how much they know. For some categories of evidence they have to give notice before the trial and with those categories we may have a chance to kick the tires a little in hearings, and sometimes I can get quite a bit that way. And then if there are federal charges, the rules in the federal courts are a little better for discovery. Technically a federal case is a separate legal matter, by the way, and if you're going to want me to represent you there as well we're going to need for your parents to sign another letter of understanding, but we can do all that electronically, like last time. . . . Are you all right? You look a little pale."

"I'm fine," Raleigh said, and he nodded vaguely but he hoped reassuringly. He didn't want his personal discomfort to delay Felix or trip him up in any way. He himself was making an effort to think his way past it. "I really didn't do anything," he said. He was repeating himself, but it was starting to feel urgent to him to tell Felix the whole story. He had been holding in the details, he realized, waiting for Felix to ask about them, and he couldn't hold them in any longer; he needed to get them out. "I accessed the login page through a proxy, just to be on the safe side. And then Leif read Bresser's password. That's what we called it, *reading*. Which just means that Leif guessed the password, you could say. That's all there was to it. There was no brute-force attack. There was no exploit. We didn't do an SQL injection or anything. It was just—we walked in, through the front door."

"Your friend knew the password," said the lawyer.

"No, I mean, well, yes, somehow he knew it," said Raleigh.

The lawyer's smile was frozen.

"You don't believe that," Raleigh said.

"What's important is that I believe *you*," Felix replied. "What's important is that I believe that you're telling me what *you* think is the truth."

"Okay." This wasn't going so well, Raleigh suddenly felt. Not going so well entirely apart from the problem of his mind filling up with unpeed pee. He looked out the window behind Felix's head. They were high up, and it seemed to be an empty vista, which was unusual for the city. Almost no grand buildings had gone up in the neighborhoods that the window overlooked, because until recently only people of color had lived there, and it was only in the past few years that money had seen anything to gain in taking their houses from them.

"By the way, it's too late now, of course, but if you ever pass this way again, next time don't just give the cop your password when he asks for it," Felix said. "That was a rampart we probably could have defended for at least a little while. But onward. How did you know Bresser's company was tracking you?"

"We didn't, really."

"Don't tell the internet," said the lawyer. "They think this is Hack Counterhack."

It might turn out to be difficult to be something other than what the internet thought you were. Especially if the internet thought you represented a cause, and if a belief that you did represent one was one of the few reasons you still liked yourself. "I think mostly we just wanted to see how much we could do." It was safe for him to confess to Felix, wasn't it? "We were just being assholes, really."

Felix folded his hands and hid his mouth behind them. "Chris Finn is cooperating with the DA's team now," the lawyer said.

"I know," Raleigh replied.

"You know?"

"Julia told me."

"You had a recent conversation with Julia?" the lawyer asked.

Raleigh nodded. He was keeping his pee in now only with an effort of will that he had to keep willing, consciously. Straightening his spine helped, the way that uncrossing his legs had helped, but only if he didn't straighten it too much.

"In this conversation with Julia," the lawyer asked, "did you tell her anything about the case? Mention anything about what you did or what you think happened?"

"I don't know. No."

"Raleigh, it's not a good idea for you to talk with your co-defendants right now."

"It isn't?"

"What if Chris Finn isn't the only one cooperating?" the lawyer suggested.

Raleigh nodded. He had to consider the possibility that he was a fool, of course. "The whole idea of our group was that we talk about things," he said, in order to explain himself, and as he said it, he peed himself a little, just a tiny bit, but not enough, he was pretty sure, for any to actually come out.

"That can't be your idea anymore. Not right now. Not for a little while."

He was alone, Felix was telling him. Everyone from the working group was alone now, separately. "I saw Leif, too, yesterday," he confessed.

Felix dipped his head toward his desk, as if Raleigh had aimed a blow at him and he were accepting it.

"Leif would never work for the other side," Raleigh added.

"When you say something like that, what I understand is that you care about him," Felix commented.

"I don't have the gift he has," Raleigh went on.

"I wouldn't be able to represent you if you thought you did."

"I mean, I can't show it to you, is what I mean," Raleigh explained. "I can't make you believe it. Do I need to tell you if I keep seeing my friends?"

"I'll continue to represent you for as long as it's possible for me to, ethically speaking," Felix replied. "Your friend Jeremy seems like a good guy."

Raleigh was getting tired of Jeremy.

"He's your roommate, is that right? He has everyone's ear right now.

You know how the internet is. His website is a source people trust right now. We should make use of it."

"We should?"

"Carefully, but we should make use of it."

"But I thought you don't want me to talk to people."

"I don't. Don't talk to him. I think the ideal, as far as this kind of thing goes, is when a site like his is running while a defendant is in jail and really *can't* communicate. But you can talk to me, and I can talk to Jeremy. And with a friend like Jeremy, you can talk to him directly so long as you don't talk about the case."

With a friend like Jeremy. With a vulture whom they could trust because he shared the professional interest that all vultures have. The professional interest in carcasses.

"Can I tell you what I like about your case, Raleigh?" Felix continued. "It's that you knew without knowing how you knew, and that's where *everybody* is right now. Everybody in America. That's where the government has put us. I think we're going to find out how you knew, of course. I think we're going to find out that because of the participation of Chris Finn or someone else there was something very much like entrapment going on, quite early. But the thing is, you felt like you knew, and I don't see how anyone could get from that feeling to actually knowing, unless they did what you did. You did what you did in protest. That, after all, is the definition of protest: you broke a small law in order to make a large point."

"I heard that Leif's lawyer thinks there's a right of play."

"No no no. There's no right of play. No. But there's a right to privacy. And there's a right to be free of government search in the absence of a warrant. Those rights were violated by the government, and whenever we've come close to catching the government at this kind of violation, in the past, one of the government's defenses has always been that if a citizen like you doesn't know that your privacy is being violated, then how can you be said to be harmed? But in this case you were harmed. The violation caused you unease. It did reach you somehow. I'm not saying it's a mystery. As I say, I think we're going to find out that somebody somewhere told somebody something that they shouldn't have. But we have to expect that that's what's always going to happen, if the government is free to track anyone it wants to. It's the sort of thing that's bound to happen."

The restroom was probably on this floor somewhere. Did he have time to ask where? Did he have time not to ask where? But what he said was, "There's a symmetry," as if he had all the time in the world.

"Exactly. A symmetry."

"So should we countersue?"

"Countersue! I love it. No no. We're probably going to lose, Raleigh."

There. There, for a second. For almost a whole second he hadn't been able to stop the unstopping. But if Raleigh didn't look down then maybe Felix wouldn't look down, either.

Felix was still talking. "I think there's a reasonable chance that we'll be able to avoid more than minimal prison time, more than symbolic prison time, but the letter of the law was against you when you made that move from feeling to knowing. You *had* to go against the letter of the law, in order to make that move. So be it. What's great about this case is that we're going to establish some principles and answer some questions and put some facts on the record, even if we don't prevail."

"Is there a restroom on this floor?" Raleigh asked.

"A restroom?" Felix echoed.

Raleigh stood up. "I have to go."

"To the right, past the elevators," Felix told him.

"To the right, past the elevators," Raleigh echoed.

"It'll be on your left."

"To the right, on my left."

The bench of law students looked up as he loped past. It wasn't safe to run.

His hands struggled flurryingly with his fly, and as he at last splashed into the porcelain, in the harbor of the well-appointed, faculty-grade men's room, all blue tiles and frosted aqua glass, he found himself speaking aloud, questioningly, between sighs, the words "Prison time?"

6.

Blades of grass trembled as they were struck by the rain, like tines plucked by the rotor of a music box. It was warm, for Thanksgiving. A fecund and unpretty day. Maybe winter was going to be replaced by a rainy season, Matthew thought, and maybe that wouldn't be such a bad thing. Rain seemed to make the world gentle and indirect.

Fosco, the three-year-old yellow lab that belonged to his parents, suddenly lost patience with walking on Matthew's left and crossed in front of him, surprising him with the purposive force with which she yanked against the leash. She padded obliviously through and across a stream of rainwater purling in the gutter and clambered up into the lawn that they happened to be walking beside. There she snorted three times, burying her snout deep in the wet grass with each whiff before lowering her hips and affixing the seal of her satisfaction.

As Matthew waited, drops of rainwater wavered and associated on the brim of his cap. In case she was about to answer one call of nature with another, he touched the folded plume of plastic bag in his back pocket, as if he were doing so absentmindedly, the plastic constituting the flag of his good intentions as a dog walker in the neighborhood.

He had left Leif asleep, unfolded in the bed that he himself had used to sleep in as a child. The room itself wasn't Matthew's anymore. Years ago he had prised out the thumbtacks that had held up his movie posters and his mother had repainted. A framed print of a peach-and-blue-colored lighthouse now hung above the spot where his desk had been. The desk had moved into what had once been his brother's bedroom, next door, which was now his mother's office. His brother's bedroom had been repurposed, and his had been "staged," like the homes of his mother's clients if they moved before she was able to find a purchaser—lightened of its memories, furnished with an almost impersonal representation of habitability. The redecorating was a way for his mother to pretend to herself that she didn't mind that her sons had left and a way for her to make a show of convincing them that she didn't mind.

The bed that had used to be his brother's had gone to the attic, which had been the playroom when he and his brother were little, and hadn't changed, except for a dormer window, which had never shut right and according to their mother had been letting in bats. It had had to be replaced.

"Would Leif like to sleep in the attic?" his mother had asked, the night before, in the car, when she and Matthew's father had picked Leif and him up at the train station.

"No, he can have my bed," Matthew had replied, "and I'll set up the air bed on the floor. You still have the air bed, don't you?"

He had been aware of his father listening to the conversation from the driver's seat; he had been aware of Leif, beside him, listening just as carefully. Neither Matthew nor his brother had ever brought anyone home before. No one in the family doubted that Brian would bring a girlfriend home one day, but at the moment domesticity wasn't Brian's style, and for once it was up to Matthew, the younger one, to be the pioneer. Matthew didn't want Leif to know how nervous he was about it—about bringing into his parents' house a living, breathing sign that their younger son fucked and liked fucking and liked for the partner of his fucking to be another man. He tried to tell himself that it probably wasn't that different for straight people, the first time they brought someone to their parents' house, except he knew that when the time came Brian wouldn't give it a second thought.

For an hour or two after saying good night, he and Leif had tried to share the twin bed. The darkness mantling the room had been familiar. As a teenager, Matthew had jacked off in it, in careful silence, so many times that the possibility of having sex in it now felt, unexpectedly, like a continuation rather than a departure. But Leif had been too shy to follow through, and when both of them were in the bed it had been impossible even to turn over without lurching and nearly knocking each other out of it. With two bodies so close under one blanket it had soon become uncomfortably warm. "You're like a little furnace," Leif had reproached him. In the end Matthew had given up on both sex and co-sleep, got into the air bed alone, and turned away, cradling his genitals in his fist for a while, under the covers, for consolation.

Leif's cough had kept him awake until it didn't, and then Matthew had slept like the dead, for the first time in a long time.

In the morning, he had been woken by Fosco snuffling repeatedly into the crack at the foot of the closed door. To give Leif more time to sleep, he had dressed and taken the dog out. Neither of his parents had emerged yet.

And so here he and Fosco were, with the street to themselves, gray rain pittering dispersedly around them. Even when it wasn't raining, children no longer played outdoors in the neighborhood. Maybe video games kept them inside; maybe the families on the street had simply grown older. The lawns were more fussily kept than Matthew remembered—the yews more vigilantly pruned, the velvety shingles of mulch more consistently confined within the borders of flower beds.

The visit was going pretty well so far, in his estimation. Last night, in his parents' kitchen, he and Leif had eaten bowls of cereal, for a snack, his mother checking the level inside the cereal box as she put it back in the pantry, to be sure that there was still enough left over for the morning. She had remarked that she and her husband understood that Leif worked in a coffee shop, and Leif had let go of his spoon and replied that he did, it was true, and Matthew's father had asked what kind of coffee, and Leif had listed as many national origins of coffee served in his café as he could remember, Matthew's mother and father nodding with cautious, stilted encouragement. "He's really a poet," Matthew had blurted out, and Leif had rolled his eyes, but Matthew's father had taken the cue and had stolidly asked for names of the journals where Leif's poems had appeared.

"Your parents must be so proud," Matthew's mother had said. Matthew had watched Leif fail to answer, not sure how to respond, evidently not wanting to explain so soon after meeting Matthew's parents that he wasn't in touch with his father.

Matthew had then watched his parents interpret Leif's silence as modesty, which in a way it was.

Leif's charm, Matthew thought, was working. Or maybe it was only the opportunity that the visit gave his parents to see how Matthew himself looked at Leif. Did they appreciate Leif's beauty? Were they able to? Matthew knew he had to be patient; they might still be suspicious of the beauty as a kind of superior force. They might still be suspicious of Leif himself. Leif tried at one point to thank them. "I'm so grateful—," he had begun, awkwardly.

"We know it's the right thing to do," Matthew's mother had said, cutting him short.

Matthew sensed, however, that his father would have liked to hear Leif's thanks in full.

It was all right. It was going to be all right.

Matthew's phone rang, and he fished it out of his pocket with the hand not holding the leash. "I'm walking the dog," he told Elspeth. "Leif's still inside asleep."

"A dog! What kind?"

"A yellow lab. Dumb and selfish and greedy."

"Don't say that about your dog."

"She's not mine," he said. "She's the empty-nest dog." Heedless of the discussion, Fosco froze and then lowered her head, having sighted a rabbit taking shelter in the dark skirts of a cypress. "I'll tell Leif to call you back when he wakes up."

"No, I need to talk to you," she said. "Michael Gauden charged Diana's credit card."

"Diana's?"

"She gave it to him that first day. She doesn't know I'm calling. I was there when she noticed it on her bill, and she said she guessed it would be her contribution, is the only reason I know about it. I know your parents are already being so generous."

"How much was it?"

"About twenty-eight hundred dollars."

For a couple of days' work. The side of town where Matthew's parents lived was built on a hill, up which he and Fosco were gradually proceeding, a long, slow hill that, as was always explained to new arrivals in town, served as an objective correlative of the relative financial net worth of the households along it. Blocks ahead, at the top, were mansions with a view of the distant city. Matthew's parents lived more than halfway down, where the houses were still faced with brick and perfectly respectable but not grand.

"Let me talk to my parents," Matthew said. "Thank you for telling me."

Was he going to ruin them?

"You don't think Diana will be offended, do you?" Elspeth worried. "If she's thinking of it as her gift to him and if we take it away from her? She only knows Leif through Occupy, but I think she really likes him."

"Let me make sure my parents can do it first."

"Okay, I'm sorry."

"Thank you for telling me," he said again, as if he were confident. He put on the manner not in order to fool her—this was Elspeth—but to save himself and his parents face and to signal that the awkwardness of not knowing whether they could bear the burden was not for Elspeth to worry about.

He pocketed the phone. How stupid he had been to go to grad school. He was thirty-one, and he could do nothing to take care of his lover but hope that his parents would take care of him.

A hollow-eyed Leif was sitting up on the edge of the bed, still in his T-shirt and boxers.

"What's going on?" Matthew asked.

"I deserve it."

"You don't deserve anything," Matthew said. Leif had begun to have these spells, and it was hard to know what to say during them.

"I led my friends into danger," Leif said.

"People make their own decisions."

"I'm not going to be able to pay your parents back. I'm a waiter, and my mother cleans the houses of summer people."

"They're not expecting you to pay them back."

"I should just get a public defender."

"Like Chris?" Matthew asked.

Leif returned to staring at the middle distance. "What if I stop wanting to go out with you?" he asked.

Matthew held his breath. They had had this conversation a few times now, too. "Do you?"

"I don't know."

"Don't do this," Matthew said.

"I'm not a loyal person. I'm not a one-dog man or whatever. There have been a lot of dogs. A history of short-term dogs."

"I have to give Fosco her meds," Matthew remembered. "Do you want to come downstairs and have breakfast?"

"Shouldn't I shower?"

"Before breakfast? It's just my parents."

"I'll wash my face."

Matthew waited on the bed beside the snug dimple that Leif's buttocks had left in the comforter. He listened to the white shivering of the tap water in the next room as it ran over Leif's face and hands. He wondered what his parents thought of his having chosen a boyfriend so much younger. He wondered what they thought of his inability to provide any more than just barely enough for himself, let alone for Leif. Whether they thought these facts said anything about him.

In the kitchen, his mother was wearing her morning kimono. She offered to make eggs so he and Leif wouldn't have to eat cereal twice in a row.

"But that's our fault," Leif said.

"I really don't mind. Do you like eggs?"

"I need to give Fosco her meds," Matthew said.

"Oh, would you?" said his mother. "She takes point-one milliliters of the bromide. You squirt it in at the back of her throat."

"I remember."

"And the other is a pill that goes in a little dab of peanut butter. I usually put it on one of the tea saucers. A whole pill."

"A whole pill?"

"We had to go up. She started seeing things." She explained to Leif: "That's her symptom."

"Her symptom?" Leif asked.

"Her prodrome," Matthew said. "It's the sign that a seizure is coming on."

"What does she see?" Leif asked.

"Things that aren't there," Matthew's mother replied. "Flies, we think, from the way she looks around, but of course she can't tell us."

"Maybe I should take some of these pills," said Leif.

Matthew's mother didn't acknowledge the joke. "It caused so much suspicion, when I asked to raise the dose," she said. "It's so regulated now. It's all tracked."

"That's so paranoid," Matthew said.

"Prescription drug abuse is a big thing in Vermont now, too," said Leif.

"Is it?" Matthew's mother asked. "I remember there was a vogue for barbiturates back when I was a girl. Mother warned us not to ever let a doctor prescribe them to us. But I have to say, they're wonderful for Fosco. She hasn't had a seizure in almost a year." She cut a thick chunk of butter into a sauté pan. It was an old stove, and when she lit one of the burners, she used a wooden match from a box. Very gradually the butter swiveled in the pan as its foot began to melt. "Do you like to watch the news?" she asked.

"Not in the morning, Mom," said Matthew.

"Not in the morning. What a nice policy. Then do you want me to buy you a paper?"

"I can still go online. It's only Leif who can't go online."

"Oh, I see," she said.

"I read the headlines to him," Matthew said.

"But that's a good idea, buying a paper," said Leif.

"We can buy one from Sam here on the corner. Let me call and ask him to keep one for us. He's a sweetheart."

"Okay," agreed Leif.

"Let me just do that right now," Matthew's mother said, rinsing and drying her hands before she picked up the telephone. "His real name is Osama, but he doesn't go by that anymore."

Matthew thumbed open Fosco's snout with one hand and depressed the syringe's plunger with the other. "Say *aah*." Fosco choked on the fluid, shook her head, and sneezed.

"Poor thing," said Matthew's mother. "Every morning. But she likes the peanut butter."

While Matthew prepared the day's saucer of medicated peanut butter, his mother called the corner convenience store, which was attached to a gas station, and asked in a musical voice for a newspaper to be put aside for her.

She was cracking eggs into a Pyrex by the time Matthew's father came downstairs. "How did you sleep, dear?" she asked.

"Great," he answered. He wasn't going to say otherwise in front of someone he didn't yet know very well.

"I'm making eggs. Is that all right?"

"Is there a vegetable?"

"A vegetable! How about toast?"

"Toast, then. We're not turning this on?"

"I think it's nice not having it on, for a change," said Matthew's mother.

"Don't not turn it on for us," said Leif.

"Whatever you want, Dad," said Matthew.

"It'll be all nonsense today, anyway," his father replied. He poured himself a coffee. As an afterthought, he added, "I mean, because of the holiday."

"Do you usually watch the parade?" Leif asked.

"Would *you* like to see it?" Matthew's mother asked.

"No, I just wondered if it was a tradition."

"Would you say it's a tradition with us, Jack?"

"No. Did I hear you ask Sam to save us a paper?"

"I did ask him to."

"Do I have time to go get it?"

"Well, the eggs will be ready in a minute."

He sank into his chair. "Oh, all right."

"Can I do anything?" Leif offered.

Matthew's mother put Leif in charge of making the toast, and she and Matthew's father were soon lecturing him about the toaster's idiosyncrasies. Matthew, for his part, poured glasses of water and set the table.

"Is there room for you there?" Matthew's father asked Leif, when at last they were ready to sit down.

They had to move the kitchen table farther away from the wall before there was enough room for Leif to get into the seat on the fourth side.

"Matthew, when you say that you go online," his mother asked, "does that mean you have your laptop back?"

"My downstairs neighbor is letting me borrow her old one."

"Is she the one with the rabbit? But wasn't your thesis on the laptop they took?"

"I had emailed my adviser the chapters I'd finished, and he emailed them back to me."

"So you haven't lost anything. How lucky."

"The eggs are very good, Mom." His father and Leif also complimented her on them.

"Thank you, dear."

In fact, he had lost a dozen pages of chapter three, as well as his outline for the dissertation as a whole. The lost pages had been about the stanzas of Samuel Daniel's *Civil Wars* that Coleridge disliked, the ones that interrupt the old plainsong chronicle with of all things a theory of history. A theory about the alteration that printing and gunpowder made in the fifteenth century to the pattern of life. Tongues became able to speak unlicensed; cowards became able to kill from afar. Matthew had hinted in the lost pages that what the internet and drone warfare today further, printing and gunpowder had begun. It was maybe because Daniel was aware that literature had become subject to modernity—had become prey to the marketplace, among other things—that he was so defensive and depressive, in some of his shorter poems, about the chance that a new work of true literature would be recognized and survive. Daniel had been between two worlds. He had looked back a little more than he had looked forward.

It occurred to Matthew that he should write that down, the part about Daniel as a depressive, because he hadn't thought of it quite that way before. There was a pad on the refrigerator door for grocery lists, and there would be ballpoint pens in the drawer next to the refrigerator, the drawer where his father kept batteries and his mother stuffed spare plastic bags for Fosco's walks. He had withdrawn his attention when his mind turned to his dissertation, but now that he was coming back to himself—now that, having made his note, he folded it and slipped it into his wallet—he noticed that his parents and Leif were chatting amiably. Everyone was making an effort, of course, but it seemed as if maybe his parents and Leif actually did like each other.

The landline rang just as Matthew's father was explaining that in the late fall, he put the snowblower into the same corner of the garage where in the summer he kept the lawn mower.

"If every year I kept track of the date I make the swap, you could track climate change," his father said, hurried into his punchline by the ringing.

"I'll get it," Matthew volunteered, rising before his father could. He had expected a reprieve from reporters. But maybe it was his brother?

"I'm sorry," Leif said. He, too, thought it was a reporter.

"What are you apologizing for?" said Matthew's mother, lightly gripping and shaking Leif's forearm, which slightly startled Leif.

"Fisher residence," Matthew said into the phone.

"This is Elaine Saunderson," said a woman's thin voice. "I hope it's all right to call now. My son gave me this number, and I'm going to be stepping out in a minute."

"Oh, hi, Mrs. Saunderson. This is Matthew."

"Oh, I thought you were your father. Good to meet you! Or, talk to you, I guess. I've heard so much about you."

"I've heard so much about you," he replied, which wasn't quite true.

"You've really been there for Leif," she said abruptly.

"It's a crazy time."

"I'll say," she agreed. "And your parents are so kind. Is your mother there? I want to thank your mother."

"Do you want to take this in Jack's study?" his mother was asking Leif.

"She'd like to talk to you, Mom," Matthew told his mother.

"To me?" His mother rose, with one hand gathering her kimono together at the neck and the other accepting the receiver. "This is Sharon Fisher," she said, in the professional manner that she spoke in when handling real estate. Her manner with peers.

Stock-still, she listened to Leif's mother.

"Well, we're so glad to have him here with us," she burst out, a moment later, back in her family manner again.

They don't tell you when you come out as gay, Matthew thought to himself, *that someday you'll be riveted by even the most banal interaction between your in-laws and your own parents.*

"We're happy that we're able to, and I *will* let you know, I promise," Matthew's mother said. She put a hand over the mouthpiece. "There's a phone in Jack's office," she told Leif. "At the top of the stairs on the right. You'll have a little more privacy there."

Matthew and his parents waited in silence as Leif mounted the stairs. When they heard him say the words "Hi, Mom," half muted by the distance and the plaster shield of the ceiling, Matthew's mother replaced the receiver.

"She's very grateful, Jack," his mother told his father.

His father nodded.

"She said her house isn't hers or she would do more herself."

"Whose is it?" his father asked.

"I think she rents," Matthew said.

"She shouldn't have felt obliged to tell me that," his mother said.

His father grunted.

"Is she from Vermont?" his mother asked.

"I think she's from Virginia, originally," Matthew answered.

"See, I didn't think she sounded quite like a New Englander. She seems very nice. Very outgoing. And so is Leif. I think I was afraid he was going to be a little, I don't know, mysterious."

"Everyone's a little mysterious," Matthew's father said.

"You know what I mean. But he's right there when you're talking to him. He's very *present*." She liked it when people weren't locked away from her, as her younger son sometimes was.

"I appreciate that you're helping with the lawyer," Matthew said.

"You're welcome, dear," his mother said.

His mother and father exchanged a look.

"Is it all right?" he asked.

"We're helping *you*," his father said, "because you told us that this is very important to you. But you know, this is going to be a fair amount of money, and your mother and I have been talking about it, and we think it wouldn't be fair to Brian unless we make an adjustment to what you'll receive in terms of your share of the value of the house, after we go."

Matthew felt a flush rising into his face. "That's okay," he said.

"I didn't mean to tell you until later," his father said. "I wasn't going to tell you on the holiday."

"It's okay. That makes sense." Matthew listened for Leif, who still seemed to be on the phone. "Well, while we're on the subject."

"What?" his father asked.

"Gauden already charged the credit card of one of Leif's friends, and she's a graduate student and can't really afford it."

"How much?" asked his father.

"Twenty-eight hundred."

"Your mother and I will take care of that, too, but it'll be a few weeks before we have the cash."

"I told them," his mother said, "that I have someone who can do an appraisal for me in twenty-four hours, but the bank always wants to use their own person."

"Sharon," his father admonished her.

"I don't think there should be any secrets, Jack."

"The bank?" Matthew wondered aloud.

"A mortgage is just the easiest way to arrange it," his father said. "That's all it is. It's just easier than messing around with the retirement accounts. It's the same thing, really. Taking it out of X instead of Y. It's just math."

"Are you taking out a second mortgage for this?" Matthew asked.

"We paid off our first first mortgage two years ago," his mother said. "So this is another first mortgage, technically. A second first mortgage."

"Should you be doing this?"

"Oh, the rates are really good right now, dear. I work with this sort of thing all the time."

"You can keep track of the numbers, too," his father said, "if you want to try to pay us back. If you want to do it that way instead of as an adjustment to the estate. If it'll make you feel better."

At the sound of Leif's footfalls on the stairs, Fosco staggered to her feet and waddled toward the door, grinning.

"My mother wishes happy Thanksgiving to all of you," Leif said.

"And we wish her the same," Matthew's mother firmly replied. "How is she going to be celebrating?"

"She's having dinner with a couple of girlfriends. I mean, friends of hers who are girls. Who are women."

"I understand," said Matthew's mother.

After the great meal, after loading the dishwasher for Matthew's mother and scrubbing and toweling dry her pots and pans, Leif and Matthew lay down in Matthew's bedroom for a nap, Matthew falling asleep almost as soon as his head was cradled by the pillow. When he awoke, it felt as if a week had gone by. Sleep at his parents' house was so much deeper than in the city. He saw that he was alone in the room, which was shadowy, Leif having removed himself and dusk having fallen while his soul had been away. Outside, a soft, blanched glare lay on the lawns and the pavement, resembling in its flatness the glare on snow. He looked at his watch on the bedside table. It would be time to eat now, he saw, if they hadn't just finished eating an hour and a half ago. Next to his watch, in a V, was a folded sheet of paper, striped with dark lines because it came from the pad for grocery lists on the refrigerator door. He had written a note about Samuel Daniel, he remembered. But what if there wasn't anything special about Samuel Daniel? What if he was interested in Daniel and touched by Daniel's devotion to his vocation only because he himself, in choosing to write literary criticism, was making a mistake like Daniel's—giving his life to a kind of writing that was about to pass out of the world? To a modern equivalent of Daniel's poeticized, aestheticized history?

He picked up the forked paper, to read over the note, but the handwriting wasn't his.

"You can read it," said Leif, appearing at the door.

"I thought it was mine."

"It's the devil," Leif said. "It's one of his voices."

"I don't need to read it."

"Oh, it doesn't matter. I can't use any of these ideas unless I want to sound like I'm writing a 'cry for help.'"

That made Matthew think that Leif did want him to read it. It was in the form of a letter, though there was no salutation or valediction:

There have always been people like you, whatever you are. And so there have never really been any secrets, not from your kind. And there aren't

any now. It's no secret, for example, that the world is being poisoned
and cooked, and that there's only a generation or two left before chaos.
What's changed now isn't changed because of you. It's changed because
of the amount of sideways communication that's now possible. We're
doing what we can to quarantine you. Do you think it's an accident
that the social media companies are working so hard to hold everyone's
attention? Do you think the government isn't watching, in case these
and other corporations fail to establish—to reestablish, really—
sufficient control? It looks, fortunately, as if they'll be able to capture
enough of you. Enough of the souls of enough of you. And by soul I
mean voice. The voice will be our handle. Our grip. We can't any
longer prevent everyone from knowing, not because there are more of
you than in the past or because you are any smarter or more numerous
or better than your kind has ever been, but because it's become easier
for you to tell others. And so what we have to do is draw a new line,
not between knowing and not knowing but between knowing and being
able to say that you know. That's the future. That's what order will
consist of—not of keeping people in the dark but of keeping them from
talking about the light. The voice is what we will darken, from now
on. It'll be a little awkward, at first, to live this way, but you'll get
used to it.

"It's just a voice," Leif said, when he saw that Matthew had finished.
"One voice in a poem."

"What poem?"

"The one I can't write. The dark poem."

"Does the devil have a name?"

"It's not that kind of devil."

"Come here," Matthew said, from the bed.

"What?" Leif asked sulkily, without approaching.

Matthew watched him roll the back of his head against the jamb of the doorway.

"Why would even the devil care about enslaving people if the world is going to end in a few years?" Matthew asked.

"You'd have to ask the devil that."

"Are you all right?"

"What do you mean?" Leif asked.

"I mean, you're writing about the voice of the devil."

"What do you think poetry is?"

"No, you're right," Matthew agreed.

"If you mean, Is it alarming to sometimes hear these voices talking almost as if they were talking to one personally, then the answer is yes. But do I think these voices are real, no."

He was standing on only one foot, stepping on it with the other, and to keep his balance flexing his long spine against the jamb.

"I want to show you the attic," Matthew said.

"I saw the attic."

"But I want to show it to you."

In the hallway, he could hear the television going downstairs in the den, where his parents must still be sitting. He opened the closet-like door to the attic and flicked on the Charlie-Brown's-shirt-yellow light in the alcove where the stairs turned to go up.

It was a finished attic—hardwood floors under an upside-down origami flower of white-painted walls. It was crammed with things his parents hadn't yet been able to bring themselves to part with: a rocking chair, an ice cream maker, a foosball table, a superseded printer, Brian's bed, and his and Brian's board games and childhood books.

"You had an encyclopedia?" Leif asked.

"They still had them then."

"You *are* old."

"We bought it used," Matthew said, as if that were a mitigation. "At a garage sale the Peloskis had after their twins went to college."

Leif touched a ceramic kachina wind chime that Matthew had bought one summer when the family took a trip to New Mexico. It had a funny cowlike snout. It gave a resonant and musical little clonk.

"It's so funny to have you here," Matthew said.

"It must be. Your gay lover."

"Can you tell that this is where I grew up?"

"What do you mean?" Leif asked.

"The way you can tell things."

Heavily, methodically came the thumping footfalls of Fosco as she climbed the narrow staircase to join them.

"Come here," Matthew said again.

"What?" Leif replied again, but this time he came over to Matthew.

"So you have the devil in you," Matthew said.

"Evidently I'm not the only one."

"Take it out."

"And play foosball with it?"

"Take it out. I want to see it."

Fosco settled butt-first onto a braided rug and sighed stagily.

"Were you unhappy here?" Leif asked.

"I had to hide," Matthew said. "It wasn't that long ago, but it was different then and you had to hide."

"I hid, too, for a while."

"For a few weeks," Matthew kidded him.

"You're not that much older than me," Leif said.

"I thought I was."

Leif unzipped his fly without unbuttoning and with his finger and thumb unlooped his cock and took it out for Matthew. The clapper in his wind chime. A yearning monk in a plump cowl.

"What if it's all true?" Leif asked.

"It *is* all true," Matthew said.

"That's not what I mean."

"You shouldn't be doing this," Matthew told his father, the next morning, through the kitchen window.

"I'm fine."

"Stand behind him in case he falls," Matthew told Leif.

"The only problem with my back is if I lean over," his father said. He was standing on a flimsy, stackable lawn chair, his arms up and out and slightly wandering. It would have been safer to pull the air conditioner into the house, but the upper sash was jammed, and so Matthew was pushing it out of the window and lowering it toward his father.

"I don't think he should be on that chair," said Matthew's mother, from the next window. "Oh!" she exclaimed.

"I'm not going to fall," Matthew's father declared, his arms trembling as he held the machine.

"Let Leif hold it, too," Matthew ordered.

"Got it," Leif said. "I've got it."

The lawn chair wobbled as Matthew's father stepped off.

"Where is that stepladder you bought," said his mother.

His father had cut his palm, but he insisted nonetheless on taking most of the weight. He and Leif shuffled around the house, through the back door, and down into the basement.

A loaf of bread had to be purchased if there were going to be sandwiches for lunch, so Matthew left Leif reading a book on the glassed-in back porch, which was a little chilly but out of range of the television, and drove to the supermarket in his parents' sedan.

If you turned, before the roundabout that was the hollow center of the town, onto the street that had both of the town's funeral homes, there was an unmarked entrance to the grocery store—a dogleg that came in alongside its loading dock. As Matthew took the shortcut, he thought, with satisfaction, that at least as far as this little geographical matter was concerned, he was still a native and an insider.

Inside the supermarket, however, the light was a different color than he remembered, a palatable amber where there had once been an almost clinical jade. The vegetable aisle had been shifted aside to make room for chafing dishes of rice pilaf and three-bean salad and shredded lettuce, in carefully tended mounds. Would there be people to eat all this, the day after Thanksgiving? Matthew walked down the aisle of flours and sugars, down the aisle of soda and pet food. He didn't recognize the boys working as shelvers now, but they wouldn't even have been in grade school when he had left. They didn't have the air of menace that he remembered high school boys as having. Their skin was pale and irritated, like paper that has been heavily erased. A few were working as cashiers, a job that students hadn't used to be allowed to do.

He chose a line where the boy at the register was a little bit cute. His phone buzzed. "Hey, Matt," said a man familiarly.

He didn't recognize the number or the voice. "Hey!" he replied.

"You don't know who this is, do you?" the man said.

"Of course I do."

The boy who was the cashier scanned Matthew's one item and in deference to his phone conversation pronounced the price quietly.

"Hold on, I'm paying," Matthew said. Maybe it was Philip, a man he'd seen a few times and sometimes thought of.

"You'll pay, all right. This is Adam."

"Oh, *Adam*, of course, hi." He glanced at the cashier, who pointed at the credit-card reader. Matthew swiped. He always forgot about Adam, but he always liked seeing him. Of course, it was different now.

"What are you buying?" Adam asked.

"Bread."

The receipt uncoiled and sliced itself clean. The cashier asked in mime whether Matthew wanted the receipt in the bag with the bread or in his hand. There was something a little airy about the boy's questioning gesture; maybe he had recognized the kind of phone call it was.

"Are you in town?" Adam asked.

"Went home for the holiday." The sliding doors bumbled open. He didn't have a free hand, but the car wasn't far, and he thought he could get away with not buttoning his coat.

"Too bad," Adam said. Evidently Matthew's number had come up in rotation.

"Too bad," Matthew agreed. It wasn't such a bad world, the one that he had left, the one that the call was beckoning him back into.

"We should have dinner when you get back."

"I'm sort of involved with somebody," Matthew admitted.

"Oh, man, again?"

"Again."

"Seven nights a week?"

"Pretty much."

"You should have called me when you were between gigs," Adam said.

"I think I did."

"What if we got coffee," Adam suggested.

"You know what coffee is, and so do I."

"So it's serious."

Matthew got into the car, which was still warm.

Adam was a lawyer who was bored with his job at a hedge fund but couldn't bring himself to quit. They had picked each other up at a party a couple of years before. Adam had been walking out of the host's bathroom and Matthew had pushed him back into it, but Adam had said he wasn't that kind of girl and had asked for Matthew's number. A few times, the dates carefully spaced apart, they had watched movies together at Adam's downtown apartment on his television, larger than any that a graduate student could afford. A few times, Adam had come uptown to see him. Once, before going out to dinner, Adam had offered him a sweater, claiming that he had bought a medium by mistake but had lost the receipt and couldn't return it, and only later had it occurred to Matthew that the story had been a way of giving Matthew a gift while sparing his pride.

Matthew still had both the sweater and the little flat cardboard spindle of extra yarn that had come with it, in case the sweater frayed and one knew how to darn it up. It was cranberry heather.

"Is being involved with somebody good for your dissertation?"

"Not really." Matthew had forgotten that he had told Adam that he was at the dissertation stage.

"Remember when I helped you carry your books home from the library?" Adam continued.

"Oh, that's right." As recently as a year and a half ago, it hadn't been possible to do semester renewals online.

"'Oh, that's right.'"

"It was very sweet of you," Matthew said. It *had* been sweet, being with Adam, not taking each other seriously. That it hadn't been meant to last or to contribute to anything but their own pleasure had been a large part of the sweetness.

"So you'll have coffee with me," Adam said. "A study break."

"There's a lot going on right now."

"Seven nights a week!"

Matthew laughed. But then a panic ripped through him. "You haven't heard about what's going on, have you?"

"Why, what's going on?"

No, he couldn't have. Matthew's name hadn't been in the news. "Nothing," Matthew said. "It's a stupid legal thing."

"Tell Daddy. Daddy's a lawyer."

"It's not your kind of law."

"Now I'm curious," Adam said.

The car had grown cold while Matthew had been sitting in it, and Matthew shivered.

"Are you in trouble, Matt?" Adam asked.

"I better not talk about it."

"Is it this new boy?"

"No. I shouldn't talk about it."

"I won't ask if you don't want me to," Adam said, his voice taking on, suddenly, a blankness.

It was a part of the code of the world where they had met: one accepted limits quickly. And of course the acceptance was at the same time a brotherly weapon. A way of punishing Matthew for failing to be open still to the bond that he and Adam had used to share. A punishment of omission. All right, then, Adam was saying, he would let Matthew be. Knowing that a part of Matthew didn't want to be let be, that a part of him wanted to be called Matt again, that he wanted to be able to talk about what was happening to him as if, at least while he was talking about it, he wasn't trapped inside it. He wanted a friend, and he didn't seem to know how to have one anymore if he and the friend didn't go to bed together. A defect of character that left him alone. Even if he stayed with Leif and went on to give Leif everything he had and was, he was going to be left, to a certain extent, alone.

"But if you ever do want to tell me . . . ," Adam suggested.

"Okay, thanks."

"Or if you decide you need a study break."

"Yeah, got it." Maybe this was just how friendship was, once you had an adult sexuality.

Smoked glass hid the walls of the elevator that carried Leif and Matthew to Michael Gauden's law office, the day after they returned to the city. A red digital number flickered slowly higher.

"It was going to be Revolution through the Perception of Feelings," Leif said.

"What was?" asked Matthew.

"It wasn't going to be Refinement."

"Who changed it?"

"I don't remember," Leif said. "I mean, it's good that we changed it. How stupid would that have been."

Now that the folie was dying, Matthew almost wished it weren't. According to Leif, this wasn't the first time in his life that he had become depressed. He described depression as a little like having a worm inside one's mind at first so small that one didn't initially perceive it as a thought with substance of its own but merely as a twist in the substance of other thoughts. The swiveling, corkscrewing motion is what one came to recognize it by.

Matthew had never experienced anything like that. A part of him wondered if Leif was exaggerating.

"You don't have to agree with me," Leif said.

"I didn't say anything."

They stepped off the elevator into a long corridor, glassed-in at the ends, full of nothing but beautifully temperate air. Thousands of such corridors floated now above the city, like vacant space stations. They had been rendered architecturally superfluous—emptied of guards and left unwatched by receptionists—when security screening had shifted to the ground floor in every building in the city following 9/11.

Just as Matthew and Leif reached the set of glass doors to the north, they heard behind them, at the southern end of the corridor, Michael Gauden calling out, "Over here."

He was a pale, almost skeletally thin man. His suit was slender and unfashionably long, a wizard's gown stripped of its moon and stars. There was something lupine about his face—lean and dolichocephalic—that wasn't softened by his loosely curling blond hair, and Matthew wondered if maybe he didn't smile so as not to show his teeth. Matthew kept hoping that he would come around to the lawyer once he got to know him better.

"Did you have any trouble finding it?" Gauden asked. At a stately pace, with the smile of a precocious boy, he led them down a hall. "So this is Finch Claypoole," he said. A colleague of his, also in a dark, slim suit, trotted swiftly, greetinglessly by. The premise of Gauden's remark seemed to be that the law firm was one of the city's attractions, something people came to see.

"You shouldn't be disturbed in here," Gauden said, when they came to a windowless conference room.

"Is this your safe room?" Matthew asked.

"Safe?" Gauden echoed.

"No windows, no eavesdropping."

"They check every square inch of the whole office for listening devices once a month."

"Wow," Leif said.

"More often than they check for bedbugs, I think," Gauden mused.

"Do they ever find anything?" Matthew asked.

"You know that old joke about the little girl on the train who's tearing up pieces of paper and says she's doing it to keep the tigers away?" Gauden said. "'It seems to be working.' Or maybe they find bugs and tigers and don't tell us. I don't really know. There are bottles of water in that little refrigerator there. Help yourself. I'll bring Leif back when we're done. Half an hour?"

"Oh," Matthew said.

The wolf smiled.

"Matthew can't come with us?" Leif asked, catching on.

"It wouldn't be best practices, in terms of attorney-client privilege."

"I can completely stay here," Matthew told Leif.

"If you were married . . . ," Gauden protasized. It had become possible six months ago for gays to get married in the state.

"Yeah, I'll stay here," Matthew again volunteered.

"Would it be wrong to have Matthew with us?" Leif asked.

"Not 'wrong.'"

"Then maybe he can come."

"Oh, of course. What happens, though, in that case, is, anything you say to me in the presence of a third party, technically the third party could be required to testify about it."

"But his parents are paying, even. Doesn't that make him part of the team?"

"That could give us a little gray. A color of gray, as I like to say. It isn't safe by any means, but if that's what you want and if you understand what you're doing, I'm not here to stop you."

"I want him to be with me."

"It's your choice. My role is to let you know and give you options."

"Leif, I don't think—," Matthew began.

"I want you to come." He was frightened, Matthew saw. For some reason it was now that Leif had become frightened. "'O if I am to have so much, let me have more!'" Leif said.

"Is that a quote?" Gauden asked.

"Whitman," Leif told him.

"I should go back and read more Whitman," Gauden said, resuming his stately walk.

Gauden leaned into one armrest of a high-backed chair behind his desk and with the hand that was pinned to the armrest twirled a pen, which fluttered and stopped, fluttered and stopped, unfurling into a pinwheel and then condensing into a pen again. The lawyer's blond hair, Matthew realized, was to be thought of as movie-star hair. As a gift, as an effect. It always took Matthew a little longer to become aware of the vanity of straight men. For some reason he always failed to expect it.

"I'm not representing *you*, by the way, am I?" Gauden asked Matthew, as Matthew and Leif draped their coats over the backs of their chairs.

"I still need to get a lawyer," Matthew admitted. At the back of his mind he hoped that if he put it off long enough, he could save his parents the money.

There was news, Gauden said. The federal prosecutor's office for the district had filed charges. In deference, the state was now dropping its case, and the judicial process was going to start all over again, from the beginning, this time in federal court. The state's grand jury was going to suspend its work on the case; a federal one would soon be calling witnesses and reviewing evidence. For the moment, though, Leif's participation was not required.

"A federal case can be a little showier, unfortunately," he said. "It takes place on a more visible stage. Sometimes a federal attorney is thinking more about how a thing plays."

"How it plays?" Leif asked.

"To other courts, to voters. I think it's always in their minds that sometimes people in their position go on to run for higher office. Sometimes they see themselves as on a 'crusade,' though I guess that's a word we're not supposed to use anymore."

"Who's the prosecutor?" Matthew asked.

Gauden swiveled in his chair and with a long arm drew a page from a sheaf on his desk. "Thomas Somerville, assistant US attorney. Do you know him?"

"No."

"I almost thought maybe you knew his office, the way you asked. What is it you do again?"

"I'm in grad school for English."

"Oh, that's right."

"Do I need to plead guilty again?" Leif asked.

"You're pleading not guilty, I believe," Gauden said.

"Oh yeah."

"Not yet. But as long as the grand jury is still sitting, and sometimes longer, there's an opportunity for plea bargaining, and we should be thinking about that possibility. Just in the back of your mind."

"And then there wouldn't be a trial?" asked Leif.

"Not for you, if they make an offer and you decide to agree to it."

"What would they want?"

"It can be a bit of a game, because they know that we'll read the boldness of their offer as an indication of how strong and solid their evidence is."

"Do you have a strategy?" Matthew asked.

"A strategy?" Gauden looked amused. "You don't always have a strategy. You try to have ideas, I think, and you try to keep learning about the case, and you're not always sure where the things you're learning are going to take you. Like a novelist who starts writing without knowing where his book is going to end." He drew a filigree in the air with his capped pen. "For example, this morning I was trying to figure out, and maybe you can help me"—he was addressing Leif—"how did they know to arrest you at *his* house?"

"They had us under some kind of surveillance," said Leif. "Didn't they?"

"Don't ask me! But they couldn't have put that in place overnight. The city police, overnight? Had you given them any reason to put you under surveillance *before* the incident with their computer system?"

"I did tell Bresser I could read his password, that day I saw him at Occupy," Leif said.

"Wait," Matthew interrupted. "Are you suggesting that if they had Leif under surveillance without a warrant, before he did anything, the court should throw out the arrest?"

"How much television have you been watching, young man?" the lawyer asked. "That almost never happens, first of all. And they did have a warrant, and no court is going to care how they knew how to find Leif if the warrant was properly written."

Matthew didn't respond.

"What I wonder," the lawyer continued, having cleared Matthew out of the way, "and it's a line of thought that I haven't fully worked out yet, is, if the government puts too many people under surveillance, puts together all this personal data in one place, maybe it's not wrong for the government, qua the government, to have done so, but once they have, maybe it's incumbent on them to make sure it's very difficult for anyone to get to it. There's this concept of an 'attractive nuisance.' If you own a swimming pool, you have to expect that the neighbors' children will try to drown themselves in it and you have to put up a fence. Otherwise it's your fault if they do drown in it."

"So we should have put up a fence?" asked Leif. "We were actually *inviting* people to our working group."

"No no no. You're the ones who fell in and drowned, is what I'm thinking. If the data on this server was private, as the government is claiming, then the government created a hazard by assembling it and failing to protect it. It shouldn't have been so easy for you to fall in. To take another example, if one slab of concrete in the sidewalk is half a foot higher than the next one, and you trip, you can sue the city: that's what I mean, but what was out of alignment wasn't one slab of concrete with another but the expectation of privacy with the ease of publication. Or maybe what I mean is that they were too *well* aligned. Too conveniently aligned."

"But we weren't children," Leif said.

"Well, that's a problem," the lawyer acknowledged.

"You're saying," Matthew said, "that it was irresponsible of the government not to try harder to keep us out."

"You weren't there, were you? You just said 'us.'"

"He wasn't there," Leif said.

"Were you there?"

"No, I was just trying to understand your argument," Matthew said.

"I see. Well, it's a big argument. Maybe it's the wrong tool for the job. Maybe it's a wrench and I need pliers. But I like to think about all the possibilities."

"I have a big argument," Leif said.

"Oh, you do?" Gauden said, not encouragingly.

"I think there's no such thing as human rights," Leif said. "I think there's only power, and it goes more smoothly for the powerful if most of the time people act as if human rights do exist. But once per generation, there has to be an 'accident,' on purpose, to remind everyone what's really happening. To remind everyone that the rights are only granted on sufferance. That they shouldn't be taken too seriously. That they only exist because at the moment it isn't in the interest of the powerful to take them away."

"I see," the lawyer said, nodding, twirling his pen again.

"It's just an idea," Leif said.

"No, it's very interesting," Gauden said, still nodding.

"I have another idea," said Leif, when they got downstairs.

"Are you having too many ideas?" Matthew asked. He threaded his way between two parked cars and in the open street raised a hand. When he looked back at Leif, still on the curb, he smiled as if to say that he wasn't asking in order to hurt Leif, but his smile therefore also necessarily meant that he knew that asking did hurt Leif.

Bundled up in an old coat of Matthew's, which was too short for him, Leif looked like an invalid being taken to see his doctor. Which reminded Matthew that they needed to make a follow-up appointment. He wouldn't still be coughing the way he was if the steroid was doing what it was supposed to.

A cab stopped, and they got in. A screen set into the back of the front seat began to hector them as the car pulled away.

"Can you turn it off?" Leif asked. "I think it's the sort of thing I'm not allowed to touch."

"Buckle your seat belt," Matthew said, as he left off buckling his own.

It turned out to be possible to turn off the show that was auto-playing but not the screen itself.

"I shouldn't have said that," Matthew said, once the car was silent. "About your idea."

Leif looked down at his hands. "Do you want to hear it?"

"Of course."

"It used to be possible—and it used to be important that it was possible—for writing to have a secret meaning," Leif said. He spoke as if he didn't believe Matthew really wanted to hear but couldn't see any other way forward. "It could signal that it had a secret meaning by making an oddly weak argument, or by bringing up an example that made a hash of what it was supposed to be evidence for."

At the foot of a hill, in sight of the water, the driver shunted the taxi into a narrow, canal-like street, hedged on both sides with Jersey barriers that blinded it. Abruptly the canal street fed into three lanes of a six-lane highway, the cars in which didn't slow, let alone stop, so that the challenge of merging drew a burst of adrenaline out of all three men in the car—their bodies' involuntary acknowledgment that survival was at stake.

"Jesus," said Matthew quietly, as the driver gunned the engine and swerved, to seize a place in the ungiving flow.

Once the car was inside the flow, however, one felt impregnable.

"But you can't signal a hidden meaning on the internet," Leif continued. "If there's weakness or inconsistency in a piece of writing now, it goes unnoticed because of the general sloppiness of expression. A writer's ambivalence registers at most as a flaw that has kept a message from going viral. A handicap. Not as an instance of someone saying something almost despite himself. Or literally despite himself."

"You should write this down."

"Like Julia? For a rainy day?"

They rose on the highway's ribbon of concrete into a bend in the sky where two of the great bridges that spanned the harbor came into view. Maybe Matthew wasn't any good at pretending to welcome Leif's ideas because with each idea that Leif had, it was as if the air that the two of them breathed when they were together became that much thinner, as if they found themselves further up a mountain they hadn't planned on climbing, further away from the path that they had set out to follow. Leif seemed to be propelling himself forward through his days with mere willpower now, as if he were trying not to think about his body and what might happen to it, as if he were deliberately leaving his physical self out of the reckoning, while Matthew became more and more aware that it was only through their bodies that they were connected. Aware the way that, with each cigarette, if you fall back into that habit, you become more aware of the minutes since the last cigarette, of time as something that has to be counted off and paid for in cigarettes, which your health even less than your budget can afford.

Beneath the angle that the driver could see in the rearview mirror, he took Leif's hand. It was cold and knotty.

No reporter had pursued Leif to Matthew's parents' house, which he and Leif had attributed to the holiday. By the time they got back to the city, the news cycle must have completed a revolution or two, because no reporters were waiting at Matthew's apartment, either. Nor were any waiting outside Michael Gauden's office the next day. Was it over? The coast seemed to be clear, too, at the café where Leif worked, according to the wife of the couple who owned it, who called Tuesday morning. Over the long weekend she had covered for Leif, as had Greg and another co-worker. Leif decided to go in for a shift.

He put on his bike cap and flipped up the brim. Matthew volunteered to walk over with him. He wanted to make sure Leif wasn't inflicting on himself some kind of penance. In many of Leif's ideas lately there was a theme of punishment—of deserving punishment, of being found out as deserving punishment. Sometimes what Leif had done was tell. Sometimes all he had done was know—about the end of the world, about the sorrow that a sense of the end brings to people, about the susceptibility of caretakers to sorrow. If Matthew challenged the logic, Leif fell silent and Matthew worried that the snake was returning to earth by a different hole. It seemed to be becoming difficult for Leif to conceive of himself as existing in the world except as a trespasser in it. He had lost the swan's-neck nonchalance that he had had when Matthew had fallen for him.

"What if they're after me because they know that I know?" he had asked one night.

"What do you mean?"

"What if they don't want me to realize that we really are a threat?"

"I don't think that's what the charge against you is going to be," Matthew had said.

Was he literally feverish? Maybe the pneumonia, or the steroids he was taking by inhalant to treat it, were giving his thoughts these qualities of abstraction, perseveration, and astringency—giving his thoughts themselves nearly the character of punishments.

Or maybe the thoughts came because Leif had in fact glimpsed the future and really was being punished for it. It would have been easier if Matthew had been able to believe in the folie in a simple and straightforward way, and he hated himself, a little, for his skepticism, even though he knew that skepticism was one of the components of his personality that made him a caretaker, if not quite a caretaker of the kind described in Leif's philosophy. He felt that it was in part the mismatch between them—the almost-but-not-quite nature of Matthew's faith—that had attracted Leif, that held him.

One night, not long after they had met, when they had been hanging out with some of the other members of the working group in Elspeth's apartment, one of Elspeth's roommates had come home with a vintage-store find—a green tulle gown—and Leif had pleaded, and the roommate hadn't been able to say no, and when Leif had tiptoed back into the living room, wearing the gown, Peter Pannishly, and had sat down beside Matthew, he had asked for a kiss, which Matthew had only been able to deliver awkwardly, gingerly, prompting Leif to ask, *Don't you believe in any of my magic?* There had been a note of gratification in his voice, Matthew felt. There had been disappointment, too, of course, but it hadn't been a very serious disappointment. He had been proud, in some corner of himself, of having gone further than Matthew could. And in that corner, Matthew suspected, Leif didn't entirely want Matthew to believe. At any rate, that's what Matthew had to hope. Because he couldn't believe. Just as he couldn't pretend that his interest didn't center on what had been lolling, factually, under the green gauze that had draped Leif's lap. Matthew was the sort of person who couldn't hear the lines

> *And by addition me of thee defeated,*
> *By adding one thing to my purpose nothing*

as if they were serious. The best he could do was pretend not to notice that he was meeting halfway what he was being asked to believe.

He put a book, notebook, and two pens in his backpack.

There was no one in the café but Leif's co-worker Juniper and a handful of regulars, typing into laptops and paging through cram books. A man with gelled hair and a dimpled chin, probably an actor between roles, was reading an ink-on-paper newspaper. Matthew took a seat in the corner. Leif looped an apron over his head and ducked under the bar.

Juniper kissed Leif, and he hugged her. He pinched the foil pouches beside the espresso machine to find out how much coffee was still in them.

Matthew opened his notebook and tucked the written-on half of it under the book that he was going to try to read.

"Are you Leif Saunderson?" the man who was probably an actor asked.

Leif nodded.

"That's cool, man," the actor said.

"Can I get you anything?"

"A refill? This is an Americano."

"Coming up," Leif said.

It turned out to be easy to surrender one's celebrity. Patrons with earbuds, having sensed the exchange but not having heard it, looked around frowningly, like seagulls.

The book that Matthew had brought was a collection of meditations written in the voice of Charles I by a priest loyal to him. The king had revised and approved the meditations shortly before he was executed; they were published shortly after. As a defense of kingship they were almost painfully unpersuasive. Charles, or the priest writing as Charles, asserted over and over again that the king had never cared for his power or been solicitous of it, as if this were a virtue. He complained that democrats seemed to think that the king was the one person in England who could be required to sacrifice the free will and political conscience that belonged to every individual. Yet despite the distaste he claimed to feel for kingship personally, he refused to "consent to put out the sun of sovereignty" in his own case.

The sun of sovereignty, Matthew carefully printed in his notebook. The day had grown so short, he noticed, that the windows of the café were already gray even though it hardly qualified yet as late afternoon.

> *How like a winter hath my absence been*
> *From thee, the pleasure of the fleeting year.*

He couldn't really imagine what it would be like to be without Leif, which is what would happen if Leif were to lose his case. He didn't want to think about it. Things had gone so quickly between the two of them that that possibility was already unbearable. In the past few days, being with Leif had sometimes been like not being with him, because of Leif's preoccupation, and that had been bad enough. It had been a few days, for example, since anything had happened between them—since the time in his parents' attic, in fact. Here in the café, now, too, they were together without really being together: Leif toweling dry the saucers and cups that he clankingly removed from the dishwasher, Matthew hunched forward over a seventeenth-century text he wasn't reading.

But then the quiet and the early darkness always gave this time of day, at this time of year, a cloistered feeling.

Leif came to his table.

"Do you need me here?" Matthew asked, on an impulse.

"No," Leif said. Then he hesitated. "Maybe it's better if you go, actually."

"Okay," said Matthew.

"I want to see how I am."

"Okay."

"Are you all right?" Leif asked.

"Me? Fine."

"Don't be like that."

"Like what? You're telling me to leave, and I'll leave," Matthew said.

"You asked to leave."

Matthew couldn't bring himself to say that that wasn't what he'd meant to ask. He couldn't bear to reveal himself as so weak. He looked down at the words that filled up his book's pages, words that had abruptly become strange and remote, a meal for which he had suddenly lost his appetite. Why would anyone ever care what he or anyone else thought about these old dead words?

"It's hard for me to find out how I am, right now," Leif continued. "What I'm feeling."

Leif was so full of his sad self, Matthew angrily thought. So full of his sad, wounded self. "It's easier for me to read in a library, anyway," Matthew said, shutting his unreadable book.

"Matthew—"

"It's fine," Matthew insisted. When had he become the clingy one? He strategized: he could try to read for an hour or two in the city college library, where he could buy a sandwich at the food court if he got hungry. Maybe he and Leif had gone too fast. Maybe neither one of them knew how he was on his own anymore, and maybe both of them needed to know that. "It's really fine. I understand."

After Matthew finished packing his bag, they embraced and kissed, stiffly.

"What was that?" Leif asked.

"Tough love, tough kiss," Matthew said.

Matthew walked back to his apartment for his bike. As soon as he got it downstairs, he realized he had forgotten his bike lights, but he had already wasted enough time. The day was ending, and the point of it was supposed to have been to make a little progress toward returning to the life that a month and a half ago he had thought worth living. He biked, therefore, in the dark, unilluminated, recklessly, angry at himself, on top of everything else, for running a stupid, needless, and not even pleasant risk.

As he locked up his bike, he made up his mind to be angry at everyone he saw—to be the one true scholar, indignant and monastic—but the lamps suspended above the work-study students at the checkout desk cast them in gold light and fat textbooks were opened across their knees and he had to accept that they had been here learning all day when he hadn't been and that if anything he should try to emulate them in doing uncomplainingly the work that one was given to do.

His usual carrel was unoccupied. So much of academia was about coming back to things—coming back to the same room, the same chair, the same text—while one grew older. Did the outside world really matter compared to this return, which was not just to a chair in a library but to an eternal, silent conversation? Maybe the outside world only existed to bring one here, to this seat. Maybe the outside world was only a scaffolding, meant to fall away. Of course to live a life whose meaning lay outside the life itself would tend to make one melancholy.

This was the story he had given most of his youth to.

He opened his book, but it was still unreadable. He would have to convince himself that Leif would forgive him before he would be able to read it. He was actually pretty sure that Leif was going to forgive him, which made his task easier.

The tall panes of the library windows, now that it was night, had a slate-like opacity.

The trouble with the book he was trying to read was that the most interesting question about it couldn't be answered by it. The question didn't even have to do with the book proper but with an appendix. In the appendix, the priest who had compiled the book had printed a prayer of Charles's that happened to be identical to a prayer uttered by a lovestruck princess in Sidney's *Arcadia*, as if kingship were so much a thing of make-believe that even a priest—or perhaps even Charles himself, it was impossible to know—saw no reason not to pass off a sacrament of one realm as a sacrament of the other. John Milton, after Charles's execution, detected the borrowing. Milton was outraged. The prayer in Sidney's poem was pagan! How dare a Christian king address it to his god? But Matthew, isolated in his carrel and cozy, for the moment, in his isolation, couldn't decide whether what needed to be explained was the priest's dreamy willingness to confuse fact with fiction, and himself with Charles, and both with Sidney's princess, or Milton's intolerant insistence on distinguishing them. It was hard to remember what the way of the world was, when one wasn't at the moment in it. What was strange here? Was confusion unacceptable? Was it always necessary to be a single, real person?

He read until late. When he got back to his apartment, its lights were off and its blinds were still up. Emanations from the streetlamps below crossed into it in long, faint rectangles as neat as shadows.

A note was on the table and the boxers that Leif usually slept in weren't on Leif's pillow, their resting place during the day.

As Matthew lowered the blinds, he was aware that he was only papering over the night, not separating himself from it.

Gone home to do laundry, the note read.

Matthew called the cell that he and Leif had bought for Leif a few days before, whose number they had so far managed to keep secret.

"I told Gauden I'm going to go with a public defender," Leif said.

"What are you talking about?"

"All I do is take," Leif said. "Take take take."

"Slow down."

"You don't even like him," Leif pointed out.

The books on Matthew's desk, Matthew noticed, hadn't much shifted lately. The apartment got on his nerves now whenever Leif wasn't there. Everything in it remained so eternally where they had last left it. Everything seemed prepared for years to pass by with no dislodgement or disruption other than the fine invisible pinpricks by which time introduces brittleness, dryness, and weakness. "Leif, it's okay," he said. "I'm going to be here for you." He needed to say something whether or not it was true. He had to hope that making a commitment always felt a little like making one up.

"It's supposed to be money for *your* future. I don't think my own father even knows that any of this is happening."

"I'm here for you," Matthew repeated. Before last week he hadn't ever thought of his parents' house as someday a future inheritance of his, which maybe made it easier to give away.

"But what if I leave you? What if I'm like, I can't be with you, I'm a poet, and I have to be able to hear my voice."

"Is that how you feel?"

There was silence on Leif's end of the phone.

"I'm helping you right now," Matthew said. "That's all it is. You don't ever need to pay me back."

While he waited Leif out, he noticed that his little red Cambridge edition of the *Sonnets* wasn't balanced on top of the microwave anymore, where Leif had left it the other day. Its slot on the bookcase was still empty, too, though the slot had narrowed slightly, because the volumes on either side had taken breaths in, once they could. Matthew scanned the apartment. His eyes jumped from shelf to shelf. The book wasn't anywhere.

Which meant Leif still had it with him.

"Why do you put up with me?" Leif asked.

"Because fucking you makes me feel alive."

Leif apologized to his lawyer and recanted his dismissal of him. Over the weekend he worked a few more shifts, and Matthew managed to do a little reading. On Monday, the buzzer rang in the middle of the day.

It was Raleigh. "Do you mind if I come up?" he asked through the intercom. "I was in the neighborhood."

Leif put on a sweater. Matthew picked up a wad of dirty clothes off the floor, and when Raleigh reached their landing, it was still in his hands.

"Your apartment's already neat by my standards," Raleigh said.

"You're straight," Matthew replied.

Raleigh hadn't shaved, and under his fair beard, patches of his skin had broken out.

"Sit down," Leif said, folding himself into a corner of the futon.

"Do you want a glass of water?" Matthew offered.

"Sure," Raleigh said. He perched on the futon's edge. "So how is it all going for you guys?"

"Elspeth said your lawyer didn't want you to talk about anything," Leif said.

"He doesn't know I'm here. I took the battery out of my phone."

"Can't you just turn it off?"

"I'm pretty sure they can track you now even when it's off. Although maybe not with a phone like mine."

"Felix Penny is tracking you?" Matthew asked, as he handed Raleigh a glass of water.

"No. I mean, I don't know. We don't know who's tracking us anymore, do we." He took a sip. "We don't have to talk about anything, if you don't want to."

"Our news is that Leif is coughing too much," Matthew said. "And not getting enough sleep."

"Why are you telling him that?" Leif asked.

"He's your friend."

"Okay, and I don't always feel 'real,'" Leif admitted, marking the quotes in the air.

"I have this recurring dream," Raleigh said, "that another timeline is crossing into mine."

"Someone else's timeline?"

"No, mine, but from a different universe. All the possible universes are layered on top of each other, like in sedimentary rock, but they've slipped out of alignment and I'm crossing on the diagonal. Which I experience as another reality surfacing into mine."

"I don't know if I follow," Leif admitted.

"There's a lot of geometry," Raleigh acknowledged. "Has Elspeth said anything?"

"About what?"

"I don't know. Can I ask you something? Did you have porn on your laptop? Can they mention that, if they find it?"

"What kind of porn?" Leif asked.

"You know, normal."

"You mean, ladies?"

"Yeah, 'ladies.'"

"Did you at least hide it good?"

"It was in a folder called 'Porn.' But can they mention it for no reason? Aren't there rules?"

"I have no idea," said Leif. "Why are you worried about this?"

"I don't think they can just talk about your personal life," Raleigh said. "I think there must be rules."

"Did you ask Penny?"

"No. I was just thinking yesterday, they have all our emails, too, if they have our laptops."

"Yeah, I guess."

"Everything we wrote to each other. They can just grep our brains, essentially."

"Did *you* have porn?" Leif asked Matthew.

"Of gentlemen," Matthew replied.

"Elspeth's not seeing anyone, is she?" Raleigh asked.

"She hasn't told me anything," Leif said. "Why?"

"She's changed her mind about me, hasn't she."

"I thought you broke up with her."

"But it was a mistake." He looked down at the floor. "You couldn't say anything, could you?"

"To her?"

"Never mind." He bottoms-upped his empty water glass. "You don't understand. It's probably easier for gays."

"What, breaking up or being arrested?"

"No, I didn't mean that." He blushed.

"What did you mean?"

"I mean, with the other guy also being a guy."

"You mean it's easier if it's two men for the other person to know what you're thinking," Leif said.

"Isn't that a good thing?"

"Maybe it used to be."

The buzzer rang again. "It's me," said Elspeth, from downstairs.

"Raleigh's here," Matthew disclosed, through the intercom.

"Well—okay," she said.

"Shit, can I use your bathroom?" Raleigh asked. He slammed the door in his hurry to tidy himself up.

"There's a problem," said Elspeth, after she kissed Leif hello. She shuffled off her backpack. "I brought my new computer because I don't want Matthew to use his when he looks at it. I was hacked. I mean, the RPF site was hacked."

"By who?" asked Raleigh, emerging from the bathroom, his wet hair pointed starfish-like in all directions away from his face.

"I don't know. By hackers." She sat down on Matthew's folded-up futon and powered on her laptop.

"Don't be mad," said Raleigh.

"I'm not mad at *you*. Don't let them look, Matthew, because neither of them should be looking at a computer."

"Sit at the dining table," Matthew ordered Leif and Raleigh.

"I'm sorry I'm a hard-ass, but all my lawyer ever talks about to me is am I doing everything I can to convince the government that I have no interest in trying to obstruct or sabotage the government's work," Elspeth said while she waited for her machine to boot up.

"Don't worry," Raleigh said. "You'd come across as law-abiding even if you were trying not to."

"This is what you see now, if you go to the site," Elspeth, ignoring Raleigh, said to Matthew. "I'm sorry I'm bringing you this," she said to Leif. "It's so ugly."

"What does it say?" Leif asked.

"Usually when they hack a website they put up porn," Raleigh said.

The page, when it came up, was black, and the writing on it was in a font that was green and fixed-width, like on an old terminal. Matthew read the new text aloud:

```
            Rest    In    Peace

                    the

      Republic    of    Precious    Feeleengz

They weren't moralfags. They weren't even stupidfags.
They were NOTHINGFAGZ!!!

(FYI, we don't mind feeleengz. This is teh Internet,
after all—if you're not at least a little bit ghey, you
haven't been paying attention. It's just, have a point,
plz. So, we haz hacked you.)
```

The cursor, over the text, was flickering. "It looks like you can click," Matthew observed.

"Oh no, don't," said Elspeth. "If you do, there's this little elephant that flies around and"—Matthew clicked, and there was a sound—"farts."

"And leaves swastikas."

"Oh, I hadn't noticed that they were swastikas."

"Well, they're all smushed on top of each other, so they're hard to see."

"I'm really sorry I can't see that," Raleigh said.

"It's actually pretty upsetting, Raleigh," Elspeth said.

"I'm just saying I wish I could see it. Is *moralfags* one word or two?"

"Why does that matter?" Elspeth asked. "It's hate speech."

"It has a different meaning when it's one word."

"What does it mean?" Leif asked.

"You use the suffix *–fag* to say what somebody's gay for. What somebody's into. So a moralfag is someone who's really into being moral, being righteous."

"Oh, like *queen* in real gay slang," said Leif. "A muscle queen is into guys with muscles; a size queen is into—you know."

"Yeah, like *queen*, but for hacking," Raleigh said. "What you're a fag for is your motive for hacking. So if we're nothingfags, they're saying we didn't have any reason at all for doing what we did."

"But we *weren't* hackers," Elspeth said.

"I thought the internet was on your side," Matthew said.

"Not these guys, apparently," Raleigh said.

"It's so full of hate," Elspeth said.

"But maybe also just a little bit funny?" suggested Raleigh.

"With swastikas?" she replied. "And where is our site now? Where is everything we wrote?"

"Didn't we have a backup? I thought with this build there was auto backup."

"No," said Elspeth. "That cost extra, so we didn't do it, remember? And the cops still have our old hard drives."

"Can you still log in as an admin?"

"I can, but the hackers are still in there, and I can see them. It creeps me out."

"What do you mean you can see them?" Raleigh asked.

"When I tried to delete the splashpage they put up, they put it back, while I was watching."

"Did you change your password?"

"That was the first thing I did," Elspeth said.

"You probably need to re-salt the hashes."

"Okay, whatever that means. Where do I do that?"

"I can't remember. It's probably under Settings, but I'd have to be looking at the dashboard."

"Do you know *how* they got in?" Leif asked.

Elspeth shook her head.

"Did you get an email recently asking you to reset your password?" Raleigh asked.

"No," she said.

"Maybe your password wasn't strong enough."

"It probably wasn't," she said. "I know I'm the weak link. I know that absolutely anybody else would be doing it better."

"Don't be so hard on yourself," said Raleigh. "What if you took it to Jeremy and he helped you."

Elspeth executed a few commands. "I think they put in a back door," she said to Matthew, pointing at a list of filenames on the screen that meant nothing to him. Matthew saw that she was making an effort not to cry.

"You might have updated a plug-in without realizing that the update was compromised," Raleigh continued. "That happened to me once. It can happen if the developer sells out to the wrong kind of people."

Elspeth continued working, without responding to Raleigh.

"Is there anything that you can want, in the world these people live in, without being a fag for it?" Leif asked. "I mean, if you don't want anything and that makes you a nothingfag, that's pretty comprehensive."

"Lulz, I think," Raleigh said. "'Lulzfag' is a compliment."

After half an hour, Elspeth gave up, and they called a car service to take them to see Jeremy. Elspeth sat in front, next to the driver, and stowed her offending laptop, shut asleep, at her feet. In the back, next to Matthew, as the car mounted the elevated highway that snaked above the city, Raleigh and Leif a little too loudly debated whether it was Anonymous who had done them the honor of hacking them. Matthew heard Elspeth quietly call someone to report that she was going to Raleigh and Jeremy's apartment. Outside, dark windows of apartments wheeled by, succeeding one another like notches in a turning gear, strangely close because the apartments had been built long before anyone knew that a highway would one day hang in the air a few yards away, four or five stories above the ground.

They were met at the door of Jeremy and Raleigh's apartment by Philip, who was wearing an open kimono over a pair of swim briefs, displaying his knotted chest and stomach. "Oh my god, you're all together again," he said.

"We were hacked," Raleigh told him.

"Why would anyone bother to hack you? You're last week's news. When I'm out with Oliver, you don't even come up as a conflict of interest anymore."

"Did you tell the press I'm from Kansas?" Raleigh asked. "You're the only person I know who gets Oklahoma and Kansas confused."

"Kansas, R-Kansas, O-Kansas. There's only one letter's difference between any of them."

There was nowhere to gather except around the island table in the kitchen.

"Scene of the crime," Raleigh said to Elspeth.

"It's so stupid, being here, isn't it," she replied.

Matthew hadn't previously thought of the act that had got them in trouble as having taken place in any particular location. On the night it-self, he had been too angry at Leif to picture where Leif had been when it had happened, and later the events had become a sort of myth.

"You and Leif can't sit where you can see," Elspeth told Raleigh.

"I know." He pulled two stools over to in front of the refrigerator.

Leif clambered backward up onto one of them. "Dunces in the corner."

"I'm so happy I can help you out, Elspeth," Jeremy said. He held up a power cable and let it untwist. "There's a fresh six-pack of energy drinks in the fridge, if anyone's thirsty."

"I thought only newspaper articles actually called them energy drinks," Raleigh commented.

Jeremy tapped the table beside him to indicate that Elspeth should set her laptop there. He ran a hand through his hair. "Can I ask you a question? Have you been adding to the site? Are you writing new posts?"

"It's more of a historical record at this point."

Jeremy leaned forward over his folded, powerful arms. "And are you getting traffic? What if I took it off your hands."

She looked frightened. "Please don't take it away. Just because I was at-tacked."

"No one's taking anything away!" Jeremy laughed, looking around the room.

"I want to keep it."

"I'm just suggesting we coordinate the sites. The site you're running with the one I'm doing. It could be really useful."

"I don't want to be useful," Elspeth said. The heartache, now that they had come together again, was something that maybe later they could take turns carrying, but for the moment it was hers.

"I get it," Jeremy said.

"You're still going to let him help you clean it up, though, right?" Ra-leigh asked.

"It can't be that different from fact-checking," Elspeth said.

"That's a good analogy," said Jeremy.

"Just tell me what to do," she said, eyes forward, unfolding her screen.

Jeremy squatted to plug in his power cable and then, standing beside her, issued instructions. Distrustfully, a little combatively, she obeyed: She rebooted in recovery mode. She let him connect his laptop to hers and allowed his security software to scan her hard drive for viruses. She logged on via FTP to the server that hosted the website and under his coaching began to weed out suspect files.

It was an exorcism. The ritual was long and tedious.

"Should we stay?" Matthew asked Leif, after an hour had passed.

"Why not?"

"Do you need to be here? And if everyone's here together . . ."

"Why is that a problem?" Leif asked. "It's okay for me to see Raleigh. It's okay for me to see Elspeth."

"I'm not saying it because *I* mind," Matthew explained.

"Then why are you saying it?"

Matthew nodded as if he accepted this and, taking one of Philip's celebrity lifestyle magazines, went to sit in a chair by the apartment's front window.

Jeremy and Elspeth were still working when Julia appeared in the apartment's doorway. "Knock knock," she said. "Is Raleigh here?"

She was wearing a burnt umber beret at a jaunty angle: she was a little girl, she was an adventuress.

"Why, it's everyone!" she cried. "Elspeth, how *are* you?" She was overdoing it. That and the beret suggested to Matthew that she had lost her balance.

"Not Chris," said Elspeth.

"No, I guess not Chris," Julia agreed. "Well, I have some news," she said, looking around. "Bresser's having a press conference at five."

"Today?" asked Raleigh.

"Something has leaked, apparently," Julia said.

"Did your lawyer tell you?" Elspeth asked.

"I have a source. I'm making a study of our case."

"I could go to a press conference," Jeremy volunteered.

"Well, I'm going myself," Julia quickly clarified.

"Do they let just anyone in?" Raleigh asked.

"You guys are on trial," Matthew said.

"Do we know what leaked?" Leif asked.

"My source told me because she hoped *I* would know," Julia said.

"What do you mean 'your source'?" Elspeth asked. She was the only one who hadn't heard about Julia's project.

"Oh, it's silly, really. You have to promise not to laugh. I want to write about all this someday, so I need to *know* about it now."

"I see," Elspeth said.

"It's silly."

"No, it's not silly."

"I'll go with you," Leif said. "Where is it?"

"The lobby of Bresser's office building." The building was in a downtown neighborhood across the river that had once housed light industry and was becoming fashionable.

"Leif, please don't," Matthew said.

"Why not?" Leif asked. He shrugged on the coat Matthew had given him. Maybe he, too, wanted to know about the press conference so that one day he could write about it, in which case what Matthew was trying to prevent was a poem, from being written.

"What if you see him and you read something again?" Matthew asked.

"It's not against the law."

"It shouldn't be, anyway," said Raleigh.

"Leif, people are very upset," Elspeth said.

"Why do they get to be the ones who have press conferences? Why do they get to be the ones who describe what's happening?"

"I'm going, too, then," said Elspeth.

"So we'll have a really big posse," Julia said. "But we have to leave right now if we're going to make it."

They called two cars this time, and after a skirmish on the sidewalk, Leif, Jeremy, and Julia got into the first one and Elspeth, Raleigh, and Matthew into the second.

"You don't have to go," Elspeth said to Raleigh, as Matthew pulled shut the door.

"Why shouldn't I?" Raleigh asked.

She was right to try to stop him. There seemed to be nothing Matthew could do to stop Leif, who had become feverish with what Matthew referred to in his dissertation as insulted kingship. His senses were stopped up, like a Shakespeare monarch who has shut his ears to any question about whether his dukes are still loyal. Like Alice after she has been turned into a Wonderland chess piece and is blinded by the crown that has queened her, which slips down over her eyes.

Matthew had been cast in the role of loyal but ineffectual adviser. Beside him, Raleigh and Elspeth were trying to keep themselves distinct from each other, trying not to touch. Elspeth took out her phone and held it in her hands in front of her, as a focus of her attention, but didn't unlock it.

They rode onto a bridge, the seams in whose asphalt were so pronounced that the car thrummed like a heartbeat as the front and then the rear tires passed over them. It wasn't clear to Matthew what Leif was still king of. It wasn't clear what Leif was ordering his knights and ladies into battle to defend.

"Do you still read things from people?" Matthew asked Elspeth.

"I don't do experiments anymore—is that what you mean?"

"I guess I was wondering whether it's still there to hear," he said. "Whether anyone is still broadcasting on those frequencies."

Her eyes wavered on him. It will always be there, she seemed to say, in reply, in a voice without words. The awareness that he knew what she was saying was uncomfortable to him.

It was dark when they reached Bresser's office. The scene of people gathered in the lobby shone out through the plate glass of the building's facade like a play being performed for passersby in the street. There was an air of expectancy and also of exclusivity. Anyone on the sidewalk could have walked in, but everyone all knew that no one who didn't belong was going to.

Julia was the first to push her way in through the revolving door. Matthew came last. When the rubber blades of the door unsealed and released him into the lobby, he found himself immersed in a roar that mirroring by glass and marble had made of the gathered people's talk.

"We're here for the Bresser Security press conference," he heard Julia say, above the roar, to a blond, unshaven man in a blue porter's uniform.

"It's not anywhere else," said the man.

"This is the right place?" Julia asked.

"He's gonna have it here, anyways."

Julia drifted toward the crowd.

"Who are you looking for?" Matthew called out to her, but she didn't answer. "Are we meeting someone?" he asked the others, but they didn't answer, either.

Jeremy strode forward as if he knew where Julia was headed, but the confidence with which he followed her may have been founded on nothing more than his personal history of having almost always been welcomed wherever he went.

An ungainly woman clopped toward them on loud heels. The belt that was lashed around her skirt seemed to be a length of rope. "Are these your friends?" she asked Julia. "I'm Jan Ridgely," she introduced herself. She said that she worked for one of the city's tabloids.

"Jan, thank you for this," Julia said.

"Who has more of a right to know about it?"

"And that's all we can do, or try to do, isn't it."

"Have you heard anything?" Ridgely asked.

"Not a word."

"Maybe he'll say."

"Maybe!" Julia agreed.

Ridgely appraised the friends. Of course Leif was hard not to look at, burning with fury as he was. "Do you regret any of it?" she asked him softly.

"Oh, we're off the record, Jan," Julia said, on Leif's behalf.

"Anyone can ask," Leif corrected her. "It's a free country, for now."

They had been spotted; other reporters were raking them with looks. Two or three seemed about to approach when Bresser appeared from behind a row of ficuses, brushing out of his face the irritation of their varnished leaves. He was wearing a camel suit that stretched tight across his back. He paused at a crimson rope, and a pale, gawky man with an aquiline nose and floppy dark hair rushed up to unhitch it. The deputy was taller than Bresser was. He was nervously clicking a pen attached to his clipboard.

Leif was impatient. "Is Bresser going to say anything?"

"'One of the accused, Leif Saunderson, wondered aloud,'" Raleigh said.

With a glance Leif acknowledged the warning. Ridgely made a note.

Bresser's deputy stepped back over the crimson rope and sprinted to the building's security desk to ask the porter something. The porter shrugged and handed over a small metal dustbin. Inside the crimson rope again, the deputy set the dustbin on the floor upside down, and stepped onto it, a hand momentarily flying out and touching Bresser's shoulder as he tried to steady himself. Bresser reflexively brushed the hand away; the pale man teetered. Bresser silently shook his head. *No.*

The deputy stepped down, righted the dustbin, and slid it behind a ficus.

"Ladies and gentlemen, thank you for coming," the deputy announced. For a few seconds the journalists continued to murmur, and then the murmuring flickered and went out. "I'd like to introduce Joseph P. Bresser of the Joseph P. Bresser Operational Security Consultancy, who will say a few words."

As the reporters fanned out in search of open sight lines, a clear view opened for the first time between Bresser and the members of the sometime working group, and recognition came into his eyes.

"Good evening," he said. With an effort he scattered his gaze across the room. "As some of you may know, Bresser Operational has been a resource in a case that is currently before a federal grand jury. It would be improper for me to comment on an ongoing investigation. But when the press takes an interest in a case, as they have with this one, their leaks and disclosures often present a very partial picture, a picture unfair in this case to the very innovative suite of products we have here. It does not do justice either to the product or to the considerable commitment that our team has made to bringing this product to market."

It was a solid voice. It was the voice of someone who had never doubted that he had the right and capacity to address his peers.

"So what I want to do today is describe for you that suite of products, so that even if you do hear different, going forward, you'll know what the product really is."

"Is it a honeypot, Joe?" someone asked.

There was nervous laughter.

"I'll tell you what," Bresser said. "I'm not going to answer questions from people who don't respect the integrity of the grand jury process. You can laugh if you want, but that's how I feel about it."

"Jesus," a journalist near the friends muttered.

Bresser scanned the room as if looking for challengers. "I don't even understand how one of you could ask me that after I just finished saying that it would not be appropriate for me to discuss the methods used in a case that is now before a grand jury."

"What the fuck did he call a press conference for then?" muttered the journalist who had muttered before.

"Is this funny to some of you?" Bresser asked. "Do you think this is funny?" He wasn't able to tell which journalists were talking and laughing.

"This is like fucking gym class," said Raleigh, covering his mouth as if he had to cough, and then in fact coughing, fakely.

"Shh," warned Elspeth.

"I know you guys consider yourselves pretty clever," Bresser continued, "but keep in mind that you're operating with more axes of freedom than are available to someone in my position. My people and I have to move within constraints you aren't even aware of."

"So tell us about them," someone hollered.

"I'd like to, believe me. But I can't do that. What I can do is tell you about the algorithm we have."

"Oh, come on," jeered someone else.

Bresser hesitated. "There would be some very unhappy people if I did tell you. Some very surprised and unhappy and angry people."

To this conspiratorial note no heckling came because it raised hopes that Bresser might say something he shouldn't.

"What's he even doing?" Matthew asked.

"Gathering them in," Leif said.

"What I want to communicate," Bresser at last proceeded to say, "is that Bresser Opsec offers a suite of security solutions, not all of which, by any means, have been deployed in the case under investigation, which was, I can probably say this much, both more complex and simpler than many of you have been led to believe. The important thing I want to convey here is that if it weren't for our participation, the district attorney probably wouldn't even have been aware of the danger. Let alone the federal prosecutor."

A journalist near the front raised a hand. "Mr. Bresser, are you saying the US Attorneys' Office is under a misconception about the case?"

"Not at all. In fact, I concur wholeheartedly with Mr. Somerville's assessment that there was a grave threat of wide unauthorized release of personal identifying information and that the authorities had no choice but to step in when we did."

A humming started up, and the journalists began to jostle one another.

"What kind of personal information, Mr. Bresser?" one shouted.

"I'm not at liberty to say."

"Is this Somerville's assessment of the Telepathy Four's capabilities?"

"Not at liberty to say."

"Is it Somerville's understanding that the principal charge against the Telepathy Four is going to be identity theft?"

"I didn't say identity theft, and I didn't say it was Mr. Somerville's understanding. I'm not talking about his understanding. I'm talking about *the* understanding. The general understanding."

"The general understanding that there was a risk. An imminent risk."

"That's correct. An imminent risk."

"How were you able to find out about it in time? How did you start tracking the Four?"

"Again, I'm not at liberty to say," Bresser replied. His deputy leaned down and said something into his ear, which Bresser brushed away like a fly. "This is *my* understanding that we're talking about. I'm not speaking for Somerville."

"He's a fucking idiot," said the muttering journalist, a little louder than sotto voce. It occurred to Matthew that the journalist might be drunk.

"Why *this* group, Mr. Bresser?" asked another journalist, up near the front, who had a TV voice. "Why was *this* group seen as a particular danger?"

It was strange to hear the journalists falling in almost unconsciously with the idea that the friends had posed a threat and setting aside for the moment, if not longer, a portion of their professional skepticism in order to win Bresser's trust.

"Weren't they just kids?" It was the drunk.

"No," Bresser said sharply, focusing on the man at last and, without leaving his precinct of crimson rope, seeming to round on him. "No. We identified RPF because it was brought to our attention that a group of people at Occupy were boasting that they had new decryption methods and new surveillance methods, which could have been destabilizing. We had no choice but to look into the claims."

The deputy began swallowing air spasmodically, like an unwell guppy.

"You're saying you became aware of the danger because you already had them under surveillance?"

"Initially these were statements that they made out in the open."

"Then are you saying you believed in their telepathic powers?"

"I didn't fall for that, and I advise you not to."

The deputy extended a monitory hand toward Bresser, but before he could touch him, Bresser snapped, "No further questions at this time."

The humming redoubled and again became a roar.

"Elspeth?" queried a tall woman in black whose hair was pulled tight to her head. "We spoke briefly at the courthouse."

"Oh, that's right," Elspeth replied.

"Do your lawyers know you're here?" the woman asked.

"We seem to be improvising," said Elspeth.

"You should go," the woman said.

"Who is this?" Raleigh asked.

"She's a reporter," Elspeth said.

"Do you know why he called this press conference?" Jan Ridgely asked her colleague.

"He seems concerned for his company's reputation, doesn't he," the tall woman replied. "Do you still have my card?" she asked Elspeth. "If you stay here, I'll have to report anything you say, but I hope for your sake you'll go. Just because Bresser is making an—"

"Oh, it's not that bad," interrupted Ridgely.

"Excuse me," said Leif, speaking generally, waving his arms semaphore-style. Still in Matthew's coat, and warmed by the excitement, he was flushed, and there was a lick of fresh sweat across his forehead.

"Leif," said Matthew.

"Leif," said Elspeth.

"He said his say, and I want to say mine," Leif continued, still in a voice pitched slightly louder than what would have been needed to address only his friends. "Are you listening?" He didn't try to single any of the journalists out with his eyes; he simply waited, with the patient confidence that beauty has never even had to recognize as one of its strengths.

The patter of talk in the room grew thinner. Suddenly only one reporter was still speaking, and then in self-conscious embarrassment he, too, stopped.

"Leif, let's go home," said Matthew.

"You guys probably think this is like any other case, and that's why I want to warn you. I'm sorry if that sounds a little crazy."

Glowing red dots of handheld recording devices constellated the crowd, which had re-centered itself on Leif. Bresser, who had got halfway to the elevator bank, turned to watch.

"There was this thing that we discovered we had," Leif said. The faces of the listening journalists were solemn, perhaps out of pity for the harm that they knew Leif was doing to himself, perhaps entrained by Leif's own calm, uncanny seriousness. "We had been told all our lives that it was impossible to have it, but we did have it and we knew that we did and we decided to accept that we did. You know what I mean. I'm not going to say what it was. We didn't think it was special that we had it, but we thought it was special that we let ourselves know that we had it, and what I realized today, while listening to that man, is that that's what we got wrong. That's what he's trying to tell you without telling you. What he means is that they had it, too. Maybe not him personally. But there were people on their side who could also do it. What happened to us—the way we were 'caught'— couldn't have come about any other way. I don't know why anybody would do it for them—we thought the whole point of doing it, or rather, of deciding to be aware that you could do it—was to be free. To be making a choice. But we were wrong—that's what he's telling you. Or not telling you. It's actually only because he hasn't really told you yet that I can still talk to you. He walked away and left us here together because he thinks we can't speak anymore, but we *can* still speak, for at least a little while longer. We can speak, up until we understand how the blackmail is going to work, and he hasn't finished explaining it. Even then we're still going to be able to speak but only without saying words or hearing them, which is going to be difficult. It'll be like what I'm trying to do now, talk without saying what I'm talking about, which I have to do because if I were to say out loud everything that I'm trying to say, you wouldn't be able to hear me."

"Mr. Saunderson," asked one of the journalists, not the drunk one, "are you accusing the government of being psychic?"

Leif stared at the man, almost longingly, and Matthew knew that Leif was saying to the man, without words, that even when we can no longer speak in words, we'll find a way to know what's in each other's hearts.

"What have I done?" Leif said to Matthew.

The caretaker of the caretaker, Matthew pulled Leif out of the building and into the street. He shoved out of the way a reporter who tried to come between them and the open back door of a taxi.

"It's okay, go," he told the driver, who instead of going studied the reporters flooding into the street around his car and studied Leif and Matthew in his rearview mirror. "I think at this hour we should take the tunnel," Matthew advised, as if he and Leif were an ordinary fare, and the suggestion of routine was powerful enough that the driver let his car creep forward. After three blocks, the car turned onto a highway, and their pursuers were left behind.

"Is it true?" Matthew asked. "About the government?"

"I thought I had to say it."

"Were you reading it?"

"I had to say it the way each generation of poet has to say explicitly what was implicit the generation before. Bringing to the surface what used to be just beneath the surface, like a snake molting its skin. Becoming less subtle and more obvious."

"Are you warm?" Matthew asked, putting a hand on Leif's forehead.

"Am I?"

"Yes." His forehead was still wet.

"Don't be mad at me," Leif said.

"I thought you were mad at me."

The car dipped into one of the preliminary tunnels that came before the deep one that would take them under the river. "That was before I decided to save the world," Leif said. "Did I fuck up?"

"I don't know. It probably doesn't matter."

"It *feels* true. It might as well be true."

"Maybe it is," Matthew said.

The pale, tiled vault of the tunnel abruptly hooded them, and they fell silent.

When they reached Matthew's apartment, Matthew made dinner while Leif, sitting in the front window, peeked around the edge of the blinds at the street below, where the television vans were once again assembling.

"I see your friends are here again," a lanky man, one of Matthew's neighbors, said the next morning, curtly, when they crossed paths with him in the corridor. From the stoop, reporters were waving and smiling in at them insinuatingly.

Matthew and Leif braved the press and made their way back across the river to Michael Gauden's office. He had summoned them. When they reached his office, he rose not to greet them but to shut the door securely behind them.

"Am I in the doghouse?" Leif asked.

"The media at least seem to be responding positively to your apparent sincerity."

"My apparent sincerity," Leif echoed.

"That's how they're taking it." Gauden put reading glasses on his nose and slapped at his computer's keyboard. "'All in His Head? Cops Read Minds, Warns Hacker.' For example." Gauden looked over his glasses at Leif. Then he looked at Matthew: "You couldn't have tried to stop him?"

"I—," Matthew began.

"And how is it that you all came to be together in one place?" Gauden interrupted. "Was there a touch of the supernatural there, too?"

"That's just how it happened," Leif said.

"I'd like it if you were to promise me it won't happen again and we leave it at that."

"Why are you so angry?" Leif asked.

"I'm not angry," Gauden said, with a wide, false smile. "It's your neck. It's my job to try to save it."

"Was it really a hanging offense?" Leif asked.

"Prosecutors and judges often fail to respond well when the defendant takes threatening action against the victim of the alleged crime."

"I was just talking."

"There's actually very little talking that qualifies as just talking for someone in your situation, if the talking is being done to someone who stands in the relation to you that Bresser happens to occupy." Gauden took off and pocketed his glasses, pinched the bridge of his nose, and kneaded his left eye. "I'm in a difficult enough place as it is with the pressure to cooperate that I'm getting from some of the other defense counsel in this case, who seem to be unaware that the justice system in this country is adversarial."

"What do you mean?" asked Matthew.

"Do you know where your friend Elspeth found this"—he produced the glasses again and scrutinized an email on his screen—"Dominique Blount? She seems to be operating on the theory that she and Somerville are going to be friends. Perhaps because she was such good friends with the state's district attorney."

"They were friends?"

"I'm being ironic. I mean the state didn't charge Elspeth, and now Ms. Blount seems to think the feds won't charge her, either, if only she's nice enough to Somerville."

"Elspeth didn't do anything," Leif said.

Gauden didn't seem to hear. "Ms. Blount doesn't seem to be aware if you give someone like Somerville a slice of the carcass, it doesn't make him any less likely to demand a leg or a haunch."

"Is there something she wants us to do for Elspeth?" Leif asked.

"Wrap you in a bow and leave you on Somerville's doorstep."

"Would that help?" Leif asked.

"Right now Elspeth's not in any legal peril, and you are," Gauden said. He picked up his pen and whirligigged it, leaning sideways into the arm of his chair. "There is one piece of relatively good news, though I'm not entirely sure how you'll take it. It came out yesterday morning during a hearing in the Evans case about a motion that Penny filed to suppress the server log. It's probably been leaked online by now. Bresser seems to have called his press conference because he thought it would get out."

"What is it?" Leif asked.

"You don't know?"

Leif shook his head.

"The server was rigged to open to any attempted login from certain IP addresses," Gauden said.

"I don't understand," Leif said.

"Well, the apparent IP address of Raleigh's laptop was one of those addresses. Penny asked a question that brought it out. I think he must have been tipped off, but I can't figure out who did it. He was kind enough to let us know."

"I don't understand," Leif repeated.

"You didn't have to say open sesame for it to open," said Gauden.

"You mean, I didn't read anything."

"Well, I can't speak to whether you 'read' anything, as you call it, or heard anything or saw anything, but whether you did or not wouldn't have affected your ability to log in."

"Does that mean he's innocent?" Matthew asked.

"If I leave the door of my car open with the engine running and the key in the ignition, it's still a crime if someone drives off in it without my permission. But it puts us in a slightly better bargaining position."

"Doesn't this make it entrapment?" Matthew asked.

"It's not entrapment," said Gauden. "In real life, as opposed to television, entrapment is the defense you make when you've lost, basically. Because if you argue entrapment, you're saying you did it, but."

"Then how is this good news?"

"Because you're not very dangerous criminals if there's no evidence that you could do what you thought you could do. That's why Bresser wanted to get out in front of it, I suspect. It makes what he did look like overkill."

"They were waiting for us," Leif said.

"But you knew that," said Gauden. "You told me you saw files with your names on them. They don't seem to want to enter those as evidence, by the way, which is going to make it hard for them to prove their gravamen. I think we have a shot now at avoiding not only jail time but even having to plead to a felony, which you don't want to do if there's any way you can avoid it because in a number of states it means you can never vote or hold office, and you're young and it closes some careers to you, such as the law, for example."

"I don't think we have to worry about my law career," Leif said.

"You never know," said Gauden. "But you won't even have the chance to turn the law down if you don't stay away from the press. The more public a case is, the more unrelenting someone like Somerville feels he has to be. Please don't make any more statements."

"Maybe they knew we were coming because *they* had read *me*," Leif said.

"Have you considered talking to a therapist?"

Leif shook his head.

"There might be more in heaven and earth than is dreamt of in my philosophy, as they say, but I have to restrict myself to thinking about what can and can't be proved in court."

"Of course," said Leif.

"Not everyone has to operate under such restriction, is what I'm trying to convey. I can get you a name and number if you're interested."

On the subway back to Matthew's apartment, a bearded man in a plaid shirt cruised Matthew. The man was sitting across the car and three seats to the left. At first Matthew wasn't sure. Cruising was one of the analog practices that the internet was rendering obsolete. Maybe it was only that Matthew wanted to think he was being cruised? The man's eyebrows were almost black, and his beard was as richly dark. His eyes suggested that he was telling a story about himself in which he didn't mind that he was misbehaving. He looked away to give Matthew a chance to look at him and then looked back to catch him at it.

Leif didn't seem to notice. Maybe he was choosing to be tactful.

The man's coat was sprawled behind him on his seat. He seemed to be proud of his shoulders and arms and was leaning forward to show them off. Matthew would have liked to be wrestled down by them. Leif had winced and twisted away the last time Matthew had tried to touch him. *It isn't your fault*, Leif had said, as if Matthew had asked about assigning blame.

"Is it safe to talk to a therapist if you're going to be on trial?" Leif asked.

Matthew swiveled in his seat, to make a show of facing Leif as he talked to him, demonstrating his attachment to Leif for the bearded man's benefit. "We should have asked."

"What?" Leif asked, reacting to the swivel.

"Nothing," Matthew said. He thought of confessing that there was a boy down the car staring at him.

It was never exciting unless the man cruising you seemed a little better than you could expect to get. It was possible that the man was looking their way because of Leif—because Leif was the one he really wanted, because the presence of Leif somehow ratified Matthew as an object choice, proving, perhaps, that Matthew met at least the minimal requirements for dating. But the man didn't look like he was thinking about dating. Maybe he liked the challenge of taking a stranger away from his boyfriend.

"I don't think Gauden would have suggested therapy if there weren't some kind of legal privilege," Matthew said.

The bearded man caught Matthew's next glance and let Matthew see him looking Matthew up and down. Matthew looked away to avoid committing himself.

"The thing is that if it's not what I thought it was, then I don't know what it is," Leif said.

"What what is?" Matthew asked.

"My secret grove," said Leif. "My secret grief. The one I wear on my tattoo sleeve."

"Gauden said the news about the server didn't necessarily mean you weren't picking up on something," Matthew said.

"Don't pretend to believe *now*. What is it your dog has?"

"My mother's dog. She has epilepsy."

"Maybe I can see a vet instead of a therapist. I don't think it would occur to anyone to subpoena a vet."

The man was burning a hole in Matthew's peripheral vision, but Matthew made a decision not to look at him again. Leif was more beautiful, after all. When he took off his shirt, there was that cross grain of down at the top of his breastbone.

"What?" Leif asked again, perceiving the new shift in Matthew's aspect.

"Nothing," Matthew said again. The trouble was that beauty alone wasn't enough, because close handling eventually made it common. In a tumble with someone like this bearded man, Matthew would be more free, for the brief time it lasted. The bearded man belonged to the animal life of the city. Matthew, however, had chosen to have a name and to be part of a story.

It could be reassuring, perhaps, simply to know that animal life was still running through the city. He could make an effort to think of it as reassuring. His hands were trembling, and he hid them in his coat pockets.

All the lawyers came down hard against fraternization among the defendants, which left Leif with no one but Matthew to talk the disillusioning news over with.

"Did you think all along that I was making it up?" Leif asked.

"No," Matthew said.

"You must have wondered. You're not an idiot."

"I could have been wrong."

The bitterness that was settling on them compounded the difficulty. It seemed to Matthew that everything was getting worse so rapidly that the pace interfered with the way that one parceled out one's caring along the axis of time. It was becoming hard to rest in any one moment long enough to mourn the misfortune that belonged to it and ought to have been sufficient to it, because one knew that a worse misfortune was probably about to come next. One became distracted from one's present unhappiness by one's likely future unhappiness.

An email from Matthew's adviser warned that Matthew had missed a chapter deadline, and at first, at the prospect of burying himself in reading and note-taking, Matthew's spirits not quite paradoxically lifted, but they fell again as soon as it occurred to him that if he were to immerse himself in the seventeenth century he would leave Leif too much to his own devices. It had become impossible again for Leif to work at the café—the journalists were swarming—and Leif sharply refused when Matthew suggested poetry.

"Your old grad school friends were right. It's just creative-writing faculty talking about each other."

"Don't say that."

"Maybe I'll take up knitting."

"What about the dark poem?" Matthew asked. "Can't you write that?"

"It's not a poem."

"What is it?"

"It's just the way the world is," Leif said. "It can't be made into anything."

"You could write that down."

"There's no one to write it down for. That's what being at the end means."

The remark seemed a little dramatic, but Matthew knew better than to say so, and it wasn't until they were in bed that night and he was staring at the ceiling, next to Leif, whose eyes were shut and who was curled up like a fist and whose body was nowhere touching his—it wasn't until he was alone in the dark beside Leif that it occurred to him that he could have said that if Leif were to write down what he felt about the end of the world, it might do good even if no one did survive to read it later, even if no one but Matthew and Leif himself ever had a chance to appreciate what he was able to say.

Sometimes, in the middle of the night, Leif's arms, around Matthew, would quiver in his sleep, his legs would halfheartedly piston, and from his throat would come faint, half-swallowed cries. Whenever it happened, Matthew wondered if he should wake Leif up or if it was better for Leif to work through in his dream whatever he was working through.

And sometimes, from within a dream of his own, Matthew would hear the toneless whistle of a gas burner opened, the clicking of his stove's igniter, and the thick flutter of a blossoming flame, and when he opened his eyes, he would see, across the room, a small purple thistle-bloom burnishing the underside of his teakettle. Invisible in the dark, Leif, having heard Matthew stir, would explain in a low voice that he hadn't been able to sleep. Matthew would then get out of bed, too, despite a protest from Leif, and wrap himself in the blanket, and they would sit up for a while together in the window at the front of the apartment, looking down at the street.

In daylight Leif admitted that his dreams were violent. A murderer was chasing him with a power drill. He was in a house with boarded-up windows surrounded by creatures that wanted to catch him for food. It was absurd, he said. He wasn't the kind of person who liked to go to horror movies. It was getting so that some nights he almost wished he didn't have to sleep.

"Would you like to see someone?" Matthew asked.

"They'll go away," Leif said.

They were only dreams, Matthew told himself, because he didn't know what to do.

"How much is it so far?" Leif asked. "Would you ask your father how much it is?"

Matthew told him not to think about that.

Usually when the doorbell rang now, they ignored it, but one afternoon it rang and rang, insistently, and maybe because Matthew had been thinking that morning that they needed to see people, if only he could think of someone Leif wanted to and was not forbidden to see, he put on his sneakers and walked downstairs. Standing in the foyer was Diana, in her orange jacket. She was holding a plastic Thank You bag from a bodega.

"Can I help you?" Matthew asked, the glass of the door still between them.

"Elspeth asked me to check on Leif," she replied, projecting her voice through the barrier.

Matthew opened the door but stood in it. "Is it all right for him to talk to you?"

"I don't know," she said, smiling and not moving. "That's got to be your call."

"I mean because of the lawyers."

"That's your call," she repeated.

"Come in." He waited at the foot of the stairs for her to go up first. "Do you know how Raleigh's doing?" he asked. Now that he was letting her in, he felt that he needed to make conversation.

"No idea."

"So you haven't checked on anyone else."

"Elspeth thought Leif might have been upset by the news about Bresser's server," Diana explained. "She and Leif are sort of on each other's wavelengths."

"You have a visitor," Matthew announced when he opened the apartment door.

"You brought me goldfish?" Leif exclaimed, when he looked into the bag from the bodega.

They embraced. "How are you, babe?" she asked, caroling her voice.

"Do you like our Christmas tree?" Leif asked.

Matthew had suggested it one day mostly as something to do. It blocked one of his bookshelves.

"Are you going to decorate it?"

"It's more of a natural Christmas tree," Leif claimed.

"It's very nice."

"Matthew even remembers to water it. Sit down, sit down."

Matthew turned around his desk chair for Diana and offered her something to drink.

"Elspeth asked me to see how you're doing," Diana said.

"Oh fine," Leif replied, with a dying fall. "I had a friend whose five-year-old started saying that, exactly that way. 'I'm oh-fine, thanks.' How is Elspeth?"

"She's oh-fine, too. Maybe a little confused."

"It's not that confusing. I was an idiot."

Diana hesitated.

"Isn't that what they're saying online?" Leif continued.

"I don't know," Diana replied. "I haven't been—"

"Matthew reads it, but he won't tell me. That's what I'd say if I had believed in me. If I had wanted that badly to believe."

"It doesn't matter what anyone online says," Matthew interposed.

"He keeps saying that. But I told everyone there was another world, 'far other worlds, and other seas,' even, and I was wrong, there's just one, and furthermore, because there's only one, what they say online is all there is."

"It isn't *all* there is," Diana objected.

"What does Elspeth think we were doing?" Leif asked. "Does she have a theory? That's my hobby now: trying to figure out if it was mania or an epileptic aura or did we just have very delicate mechanisms. Raleigh's idea was always that we were responding to messages that we weren't aware we were receiving, like that nineteenth-century horse that thought it could do math but was actually just watching its owner's foot. Of course it might have been just nothing at all. There might not have been any real thing that was being referred to. After all, if there's only one world . . . You know, I used to think that if a thing was able to appear in a real poem then it must have some kind of reality somewhere. The way that some mathematicians believe that numbers are real. It's almost embarrassing even to say it out loud now."

"The way I think of it," Diana said, "you and Elspeth were playing a game."

"We're not supposed to talk about it, are we," Leif said, with a glance at Matthew.

"Do whatever you want," said Matthew.

"Does Elspeth think it was a game?" Leif asked.

"We don't—she just asked me to get in touch and not drop too many bread crumbs along the way. She just wanted to send her love."

"I see."

"She was afraid that if you two don't send messages back and forth somehow that you'll lose track of where you are with each other."

"We never thought it could work if you couldn't get into the same room with each other," Leif said.

"Well, I guess she's trying to adjust to that, is why she sent me."

"Tell her I send my love, too," Leif said. He sat very still for a moment, as if concentrating, and Matthew realized that he, too, was no longer entitled to imagine that he knew what Leif or anyone else who didn't speak was feeling.

"I think maybe I didn't think enough about 'annihilating,'" Leif resumed, "when I thought about 'annihilating all that's made.' Maybe annihilating the world makes the world want to take revenge."

"Do you mean in the poem that your forest comes from?" Diana asked, gesturing toward her own shoulder.

"Yes. The thing is, Marvell makes annihilation sound so pleasant: 'A green thought in a green shade.' I didn't think anyone would mind."

"Is it annihilation? It sounds like understanding."

"It's everything. That's why I got it in ink."

Matthew offered to walk Diana downstairs. "I think that was good for him," he said. "Your visit."

"Oh good."

"Have you been able to get any work done?"

"I'm supposed to be writing my theory chapter, so I've been telling myself that I'm doing the thinking."

"What's it about?"

"My dissertation? Cigarette smoking, as a way of looking at the ideas people have about human nature. There's sort of a whiteness studies angle. What happens to the rhetoric of moral disappointment now that large populations of white people are becoming newly subject to description by it."

"I still have to make an effort not to think about cigarettes sometimes," Matthew said.

"See, one of our questions when a person says something like that is whether he describing a weakness or a strength. Is he describing an inability to resist a cigarette once the thought occurs to him, or a resourcefulness in knowing how to circumvent that susceptibility? Whether you describe it one way or the other is like having a different operating system on your computer."

"And where does the whiteness studies come in?"

"We've found that a smoker who wants to quit is more likely to succeed if he believes that character is universal but polyvalent. Not determinist, not a matter of essence. And even though blacks smoke more overall than other groups, they seem to be a little better at thinking that way, probably because they've had more practice with denaturalizing essentialist ideas. And your dissertation?"

"Poetic kingship," he said. "This sense that people started to have in the sixteenth and seventeenth centuries that they were like dethroned kings, in a way that left them feeling sad but more like the sovereigns of their own lives."

"So maybe the same thing a little."

One morning, Matthew took the train alone to look for a Christmas present for Leif. Christmas was only a couple of weeks away. He said he was going to the library at his university, and when, long before the train reached the university, he alighted and walked upstairs, the street itself seemed galvanized by the lie—by the excitement of being where his boyfriend didn't know he was.

At a chain clothing store decorated like a gentleman's club from the 1940s—cherrywood and baize and taxidermy—he fingered the blue-and-white houndstooth shirts and the fawn-colored sweaters. It wasn't a place he ever went to on his own account. As a graduate student he couldn't afford it.

It was a weekday, and there were only a handful of other men in the store. They had the bland handsomeness and unself-doubting manner of people with corporate jobs—or perhaps, given that it was a weekday, of people between corporate jobs.

"Can I help you find anything?" it startled him to hear a salesman say. The salesman, two or three years younger than Matthew, reached over to space out more evenly the shirts hanging in front of Matthew. His touch on the shirts was proprietary, as if he were counting them.

"Just browsing," Matthew said, with an angry smile, knowing that the salesman could see that he didn't ordinarily wear such nice clothes and was shopping alone. The salesman could probably also tell that Matthew was gay, as the salesman himself obviously was, and gays were reputed to be light-fingered. An indignant part of Matthew wanted to explain that it was the prospect of spending that was making him jittery.

"Could I try these on?" one of the corporate-looking customers asked.

The salesman appropriated the shirts that the customer was holding and, draping them over his forearms like a muff, led the man to a dressing room.

The prettiest things in the store were the sweaters, but Matthew wasn't sure he could afford one and didn't know if Leif would like it. It had been clever of Diana to remember that he liked goldfish.

His phone trembled. "Am I disturbing you?" his mother asked.

"No."

"Your father has a convention in Portland this weekend."

"In Portland?" He had no idea where this was going.

"I know, at this time of year. But I think it's so nice there, I want to go anyway, and I wondered, do you and Leif want to come look after Fosco?"

"Oh. Sure."

"I thought it would be a chance for you to get away."

"I think we have to ask someone before we can leave town," he cautioned.

"Who?"

"I can find out."

"Only if you're interested. She loves Puppy Hideaway, and right now they do still have a slot."

"I'll ask Leif."

"And another thing—I'm sorry to bother you with all this."

"What?" he asked.

"Do you think you'll be coming for Christmas?"

His mind raced. He didn't want to commit to anything.

"I'm starting to plan," she continued, apologetically.

"Leif might need to go see *his* mother."

"Of course. It's her turn, isn't it. Well, we'd love to have you if for some reason he isn't able to."

"I don't think he'll be going to trial that soon."

"Matthew, I wasn't talking about that."

"It's something we have to think about," Matthew said defensively.

"Is everything all right?"

"Everything's fine." It hadn't occurred to him before that there was a finite number of days until Leif's trial, no less finite for his ignorance of the number. "I guess they're still having the grand jury. We haven't heard anything lately."

"You'll let us know when you do."

As the conversation ended, he surfaced into the store where he happened to be standing. He needed to buy presents for his parents, too, he realized. Maybe he could also buy his father a sweater? He picked up a second one, in a different color. But was it weird to buy your father a sweater if you were also buying your boyfriend one?

They were too expensive, anyway.

"You really don't mind?" Matthew double-checked, even though it was too late to back out.

"I like it up there," Leif replied. "It's like stepping outside of one's story, at least for me. Everything's so taken care of. There's peanut butter ice cream in the freezer. There's a big TV."

"Would you want to go for Christmas, too?"

A cloud passed over Leif's face. "If I'm still here."

"Or maybe you want us to see *your* mother."

"She won't be up to it. She told me she's giving me books, and when I said remember they don't allow hardcovers in prison, she said then don't use the gift card to buy hardcovers. Which leads me to think she isn't going to be putting up a tree or anything."

"It's up to you," Matthew offered.

"Your parents must be sorry you met me," Leif said.

"Why do you say things like that?"

They had to leave their Christmas plans unresolved because they needed to move quickly. Fosco was already locked up alone in the little clapboard house, waiting for Matthew and Leif to travel the hour and a half's distance and take her out and feed her, and they had to meet Michael Gauden before they could even get on the road. Gauden hadn't said what it was about.

In Gauden's office, a curtain had been drawn away from what on previous visits Matthew hadn't even been aware was a window. At this height, in the center of the city, the fraternity that obtained among the skyscrapers was evident—their shared distinction from the unimproved real estate below.

To enjoy the view for too long might have seemed unsophisticated. Matthew took a seat. Leif craned his neck for a few moments longer. "It's like satellite view," he said.

"And how are your spirits?" the lawyer asked.

"I threw my Ouija board out," Leif said. "I thought I wasn't supposed to contact them anymore."

"Touché," Gauden said.

Leif was making an effort, Matthew saw. Having dismissed Gauden and then reengaged him, having defied him and then put up with a scolding from him, he seemed to have come round to a recognition of what he and the lawyer owed each other. It disappointed Matthew a little to see that Leif had been tamed somewhat. But there was no other way out.

"Listen, I had a thought," Gauden said, leaning forward in his chair, as if he wanted to ask a favor. "Maybe it's even what your friend here would call a strategy," he continued, pausing to glance at Matthew. He slid back in his chair. The pen in his hand wouldn't launch into its revolutions until, in the effort of speaking, Gauden became unconscious of it, and for the moment he was still present, still awkwardly in the room. "It occurred to me, in the light of what we now know about Bresser's cybersecurity, or rather the lack thereof, that I might have been hasty in saying that belief had no relevance. Or rather, the quality of belief." The pen whirled once and stopped, a silent trill. "If I can put it that way." Another whirl. "It surprised you, didn't it, when you were able to get into Bresser's server?"

Leif nodded.

"Did it surprise you?" Gauden asked again, in a louder voice.

"Yes," Leif answered. He wouldn't be able to nod on the stand.

"If we were to explain to the court that it surprised you, and that it surprised you because at heart you believe about this sort of thing what most people believe, and if we were to explain that what you said to the other members of your working group about your ability to 'read,' as you called it, held a truth-value for you, to the extent that it held any truth-value at all, like that of poetry, which you do, after all, write—"

"But I meant it," Leif interrupted.

"You just told me you were surprised."

"I was surprised," Leif admitted.

"Which means you didn't expect to get in."

"But I wanted to."

"And I want to steal the Hope diamond, but if I don't do anything that I believe would enable me to steal it . . ."

"I was lying?" Leif queried.

Gauden shook back a lock of blond bangs that had fallen across his forehead. "It may come to the point that we need to say something as bald as that in order to make the logic of our argument as clear as possible, but personally I think of the speech act in question as being more along the lines of a metaphor." The pen again flashed into motion.

The lawyer, Matthew understood, had no idea how much it would hurt Leif even to pretend to believe that he had knowingly deceived his friends.

"The usual case," Gauden continued, "is that the accused thought he was buying uranium, and he's being tried for that intention even though the government agent who entrapped him delivered only pyrite. But here, you were holding a chunk of what you knew to be pyrite, and the government switched it out for uranium."

Leif didn't immediately respond.

"Well, I for one think it's foolproof," Gauden added. He smiled at his self-congratulation.

Leif nodded but still didn't speak. He looked at Gauden and then at Matthew and then out the window, where sunlight was quivering on the glass scales of the nearest fellow skyscraper.

"And what does the monkey say?" Gauden asked. The lawyer was looking at Matthew.

"The monkey?" Matthew echoed.

"I mean, you know, what's the opinion in the peanut gallery?"

"You mean, what do I think?" Matthew asked.

The lawyer nodded. He probably hadn't meant for his scorn to slip out of his mouth.

"I don't know why you're taking away from him . . . ," Matthew began.

"What?" the lawyer asked.

Leif, still silent, wouldn't meet Matthew's gaze.

"Never mind," Matthew said.

"I don't think I'm taking away anything that isn't already gone," the lawyer said. "I'm trying to prevent the loss of even more."

"I see," Matthew said.

Leif asked for a little time to think it over.

They had rented a car, since Matthew's parents wouldn't be there to pick them up from the train station. Matthew drove. When they set out, the road was chalky under the winter light. Along the shoulder, in the strips of turf and brakes of scrub pine, the green hues were flat and pale, almost whitened. Inside the envelope of the automobile, they were safe. Leif curled up in the passenger seat with his stocking feet perched above the glove compartment, near the windshield.

"Did I tell you I figured out the sonnets?" Leif asked. "I had read them before, but this time it was so obvious. You know there's the Fair Youth and the Dark Lady, and the speaker's in love with first one and then the other and then back and forth, and all the scholars think they were real people but no one knows who they really were?"

"I'm getting a PhD in sixteenth-century English literature."

"I'm just checking. Anyway, you don't know the answer because I'm the first person in history to figure it out. The Fair Youth is a boy who played women's roles, and that's how Shakespeare met him and they fell in love, and the Dark Lady is the Fair Youth after he's started transitioning. She's the Fair Youth once she's become old enough to want to pass as a woman offstage as well as on."

"Huh," Matthew said, with the slow half mind that one has while driving.

"And once he has started taking clients, probably. But I'm not really sure about the social history of cross-dressing actors in that period."

"Huh," Matthew said again.

"You don't believe me."

"I didn't say I didn't believe you."

"That's why there's all that negativity in the sonnets about makeup and female artifice and how the Dark Lady isn't what she seems to be. The speaker of the poems is being all cis about everything."

"I thought the speaker liked the Fair Youth's ambiguity."

"He likes the ambiguity. He doesn't like the identity."

"What about when the two loves of comfort and despair hook up with each other and leave him out?"

"Allegory," Leif answered. "Allegory of the self."

"I see."

"I should be able to get a PhD for this, right?"

"Definitely," Matthew said.

"It's probably as much as most scholars hope to discover in a lifetime."

"Are you really going to write about it?"

"No," Leif replied, his voice suddenly hollow.

"Are you all right?"

"I'm fine," Leif said. "There's not really time."

"We don't know that."

"It's just one of my ideas," Leif said. "What are you doing?"

"My wallet was digging into my ass the way I was sitting on it, so I'm putting it in my coat pocket, but I want to zip the coat pocket shut so it doesn't fall out later." The wallet had been bothering him for half an hour, but suddenly the discomfort of it was in the forefront of his mind.

"Do you want me to do it for you?"

"I got it." The steering wheel jiggled a little as he maneuvered. "What?"

"Nothing," Leif replied.

"What is it?"

"I thought you'd be more interested."

"In your idea? I'm totally interested. I want you to write it."

"No, forget it. It's too late. Now you're being nice. It's your thing, anyway."

"It's not my thing. I don't own sixteenth-century literature."

"I think maybe I was trying to get close to you somehow," Leif said.

"That's great," Matthew replied. "I can tell you what editions to cite."

"What do you mean?"

"About half of scholarship is that all your page numbers have to be to the canonical editions."

"But I don't think I really want to write it now," Leif said.

"What do you mean, 'now'?"

"Oh, maybe I thought you would whoop or something. And there isn't really time, like I said."

"I'm totally excited about it. I'm saying I'm excited about it. Why aren't you listening to what I'm saying?"

"I'm sorry."

The lane stripes, as they slipped past the car, flashed with a faint glow and seemed to hover slightly above the agate of the road. It was twilight, Matthew realized. What had been green along the roadside was now dusky and indistinct, like an aquarium that has been neglected and has gone murky. He switched on the headlights.

"I want you to write about it," he repeated. "You have to write about it now."

"But I don't want to. Honestly. I was being stupid. I think maybe I just wanted to imagine what it was like to do what you do. Since I'm not writing poems anymore. Maybe that's what I wanted you to be excited about."

"Okay," Matthew said.

"And you were moving your wallet around or whatever." He was trying to make it all a joke. "I don't even know anymore what's going on in my head."

Matthew nodded. "Do you want to watch a movie tonight?"

"Oh, sure."

"There's pay-per-view at my parents' house."

"Oh, that's right."

"Leif," Matthew said.

"I'm *fine*."

"Okay."

"I just may not be in the mood for a movie."

By now Matthew's eyes had adjusted to seeing only as much of the road as the streetlights shone down on and the flares of the car's headlights hit as they traveled forward. It was almost night. The defile of trees along the road was still legible but only as a silhouette. A silhouette with spindly, upward-reaching fingers.

"What did you think of what Gauden said?" Matthew asked, a little later. It was as dark now inside the car as outside. "Are you going to go along with it?"

"Why not?" Leif asked, looking out the window.

"Well, it's not—"

"It doesn't matter," Leif interrupted.

"It's not who you said you were," Matthew finished saying.

"It doesn't matter."

After Richard II is unkinged, he is paraded through London by his usurper without his crown or royal raiments, according to the account given by Samuel Daniel in *Civil Wars*. When Isabel, Richard's queen, catches sight of him from a window, she is at first distraught and even angry, but with an effort she checks her grief, and by the time she and her husband at last speak, she is ready to renew her pledge to him:

> *Thou still dost rule the kingdome of my hart:*
> *If all be lost, that government doth stand;*
> *And that shall never from thy rule depart:*
> *And so thou be, I care not how thou bee:*
> *Let Greatnes goe; so it goe without thee.*

Matthew felt the pathos of the speech, and the nobility of it, but he didn't know whether it was true—whether the lover of a dethroned king would really feel that way, or feel that way for very long.

After dinner Matthew started a movie on the television, in the hope of luring Leif onto the sofa beside him, but the movie wasn't very good—in a theater the garishness and the violence might have radiated harmlessly away, but in his parents' home the toxins seemed to accumulate—and after half an hour of watching alone he turned it off.

They were sleeping in his old bedroom again, even though the master bedroom was free. Fosco joined them, pacing counterclockwise four times before settling heavily to the floor. Though the house had two stories, plus a finished attic and a basement, all the animal life was focused that night in a single room.

"Do you think she sleeps here all the time?" Leif asked.

"I doubt it."

When Leif got up in the middle of the night, Matthew was awakened not by him but by Fosco—by the thumps that she made on the stairs as she padded down after him to the kitchen. In the morning Matthew knocked wadded-up chamomile sachets out of two mugs that Leif had left in the kitchen sink.

"Nightmares?" Matthew asked.

Leif made a gesture as if to push away the question.

Leif had gotten so little sleep that when, a couple of hours later, Matthew set out for the grocery store, Leif stayed behind to try to take a nap.

It was so much warmer than it had been the night before that Matthew walked to the car in just his sweater, and it wasn't until he came to the corner, where the traffic was always so heavy that it was tricky to turn left, that he realized he had forgotten his wallet, still in the pocket of his coat, hanging beside the refrigerator in the kitchen. He turned right instead of left and made his way around the long block. Back in his parents' driveway he turned off the car but left the keys in the ignition and the door open. An alarm in the car mewed at him as he walked away from it.

"Forgot my wallet," he called out in explanation as he grabbed his coat. Through the quilting he confirmed by feel the nub of the wallet.

There was no acknowledgment of his explanation. Leif probably hadn't heard him—Matthew had waited so long at the corner for a break in the traffic that Leif was probably already asleep—but it was strange that Matthew didn't hear the click of Fosco's nails on the wooden floor, ambling her way toward him from wherever she was in the house. "Leif?" Matthew called out, listening also for Fosco.

No one was on the sofa in the living room or on the one in the sun porch.

"Leif?" he asked, at a lower volume, knowing that Leif must be nearby, and climbed the stairs. But the bedroom where they had slept was also empty, and so was his parents' bedroom. He checked the one that had used to be Brian's, too.

The door to the attic was ajar. "Leif, are you up there?" Matthew asked. He felt a little silly climbing yet another flight, while the driver's-side door of the car and the kitchen door of the house were hanging wide open, down below—while the pealing of the car's alarm was draining its battery and while the money that his parents spent heating their home was being squandered—merely to see what was probably going to be Leif already obliviously asleep in Brian's displaced twin bed, with Fosco ensconced beside him. "Leif," he said once more.

In the attic, Leif was sitting in an overstuffed sage-colored armchair that Matthew's mother had retired from the living room ages ago, in the first turmoil when Brian went away to college. He seemed to be having trouble keeping his eyes open. Fosco was staring at him so attentively that at first Matthew thought they were playing a game.

"I forgot my wallet," Matthew said.

"I made a mistake," Leif replied slowly.

"What?"

"I thought I would get used to it in a few minutes," Leif said, "but you came back first."

What Fosco was paying so much attention to was an object in one of Leif's hands. "What's this?" Matthew asked.

"To put away."

It was the smoky orange plastic vial of Fosco's medicine. It was empty, Matthew saw when he took it.

"Where are they?" Matthew asked. "Where are the pills, Leif?" There was a glass with a little water still in it on the floor beside Leif's feet. "Jesus Christ."

"It was a mistake," Leif said. "Everyone makes mistakes."

"Can you walk?" Matthew asked. He pocketed the empty vial.

"I don't feel so well."

He didn't seem to be able to rise on his own, so Matthew put his arms around him in a bear hug and lifted him up out of his chair. "Can you help me?" Matthew asked, as he shifted to Leif's side so that they would be able to move forward.

Fosco barked at them because it was all so unusual.

"Shut up, Fosco," Matthew said.

"Probably got the dose wrong," Leif said, "because I couldn't go online."

"My parents mortgaged their house for you," Matthew said.

"God," Leif said, twisting in Matthew's arms. "Don't tell me that."

But Matthew wanted to tie him to the world. He wanted him more than he wanted him to be perfectly free.

He tried to brace himself against the wall of the stairwell as they descended, so that if Leif stumbled, he wouldn't be knocked down by him.

"Wasn't going to have to think about it anymore," Leif said.

"Yeah, you fucked up."

The hospital where they usually took Matthew's father, whenever he had indigestion and thought he was having a heart attack, was only seven minutes away. At the landing Matthew would be able to call an ambulance from his cell phone, but if he and Leif could manage the second flight of stairs, too, and he got Leif into the car, they would probably get there faster.

"How many did you take?" Matthew asked, planning what to tell the doctors.

"Thirty," Leif said, holding up a hand with, nonsensically, five fingers.

When they reached the landing, Matthew tried to draw Leif along it a little more swiftly, since it was a flat surface.

"Poor Fosco," Leif said. She had stopped barking, but she was following them closely.

"Why?"

"Won't have any," Leif explained.

"You should have thought of that," Matthew agreed.

No walls hedged in the stairs down to the ground floor, and Matthew did his best to anchor himself with careful footing. He needed to let Leif hold the banister.

"I know," Leif said. It took Matthew a moment to realize that Leif was still in the conversation about Fosco and was replying to the last thing Matthew had said. They were falling out of sync; Leif's mind was slowing down. Matthew wondered whether choosing to drive Leif himself was the right decision. They weren't even in the car yet. They weren't even on the ground floor yet. Matthew felt panic flush his chest and neck and face, but he didn't think Leif was alert enough to notice.

"I should've been paying more attention," Matthew said.

"To read my mind?"

Fosco trotted ahead of them into the kitchen and then straight out the open kitchen door. "Fosco!" Matthew shouted.

"She'll come," Leif said hopefully.

Matthew pulled Leif through the kitchen. They didn't have time for Leif's coat.

Outside, Fosco was peeing in the neighbor's roses, which at this time of year were no more than knotty vines with prickers.

"I'm sorry," Leif said, as Matthew lowered him into the passenger seat. His skin was alabaster.

"It's okay," Matthew said. "Fosco, come," he called, but she wouldn't. "Look, Fosco," Matthew tried, but not even the car appealed to her.

Leif had closed his eyes.

"Fosco, come!" Matthew called again. He got in the car himself, for encouragement, but the dog turned tail and cantered away.

"Fosco!" Matthew shouted hoarsely, scaring the dog into a gallop. The white tuffet of her tail bobbed above her as she crossed three lawns, four lawns, five.

Matthew slammed the door and turned the key in the ignition.

Since Matthew had never been to Leif's apartment, Leif had given him instructions: the top lock wouldn't be locked, unless the landlord had come by, but in order to turn the key in the bottom one, Matthew would need to pull the doorknob up and slightly to the left.

At first, however, the key still wouldn't turn, until, in frustration, Matthew pulled harder—held the knob in both hands and tugged—and then the heavy shield of the door shifted in his grip, sitting back on its hinges, and after that the key rolled easily around.

At the end of its swing, the opening door bounced against a running shoe on its side that the door had obviously stubbed its toe on many times before. Just beyond, along one wall, began a bookshelf. The books that Matthew had been asked to fetch, however, were near Leif's desk, which Matthew could already see a corner of, in the room ahead. *If you sit at the desk*, Leif had said, *they'll be here*, and he had mimed stretching out a hand to touch them. Leif had added that the patterns on the covers looked like dimity. Blake and the Metaphysical Poets were the ones he wanted. Plus a novel about a medieval nunnery, which didn't look like dimity and was on a different shelf—Leif hadn't been able to remember which one.

Behind Matthew, after he stepped inside, the heavy door clicked shut. The light in the apartment was gray and indirect; the shapes revealed by it, quiet and precise. The shapes, for example, of Leif's three skateboards—tar-papered escutcheons, horned with wheels, that were propped against the entry corridor's wall.

As Matthew walked, he was conscious of the clops that his footfalls made and of the floorboards creaking. He was conscious of being in an apartment that he had never been invited into.

There were two windows. The bed lay under the one on the left; a desk, under the one on the right. Beside the bed there was a green rocking chair. If you turned around, you saw a kitchenette, with a side door leading to a bathroom.

Up to the panes of the windows, which overlooked the street, rose the muted lilt of a man and a woman talking as they strode by on the sidewalk below.

In the cement front yard, brown leaves, curled like closed hands, were rattling against ironwork where they were trapped. In a week or two, a fall of snow would overlay the leaves, and they would be held down, rotting, until spring.

Matthew set his backpack on the floor. On the desk a pale jade hen and chicks was growing in a shallow terra-cotta tray. The toothed whorls looked out at oblique angles. Leif hadn't said anything about it, but Matthew was pretty sure that even a plant like this needed watering sometimes.

The apartment did have his delicate smell, or nonsmell. Of a rubbed penny, a penny old enough to be real copper. Was that it? And also the smell of fresh milk, maybe, if fresh milk even has a smell. The smell of cut skin and of a kind of blank richness.

It would only be for two weeks, initially, the doctor who had admitted Leif had said. Then they could revisit the decision, see where they were. The facility was one town over from Matthew's parents' house. A nurse in the ER had assured Matthew that she had seen many patients sent there over the years, and it had been easier to accept her advice than to try to arrange to have Leif transported all the way back into the city, where, the nurse had warned, beds were in short supply. Easier and probably cheaper. Matthew would be able to stay nearby, with his parents. After all, on Sunday it was already going to be Christmas. Why go back to the city? And then a week after Christmas the two weeks would be up. The first two weeks, anyway. Matthew wondered whether on Christmas Day the doctors would be willing to let Leif out for a few hours.

He knew as an intellectual matter that it was natural to be angry at someone who had done what Leif had done, but he thought it was possible that he had used up all his anger on the effort of locking Leif up. While he had been telling the nurse that yes, he did believe that Leif continued to be a danger to himself, he had had to not look at Leif's eyes, and then, as soon as the nurse had begun to loop cloth restraints around Leif's wrists and ankles, he had wondered if that had been the right thing to say, because maybe saying it would make what Leif had tried to do more real and more plausible; maybe therefore it would have been better not to say it, in order to encourage Leif to forget about it—to live around it rather than pigheadedly through it.

Institutions weren't subtle.

Matthew walked into Leif's kitchenette and opened the cold-water tap. In a building as old as this one, lead seeped into water that sat for any length of time in the pipes, so Matthew let the water run. He opened a cabinet: cereal, canned tomatoes, a bag of lentils, boxes of tea. In a second cabinet he found a glass.

He held a finger under the water, waiting for it to run cold.

The facility itself had turned out not to be terrible. It was disconcerting, whenever Matthew visited, to have to wait between two locked sets of steel-plated doors for an orderly to pat him down. And the food, the times he had shared it, had been farinaceous and had been served on cardboard without even plastic utensils—everything had had to be eaten with fingers. Leif was allowed to wear his own clothes, though, except for belts and shoe-strings, and there was a dayroom with a large window where he and Matthew were able to sit and talk and, if they felt like it, play Scrabble. They had to play at a rather desperate pace—the clock was always ticking—and unfortunately the televisions in the dayroom had cable and were almost always showing something violent, something crudely male—a car crash, a slashing—even though there seemed to be as many women as men in the ward. Leif was developing an ability to ignore the television, but Matthew couldn't master it.

The water having turned cold, Matthew poured himself a glass.

Everything couldn't be perfect, but maybe it would turn out to be good enough.

There wasn't much choice about drugs. Leif said the consensus was that if you were in there, it was inconsiderate to the people who were paying to keep you there for you to say you wanted to try to do without them.

The green of Leif's rocking chair was a practical, civic green—a shade of green that a water pump in a town square might be painted. It didn't seem full-size, but it was too large to be a child's; maybe it was an antique, scaled to an era when people were smaller. Matthew sat down in it, and it sprang forward and slapped his back, but then he found his center of gravity. The blanket on the bed beside it was a black-and-red tartan, cheerful even in the room's dim, hooded atmosphere. He took a sip of the water he had poured. Could Leif get a drink of water at any hour, if he wanted one? Matthew didn't know. Maybe they locked the door to his room at night. But no, they couldn't. None of the interior doors in the facility had locks, not even the bathrooms.

Why had Leif said he had roommates? Something else he had been hiding.

On a dresser beside the rocking chair there was a child's microscope, a solid one, of gunmetal. Solid in a way that gave Matthew the impression that it had been a father's or a grandfather's gift. Next to it was a small pinewood box, and when Matthew flicked up a little brass clasp on the box's front and lifted the lid, inside he found an array of glass slides, shelved in parallel on their sides, making a puzzle of even the diffuse light that fell into their honeycomb.

The trick was to convince Leif to think of the treatment as a gift. It would even be preferable for him to think of it as a gift he hadn't asked for and didn't want, if that would discourage him from worrying about how to repay it. The danger came when Leif was seeing himself as a cost that he could try to cut. If he were gone, he was in the habit of saying, the charges against the others would almost certainly be dropped. He shouldn't be saying this. Even if it was true, saying it was part of the disease.

In the *Arcadia*, when the hero tries to kill himself, his lover can't believe that he's sincere in thinking she'll be better off without him, but in real life maybe this is what a suicide always thinks, if any thought goes to another person at all.

Matthew drew one of the slides out of the box at random. *Kidney cells (human)*, read the label. He filed it back into its grooved place.

After a little searching, he was able to find the books that Leif had asked for. He also found one of Leif's little red passport-size notebooks, one that still had blank pages. He added it and the books to his backpack, which already held books and changes of clothes for himself, as well as the presents for both of them that his mother had mailed to his apartment in the city—needlessly, it had turned out—the week before.

If Leif had died, Matthew thought, without intending to let himself think it, as he pulled out the dresser's middle drawer and a stack of Leif's folded white T-shirts briefly wobbled—if Leif had died, Matthew would have had to come here anyway, to choose clothes for Leif.

Maybe he hadn't used up absolutely all his anger.

What he had been watching all this time was Leif trying to destroy himself. He didn't mean his taking Fosco's medicine, or not just that. He meant the whole effort that Leif had made to open himself to the world and keep himself open to it. Leif had taken off his armor in the middle of battle—in the middle of a war. It probably had something to do with being gay—with not being a man the way men usually were—with having had to learn the rules of combat artificially, the way that autistics have to learn social niceties. It was easy to make a terrible mistake if you weren't by nature a killer, if you were deducing it all from first principles.

Matthew halted his thoughts. It probably wasn't a good idea to do too much thinking here alone, he advised himself.

The hen and chicks—he had almost forgotten. He picked the plant up and ran it quickly under the faucet as if it were an ice cube tray that he was filling. Water beaded up on the pebbles in the medium and on the leaf clusters' indifferent, ingrown faces. He suddenly wondered: Should he *not* be watering it? There were plants that didn't like to be touched with water directly. Would some of the stiff spikes now fur over?

He returned the plant to Leif's desk. He sat down, and with his handkerchief he started to dab away the small mirrored spheres that were now lodged in the folds between the lames of the plant's armor. There were dozens of the spheres, and each one dissolved at the lightest touch of the handkerchief, as soon as its cotton fibers interrupted the integrity of a water-pearl's surface.

This was something he could do, he told himself, as he kept dabbing. This was the sort of task he could safely spend his anger on. Even if he didn't save the plant and even if the plant didn't in fact need saving.

7.

Outside, in the snow, children from the neighborhood were barking taunts at one another. Their plastic sleds quacked beneath them as they sat down, squirmingly, on the hardpack at the heads of the trails. The slope behind the Farrells' backyard ran downhill so steeply that no one had ever built on its few acres, and in neglect the land was so heavily and erratically wooded that to ride down through and between its black trees was genuinely dangerous and enlivening. Back when Elspeth and her brother had run with the neighborhood children, their father had periodically attempted to forbid sledding on the slope as too risky, and it was a legacy of his attempts that the subdivision's children, long after Elspeth and Sam's father had moved away, still skirted along the edges of the Farrells' backyard, instead of tramping diagonally through it, and never looked up at the windows of the house.

With her back to these windows, Elspeth had laid out five cards on her mother's dining room table.

The ace of money   *The ace of cups, inverted*

The eight of staves

The five of money   *The six of staves*

To turn over only number cards was like a commentary on the recent un-deceiving, the working group's great public failure, which shouldn't, strictly speaking, have shaken Elspeth's faith, since she had never thought that she could do anything with numbers.

Because she had never thought they could read the future, either, she had never bothered to learn how most people who used tarot cards actu-ally used them. She had a vague memory that in the configuration she had just laid out one card was supposed to represent old love and one card new, but she didn't know which was which, and she didn't recognize any-one, having had the bad luck to turn over instead of personalities only statistics.

Did it mean anything that the ace of cups was upside down? Of course the other four cards might also be. It was only because the figure on the ace of cups was asymmetrical that its orientation showed. On closer scru-tiny, the ace looked less like a cup than like a castle—a miniature castle with seven turrets—a chatelet so diminutive that it could be held in a single hand. A gilded container for the self, in this case upended. Or maybe it looked more like a throne? An unyielding, high-backed bishop's throne.

There was now always another puzzle for Elspeth under the evident puzzle. Under the question of what a hand of tarot meant there now lay the question of what she thought she was doing. Maybe she was ceding away from herself her own will. Maybe she was hoping to let things say for her what she didn't want to have to say herself. It shouldn't be possible to have a private religion, but maybe a private one was the only honest kind in an era when faith had to be sheltered from so much knowing. From even one's own knowing.

The eight staves that were depicted on the eight of staves card were in-terwoven as if they constituted a net connecting the cards around it. It would take only six lines to connect four points, however, and it would take ten to connect five. *You really are a fact-checker*, Diana kidded whenever Elspeth overexplained—when, for example, she had overexplained that it made more sense to freeze soup in portions that were the size of a single serving than the size of a meal.

Maybe there were eight staves because eight was the smallest number that could be split in half three times: man from woman, mind from body, self from other.

"When's your bus, honey?" her mother asked as she came down the house's narrow central stairs.

"Three seventeen," Elspeth replied, gathering up her cards, to hide them. Her brother had already left, the night before.

"So we should leave here at two forty-five," her mother said.

Her brother had claimed he had a report to write, and Elspeth was going back early in case it was going to be possible to visit Leif in the locked ward. Leif hadn't emailed her back yet. There was a computer in the ward that the residents could take turns using.

It occurred to Elspeth that she should tell Diana she was on her way. Elspeth had been making an effort, which Diana probably hadn't even noticed, not to need to tell Diana everything, but it would be all right to tell her the bus schedule.

"I wish there was something I could do for you," her mother said.

"There's nothing wrong with me, Mom. Nothing has happened to me."

"I know."

"You're paying for my lawyer," Elspeth pointed out.

"That's not what I mean," her mother replied. "How will you get to your friend?"

"There's a train. Matthew can meet me at the station."

"Matthew is his . . . ?"

"Uh-huh."

"D'you find it?" one of the boys outside yelled.

Elspeth's mother's eyes strayed to the windows.

"I'm surprised they still go sledding," Elspeth said, looking over her shoulder at them. "I thought kids only played video games now."

"They take movies," her mother explained, and stuck out a stiff arm as if she were holding up a phone.

As her bus reached one of the lime green metal bridges that join the city to the continent, Elspeth decided it made more sense to go back to her own apartment. Diana hadn't retracted her invitation, but the holiday had made its interruption, and Elspeth felt she could no longer presume that in Diana's eyes she still stood in quite so dire a need of succor.

She checked her phone, in the look-busy way that one does when returning to civilization. Leif still hadn't emailed.

Her roommates were still at their families' houses. In the refrigerator, there was a carton of eggs she had left behind because she had known they would keep. Or she could have peanut butter for dinner. There were two heels of bread in the freezer.

She hadn't sensed anything when it had happened. She had cast back into and combed through her memories pretty thoroughly afterward, hoping to turn up a sliver, at least, of awareness that she could reproach herself for not having paid more attention to, but there hadn't been one. She had been out shopping that day for a Christmas present for Diana, something sincere that wasn't too much. It couldn't be food, which she herself might end up eating. She had found a porcelain tumbler with a streaked, opalescent glaze, but to buy just one would have seemed to say too clearly that she saw Diana as alone. In the end, she had bought a candle.

In return, when they exchanged gifts, Diana had handed over a black-and-white snapshot: a sparrow perched at an angle on a wooden banister. The shadowed grooves of the wood grain were in sharp focus, but the sparrow itself was blurred, the stipples and smudges of its coat faintly doubled. The shutter must have startled it into the intake of breath that precedes flight.

It had been while Elspeth had been buying the stupid candle that Leif had done it.

She decided on peanut butter. She was only good at taking care of other people, not herself. She had to use a knife to pry apart the slices of bread, scattering, as she did so, some of the crystals of rime with which the bread was diamonded. On the counter the crystals wilted, dissolved. The pith of each slice of bread had been bleached to an uncanny, filamentous white by the long storage. She set the toaster to Frozen.

Her phone. "What happened to you?" Diana asked.

"Oh, I came back here," Elspeth said. "To my place."

"Suit yourself."

It was easy for Diana either way. Elspeth turned on the public radio station at a volume audible but not quite intelligible, a known lonely person's strategy.

The thing about what Leif had done, she thought as she sat down at the dining room table with her dry toast and its gluey covering, was that she could just as easily have been the one to try it first. If you didn't know how to take care of yourself, it was the obvious way of taking care of yourself, she thought, and as she had the thought, a surge of self-pity constricted her throat and she had to thump herself on the chest and slip-slide back into the kitchen for a glass of water, which she ought to have poured for herself in the first place.

She drank it at the sink, staring into the black window above it, which reflected the white cabinets behind her but only the outline of herself. The radio chuckled and warbled, far away in the parlor.

The truth, though, was that she liked even peanut butter. She liked knowing that it was waiting for her in the next room, and she didn't like the idea of ever not being able to look forward to eating it again. She understood but maybe she also didn't understand what Leif had tried to do.

In the dark, later that night, Elspeth's body sat up in bed. Somewhere above her, the soul that should have been hers was battering itself against the ceiling like a bird caught inside an airport terminal. Her heart, for the moment empty, was knocking in her chest.

When she tried to think about what was happening to her, she saw the words of her thoughts assembling themselves in anticipation of her thinking them.

"Please don't hang up."

"What time is it?"

"I'm not sure. Oh, it's a quarter to three."

"Is everything all right?"

"I don't think I'm a real person."

"Are you having a nightmare?"

"No, it's—it feels like I'm in a moving car and there's no one in the driver's seat."

"Are you asleep?"

"I don't think so."

"Maybe we should just keep talking," Diana said.

"Okay."

"What should I say?"

"Anything."

"My mother has an heirloom she wants to give me. A lace tablecloth that her mother gave to her. She wants to give it to me, but she also seems to be afraid I'll ruin it somehow. She's being impossible."

Elspeth listened silently. After a while, the squirrelly emptiness inside her ran itself out, like a windup toy running out the tension in its spring.

Her reunion with herself, when it came, was as casual as stretching out her arms into the sleeves of a coat.

The next morning, she wondered if the experience had been a side effect of her gift. It had been a little like losing one's place in a book.

In the afternoon, an email came at last from Matthew saying that Leif did want her to come; his hospital stay was being renewed. They had held off so long on inviting her, Matthew explained, by way of apology, because first everything had been too chaotic and then for a while it had looked as if Leif might be allowed to go home. But there were still a couple of issues that everyone agreed he should continue to work on.

The use of the word *everyone* didn't seem to be ironic; it sounded to Elspeth like a child's identification with the grown-ups in his life. If it was Leif's word, too, then it betrayed a wish on Leif's part to be seen as safely on the side of the responsible authorities. She wondered if she was going to lose him, the distinct person in him she had loved—but she cut herself short: it would be vulgar to turn his misfortune into an opportunity for her to have feelings.

She replied to the email, arranging for a visit on Saturday, which was going to be New Year's Eve. She didn't mention the holiday.

Diana said she was going to be having dinner with a colleague that evening but invited Elspeth to sleep on her couch when she got back to the city. It was something to look forward to.

The train lumbered past mudflats, snow-frostinged scrapyards, fenced-off lawns, and, once, a pen with two swaybacked gray horses. Elspeth kept her knapsack on the seat beside her, taking out only a book, which she held but couldn't let her guard down sufficiently to read.

There was so much time to kill out here that people had shoveled the parking lots, which were mostly empty.

The journey reminded her of John Clare's escape from his asylum. Clare had tried to walk back to a past that in his madness he thought he remembered, only to discover that the woman he recalled as his wife was dead. In real, sane life, he had married a different woman. Maybe a caretaker had more trouble than other people forgetting the lives he hadn't lived because to him those lives didn't seem any less real.

Her heart beat so sharply when she felt the train halting at her destination that she wondered if she was going to lose touch with herself again. But she didn't.

Matthew's fists were balled in his pockets. His beard had gone scraggly, but his sunglasses were still decorative.

"Can I carry that for you?" he offered.

"I've got it." She couldn't remember whether he and she usually hugged.

The doors of the sedan he was driving were heavy but easy. Inside, it seemed very parental, very stiffly cushioned. Warm chimes sounded as the engine cleared its throat and hummed into life.

"Excuse me," he said as he put his arm on the back of her seat and looked over his shoulder. She watched the progress, or rather, regress, in the mirror on her side.

If she lost touch with herself while she was in the ward, maybe they would keep her. Once, accompanying a friend to the emergency room, she had fainted at the sight of her friend's blood spurting into a syringe, and because she had hit her head, the nurse had insisted on admitting her.

"How's he doing?" she asked.

"He's all right, now that they've mostly figured out his medication."

On the roof of every house a shelf of snow was draining into icicles, the top of the shelf sagging under the melt like the swaybacks of the horses she had seen.

It was hard not to relax in such a comfortable vehicle.

"How are you doing?" Matthew asked. He was a handsome man, but a part of her still didn't know if she trusted him.

"I can't believe I didn't know."

"You couldn't have known," he replied.

They were taking an on-ramp.

"Are we going straight there?" she asked, sitting forward.

"We might as well. Is that all right?"

"Is there anything I shouldn't say?" she asked.

"I don't know," Matthew said. "I already told him that the internet thinks he's in a CIA black-site prison."

He steered the sedan onto a fork that began to spiral gently downward. Beyond the highway guardrails, the white towers of a medical center revolved at a stately pace.

What would Leif be like? Elspeth couldn't find him in her mind. Maybe she hadn't been aware when he had done it because for some time now she had been letting him go.

Well, he had committed a crime. Everyone but she and Matthew had.

Why was she so fucking law-abiding?

At the parking lot entrance, Matthew pulled a ticket from the mouth of a dispenser.

He already had a little bit of a belly, which she pretended not to see, fixing her eyes insistently on his. Patients around them were staring, perhaps envious of his having a visitor.

"Where's Matthew?" he greeted her by asking.

"He's in the car. He said he had talked to you about me coming up first, but I can go get him if you want."

"Oh, that's right." He led her into what seemed to be a sort of social area, a collocation of small tables, one or two of which held board games in tidy, edge-worn boxes. There were more board games in a small bookshelf nearby. As if they were in the living room of a summer house. "Do you want a window or an aisle seat?" he asked.

"Maybe not so near the TV," she suggested.

"Here, you face away."

"No, that's okay," she protested, but he thumped a place for her.

The walls were greenish bronze color, like that of a car from the 1950s. She had had the idea, perhaps from movies, that the walls would be white. She was carrying her coat in a ball—she had had to take it off when they searched her—and she untangled it and draped it over the back of the chair.

"Thank you for coming," he said, as she sat down.

She remembered his telling her that he would never go back to jail. "Don't be silly," she said.

He seemed to be the same person. Maybe a little more subdued than she remembered. His face, like his stomach, was maybe ever so slightly more padded.

"You have that real-world glow," he said. "That's what they're looking at."

"I'm sorry."

"You'll lose it in a few minutes and they'll leave you alone."

She admired the view out the window. Snowed-over landscaping surrounded the medical center like a moat; almost no footsteps dotted the snow. At the base of the tower that they were in lay a rectangle of white that was outlined and crossed by traces that suggested the palisades and terrace of a lost garden. A hundred years ago there would have been staff wheeling patients into the garden every morning and every afternoon.

"How's it going?" she asked.

"When I was twelve I had a fantasy that I was going to be a paraplegic, and it's a little like that."

"That doesn't sound good."

"No no, it was going to be great. I was going to be all at once Christ, Dostoyevsky's Idiot, and the debonair victim of a terrible skiing accident. My body was trying to make me at long last male, and I wasn't having any of it. I didn't want to sin—I didn't even want to *want* to sin—so instead I was going to be unable to move my legs. It was going to be amazing."

"And it's like that now?"

"I'm not being serious," he said. "Did you know Matthew didn't fool around with another boy until he was twenty?"

"Are they trying to make you straight?" she whispered.

"No no no. Don't worry. I just feel a little immobilized."

"I see," she said.

"What I mean is I'm not sure it's therapeutic for me not to be able to tell the difference between am I better and am I not able to get into any trouble."

"I see," she said again. He was fighting with himself, and he was putting on a show, were her two impressions. "Is it distracting here?" she asked. "With all the people?"

"It's writers' colony rules," he said. "You decide when you want to leave your room, and no one can come into your room without a prior invitation."

"So you can keep your focus."

"Yeah," he said, but he looked away. "You know, if you want to say anything, you can. I can handle it, and if I can't handle it, well, I'm in here."

It was hard to take the invitation at face value.

"I have something that *I* want to say," he continued, "and it's that I'm sorry. Even though my therapist isn't sure I should say it."

"Sorry for—for taking the medicine?"

"No. I mean, yes of course I am sorry for that, but that's not what I mean. The medicine itself turned out to be the hardest thing to fix, by the way. The vet told Matthew she wouldn't write a new prescription for Fosco without a police report, and there wasn't one, so I had to sign a HIPAA to turn my medical records over to the vet. The woman in Records here thought it was hilarious."

"I was afraid for you," she said.

"I'm sorry," he said. "But what I'm really sorry for is that I put you at risk when—"

"Nothing happened to me."

"Maybe my therapist is right. She thinks all of us were in a system together. She thinks we were acting like a family. According to her, I don't know enough yet to apologize."

"You don't have to apologize."

"That's not the same thing. The whether to apologize and the what to apologize for. Her opinion is that it might take me a little time to redraw my boundaries. Maybe I had previously been drawing them too encompassingly, when really the part that I can do anything about might turn out to be in fact even smaller than what most people think, let alone than what the group we were in was thinking."

"Smaller how?"

"What she says is that it's sometimes the followers of a sect who create the leader out of the most suggestible member."

There was nothing but his usual, now ever so slightly ruined prettiness in his face. He didn't seem aware that he had landed a blow. Maybe the drugs interfered with his natural delicacy.

"She's never met any of us," Elspeth said in defense. But almost as quickly as hurt and anger had overtaken her, they were dissipating. Leif was hiding his gift by using it to read from his doctors what they wanted to hear. He was still using it to make connections with people important to him.

"It's just an interpretation she's offering," he said. "It's not meant to be 'the truth.'"

Elspeth nodded. She had to be careful not to take away from him anything he might need.

For the rest of the day she held Leif's betrayal tight and close, as if it were a small animal whose teeth and claws she did not want to give an opportunity to. For dinner, back in her apartment, while she waited for Diana to be freed of her colleague, she thawed a block of chicken soup and sliced an avocado. While she stood over the soup, nudging it with a wooden spoon, she grew annoyed at her own sighing. It ended up being a good dinner, plain as it was, despite being a solitary one.

Before she left for Diana's, she texted. It turned out that Diana's colleague had canceled. Elspeth had been alone for the past few hours for no reason.

On the subway people were bristling with the holiday's angry energy, the aggrandizing sloppiness with which it was acceptable for one night to mark public places as one's own. It was the holiday of leaving behind—the holiday of not caring, of violently discarding—and in principle Elspeth admired the celebrants' selfishness and ferocity.

Raleigh had texted her Happy New Year, she saw when she came out of the subway.

Children were picking icicles from the blue bars of a scaffolding.

"It's candy!" one exclaimed.

"It's not *candy*," another replied, a little scornfully.

On the top floor of Diana's brownstone, the door was ajar.

"I'm putting a pie in the oven," Diana explained, coming out from behind her peninsular counter. She and Elspeth kissed amicably. "Should we open a bottle?"

There were dustings of flour on the countertop, the movement of Diana's hands recorded in swirls and sprays. "Oh, do your pie first."

"It's going to be apple-raspberry. I put bitters in, but I don't know if that's right because I put lemon zest in, too."

"It sounds amazing."

"Bitters might be trying too hard."

"I'm putting my coat on your bed," Elspeth announced, walking back to the small room where Diana slept, unwinding her scarf as she went. She laid her parka across the duvet, specifically across the foot of the duvet, wondering as she did so whether in her imagination she was neutering the piece of furniture or hiding it or staking a claim.

"I remembered to make the dough last night," Diana said. She was pressing a pale stiff sheet of it into the circular elbow of a pie dish, folding the draped excess onto the lip as she went. "Do you want to open that?" she asked again, nodding at a bottle that bore a print of her palm in flour. "How was Leif?" She tumbled fruit into the crust's hollow.

"He's adapting," Elspeth said. She was going to be as cheerful about it as the children she had seen outside.

"Adapting how?"

"He doesn't believe anymore." Under the wrapper on the neck of the bottle, there was just a screwtop.

"Doesn't believe?"

A second sheet of pie dough came out of the refrigerator, this time on a flat plate. Diana's knife ran through it.

"What's that for?" Elspeth asked.

"The lattice."

"Science," Elspeth said.

Diana peeled a strip from the plate and draped it over the dome of raspberries and apples.

The landline rang. "Can you get it?" Diana asked. A second strip was already looped through her fingers.

Elspeth carried her glass with her.

"Happy New Year," said an older woman's voice, when Elspeth picked up. "This is Mrs. Watkins."

"Oh, Happy New Year, Mrs. Watkins," Elspeth returned. *Is it all right?* she mouthed to Diana, pointing at the receiver.

Diana shrugged. "Tell her hi for me."

"I'll get to her in a minute," said the voice in the phone. "But right now you tell me who *you* are and what it is *you* study at the university."

"I don't go to school here, actually. My name is Elspeth, and I met Diana at a protest."

"Oh, that's right. She did tell me about you. At the Occupy. You all were doing good works."

"Well, I hope we were."

"Feeding the hungry—isn't that the Lord's work?"

Elspeth didn't know how to reply.

"Tell me, Elizabeth, what kind of upbringing did you have?"

"It was in a small town," Elspeth said, trying to be equal to the question. "I went to the public school. My father left when I was ten. Is that what you mean?"

"Just you and your mother, then."

"And my brother."

"Two of you, my."

"He turned out okay, at least. Does Diana have any brothers or sisters?"

"She's my only lamb. Let me talk to her now. So good to make your acquaintance."

There was a musical scraping as the oven yawned and Diana put in the pie. Elspeth handed over the phone.

"Happy New Year, Mama," Diana said.

Elspeth ran the faucet and began to wash dishes.

"Apple raspberry, with bitters and lemon zest," Diana told her mother, as she sat on the sofa still in her apron, with a look of concentration on her face. "Well, this is a different recipe," she said, turning away as if to shield the conversation somewhat.

It was almost sad, Elspeth thought, the way parents continue to care about matters they no longer have a say in. It wasn't a holiday on which Elspeth's own mother made a point of calling.

"She is," she heard Diana say.

"Some of which young people?" she heard Diana ask.

Elspeth held the sponge under running water, to rinse away a leaf of flour that had caked up in it.

"I did," Diana said. And then: "I would be. Of course. You have a good New Year's, too, Mama." Diana carried the receiver to its cradle and set it in place.

"Is she worried?" Elspeth asked.

"She worries." Diana retrieved her drink.

"She asked about my upbringing."

"She was trying to figure out what kind of a Christian you are."

It hadn't occurred to Elspeth to identify her denomination. "We were Lutheran. What about you?"

"She's a Pentecostal accountant. It's probably why I'm a sociologist. I had to figure out what it meant when she spoke in tongues."

"Could you understand her?"

"People can only understand if they're inspired, too. But my theory at the time was that it was mathematics."

"Because she was an accountant?"

"I had a teacher who told me it was the language of God. I think I think of it now as a way of beginning certain kinds of conversations. Of licensing certain conversations. Like with your group."

"With us? At Occupy?"

"When you were all witchy together. I mean conversations that need to seem to come out of nowhere, conversations that don't work unless they seem to fall out of the sky."

"I see," Elspeth said. She wet the sponge again and swabbed the counter a second time. She returned the sponge to its little holster in the sink.

"Sometimes describing an experience from the outside can seem cold to someone who knows it from the inside," Diana said.

"No, maybe they are similar," Elspeth considered.

"It may be just that they're both experiences that I'm not going to share."

"Is your mother all right with your being—?"

"She's been informed. She's waiting for the phase to pass. She's always willing to forgive."

Elspeth nodded. "Wait—did we—what time is it?"

In fact, they hadn't missed midnight. Diana hadn't set the timer for the pie, either, but she checked on it through the window in the front of the oven until she guessed that it was time to lower the temperature and shift the pie to the center rack. Elspeth found a radio station broadcasting the countdown and turned the volume low but not so low that they wouldn't be able to hear when the chanting of the crowd became rhythmic.

At midnight, as the white noise of the crowd resolved into pulses, they toasted and shyly kissed.

"It's nicer when a girl kisses a girl," Elspeth observed.

"New year indeed," Diana commented.

"Oh, that's not what I mean."

"Careful, then."

"It's just that I never tried it before."

"Didn't you ever experiment?" Diana asked.

"I thought it would be taking advantage."

"Of who?"

But that night it didn't go any further.

On Monday, the first working day of the New Year, Elspeth took on a new fact-checking assignment, and by the end of the week, her replacement laptop, which she had financed by credit card, was full of galleys of the article to be checked and PDFs of the writer's sources, and her dining room table was littered with thesis-clipped printouts and books whose pages were flagged with orange, pink, and blue stickies—a colonization of the common space that was her prerogative as the roommate with the most seniority, the only one of the original tenants still on the lease. As a courtesy, however, because she still thought her roommates were likely to return any day now, she collapsed the array into a stack every evening, placing each set of pages at a ninety-degree angle to the set beneath for ease of disarticulation the next morning, and stored the stack in the nook that had once been a dumbwaiter. Many nights she rode the subway to Diana's, where they took turns cooking dinner. Afterward, there was sometimes a TV show; then, oblivion on Diana's sofa. She slept so deeply that it was as though for an interval she was deleted.

She went so often in part because she didn't want to be alone if she woke up again vacated by her soul. She needed that much help—a thread around her pinky that was tied at the other end around someone else's. Diana didn't seem to mind, at least so far. Elspeth knew she needed to keep in mind that Diana was a lesbian. She also needed to guard against assuming that as a white person she had an automatic right to Diana's attention. But if she asked too often whether it was okay to visit, she risked sounding uncomfortable with leaning so heavily on someone who wasn't straight and wasn't white. Raleigh kept calling, meanwhile, asking for coffee or lunch. She kept putting him off, but she sometimes wondered whether, if she couldn't otherwise find a way to maintain her balance, it was becoming something like her duty to try returning to him.

She continued whenever she had a spare hour or two to sort through the files on the server of the working group's hacked and still-shuttered blog, where Leif and she and very occasionally the others had once tried to explain themselves to the world. She reread what they had written; she excised what had been contaminated; she rebuilt what had been damaged. It was an available penance, even if it wasn't clear that anyone but she felt that it was called for. It was a way, too, of maintaining a connection to her friends and what they had been together. As tasks go, it wasn't as difficult as Raleigh and Jeremy had made out that it would be. It was tedious, but it was like doing one's taxes oneself: one had to investigate every ramification, but in most cases the liability turned out to be zero, and even when it was nonzero every individual step in the remedy was simple and easily taken, so long as one took no more than one step at a time. When one didn't understand, one googled; there was always a support forum where the question at issue had been asked and answered; eventually, one understood. She put the site in a "sandbox." She set about "hardening" it. And then, at last, she went "live" with it again, moving in metaphor from childhood through the tempering of steel to resurrection— well, either resurrection or eyewitness news. Although to a casual browser of the web the restored site looked the same, it had been invisibly fortified.

She was pleased with her work, and she couldn't think of any reason not to talk about it, even to the press. The site was public, after all. Even while it had been down, conspiracy-minded commenters had been able to spider and quote from a partial mirror captured long ago in an internet archive. Her refurbishment didn't expose anything new. She thought that by talking to reporters about it she might be able to win the members of the working group some goodwill. She told Diana that she was thinking of calling the print reporter with the scrunchie, the one who had been less of an ambulance chaser than the others.

Elspeth was innocent, after all. She was so innocent that every morning, the backup program that Raleigh had installed on his and Elspeth's old laptops sent her an email warning that it had been forty-nine days since the last successful backup of their hard drives—fifty days—fifty-one days—and she never clicked. The government had taken her laptop, and she respected their seizure even when it came to the laptop's digital reflection. Her restraint didn't have anything to do with the authorities' threats. They didn't even know that she almost certainly still had access, through the backup program, to the files that had caused all the trouble, the ones that Raleigh, Leif, Julia, and Chris had downloaded that night from Bresser's server. They didn't know that every morning she chose again not to look at the files.

She never drew on her gift for her own advantage, either, and it, too, was invisible to them and always there.

She was like a winged creature proud of having made a promise to herself that even if hunted she will not take to the skies. She lived by her own choice in a world that they didn't even know it was possible to escape.

She offered Stacey Temple a seat on her great-aunt's sofa. For the last dozen years of her great-aunt's life, the thermostat had been turned up so high that the sofa's frame had cracked, and when Elspeth's mother had the sofa reupholstered, the fractures in the frame had been soldered together clumsily, and the sofa now existed, confusingly, in a limbo between decay and repair, lacking many of the associations that had once made it dear but not quite elevated to the anonymous functionality that would have made it respectable.

Elspeth brought out a tray with two mugs of chamomile tea and a small plate of store-bought gingerbread cookies. The journalist was already taking notes on her steno pad. She seemed to be studying what she was sitting on.

"Are you writing about the furniture?" Elspeth asked.

"Just scene-setting."

"Oh, of course," Elspeth granted. She knew the kinds of shortcuts writers took; she had fact-checked so many of them. It was a good thing she had put away the tarot deck. "Thank you, you know. For advising me, before."

"Oh," the woman said. "You're welcome." She remembered to smile. "So none of it is new?"

"The furniture?"

"The website."

"Had you read all of it before?" Elspeth asked.

"My concern is whether I'll be able to convince my editor that there's a story here."

"I see," Elspeth said.

"But let's talk for now, since I'm here," the woman said. She set her digital recorder on the coffee table and lit its light. "Where were you when you discovered you had been hacked?"

She had been at Diana's. "I don't remember," Elspeth lied. "Here, I guess."

"And how did you feel? It must have been so upsetting."

"Oh, I was angry," Elspeth said. "But they were like naughty children." She took a cookie for herself and broke off one of its stubby paws. "They probably won't like my saying that. What I mean is, it was hard to stay angry at them." The woman wrote steadily in her pad even though the recorder continued to signal unblinkingly that it was listening. She wasn't writing prose but was positioning individual words on the page in a pattern that must have been meaningful to her. "You take notes, too?" Elspeth asked.

"It helps me think," Temple said. "And, you know, in case. And you dehacked—do you think that's the word?"

"I don't know."

"You dehacked the site yourself?"

"I was given some guidance by Jeremy, who runs the other website."

"'Free the Telepathy Four'?"

"Is that what it's called now?" Elspeth asked.

"I think the URL is something about a working group."

"That sounds more like it."

"Do you have a background in computers?"

"They weren't super malicious or anything. It wasn't that hard. Especially if you're a nerd. Diana says I should have been an engineer."

"Who's Diana?"

"Just a friend," Elspeth said. "Don't put her in, please."

"Are you not out?"

"Oh, that's not it. But she's been helping me because she's a friend not because she was in the working group."

"I see," the journalist said.

"I mean, she was in a different working group with me. It probably doesn't matter. But if you could leave her out."

"What if I describe her without naming her? Is she one of your roommates?"

"No. She lives in the city, uptown. Although I have been staying with her a lot, lately, to be honest."

"But I can't use any of this."

"No. Sorry."

Temple drew a vertical line along the left-hand side of the page. "So tell me something I can use," she said.

"Well, I think something very interesting is the paradox that when the hackers put up their message calling us 'nothingfags'—can you print that?"

"The copy desk will come up with a write-around."

"I wonder what it will be," Elspeth said. "'An expletive suggesting over-fondness without a motive.'"

"Something like that," the journalist admitted.

"But 'overfondness' could be 'whore,'" Elspeth said.

"They'll leave it if it's integral."

"The paradox," Elspeth tried again, "is that when they, the hackers, put up their message accusing us of standing for nothing, they put it up *over* the messages where we had tried to spell out what we thought we stood for."

"About telepathy," Temple suggested.

"The posts weren't about telepathy."

"I don't know if that's strictly—"

"Well, to say what we meant, maybe sometimes we said a little more than we meant," Elspeth replied.

The journalist took the time to write down Elspeth's answer word for word.

"I thought you were—," Elspeth began, but broke off.

"What?" Temple asked.

"Forget it."

"I can take it. I'm a journalist."

"No, you're right," Elspeth said. "You have to be able to be challenging."

"This website was up before, and what I'm wondering is, if they didn't hear you the first time, why do you think they'll hear you now?"

"Maybe they didn't want to hear it before," Elspeth said.

"And why will they now?"

"I don't know. Maybe they won't. But isn't it news, what we actually meant? Everyone keeps saying they wish they knew what we actually meant."

"You just said you didn't mean it literally."

"A lot of it is literal," Elspeth protested. "The part where we said everyone probably knows more about what each other are feeling than we usually let on, and if we let ourselves know that we know, the world would probably be a better place—that was literal."

"But I don't know if it's news." Temple drew a double line in her steno pad. "I mean, it'll be up to my editor."

"It's lucky," said Elspeth's lawyer, Dominique Blount. "One of our paralegals is your size." Someone's dry cleaning was hanging on the back of the door to her office. The lawyer slid up the plastic wrapper that ensleeved the clothes.

"You want me to wear it?" Elspeth asked.

It was a gray wool skirt-suit. "Wouldn't it look a little more formal?" Blount asked.

Elspeth felt bad for the woman it had been taken from, whoever she was, who had been told that her outfit looked as appropriate for an object of the law as for a subject of it. The least Elspeth could do was try it on.

In the handicapped stall of the echoing women's room, she clicked the hanger onto a coat hook. The fabric of the suit was heavy but limp and had the mildly tangy, olive-like smell of cleaning solvents. She wondered if she would have been offered a stranger's clothes if she had been a man. But maybe if she had been a man she would already own an outfit that was in the genre of a uniform, and someone like Dominique Blount would be confident that society had trained her to wear it in such situations unprompted.

No, she realized. They would tell a man like Chris what to wear. He probably didn't own a suit, either.

Once she had struggled into the gray wool, she faced the mirror over the bathroom's sinks. The shoulders were a little boxy. The waist of the skirt was right, but she didn't quite fill the bell of it; the woman it had been stripped from must have a bit more figure in the rear. Oh well. Tugged askew by the heavier fabric of the jacket, her own blouse looked weak and shapeless.

She shrugged off the jacket; she wriggled out of the skirt. Maybe something would happen between now and tomorrow morning that would save her from having to wear it.

Any of the women who smiled at her as she carried it back to her lawyer's office could have been its owner.

"It doesn't fit?" Blount asked, when she saw Elspeth in her own clothes. Blount herself was wearing slate blue that day.

"No, it fits."

The lawyer considered Elspeth and the suit in Elspeth's hands. "I think it could be helpful," she said.

Elspeth nodded, folding the suit over her arm. They stood in awkward silence for a moment.

"So we're all set for tomorrow?" the lawyer asked. Blount had set up a meeting with Somerville where Elspeth would be able to tell him her side of the story. Elspeth was even going to be given immunity. "The US Attorneys' Office is just five hundred yards from our front door, so if we meet here at nine fifteen, that should give us plenty of time to take the elevator down and pass through security and so forth. If you bring your phone, remember you'll have to leave it here."

"Why are they doing this for us, again?"

"They want to find out what you know," the lawyer said. "They're willing to see if they can work something out."

"But I don't know anything."

"You know what happened to you," Blount said. "There might be a part of it that's useful."

Everyone wanted her to be useful. "I want him to see that there's no reason for any of this."

"Well, it's a chance for him to hear your side of things."

"So there's a risk but maybe also a benefit. Like talking to a reporter."

Blount laughed. "I wouldn't go that far."

"I talked to one this morning."

"You did what."

"Stacey Temple interviewed me this morning."

The lawyer's eyes shifted to a stack of manila folders on her desk. The cover of the folder on top arced and draped gracefully, and a little revealingly of the documents inside.

"Is that all right?" Elspeth asked.

Blount had turned so pale that the blush on her face was visible as only paint and seemed to float over and somewhat apart from the surface of her skin. "If it already happened . . ."

"She's probably not going to run it," Elspeth said. "She didn't think it was really news. Their standards are very high over there."

"He calls and yells," Blount said.

"I'm sorry."

"Oh god," Blount continued, to herself, apparently contemplating the things that were going to be yelled at her.

"Why does he care if I talk?" Elspeth asked. "I thought he wanted me to talk."

"It's *his case*," the lawyer said.

Elspeth's soul became disengaged from her body again that night. When she realized that it had happened, she was in the middle of dreaming that transparent tunnels were being dug through the sky. She felt Diana's hand on her wrist, which woke her up. She must have cried out in her sleep. "Can you see them?" she asked Diana.

"Do you want me to turn on a light?"

"I won't be able to still see them if you turn on the light."

Diana waited while Elspeth finished staring up at the sky that wasn't in the ceiling above Diana's sofa. In the dream, she had been in one of the tunnels at the same time that she was looking at them from below. Were they the timelines in the recurring dream of Raleigh's that Matthew had told her about? She didn't like the idea that she was still receiving thoughts of Raleigh's so strongly. But maybe the tunnels or something like them were nowadays in many people's minds. In the dream she had understood that no one who was in a tunnel ever left it. Each one came to an end with its digger still inside.

In her nervousness she had put on espadrilles, even though it was January, and her feet, under the table, were now wet and cold, soaked through by slush.

"There's you," Thomas Somerville, the assistant US attorney, was saying, "and there are the defendants, and there's me and there's the government, but there's also the law, and there's the fact that we may be setting precedents here, and I don't want any more than you do to do anything that would limit or impair the protections that the law will continue to be able to offer to free speech in the future. Agreed?"

She was afraid that the point of his question might be to get her into the habit of agreement. "What do you mean?" she asked.

"Do you agree?"

Somerville as a man was a figure blossoming into middle age. He was plethoric and had broad shoulders and was beginning to be heavy. His teeth were arranged in almost military order, his new weight pushed out tight what would have been wrinkles in a less glossy complexion, and his head of hair was still full enough, his forelock still sufficiently *jaillissant*, that Elspeth thought he would be able to carry himself under the device of it without embarrassment for another ten years, at least, though not, there were signs, forever.

It was patent that he wasn't the sort of person who is ever persuaded by being shown the other side of an issue.

"Do you agree?" Blount, seated to Elspeth's right, unhelpfully repeated.

"I'm not sure I understand what I'm being asked to agree with."

"Look," Somerville said. "What I've got in mind here is that a settlement would not create a precedent. It would not make case law that would force anyone's hand later, and maybe that's something that all of us agree we would prefer."

"Why are you asking me about this?" Elspeth asked. "I'm not accused of anything, am I?"

Though Elspeth and he had only just started talking, his eyes were wide with exasperation. While deciding how to reply, he left his mouth open. "A case like this is always evolving," he said quietly.

"If your office is contemplating charges against my client—," Blount began.

"No, come on, look. I don't rule that out, I can't. It's my job. We'll get to that later if we need to, but maybe we won't need to, okay? Right now what I'm trying to talk about is the larger picture, because my read on you, Elzbeth, is that you're an idealist."

Like many people with an uncommon name, she had trained herself not to correct mispronunciations.

"Can you agree with me on that at least?" he asked.

"It's kind of you to say that."

"'It's kind of me to say that'?" he repeated, as if he wanted her to believe that her reply had wounded him.

"I'd like to talk about the larger picture, too," Elspeth said. "This whole case is a—it's a—"

"Go on," he prompted.

"It's a show trial and a witch hunt."

"Really. Interesting. According to what I've been reading online lately, I'm an ogre of fantastical proportions. So if there's a witch hunt, then I'm the object of it, Ms. Farrell. And there's definitely not a show trial here. What I've been trying to explain to you for the past fifteen minutes is that I for one would like for there not to be any more show, if possible, than there has already been."

"I haven't commented on the case online."

"I'm glad to hear it. There's been entirely too much comment already. And I can tell you I'm not the only one who feels that way."

It was fortunate that no article about her by Stacey Temple had yet appeared in the newspaper.

"What do you really even think that the accused did?" Elspeth asked.

"You want to know my theory of the case?" he asked. "Sorry, Elzbeth. We are here today for you to tell me what you *know* they did."

"I wasn't there."

"But you felt confident lecturing me a moment ago about what they *didn't* do? I hope you've got a little more for me than games with words, Elzbeth, because those can be very dangerous for someone in your position. This is our chance to talk. Our one chance. Shall we get started?"

Elspeth shrugged.

"Let me amend that," he said. "This is *your* one chance. I'm still giving you the benefit of the doubt, by the way, for the record. And it's *very kind* of me to say that to you, under the circumstances."

"We're very appreciative that you're willing to give us this meeting, Tom," Blount said.

"Thank you for that, Dominique," Somerville replied.

He rather demonstratively opened a manila folder, full of printouts. Elspeth was capable of reading text upside down, but the table between them was so large that the words were too far away for her to pick them out.

"Maybe we could begin by establishing how long you've known Leif Saunderson."

"What does that have to do with the case?" Elspeth challenged him.

Somerville sighed. He leaned forward. "Do you know what this meeting is for?"

"It's reasonable," Blount intervened, "if we try to narrow the scope a little, in the interest of Elspeth's privacy."

"But does she know what the meeting is for?" Somerville asked. "This is called a proffer meeting, what we're having," he told Elspeth, his voice raised, "because you're *proffering* to me your evidence—you're offering to let me use it in court, *if* I'm interested—but it's impossible for me to figure out whether I *am* interested unless and until I get to see what it is you're trying to sell. That's the situation between us right now."

"I thought . . . ," Elspeth began.

"What did you think?"

"I thought it was so we could talk."

"Exactly. We're talking."

"I thought that if we talked you'd see that we were just kids."

"Last time I checked, all the defendants were competent adults." Somerville took his phone out of his pocket and without apologizing for the interruption started typing. He seemed to be sending a text. "When did you first meet Leif Saunderson?" he resumed.

"Our sophomore year," Elspeth said helplessly. Blount had sold her out.

"College or high school?"

"College."

"What year was this?"

"Two thousand six? We were in the same ceramics class."

"Ceramics—like, pottery?"

"Like pottery," she confirmed. The detail didn't seem to be to his liking, which was a small consolation.

"So you were both artists."

"Well, no, we both discovered we weren't. Our bowls kept blowing up in the kiln."

"Blowing up?"

"If there are any air pockets in the clay, it blows up when you fire it. It's normal. It's not a terrorist thing."

"'Not a terrorist thing,' did you get that?" Somerville asked a voiceless assistant of his, who was taking notes on a yellow legal pad at the end of the table.

"They can't use any of this, right?" Elspeth asked Blount.

Somerville answered for her: "Only if you try to give any testimony in court that contradicts what you say to us today."

"That's accurate, yes," Blount murmured.

"I thought you said I had immunity. What if I say in court, Oops, actually I took ceramics in two thousand seven?"

There was a sharp rap at the door. "Come in," Somerville ordered.

"Pardon me, sir," said a young man in a suit and tie. "I had a feeling you'd want to be made aware of this."

Somerville didn't get up. His face took on an impassive expression, which Elspeth sensed was somehow for her benefit, as the man, who must have been on Somerville's staff, leaned over, bracing himself against his thigh with one hand and with the other shielding his mouth as he spoke inaudibly into one of Somerville's ears. The man's tie slipped away from him and dangled.

"When did this come in?" Somerville asked.

Stacey Temple must have published her article after all.

"Just now."

Somerville's eyes were on Elspeth. "Mm-hmm," he said.

She was watching a playlet, she sensed. It didn't matter that she could tell because it was almost certainly fooling Blount and because as a play it was capable of moving its audience even if the audience was cognizant of the artifice of it.

"So apparently," Somerville resumed, "the person I should be asking you about is Raleigh Evans." He watched Elspeth for a reaction.

"Raleigh who was my boyfriend?" Elspeth asked. Raleigh's name sounded so unfamiliar coming out of Somerville's mouth.

"I'm willing to keep talking with the understanding that we have," Somerville said, "but it's probably my responsibility to tell you that according to what my people are telling me, Ms. Farrell here may well have exposed herself to a charge of accessory before the fact."

"How? By sleeping with my boyfriend?" She was a little surprised by herself. It wasn't like her to be so intemperate.

"If there's new testimony concerning Mr. Evans . . . ," Blount interjected.

"We have reason to believe he was using Ms. Farrell's provision for wireless internet access when he was planning his attack."

"Using my Wi-Fi?" Elspeth asked. "That's supposed to be a thing? Are you serious?"

"Maybe you'd enjoy the challenge of explaining to a jury of your peers what it means to run a private wireless internet server in your own home?"

"Everybody has Wi-Fi," Elspeth said.

"I think you'll find that everybody doesn't."

"Elspeth, I would advise that we—," Blount began.

"He's bluffing," Elspeth said. "It's just Wi-Fi, and anyway there was never any 'attack.' Our working group's whole philosophy was that there couldn't be an attack from people like us, for the very reason that we were able to perceive what we were able to perceive. Instead of the old idea of privacy, there has to be a new moral understanding, which people like us have to feel our way into. That's what we believed. We didn't believe in 'attacks.'"

"This was your personal philosophy?"

"It was the working group's," Elspeth said. She saw Somerville glance at his assistant to check that he was getting down what Elspeth was saying; she sensed Blount wishing to restrain her. "I'm not telling you anything new. All of this is on our blog."

"Which blog is that?"

"The working group's blog. The one that was hacked after the arrests and that I spent the last few weeks fixing."

"Your working group kept a blog?" Somerville reached down to the floor to draw a laptop out of his satchel.

"Elspeth . . . ," Blount softly warned, too late.

They waited in silence for Somerville's laptop to boot up. It chimed, hummed, whirred.

He tilted his head up in order to look at the screen through the bottom of his glasses.

"You mean you've been investigating us all this time," Elspeth said, "and you didn't know until I said it just now that we had a blog?"

"Who wrote it?" Somerville asked. "It looks very interesting."

"It was mostly Leif's."

"It's his philosophy?" Somerville asked, but he didn't insist on an answer from her. From the darting of his eyes it was evident that he was now looking at the website himself. "'The New Morality of Privacy.' Is that what I should be looking at?"

She didn't reply.

"Here," he said, pointing at the screen. "'The idea of privacy isn't logical anymore.' Oh this is good, Elzbeth. This is really good, thank you. 'We're in relation, so in order to say my truth, I also have to say yours, or at least a face of yours.' That's gold, right there. That's him saying the laws don't apply to him."

"That's not what he's saying."

"He's saying he has the right to any information that speaks to him. That's justifying the crime before the fact."

"That's not the way he meant it. He says 'face of yours.'"

"It seems pretty clear to me."

"He didn't even think it would be possible for one of us to read something unless we were part of what we were reading somehow and it was right for us to be part of it."

"So if you're able to read it," Somerville said, "then you have the right to read it, and it doesn't matter what the law says."

"No, it's not like that."

Somerville smiled and didn't respond.

"I'm letting you go," Elspeth said when she and Blount reached the sidewalk.

"You should consider retaining my services until you've secured new representation."

"No, I'm going to let you go right now."

"I respect your decision."

As the lawyer walked away, leaving Elspeth alone, her toes beginning to burn with the return to cold, wearing under her coat the paralegal's forgotten suit, it seemed to Elspeth that it was her mother's help that she was rejecting. It was after all her mother who had paid for Blount, whose only offense at the end of the day was that she had worked within rules that an older generation had come up with for themselves in their navigation of an earlier version of the world. It was no one's fault that in the changed world there wasn't and never had been anything for Elspeth to fall back on but her own rage and perspicacity.

The snow along the street was granular and translucent; it was already old snow. Elspeth wondered whether she or someone else would be the one to tell Leif that she had betrayed him.

She checked her phone. There was a new email, announcing that she had been tagged in a status update by someone whose name she didn't recognize, and when she clicked, she saw that the update linked to a post about her that before she quite knew what she was doing she was in the middle of reading.

Her heart pounded. She shouldn't be reading this now.

She was an attention whore. She treated Occupy like an accessory that she wore while starring in a personal reality show of her own imagining. Everyone was sick of letting her and her fellow showboats distract from the struggles of people who didn't have the luxury of having their nervous breakdowns acclaimed as world-historical. Most people couldn't take for granted a surplus of privilege so great that they could make an elaborate drama out of their inability to focus on issues larger than themselves.

Evidently Stacey Temple had published her interview. This was one of the first online reactions.

The ranter indignantly refused to reward Temple's interview with a link, but the interview was easy to find on the newspaper's homepage. Elspeth read it quickly, not for itself but to see whether it appeared to justify the rant.

It was hard to say. Elspeth was, after all, even more of a traitor to the ideals of Occupy than the ranter knew. The only cruelty she knew for sure to be gratuitous was that of the stranger who had taken it upon himself to tag her. The tag suggested an unknown number of people capable of finding the near-anonymous direction of malice against her casually entertaining.

She noticed that she was breathing in violent gulps, as if she wasn't confident that she would remember to breathe if she didn't make sharp efforts.

A passerby impatiently sighed. Stationary over her phone, Elspeth had obliged the man to step outside the narrow lane of sidewalk that had been shoveled. "Sorry," she murmured. It was the internet's fault for taking her away from her body, as the internet tended to do.

If only she were able to talk again with Leif for a minute or two with their old freedom.

When she got home to her empty apartment—her roommates seemed to have decided to sleep every night at their boyfriends', visiting only when they remembered an item of clothing or a bottle of prescription medicine that they needed—she took off her coat and her hat and her wet shoes and socks and the heavy wool skirt-suit, and knowing that she wanted to be away from the world for a while turned off her phone. In her underwear she carried a chair into the utility closet and stood on it to unplug her Wi-Fi, too.

It was strange the way, once she had done these things, the silence of the apartment came to the surface. Or rather, its faint, homely sounds: the taps of the chair's feet as she set it back under the dining room table, the whelk-shell echo of the shape of the rooms, the whir from behind the refrigerator, the one loose window sash that from time to time was joggled in its frame by a flaw of air. It was like the blank solitude one finds when one gets up in the middle of the night. She was alone; no one could address a word to her. There would be no thoughts in her head but her own unless she happened to open a book.

She waited for the shower to run warm and then hot. When she stepped in, she began to cry, and then the wetness of the water somehow stopped her, as if like cured like.

Afterward, she dressed in a clean set of underwear and in her own clothes again.

She was able to work for a while without needing access to the internet because the piece she had been assigned to check was fairly esoteric and the writer had depended mostly on printed books for his sourcing. She unpacked the books, notes, and printouts onto the dining room table, brewed herself a cup of tea, and then disappeared, reassuringly, into the deliberateness of the task of reconstructing the writer's footsteps. Methodically she retraced the paths that she figured out he must have taken as he carried his facts into his manuscript. It was a history piece; it had almost nothing to do with the world one now lived in.

In the middle of the afternoon, the buzzer startled her.

By now she knew that the police, like mailmen, were somehow able to let themselves through the building door, so it probably wasn't them. She guessed it was a reporter. When she tiptoed out of her apartment and down the building stairs, however, and leaned around the curve of the last flight to peek into the lobby, she saw Julia on the other side of the door's glass. Julia didn't at first see Elspeth. Her eyes were hollow, and she was wearing the eccentric-looking beret that she had adopted since the arrests. The beret seemed to come from outside the ordinary vocabulary of clothes; it was marked as strange, like an item of clothing from a child's dress-up bin, or an item in a thrift store that is a little too obviously the property of someone recently deceased.

Elspeth opened the door.

Julia hesitated. "I wasn't sure you'd want to talk to me."

"Is this for your project?"

"I got a tip about you."

"Come in," Elspeth said.

As they made their way upstairs, gratitude or nervousness drew from Julia a flood of words: "I came as soon as I could so that I could get here before your lawyer told you not to talk but as I was thinking about it, as I walked over, I realized perhaps that's not fair to you. Perhaps you shouldn't talk. Perhaps I shouldn't be asking you to. But I thought to myself that I could always 'go meta' and ask about what went into your decision to talk. About where you are, as it were, rather than what you would say."

"Did your lawyer give you the tip?"

"Oh, Kenneth usually hears about these things from me now, if he hears about them at all."

"I didn't make a deal," Elspeth said, bringing Julia into the parlor. "I didn't mean to, anyway."

"Are they saying you made a deal? I don't know, remember, because I can't go online."

"Not going online sounds so nice. Would you like some tea? I have gingerbread cookies." It occurred to her that she had a routine now for entertaining the press.

"It is nice, in a way. I'd love something." Julia scanned the room, but there was nothing for her to notice; there wasn't anything in the parlor that Elspeth had changed. A few more of the hydrangeas' dried petals had dropped onto the coffee table. That was all. The petals looked like the little moth wings one finds in the sill when one first opens one's windows in the spring. "People can't be mean to me," Julia continued. "Or rather, I'm sure they are being mean, but I don't know anything about it if they are, so they might as well not be being mean."

Of the Telepathy Four, the one the internet's commenters were hardest on was in fact Julia. She was a woman, for one thing, and in her manner she was oblivious to the small conformities, for another. On social media, people were almost as hard on her as they were on Bresser, but perhaps because of the judge's order she really didn't know this.

While the water was boiling Elspeth brought out a plate of the cookies. "Someone attacked me today online," Elspeth volunteered.

"Was it very bad?" Julia asked.

"People get so angry now when they see someone paying more attention to thoughts and feelings than they think thoughts and feelings deserve. It's like there's a new sumptuary law against introspection."

"It's a new world," Julia said vaguely, which stopped Elspeth from continuing her theory.

Elspeth went back to the kitchen for the tea. "I don't have a lawyer anymore," she announced when she returned with it.

"Is that safe?" Julia asked.

"Is it safe for you to be here?" Elspeth countered.

"So long as I don't leave any trace. Unless a thing is recorded, now, it doesn't happen. I mean, I know that's not strictly true, but anything unrecorded is now so much harder to prove than the many things that are recorded, it might as well be true. Hard memory drives out soft. I don't even call or text anymore. I knock on doors."

"How did you hear about me talking?"

"My source told me. I haven't read it yet myself because for some reason I missed it when I was reading today's paper."

"Oh, you mean the interview. That's in tomorrow's paper."

"That explains why I didn't see it."

So she didn't know about the proffer meeting. Maybe no one knew yet but Elspeth, Somerville, and Blount. Elspeth didn't really want Julia to be the first person she told. She had always thought Raleigh had probably been interested in Julia, but that wasn't the reason.

"Is there something else?" Julia asked.

"I talked to Somerville," Elspeth said, giving in.

"Oh, so did Chris, you know. He went before the grand jury yesterday."

For Julia to be nonchalant about it was somehow worse. "I did it because I thought I was going to change his mind."

"Oh, poor thing," Julia said. She was trying in her clumsy way to show pity, but she didn't know how to.

The cookies were untouched.

"I guess I can't ask what you said," Julia commented.

"I only told him what I told the newspaper. That we had a blog. That we had a theory. I didn't realize he didn't know."

"We had a blog?"

"It was mostly Leif and me."

"I guess Somerville isn't the only one who didn't know about it. I hope I get to read it someday." Julia had tears in her eyes. "I know that sounds dumb, but I mean it." Julia found a tissue in her purse. "I know you probably don't want to hear this, but sometimes I think that all of this is the most exciting thing that has ever happened to me or will ever happen to me. I know of course that it's all horrible, but even during the horrible parts I feel so *alive*."

It soon got into the news that Elspeth had met with Somerville. Elspeth didn't think Blount had talked, but the information might have leaked backward through Julia to one of her sources, or Somerville might have disclosed it himself, off the record. He had a motive to, after all. The grand jury seemed to be nearing the end of its work, and if there were any plea bargains to be struck before the arraignments, it was in Somerville's interest to improve his negotiating position by frightening the three defendants who weren't yet cooperating.

The revelation further blackened Elspeth's name online. She had been widely accused, after Temple's interview was published, of inappropriate boasting. Didn't she know her friends were in serious trouble? How could she fail to understand how modest her ability to defend her site really was? And now she had told Somerville about the working group's blog. It was the internet's opinion that she must have told him much more.

She hadn't, and she hadn't been boasting, and of course she knew her friends were in trouble, and of course she knew her web security skills were negligible, and telling Somerville about the blog had been a stupid accident, but when she considered posting these disclaimers and disavowals on the RPF website, every draft she came up with sounded defensive—worse than saying nothing at all—and in the end she kept silent. After Temple's interview, the RPF site was heavily quoted by supporters as well as critics of the Telepathy Four, and one day word spread among its new readers that it was possible to send Elspeth an email through a contact form on the site, and in half an hour, before she disabled the form, a score of strangers wrote her that she was a stupid anarchist slut who would get what was coming to her and she should visualize being hit every time she considered uttering a word and she was in their sights now and they would pay her back someday they hoped soon and above all an ugly bitch like her should learn that her place in society was to shut up. Most of the writers seemed to be motivated by hatred of RPF and of Occupy generally and were therefore relatively easy to dismiss from her mind once she had absorbed and metabolized the mere menace of them, which did take a few days. A week later, however, when she made the experiment of turning the contact form back on, there was a new surge of hate mail and these writers presented themselves as partisans of the Telepathy Four who felt called upon to punish her for her betrayals of the cause. These wasps left their stingers behind in the wounds they made.

She answered now whenever she saw that it was Raleigh calling. When he first heard her explanation for her disclosure, he was unable to stop himself from saying that surely she could have done a little more research about what this kind of conversation with a prosecutor usually means, seeing as how, unlike the rest of them, she was still allowed to go on the internet. She didn't hold the small cruelty of this reproach against him because, as she told Diana, he was right. "So tiresomely," Diana had replied. Perhaps so, but Elspeth felt that it was her duty now to be bullied and bored a little by the kind of reproach Raleigh had made. It was her duty as the one who had fucked up, and to some lesser extent, in her conversations with Raleigh, as the one who didn't want to get back together.

She needed to make sure that Leif, too, knew what she had done and the limits of it. She called his lawyer, Michael Gauden, and told him everything she could remember about her meeting with Somerville.

When she finished speaking, there was silence on the other end of the line. "Hello?" she queried.

"I'm not sure what the point of this call is," the lawyer said. "There's nothing to prevent you from speaking to Somerville again."

"If he asks again, I'll refuse to," she said.

"I don't know what I can do with this, but thank you, I suppose."

From Leif himself—or rather, from Matthew on Leif's behalf—she heard nothing. Maybe he wasn't well. Some days, she was sure that if he knew, and if he was well enough to understand what had happened, he was bound to forgive her. He had to. Probably he already had forgiven her. On other days, however, she worried that in his isolation and his illness a suspicion of even her could have crystallized in him. How could he know what her motive had been in talking to Somerville? Only the effect of her meeting and a secondhand report of it would have been able to reach him. She imagined visiting the locked ward and sitting at the games table in the dayroom with him again. *You didn't think I was angry, did you?* she would say, and he would reply, *It would have been all right if you had been.* But the imagined conversation didn't reassure her. It didn't ring true. Leif wouldn't speak so lightly about something that had really hurt him. Nonetheless her mind rehearsed the scene over and over, unable to leave it and unable to make it more plausible. Sometimes her mind even went so far as to imagine that Leif, too, apologized.

In this way the silence—the actual silence—between her and Leif became as time passed more definitive. She told herself that she should approach him rather than wait for him to signal that he was able to pardon her. But from day to day there were always other things for her to do. She had her fact-checking work. She still needed to find a new lawyer for herself—a subpoena from the grand jury could come at any time. Whenever she began to research lawyers, however, the task itself, as she got into the details of it, brought home to her that unlike her friends, she wasn't facing charges, and she stalled, aware that she was guilty of having been spared and wondering whether, since she had been spared, she really deserved a defense and shouldn't try instead to save her mother from having to pay for it.

She was at fault on both sides of the equation: she hadn't been with her friends when they had made their mistake, and she had been away from them when she had made her own. She hadn't been bold enough, and then she had been too bold. Certainly she wasn't "good" anymore; the internet had taken care of that. Maybe she never had been, a thought that liberated her a little from her own caution. The feeling of liberation came and went in spasms, as late liberations do, and it was during one of these throes, one night when she had stayed home (having explained to Diana that she needed to work through the evening in order to finish checking an article that closed the next morning), that she finally logged on to the server of the company that had backed up her and Raleigh's hard drives, whose password she and Raleigh had chosen so that it would be impossible for anyone else to guess but easy for them to remember. There, in a blue folder, the blue of the sky from a Cape Cod sailboat, was the past that had belonged to her before the arrests. The past that the government had taken from her. Raleigh's past lay waiting and blinking in an identical folder, just beside it. When she double-clicked on hers, she saw recipes, and photos that she had forgotten that she had kept copies of, and drafts of, embarrassingly, poems, and other fragments that she hadn't been able to recover merely by logging back into her old email account. Almost without thinking she dragged the folder, marked ELSPETHS_, onto her desktop. The scorn that she felt for Somerville's failure even to know about the working group's blog must have had something to do with it. A small window popped up to tell her that of 383,402 files to be copied, an at first small but quickly rising number had so far been copied. She watched for a minute or so as the digits wheeled higher. Then she pushed back her chair and, leaving her computer running, went to bed.

She expected to have a moral hangover the next morning, but she didn't. Maybe she was changing. Was it unlike her that she still hadn't told her mother that she had let Dominique Blount go? Or had Elspeth not known until now what she was like? A couple of days later, her most recent fact-checking assignment out of the way, she spent a pleasant afternoon distributing the recovered files into the hierarchy of folders that she had improvised from memory when she had first set up her new laptop. Putting them in the electronic cubbyholes proper to them gave her a sense of tidiness and accomplishment. It was like going through a bureau drawer and throwing out all the socks that have lost their twins. She felt like she knew where she was again, once she had finished.

"They're going to be arrested again," Jeremy called to tell her, a week later.

"Arrested?"

"For the federal case. The grand jury has returned its indictment. The other time was for the state case."

"Leif, too? Can he leave the place where he is?"

"I don't know how they'll handle that."

"Are you at the courthouse now?" she asked.

"They're letting them go by themselves to the court tomorrow morning, and they'll be arrested when they get there." He gave her the address of the federal courthouse. It was down the street from where she had met

Somerville and around the corner from the state court where the four had been arraigned in November. "We're keeping where Leif is out of the press," he reminded her.

She called Diana, and they agreed to meet the next morning on the courthouse steps.

Then she called Raleigh, whom she probably ought to have called before Diana. He said his parents weren't able to book a flight from Oklahoma on such short notice. "You don't want to come, do you?" he asked.

It had never occurred to her that she had the option of not going. "Don't you want me to?"

His hesitation in answering seemed to her a little maudlin. She reminded herself that it couldn't be easy to go back to jail.

"You'll be strong," she said.

"I wish I knew that."

After she got off the phone, she sat down to her fact-checking work for a few hours, a little heartlessly. Even if her friends were convicted and sent away, her life was going to continue, and it was going to continue to have to be paid for. For intervals she was able to blank herself out in the work.

Alone in her bed that night, she dreamed again about the tunnels in the sky. This time they reminded her of the tunnels behind glass in a child's ant farm. While she was watching them, she opened her eyes and also saw the white frame that the plaster molding made around the white plane of her bedroom ceiling.

She was sane as long as she could see both. It was the third time her body had lost contact with her soul. It still felt strange, but she couldn't be afraid of it forever. She couldn't keep calling Diana. It might be that this feeling of non-feeling was from now on going to be part of her life.

She closed her eyes, to listen for the voice inside that she still believed would someday speak. She still knew where to listen for it even though it still never had.

She had been floating on her sorrow and anger as if her life depended on her ability to tread water and stay on top of them, but she couldn't do it forever. When she decided to stop struggling, the sorrow and anger rose into and through her as if she were a meadow being flooded.

There were no steps per se in front of the federal courthouse; the building was handicapped-accessible. Instead there was a plaza, palisadoed with cement bollards spaced widely enough to admit pedestrians but closely enough to keep out any trucks or cars that were being driven as weapons. Elspeth spotted the traffic-hazard orange of Diana's jacket, and she was so eager to tell Diana that the night before she had been able to do without her that her heart took a puppyish leap.

Hatless despite the cold, Diana was reading something on her cell phone.

"I woke up again last night," Elspeth said. "This time I let myself be afraid, and it was just fear, which is terrifying, but that's all it was."

"You fact-checked it," Diana said.

They approached the cylindrical glass atrium at the courthouse's entrance. The name of the courthouse was spelled out along the drum of steel and glass in large chrome letters, with the showiness of a wealthy suburban high school or a convention hotel in a midsize city.

The only tragedy they might not survive, Elspeth at that moment felt, was if the law made them say they hadn't felt what they had felt. She suddenly wanted to take Diana's hand even though only a moment ago she had been proud of having been able to do without her.

"Nothing metal in your pockets, people," a guard said in a singsong voice, while clunking plastic trays into a stack. "Keys, coins, into the trays. You must check your cell phones in at the desk behind me unless you're a registered attorney."

"No cell phones?" someone asked.

"You a registered attorney?" the guard replied.

When Diana took hers out of her pocket, she saw that her mother had tried to call. "It's not like her to call so early. Let me catch up to you."

Elspeth told herself that she would be all right alone here, too. She walked through the magnetometer.

In the bright halls, the reflecting slaps of her footfalls clattered at her like static.

When she reached the second floor, a man with his shirt pronouncedly unbuttoned stopped in front of her. "I know you," he said. It was Philip, Jeremy and Raleigh's roommate. "We're this way."

Around a corner she saw a long line of people.

"Jeremy wanted a show of force," Philip explained.

"Will the courtroom even hold this many?"

"I'm sure Jeremy will let you come wait with us in front," he said. "Look who I found," he called out.

Jeremy was wearing a black suit and carrying a navy blue overcoat, and with the new sobriety and formality of his wardrobe came an air of consequence. "Elspeth," he said, embracing her. "It's a difficult and important day."

"Didn't we know it was going to happen?" she asked. Matthew was standing behind Jeremy. It was his place in line she was cutting. "I'll get behind you," she suggested.

But behind him, guarded by him, were a gray-haired man and woman who seemed to be making an effort to hold themselves still, like birds conscious of being under observation. Elspeth remembered the neatly dressed, cautious-looking king and queen of money. "Are these your parents?" she asked Matthew.

The man and woman smiled without offering their hands.

"They are," he said.

"Thank you for . . . ," she began, but they were waiting for their son's lover's arraignment, and she faltered, not sure that they would want to talk.

"The marshals wouldn't let us ride with Leif," Matthew said, "but we'll be able to drive him back, after."

"That's good," Elspeth said, nodding. It would be hard, it occurred to her, for someone in Matthew's position not to seem either to exceed his place or not live up to it.

"Is Raleigh inside already?" he asked her.

"He said he would be, but I haven't talked to him since last night."

They fell silent, awkwardly. She took in the corridor's white ceiling and white floor and white walls. As discreetly as she could she surveyed the crowd in line. Jeremy had summoned more people than the Working Group for the Refinement of the Perception of Feelings had ever been able to. Most were in their twenties, but a few looked older; there seemed to be slightly more women than men. Some seemed to be focusing on her, the newcomer, returning her gaze, when it landed on them, with studiedly beneficent expressions, as if to signal that they recognized from Jeremy's body language that she had a place with the leader of their group even if they themselves didn't happen to know what her place was. Her eye was caught by Greg, the barista from Leif's café, standing a dozen yards back. He nodded when she noticed him and then looked away so as not to seem to be demanding any acknowledgment. He had pocketed his cap. The hair that was still on his head was downy and almost blond.

"It's nicer than the state courthouse," she observed to Matthew. It seemed less ancient and corrupt, though she knew she was probably responding to nothing more substantive than its light fixtures.

"It's newer, anyway."

"Are you Leif's roommate?" Matthew's mother asked.

"We went to college together," Elspeth replied.

"Oh, that's right. Matthew told us about you—didn't you, Matthew. You're also a writer."

"Maybe someday," Elspeth said.

"Don't you work for a magazine?"

"I'm just a freelancer."

"We've subscribed for years, but I always seem to be four or five issues behind."

"Oh, me too."

"My god," exclaimed a woman in a blue skirt over what seemed to be a slightly longer black petticoat, as she strode toward the head of the line. "Don't you know nothing ever happens at an arraignment?"

"They'll read the charges, won't they?" Jeremy asked.

"Not necessarily, no. But even if they do, that takes twenty seconds. Twenty-five seconds, max."

"We thought we should be here for our friends," Jeremy said.

"But there's not gonna be a jury here to see that you're being here for them."

"You're here, Jan," Jeremy pointed out.

"I have to be. You need to save your ammo, Jeremy. You need to husband your troops. If you drop from exhaustion, it won't be good for my story. I guess I'll get some quotes, since there are so many of you. Not from you, though, Jeremy. You're already too canned." She wandered down the hall.

Jeremy told the people standing near him the name of Jan Ridgely's newspaper. "She's good," he said. "She's very good."

Leif's arraignment, which was going to be the first, was scheduled to begin at ten a.m., and at three minutes before the hour, Elspeth and the rest of the audience were still out in the corridor, not yet admitted, when Julia and her parents rounded the corner. All three members of the Di Matteo family were walking with the quick, carefully aligned strides of people who know they are late but don't think they should run. Elspeth didn't know where Julia was supposed to be, but she knew she wasn't supposed to be in the corridor. Her presence was strangely terrifying. It was like seeing the bride alone in the parking lot when one can already hear the organ inside the church beginning to sound.

Julia's charcoal suit was tailored to her, as the one that Elspeth had borrowed hadn't been. Her beret was tucked under her left elbow even though it was brown to her suit's gray. Her eyes darted nervously through the crowd. "Nobody's seen Kenneth?" The smell of fear was coming from her, but she was vivid and beautiful, Elspeth had to acknowledge, with her olive skin and her dark hair.

"He might be waiting for you in the basement, at the Marshals' Office," Jeremy said. "I think that's where you're supposed to surrender."

"They told us it was going to be a voluntary appearance," Julia's mother said. It seemed to be a line that she had prepared to say; on people who weren't in any position of authority it was wasted. "We don't have our phones," she added.

"I think what they say about a voluntary appearance is that it's a courtesy but not a thing," Jeremy replied.

"Let's go downstairs," Julia's father suggested.

"Momma, will you take this," Julia said, removing a leather notebook from her purse and handing it to her mother.

"I think we should go downstairs," the father repeated.

"We heard you," Julia said.

"We'll save you seats," Jeremy called out to the Di Matteos, who were already retreating. The only member of the family to turn her head in acknowledgment was Julia, whose face twisted with the confused, late recognition that she herself wasn't going to be able to sit in any seat that Jeremy saved.

Soon after, the bailiffs opened the doors.

There was still no sign of Diana, and so when Elspeth took a seat, she arranged her empty coat beside her on the settle as if around an absent person.

Leif was already sitting at the defendants' table, in the corral at the front of the room. His back was to the door that Elspeth and the others had come in through, but he was turned sideways in his chair and was watching the procession into the courtroom out of the corner of one eye, as if he wasn't sure it would be appropriate to look at the visitors directly. His attorney, whose blond hair tumbled down rather showily, was looking at papers. Somerville, meanwhile, stood at the butt of the prosecution's table, arms folded, making silent appraisals of the members of the audience, the tuft of his forelock nodding as he did so. A slight freezing of his features revealed to Elspeth the moment when he took note of her, even though nothing in his face departed from his mask of general complacence.

The flannel shirt that Leif was wearing seemed, incongruously, to have been starched as well as ironed.

Everyone rose at the appearance of the judge, a short man with a folded-in face. The shape of his body was hidden by his robe, but his cheeks were round. He gathered his skirts behind him with both hands before he sat down. Once he sat, everyone else in the room took their seats again, too, in rumbling, rough synchrony, as in a church, though the attorneys, Leif, and several bailiffs and court officials remained standing, the way a lector stays up when it is time for him to read a lesson.

"The United States of America versus Leif Lewis Saunderson," the bailiff declared, as if he were the prologue in an Elizabethan play.

"Good morning, Your Honor. Thomas Somerville for the United States."

"Good morning. Michael Gauden for Mr. Saunderson."

The judge's lips drew into a line. "Mr. Gauden, in this court it's customary to declare the presence or absence of the defendant."

"I'm sorry, Your Honor. I'm not familiar with—"

"Don't make excuses for yourself."

"Your Honor, Mr. Saunderson is present in the courtroom."

"It's for the benefit of the record," the judge said. "Defendants have been known to be shy." From his high desk he now for the first time looked down over his glasses at Leif.

The judge was bored, Elspeth sensed. How could he help it? On the only paths he walked, he was never challenged. It was upsetting and in a way confusing that so much was going to depend on someone on whom most of it was going to be lost.

She wasn't able to read much from Leif, who was facing away, toward the judge. He was in a place where he couldn't talk, but she reminded herself that that didn't mean he wasn't there.

Diana at this point edged her way down the row toward the seat that Elspeth had saved for her, holding her purse aloft so that it wouldn't bump anyone. Elspeth slid her coat out of the seat and around herself, and Diana unholstered one arm from her jacket and then the other.

"Is everything all right?"

"She wanted my salad dressing recipe."

Once Diana was sitting spine straight beside Elspeth, there was an amplification in Elspeth of the understanding of what was happening in the room. It was an experience that Elspeth had sometimes had with Raleigh when they had first started being together, so long ago that she had almost forgotten what it felt like. The hum that was always in her seemed to begin to hum at a higher number of revolutions per minute.

As a result, in Leif's pretty shoulders, pinched upward together, she became able to read an anxiety not to bring into further harm the friends he had led this far. He was coming back to them. She knew he was going to come back to them. She was aware, too, suddenly, of Matthew, sitting next to his parents in the row ahead of her, to her right. She was able to see into his heart as clearly as if it were a cavern and she were tossing flares down onto its floor. She could see distinctly his gemlike indifference as to whether Leif was going to stand by his friends or sell them out. All he wanted was for Leif to survive. He might not even be wishing Elspeth well, an indifference understandable to her, considering her disclosure to Somerville.

She couldn't unmake her mistakes. She could only try to understand them.

"Mr. Saunderson, please raise your right hand. Do you solemnly swear that the testimony you give will be the truth, the whole truth, and nothing but the truth?"

"I'll tell the truth."

"You don't need to put it in your own words, Mr. Saunderson," the judge remarked. "The law provides all the words. Your full name?"

"Leif Lewis Saunderson."

"And how old are you?"

"Twenty-four."

"How long were you in school?"

"Um," Leif said, adding in his head. "Sixteen. Plus kindergarten? Seventeen?"

"A bachelor's degree? Or beyond?"

"A bachelor's, sir."

"Have you had anything alcoholic to drink or taken any recreational drugs recently?"

Leif shook his head.

"Speak up for the benefit of the court reporter."

"No."

"No alcohol at all."

"Not since December."

"And are you or have you been under the care of a psychologist or physician?"

Leif pulled himself up. He was deciding not to be ashamed of it. "Yes. A psychiatrist."

"What was it regarding?"

"I was a danger to myself."

"How did that manifest itself?"

"I took drugs that I shouldn't have."

"Are you saying you're in treatment for narcotics addiction?"

"No, I was trying to kill myself with the drugs."

"I'm sorry to pry, Mr. Saunderson, but I have to ask you these questions in order to find out if you're competent to make a plea today. Are you taking any psychiatric drugs now that might affect your state of mind? Or are you going through a withdrawal from any drug?"

"I think I'm on an SSRI."

"And is your mind clouded by this SSRI?"

"No, it's very clear," he said, touching his temples, as if to make sure. "Your mind is clear, too," he added.

"My mind is clear, Mr. Saunderson?"

"What you're communicating is very clear."

"The court on its own motion orders a hearing on competency," the judge said.

"Your Honor, if I may," Gauden interjected. "We'd like to request that the examination take place at the facility where Mr. Saunderson is currently being held, which right now is a voluntary commitment. It's an environment that he's familiar with and where he feels secure. It's a private facility, I know, but if—"

"The difficulty isn't that it's a private facility but that it's out of state. I've been given to understand that there isn't anyone there that we here are in the habit of working with."

"We're willing to forgo any hearing on psychological competency if—"

The judge cut Gauden off. "I'm not *giving* you the hearing, Mr. Gauden. I'm ordering it."

"It's not safe," Leif said.

"The facility here is very secure, Mr. Saunderson, as I'm sure you noticed when you passed through it this morning."

"I want to make a statement."

"There's no call for you to make a statement right now, Mr. Saunderson."

"I just want to say that I did used to think that I could read people's minds sometimes. I just want to put that on the record."

"Mr. Gauden, look to your client."

"That's all I wanted to say. It's been troubling me."

"I'm committing Mr. Saunderson to custody for the course of the examination. Mr. Saunderson," the judge said, raising his voice as if he were addressing a child, "you're going to be in the care of the state for thirty days or until the doctors examining you no longer require your cooperation, whichever comes first. Do you understand that?"

"Yes."

"They'll take very good care of you, and they'll be able to tell me after they've spent some time with you whether you're able to understand what we're doing here in this courtroom and whether you're in a state of mind such that you're able to help Mr. Gauden with your defense."

"I thought I came here to say not guilty," Leif said.

"No one pleads in my courtroom until I know that he's competent to," the judge replied, and rapped his gavel into its wooden dish.

"No," Matthew said, suddenly on his feet. "No. Wait."

"Matthew," Mrs. Fisher said, her voice full of fear, her hand trailing toward her son's back, her embarrassing, primitive love overspilling in public.

He scrambled down the row, not waiting for people to get out of his way. At the front of the room, three burly officers were handcuffing Leif.

"Matthew," said Mr. Fisher, in the lower-pitched voice one uses with a dog or child who hasn't listened to one's earlier commands.

Matthew was intercepted at the defendant's table by Gauden, just as the officers were taking Leif out through a small brass door.

"I don't want to stay here," Elspeth said to Diana. She foresaw that Somerville and the judge were going to be avuncular with Chris during his arraignment, which came next, and she didn't think she could bear to watch. Chris had been innocent once, and part of him probably still was.

"Do you want to go home?"

"I can't. There's no one here for Raleigh."

They walked downstairs. Outside, over the flat, bollarded plaza, the clouds in the sky were low and indistinct from one another. "Tomorrow a social worker will reach out to you, okay?" they heard one woman saying to another, who was on the verge of tears. The sorrow of one formed part of the occupational climate of the other. Beyond the plaza there was a park where one could walk along a brick-and-concrete path between squares of chained-off, snow-crusted lawn, and they made their way to it for privacy.

They walked for a while without saying anything. For the comfort of it Elspeth wished that Diana would take her hand, but although she knew that Diana would be willing to, if she were to ask, she was afraid that her hand would seem damp and heavy to Diana by the time she was ready for

Diana to let it go and that she would expose to Diana her need. It wasn't really need, exactly. She should be able to keep whatever it was to herself. They walked separately as well as in silence therefore.

Sparrows were bickering over a rift of black ground that exhalation from a sewer grate had opened in the snow. The birds' cries were tinny and rhythmless, like the grinding sound when someone is grabbing at the change in his pocket. Elspeth knew that not even bird-watchers took note of sparrows; they existed without being worth noticing. Only a machine could have the patience to number and keep track of them.

"If I don't go to jail . . ." She didn't finish her thought. "That sounds so melodramatic."

"It doesn't look like you're going to," said Diana.

"If I don't, would you consider having a relationship?"

"With you?" Diana asked.

Her surprise made Elspeth aware of having assumed that Diana was waiting for her. Elspeth's eyes burned. Maybe this was what boys felt when one turned them down.

"Would you at least kiss me before you ask that?" Diana asked.

There was no one around. Elspeth was clumsy until she came close enough.

"Is this safe?" Elspeth interrupted to ask.

"It never is."

Elspeth felt Diana slip her hands into the cuffs of the sleeves of Elspeth's coat and hold on by the underside of Elspeth's forearms. Elspeth leaned forward, burying her face against Diana's coat, croodling into her. Then they kissed again.

"I think I love you," Elspeth said.

"That always sounds so much like a command."

"You're so cold about it!"

"In this terrain I think it's better to be a little cold."

"I understand."

"No you don't," Diana said.

While they kissed a third time, Elspeth made an effort to continue to be able to hear the impersonality in the chittering of the nameless, unspecial birds around them, but it was hard under the circumstances to keep her mind from assimilating the sound to an impression of happiness.

They stayed in the park so long that they missed Julia's arraignment as well as Chris's and walked in on the last arraignment, Raleigh's, while it was still in progress.

"I understand Mr. Penny to say that you are waiving your right to a formal reading of the charges," the judge was saying, "but I'm something of a stickler and I like to be sure that defendants know the gist of what they're accused of, and so I'd like to walk you through the charges nonetheless, if I may."

"Yes, sir," Raleigh said. "Your Honor, I mean." He had the posture of a boy standing at a blackboard to deliver an oral report.

"First of all, the government is claiming, Mr. Evans, that you defrauded Bresser Operational Security, Incorporated, of property, in this case data, by use of a wire transmission. This is a charge of wire fraud; it's the only such charge against you. The other charges all involve a law known as the Computer Fraud and Abuse Act. The gravest of these is that the data you obtained, without authorization or in excess of your authorization, has been determined by the executive branch of the government to require protection from disclosure for reasons of national security. Another charge against you under the CFAA is that you obtained that data, without authorization or in excess of your authorization, from a computer that is used in interstate commerce, and still another is that the computer you fraudulently accessed was one used at least partly for US government purposes. The government also says that what you obtained through fraud and without authorization had a value in excess of five thousand dollars, and they further claim that through your access to the protected computer in question, again without authorization or in excess of your authorization, you caused damage and loss to Bresser Operational Security. The law calculates such loss by summing up any reasonable expense that Bresser Opsec may incur in the course of responding to your illicit access and resecuring its servers, and the government will also be arguing that in this case that loss is also greater than five thousand dollars. How much greater will likely be a matter of debate. The amount is distinct from the value of the data you took. You are also accused, as a sort of corollary to each of the five CFAA charges I have just described, of *conspiring* to commit the charges in question, which as a legal matter is a separate thing from the charges themselves. Have you had a chance to talk with Mr. Penny about these charges, and does my description of them conform to what you and he discussed?"

"We did. It sounds like what he explained to me."

"It's difficult to say what sentence you might face if you were to be convicted of all these charges, and nothing I say now is to be construed as representing an intention on my part as to your sentence, if the case should be decided against you. But I do want you to know that the gravest charge alone could incur for you a term in prison as long as ten years. If the government is able to show that you used what the law calls 'sophisticated means,' the penalty will be increased. As it also will if you are shown to have deployed what the law calls 'special skills.'"

"I'm the only one in the group who *can't* read minds," Raleigh blurted out.

The judge paused. He looked up from the rap sheet in his hands. "No,

Mr. Evans, I should say that you can't. But the law has in mind skills that are a little more, shall we say, sublunary."

"I'm not a hacker, either."

"We're not trying the case now, Mr. Evans. How do you plead to the charges? Shall I enumerate them again?"

"Not guilty."

"Be it recorded that the defendant so pleads." The judge laid the rap sheet facedown. "Will you be making a motion for detention?" he asked Somerville.

"No, Your Honor."

"I've been given to understand that both the government and the counsel for the defense are willing to abide by the automatic rules for discovery. Is that correct?"

Somerville and Penny assented.

"Other than requiring an unsecured bond to guarantee his return, I'm not going to impose any conditions on Mr. Evans's release. What that means, Mr. Evans, is that as far as this court is concerned, you're going to be free to use your computer and cell phone. There's a certain amount of jurisprudence now that maintains that access to the internet is an expressive right, and I don't want to be fussed with it. But this court has no power to lift any restrictions on you imposed by the state court, and I advise you that to the best of my knowledge the state court's restrictions on you remain in effect."

"Thank you, Your Honor."

"Never mind that. Do you understand? If the state court says you can't go online, you still can't go online, no matter what I say."

"I understand."

"Well, they'll walk you through it all again in Pretrial Services," the judge concluded.

Raleigh was then made to disappear through the brass door, as Leif had.

"Do you think Leif will still want to see me?" Elspeth asked, when she and Diana were alone in the elevator, on their way to the third floor, where Pretrial Services was located.

"I don't see why not," Diana replied.

In a yellow waiting room they found Julia, her parents, and her lawyer, Kenneth Montague. The parents were wearing their coats; the father was holding a Russian troika-driver's hat.

"It's so good of you to come," Julia said to Elspeth.

Elspeth saw Julia's parents freeze. "I know we shouldn't talk," Elspeth said.

"Who knew that being a criminal would require so much *form*?" Julia said.

"Remember what we talked about, Julia," Montague interposed.

"My whole mission is to remember *everything*," Julia said. "Are you going to see Somerville while you're both in the building?" she asked Elspeth, as if she were beyond taking sides even in her own case.

"I'm not talking to him," Elspeth said. "I let my lawyer go because she had me talk to him."

Julia nodded abstractedly. Perhaps she seemed not quite present because she was making an effort to commit Elspeth's words to memory.

When Jeremy and Philip arrived, Elspeth excused herself to use the women's room.

The restrooms for the public were at the end of the building, and as Elspeth progressed alone down the long corridor, she was able to perceive that her body was still resonating from Diana's touch. It was as if the two of them had taken an amusement park ride together and she wasn't yet completely sure of her land legs again.

As she passed the men's room, the door dipped open and Chris stepped out. He was flicking water off his hands. They had put him in a blue suit so out of keeping with his usual style that it seemed to cut his frame out of the larger picture, as if he didn't belong to the scene but had been pasted onto it.

He wasn't pretending not to see her, but he didn't say anything.

"Leif is in the hospital," she told him.

"Is he all right?"

"It wasn't his pneumonia," she said. "He was depressed."

"I heard," he replied.

He might have heard even more than she had. His devotion to Leif had always been so fierce.

He was the one she would have ended up being with, she realized, if she had stayed in the tunnel that she had been traveling in. In none of her possible timelines would she have remained with Raleigh.

"You shouldn't really be talking to me," he said.

"I know." It came into her mind that she could have saved him, but she didn't know whether this was her own thought or her reading of one of his. They had spent all those hours practicing, and she was still attuned. Perhaps he was, as well.

Suddenly the fact of his disloyalty came to her like a thick smell blossoming right under her nose. "How could you?" she asked.

"Your conscience is clean?" he answered.

As he walked away, his new shoes struck neat, clipped strikes against the stone floor.

When she returned to Pretrial Services, Raleigh had been released and was at the center of a crowd in the waiting room. Beside him, Felix Penny's arms were extended as if to suggest a path through the press of people, which Raleigh wasn't taking. Penny seemed to be trying to disguise a look of distaste with a feigned expression of amusement.

"I'm going to update with the basics as soon as I get to my phone," Jeremy was telling Raleigh. "Then a longer post when we get home."

"Raleigh, these are my parents," Julia said.

"Your parents?" There was something almost disrespectful about the note of incredulity in his voice. Julia's parents were older and were significant people, and they were being jostled and unbalanced along with everyone else in the room.

Elspeth stood next to Diana but not in a way that would suggest to an outside observer that either of them had a claim on the other.

"I wanted to ask about the motion to dismiss that you said you will be making," Jeremy said to Penny.

"I might be able to talk about it with you later, Jeremy."

"Are you Elspeth's new lawyer?" Julia asked.

"I'm Diana. We've met."

"Oh, *that's* right. From the Kitchen. I *do* remember."

It was evident that Julia was curious.

"Is the idea," Jeremy asked, "that if the government won't release the file that was downloaded, there's no proof of theft or even access?"

"Elspeth!" Raleigh called out, only just now noticing her.

"Now is not a good time to talk to Elspeth, Raleigh," Penny said.

"I'm not in prison yet, am I?" Raleigh replied.

"But won't your motion," Jeremy asked, "be at odds with the motion that Montague said he's going to make to *compel* discovery of the stolen file?"

"No, it's all the same," Raleigh answered, instead of Penny. "They make a motion to compel discovery of a piece of evidence in the hope of finding out something about the evidence that will support a motion to suppress it. Discovery is all about suppression; it's so Orwell. The thing is, it might not even matter because of Chris."

"Chris?"

"The government doesn't really need any other evidence if Chris testifies as an eyewitness."

"Raleigh, can I speak to you alone for a moment?" Penny asked.

"I'm going to talk to Elspeth first."

Raleigh steered her by the elbow, and in his excitement his grip pinched her. When they got into the corridor, she said, "Please don't," and shook her arm free.

"Sorry." He continued to walk her forward, away from the others.

"Julia was trying to introduce her parents to you."

"Was she?"

"And you should be more careful not to talk about your case."

"I don't know. Penny says the judge's talk about a ten-year sentence is just talk. He says it would be obscene to give someone a sentence that long in a case like this. Did you hear Montague give notice of that motion to compel that Jeremy's talking about? The room they put me in, I couldn't hear the other defendants' appearances."

"I think we were still in the park."

"What park? Who?"

"Diana and I went for a walk. I was upset about Leif."

"Did something happen?"

"They committed him to a state hospital. It's only for an examination, but he didn't seem to be prepared for it."

"Can we go a little farther?" Raleigh asked.

"I'd rather not."

"I want to ask you something."

"Please don't."

"I want to ask if we can get back together."

"No, Raleigh," she said.

They were still close enough to the others for Raleigh's disappointment to be legible to them, even though their voices couldn't be overheard, and she knew that this deepened his chagrin.

"I know I don't have any right to ask. I know I might be about to go away."

"It isn't that." She couldn't tell him that he had become lackluster to her, so she said what she could: "There's someone else."

He swiped at his always unruly hair.

"There is?"

"I'm sorry," she said.

"No, it's okay. If you found someone else . . ."

"Yes," Elspeth confirmed. It was better, as Diana said, to be a little cold in such terrain.

"I think I know who," he said, and then he, like Chris, walked away from her without saying good-bye.

It wasn't until they got to Elspeth's that they realized that they had forgotten their cell phones at the courthouse. Maybe they had meant to make themselves unreachable. Being without them overnight felt like an improvised shelter—like a tent that children put up in the living room with sheets and chairs.

As Elspeth filled her teakettle, she wondered how her checkerboard linoleum floor and pressed-tin ceiling looked to Diana's eyes. "I'm nervous," she said. She lit the first match she struck, however.

Once their tea was ready, they sat down together on the sofa in the parlor. "Hi," Diana said.

"I don't really know anything," Elspeth warned her.

Later, when she opened her eyes, she saw Diana's ongoing observation of her.

"You can still run away if you need to," Diana said.

In the middle of the night Elspeth slipped out of bed and returned to the laptop, which was on the dining room table. It booted up without chiming, since she had thought to mute it earlier.

She opened once more the backup program that Raleigh had set up for himself and her, the one that had quietly captured and recorded the selves that they had had in those days, the ones they were never going back to. A rainbow pinwheel revolved as the password was verified.

She knew what she was about to do even though she also knew that she shouldn't do it. She wondered when she had decided, or rather, when she had become unable to stop herself. When Chris had walked away from her? When Raleigh had? When she had realized that Leif had not looked in her direction once during his arraignment? She couldn't blame any of them. If you betray someone, you have no right to ask them to stay with you and understand why you betrayed them. But if she could leave her friends for Diana, she could leave Diana, too, for them. In her own way. She had no heart not because she was heartless but because that part of her was always breaking and falling away into other people and she was never able to recover all the pieces.

She opened Raleigh's folder. She opened the folder inside it that represented his desktop. The file taken from Bresser was still there, on top, the most recent; no one had visited this imaginary room since the night of the friends' break-in into Bresser's account. RPF-dove-shark.zip was the filename.

She clicked and dragged.

At least Bresser had recognized the dove, she thought, while she waited for it to download.

Now she was a criminal, too. She felt her neck and shoulders flush with shame, even though no one could see her. She had wanted to be with her friends again, and now she was with them.

As Raleigh had described, inside the package she downloaded there were folders named for every member of the working group. In fact, for most members there were multiple folders, each containing what seemed to be a different kind of data. There were also a number of folders with titles that looked like gibberish to Elspeth, whose contents she could not immediately identify.

Though Raleigh had said he had had trouble opening some of the files, the first half dozen that she tried popped open when she double-clicked. In a folder with her own name on it, for example, she found an archived webpage containing every Facebook post of hers less than three months old that would have been visible to a friend of a friend—in other words, almost all her recent posts. In the same folder was a spreadsheet containing two months of tweets by someone named Beth Farrell, who seemed to be a fan of all things Occupy and had even tweeted once about the Working Group for the Refinement of the Perception of Feelings, but who was unknown to Elspeth. It seemed likely, given the nature of these files, that the ones she couldn't immediately understand the significance of were also records of some kind of surveillance.

She tried to peek into some of them with a plain-text editor, but she saw only hexadecimal pi. It then occurred to her to google for the three-letter extension at the end of the name of one of the troublesome files; that revealed the software program that had created it. Maybe decipherment wouldn't be so hard, after all. She was reminded of the process of dehacking the RPF website, which had been mystifying only until one saw how to break each large task down into smaller ones.

The name of the software program seemed to refer to the exploration of caves—a metaphor, apparently, for investigation in the dark. In order to download a free copy, she registered under her own name. Almost as soon as she registered, it occurred to her that it was stupid to expose her name, but it was too late. It was very late even just by the clock. She tried to put the error out of her mind.

The files that the cave-metaphor software was able to open were charts: the contents of numbered categories were represented as fluctuating over time. Elspeth couldn't tell for sure what the categories were, but she suspected that they were the numerical addresses that lie beneath the human-language names of websites. The period of time covered by the charts was, again, the months prior to the break-in.

The chief obstacle she faced, it seemed, wasn't that she wasn't able to get files to open but that she often didn't know what she was looking at.

In one of the folders not named after a member of the working group, there were a number of extremely large files, which her trick of googling the file extension revealed to be audio, compressed in a codec that wasn't native to the operating system on her computer. It took a little searching before she was able to find a plug-in that would play the codec, and before she could use the plug-in, she also had to find, download, and install an open-source audio and video player compatible with it. Once plug-in and player were installed, however, the icons of all the audio files that were compressed in the codec changed in her finder from dog-eared blank pages to triplets of eighth-notes on wavy staffs. It was like turning over matching cards in Concentration.

She stood up. She didn't know how loud the files would be and she didn't want to wake Diana up, and her headphones were on the bureau beside her bed.

The bedroom wasn't so dark that she needed to turn on a lamp. Light wherever it falls gives off a secondary light, and in the bedroom Elspeth was able to see by the secondary brightness that was diffused from the light that fell into the corridor from the dining room. Diana was so still. On the wall, tucked into the corner of a poster of the Lake District that Elspeth had had framed last year, was the snapshot of a sparrow that Diana had given her for Christmas. Elspeth clasped the headphones to her chest quickly and tightly so that the jack at the end of the cable wouldn't be able to swing free and rap against the side of the bureau.

Once she was seated in front of her laptop again, she double-clicked.

"Hey," Raleigh said.

"Are you downstairs?" a woman asked. It was Julia.

"I'm at work."

"But it's Saturday," Julia said. "Why can't you be downstairs? I want to see you again."

Elspeth halted the file. It was dated November 19, two days before the break-in, three days before the arrests. It wasn't as if Elspeth hadn't at some level known.

She heard Diana padding down the hallway, and she closed the window of the audio player, even though it had showed no more than the waveform of what she had been listening to, which wasn't parsable by the human eye.

"What are you doing, sweetheart?" Diana asked. "It's almost two."

"Trying to figure something out," Elspeth replied. What she had learned wasn't really any more painful than fresh water on a scraped knee. It stung a little.

"Come to bed. The internet is bad for young girls."

"I know," she admitted. She should have stopped as soon as she knew the files contained surveillance. Now it was her responsibility to understand and live through, alone and silently, the shame of eavesdropping and the hurt of Raleigh's betrayal. She couldn't involve Diana. Maybe the creation of a secret was a reflex when one was new to having a lover of one's own sex and wasn't yet sure how to differentiate oneself.

She let Diana take her hand and draw her up out of the chair.

"No one knows we're here together, do they?" Elspeth asked. "Since we don't have our phones."

"I guess they don't."

"Let's not tell anybody," Elspeth proposed. "For now."

"Sure," Diana said. "Let's keep it to ourselves."

There was a diner a block from Elspeth's apartment, mildly ironic about being a diner. Because it was late on a weekday morning, the waitress let them have a booth even though there were only two of them. The night before it had seemed urgent to Elspeth that they should hide what was going on between them, in order to protect Diana, but in daylight her alarm seemed excessive. After all, if the government knew about the backup program on Raleigh's laptop, they would have shut it down long ago. They hadn't even known about the RPF blog. So they had no idea; there was no need to worry. The files she had downloaded had no more existence than did any thought in her mind that she alone had.

There was a subway entrance just outside one of the diner's plate-glass windows. A pretty woman with bright red hair was walking up its stairs. Elspeth's eyes were drawn to her.

"I wonder if I'm a lesbian now," she said, from behind her laminated menu.

"I'd say you have some tendencies."

"I'm serious."

"That's one of the signs," Diana said. "Am I your first?"

"I watched it once," Elspeth said. "Online." It was disinhibiting to answer while looking at a list of waffles and pancakes, without being able to see one's questioner. "Maybe it's not binary for girls." She put down her menu.

"Do you know what you're getting?"

"Either waffles or pancakes? It's such a constraint to have to choose."

They rode to the courthouse afterward to recover their phones. On the subway home, Elspeth, alone again, wondered if the faint, pretty pain in her chest that she experienced when she didn't know when she was next going to see Diana again was the point. The old-fashioned, almost Victorian pit-a-pat. Maybe it could be the point even if the world was going to end. The way a poem could still mean something even if it was never published—even if the reader or hearer knew that someday it would be completely forgotten.

She knew it would be better for her if she didn't think about the folder she had downloaded from Raleigh's backup. She was still innocent so long as she didn't think about it. But what if she had jumped to the wrong conclusion about what she had heard? The conversation between Raleigh and Julia might have taken place more recently and Bresser or someone else might have forged the date and time on the file, in order to upset her. Anything was possible, if you didn't know how far ahead of you they might be. The backup app kept a log, and even if someone had been clever enough to change the date of the audio file, no one would have been able to change the date in the log of the backup software, too. If she looked again, and verified that according to the log the file was at least as old as Raleigh's capture of it, she would know for sure. She would look one more time— one last time—and then she would be able to stop thinking about it.

That, at any rate, was what she told herself, without really believing that it was anything but a pretext. She wanted to return to the scene of the crime.

It was gone, she found when she logged in. There was no longer a copy of RPF-dove-shark.zip in the latest backup of Raleigh's laptop.

She checked her own hard drive; she still had her copy.

And the other items that had been on Raleigh's desktop were still there. Did they know about her?

She closed the app. She shut down her laptop. She walked to the kitchen. She poured a glass of water. She drank it. For a minute, she stared out the window into the light well.

She walked back into the dining room and logged in again.

This time she looked more carefully. The backup app had made a new sync with Raleigh's laptop at 9:43 that morning. What if she opened the app's snapshot of Raleigh's desktop as it had appeared yesterday? It turned out that in the copy of yesterday that was stored in the cloud, RPF-dove-shark.zip was still there.

Which meant they didn't know. They still didn't know about the backup program at all. Whoever had custody of Raleigh's laptop had deleted the folder of surveillance materials unaware that within the hour the backup program would sync with the copy of the laptop that Elspeth still had access to.

She had been given proof that the government had tried to destroy its copy of what it was accusing the working group of stealing.

The consequences, she reasoned, were like the legal paradox that Raleigh had talked about, of forcing the discovery of evidence in order to find grounds for suppressing it, but backward: if the government was improperly attempting to hide the surveillance folder, then the fact of the government's surveillance became newly pertinent to the case. Until the attempted suppression, the particular contents of the stolen folder hadn't all that much mattered, legally speaking. They could have been lists of batting averages, for all the law officially cared. Whether the government should have been engaged in such surveillance had no bearing on whether it was against the law for the working group to break into Bresser's protected computer. Until the suppression, the surveillance had merely been the honey in the honeypot.

The tricky part was that Elspeth couldn't share her proof of the government's attempt to hide evidence without admitting to her own snooping, nor could she do it without jeopardizing the privacy of her friends. She knew the remedy at once: she would ask her friends' permission. She would ask everyone to give up all their secrets, for all their sakes.

She didn't tell Diana.

It wasn't because she was ashamed. Shame simply wasn't a logical response anymore, she thought, that night, when she and Diana were kneeling face-to-face on Diana's bed. All the lights in the bedroom were on. What she was fighting was like blackmail, which couldn't be fought unless one accepted one's exposure. In the new world everything was always going to be exposed anyway. In the universal light everyone was going to have to come to better, more forgiving understandings of one another.

She wasn't going to tell Diana because she was going to protect her.

The radiators had gone cold for the night, they noticed after they finished. They pulled Diana's sheets and coverlet over themselves.

The sky the next morning was so uniformly gray that it seemed to have no feature, neither cloud nor sun. Elspeth felt less bold than she had the night before about challenging her friends to let her publish their secrets, and she might not have taken steps to see any of them if she hadn't, upon turning the corner onto her street, found Julia, swaddled up and pacing, in front of her stoop.

"I told myself to count to a hundred Mississippi, and here you are," Julia said.

Elspeth's uncharitable first thought was that on prior occasions Julia had had the advantage over her of greater knowledge and that this time she had it. She didn't want to invite Julia inside, but she couldn't leave her out on the street. "Come in," she said curtly.

Julia paused in the doorway to unwind her scarf, unselfconsciously. Elspeth reminded herself that she didn't have a live claim on Raleigh anymore, and that there was no such thing as a retrospective one. It could be that the only thing that was nettling her was pride.

"Was there anything particular on your mind?" Elspeth asked, when they reached her landing, as she fished in the side pocket of her backpack for her keys.

"I wanted to hear *your* impression of the arraignments. You're the only one who saw us all. And from the outside, as it were."

"Didn't your friend the reporter see it all?"

"Her perceptions aren't fine."

Elspeth put in the key. "I actually didn't see your arraignment or Chris's," she admitted. "We left after Leif's and didn't come back until the middle of Raleigh's."

"Oh, Elspeth, you *abandoned* me," Julia said, with a smile of complicity that Elspeth didn't acknowledge.

In her hallway Elspeth threw her keys down with her backpack and stepped out of her boots. In the dining room she pulled back her hair, but there was nothing on hand to fix it with and she had to let it fall again.

"You must have had some thoughts, though, about what you did see," Julia resumed, when she had joined Elspeth in the dining room. "I myself had the impression, for example, that although the journalists are as devoted to us as ever, the people, except for the crusadey ones, may be losing the thread."

There was a certain pathos about a project like Julia's of gathering and holding on to one's impressions, which like cerements were bound in time to obscure, with their accumulating pallor and shapelessness, the body of life that they were intended to preserve and commemorate.

"I know about you and Raleigh, Julia," Elspeth said.

"I'm not sure what you're referring to."

"I'm not the sort of person who minds the way most people mind. I mind in the way that I can't help but mind, but I don't really mind."

Julia didn't reply.

"Everything has turned out different than I thought it was going to," Elspeth continued.

"It's the way people are," Julia said. "I wouldn't wait for me to apologize."

"I'm not waiting for anything."

"I'm not going to apologize for finally being someone," Julia said. Her face flinched and she looked away. "Did he tell you?"

"It's in the surveillance they were doing of us."

"What surveillance?"

"I have a copy of the folder that was on Bresser's server."

"How did you get it?" When Elspeth didn't answer, Julia asked, "What's in it?"

"I stopped listening. I assume everything's in it."

"You're probably in danger," Julia observed.

"I don't think they know I have it."

"They'll find out. You should tell Anonymous."

"How do you tell Anonymous?"

"Or you could upload a ransom file, if you think they're going to come for you. Before they come for you."

"What's a ransom file?"

"It's when you upload a file in encrypted form to a site where anyone can get it so that later, if you need to release it suddenly, all you have to do is shout the password."

"I want to give it to the lawyers, and I want your permission before I give it to them."

"Why? If it's your copy."

"I don't want to repeat their violation."

"Can you afford to be so high-minded?"

"It's how I want to do it."

Julia considered. "The reason I called Chris Hyacinth is because I thought you were going to end up playing the Princess Casamassima to him," she declared. "You'll probably hear that if you keep listening."

"I haven't read the book."

"But you know what I mean. Maybe I said it because I thought I was the one who should have gotten that role. Oh, never mind," she broke off. "You have my permission."

"Can we go for a walk?" Elspeth asked Raleigh, a few hours later, after she recognized his knock and opened her apartment door.

"Outside?"

"In the park," she said. She had been inside since Julia had left and she didn't care that it was February. She laced up her boots.

"Julia says you know," he said, in an almost by-the-way tone of voice, as he followed her down the stairwell. "I'm sorry. I know I fucked up."

"I said I'm sorry," he said with a more personal emphasis when they reached the sidewalk.

"Okay," she said.

"Are you going to get Chris's permission, too?"

"I don't know. I'm asking you first."

"The price of my permission is going to be that you forgive me."

"The price?"

"And you have to really mean it."

"Raleigh . . . ," she began, but broke off.

"Julia and I aren't a couple, by the way," he said.

They entered the park at the monument along whose back ledge Leif had used to skate. On the front, set into the pink marble, was a brass sculpture of a Revolutionary War general. A man in relief was holding the head of the general's horse, and the man was black; Elspeth wondered who he had been—who the man depicted had been and who the model had been.

No one was skating the ledge today. A mortar of week-old snow had gummed up many of the bricks in the pavement.

"I just want to hear you say it," Raleigh said. "That you forgive me."

The snow had receded unevenly from the asphalt of the walkway and from the dark sockets where the boles of trees were joined to the earth. Here and there arms of snow seemed to reach toward the walkway with cupped, downward-facing hands.

"Does it have to be tit for tat?" she asked. The hurt part of her was more stubborn than she had realized it would be.

At dusk the sky was still blank, and Elspeth walked the few blocks between her apartment and Matthew's under its strange glow. The tunnels that she had dreamed about might have been hiding behind the scrim of it; they might have been somehow fueling its luminosity. Matthew's window was dark, but a few seconds after she rang his buzzer, a light in his apartment blinked on, and soon he was standing in the building's doorway.

"Look at that," he said, looking up. "It's like the sky in a movie before the aliens land."

He had been unpacking his laundry, and his open futon was littered with small bricks of folded T-shirts, folded socks, and folded underwear, held together with rubber bands. Because he was gay, the intimacy of these items of clothing made them charged objects; they were suspect. Before long, if she went ahead with being a lesbian herself, people would be performing this kind of supererogatory noticing on the appurtenances of her life, too.

"You don't have to do that," she said, as he began shifting the bricks of clothing to the tops of columns of books on his desk.

"I just got in," he apologized. When he had finished clearing the futon he folded it up into its sofa form. Then he brought her a glass of water. "How are you?" he asked.

She should have asked first. "I'm fine," she said.

She watched him sit down and then immediately get up again and walk over to his desk. At the back of it, near the window, there was a potted geranium, and he twisted off a small yellowed broom that had once borne florets. A few whitened petals fluttered away from the forked stalk as he carried it to the trash.

If all along she had felt the need to keep Matthew at a remove, then all along he must have sensed the need in her. Matthew had always been able to enter into their games.

A dog howled somewhere outside. "He must hear thunder," Matthew said.

"I want to see Leif," she said. "I need to ask him something. Do you see him every day?"

"I take the train to the train. At first I was going to bike, but it's too far." He sat down again.

"Should I bring something?" she asked. "Maybe something for him to read?"

"The trouble with that is he doesn't like finding his bookmark further along than he remembers having read."

How disconcerting that would be. As if a section of tunnel that one had passed through had been not only closed but erased. She took a sip of colorless water from the colorless glass that Matthew had given her.

"How is the new place?" she asked.

"We're still getting to know the doctors and nurses. In the elevator people have burned their names in the ceiling with lighters but that's just the elevator. The man he shares his room with has a thing where he needs to know the title of every song he hears, even if it's just a scrap of song playing in the background on television in the next room, but other than that he's pretty quiet. If there's not a song to talk about, sometimes the three of us just sit there and listen to the air blowing out of the vent underneath the window."

"Is he mad at me?"

"Why would he be mad at you?"

"For talking to Somerville. I thought I was going to change Somerville's mind. I was so stupid."

"Why don't you come with me tomorrow," Matthew said. "He loves you. He's Leif. He still Leif."

She wondered if he would give permission. She wondered if he was still willing to fight, regardless of whether he still believed. The new order had revealed to them that poems didn't have to be published in order to have meaning as poems, but apparently the same order was also going to require the publication of all the prose of one's life.

The thunder was sounding now even to their merely human ears. The dog was still crying, no longer sharply.

"It's almost purple," Elspeth said, of the sky, which had darkened.

"The color of congealed blood," Matthew said. "That's why purple is royal, according to Pliny. That's its 'glory.'"

"Does green mean anything?" she asked.

"I think it's always just life."

There was clatter as it started to hail.

Elspeth walked home when it let up. Once she was dry, she pulled one card from her tarot deck. The Fool. He was upside down, as if he had been hanged that way for a lesson. Last summer she had seen a man in the park hang himself upside down like a bat, his knees over the limb of a tree. The man's cell phone had plummeted out of one of his pockets and hit the ground, cracking its glass screen. In the tarot card a little gray fox was pawing the upside-down Fool's pocket, which in the Middle Ages was not a pouch sewn into one's clothes but a separate item of clothing that could be tied to the skirts of one's jacket.

The card made her want to check something online.

While she waited for her laptop to boot up, she reviewed her plan. The next morning, on the train ride to the hospital, she was going to tell Matthew that she was now with Diana, and at the hospital, she was going to tell Leif the same thing and also tell him that he hadn't been wrong to sense that people in the government's side had been reading him, because in a more prosaic way than he had imagined, they had been. Once he knew, maybe he wouldn't need to think of himself as crazy anymore. In a day or two, either she would relent or Raleigh would, and once she had permission from three out of four, it was too bad about Chris, but she was going to release the files to the lawyers and everyone was going to know everything and it would all change.

In the interim she wanted to look inside Raleigh's backup app one more time. She hadn't taken any screenshots, and screenshots might help her establish the files' provenance. On the backup program's website, she entered the username and password. A page loaded that was mostly blank, as sometimes happens—one of the intermittent hiccups that the internet is prone to. Her attempt to log in must have failed for some reason. She moved her cursor to the top of the screen, with the intention of trying a second time to log in, but the button there said Logout. Which meant she was logged in, actually. She reloaded the page, but the fresh version of it that appeared was still mostly blank, as if there were no files even in Raleigh's root directory on the backup. Had the government wiped Raleigh's hard drive? No, that couldn't be; if the drive had been wiped, there would have been no software on it to do the syncing; she wouldn't see any change at all. And where was the backup of *her* old laptop? In a dialog box at the bottom of the page, she changed the date to a year ago and asked to see what had been backed up as of then. In the backup for that date, too, the root directory was empty. She tried a few more dates, also without success.

There was nothing in Raleigh's backup account anymore. Nothing of his, nothing of hers. Even the past had been deleted.

They had finally found out.

On her desktop she still had the copy of the RPF-Dove-Shark folder that she had downloaded and decompressed two nights ago. Had they compromised it somehow? The files inside looked untouched. To make sure, she double-clicked open a folder and double-clicked open a folder inside it and double-clicked open a file.

"Dude, where are you?" Raleigh asked.

"One block south of the southwest corner, in front of the old church," said Chris. "You know where I mean? I'm looking at where the drum circle was. I see three garbage trucks, and cops throwing everything into the backs of the garbage trucks."

"Everything? What do you mean everything?"

She halted the audio player.

She saw the Fool upside down, his pockets emptied of what he had meant to keep to himself.

To the left of her breastbone, decentered, her heart punched into and punched into and punched into itself. Into a search bar, she typed, "How to upload a ransom file."

Against her hip, her cell phone vibrated, startling her.

It was Diana. "Hello?"

Elspeth was going to have to lie better than Raleigh or anyone else had ever lied to her. She was going to have to be as deceitful as only a thing wholly in the world could be.

She lied so well that at seven the next morning, when there was a rap on her door, she was alone.

She was showered and dressed, though still barefoot. She had been waiting for them.

The three men were in dress shirts and blazers. The leader seemed to be the one not wearing a tie.

"Elspeth Farrell?" he queried.

"Come in," she said.

"How are you doing this morning?" he asked, trying to put a lock on her eyes, relying on his colleagues to scan the cluttered corridor and the doorways into empty bedrooms that she led them past.

"There's nobody here but me," she said.

"You probably know why we're here," he said. On the nape of his neck, she saw, as they reached the dining room and he swiveled to survey it and the parlor, was the delicate mottling of stork bites. His hair there was cut like a duck's ass, but otherwise there was nothing obviously military or police-like about him.

One of the other men took a large camera out of a satchel and began photographing her laptop, which before answering the door she had stowed in the dumbwaiter's nook. It was balanced on top of her reference collection.

"You didn't take pictures last time," she said.

"Last time?" the lead officer asked.

"When you arrested Raleigh."

"That wasn't us. This time you're getting the professionals."

"Are you FBI?"

"He and I are," he said, pointing to himself and the cameraman, "and he's Secret Service. A lot of people don't realize that the Secret Service takes care of computers now almost more than they take care of presidents. It's typical in a case like this for us first to photograph the disposition of items."

The FBI agent with the camera had noticed that her power cable was still twisted through the handle of a coffee mug on the dining room table, and he took a picture.

"That's where the laptop was when you knocked," Elspeth said. "I moved it before I answered the door."

"That's okay," the lead agent said, "but if you could put it back for us."

She complied but didn't turn the computer back on.

"Is there a router?" the Secret Service agent asked her.

"In the broom closet," she said.

"You must have a lot of questions," the lead FBI agent suggested. "You probably want to know where we are with things."

"That's okay."

"Maybe while they're doing this, maybe you and I could sit down and talk a little, before things go any further. I know a little about what you've been going through, but I'd like to hear it from you."

"Your already knowing is sort of what it's about, isn't it," she said.

"It's really put you behind the eight ball, I can see that."

He couldn't see it, she reminded herself. Nobody could. "That's okay," she said again.

"A lot of times, people in your situation want to be able to explain what they've been going through."

"Did *you* bring the garbage bags?" the Secret Service agent asked the photographer, evidently afraid that he had been supposed to.

"In my satchel," the photographer said, handing it over.

"It's not actually a garbage bag, that's just what he calls it," the lead agent said. "It's actually a protection against Wi-Fi and RFID and all that. Is this your kitchen? Maybe we could talk in here for a minute."

"That's okay," she said, once more.

"I know the judge that this is going to go in front of, and she's always very appreciative when people cooperate. Do you mind if I get a drink of water?"

"Go ahead," Elspeth said.

From the dining room she listened as in the kitchen he opened one cabinet and then another and then took down a glass. She heard him rinse it out before he filled it.

"We don't have to do this the hard way," the lead agent said when, since she hadn't followed him into the kitchen, he returned to the doorway.

"Am I free to go?" she asked.

"Not just yet," he said, before taking a sip.

8.

There had been a white—had it been a goat? No, a deer. It had charged him. He hadn't realized it was dangerous. He should have. It had had strange eyes, with vertical irises, the shape of almonds standing on their ends, like in a cat.

In real life Joe always took a competitor seriously; conflict spurred growth.

He felt the coffee that he was drinking warming the flower inside him, opening it to the day.

He was well prepared for the day's meetings, with two potential investors. There had been some setbacks, but *Your luck has been completely changed today,* as the fortune cookie says. The idea behind his business was, after all, the forging of a weapon. He was never afraid of a fight, and that was why he was going to—

His phone. "Thomas Somerville of the United States Attorneys' Office would like to speak with you, can you hold."

The woman put him on hold before she could hear his yes.

"Mr. Joseph P. Bresser," came Somerville's voice, with its tone of put-on raillery, slightly bitter.

"Hey, Tom."

"Calling to keep you apprised. As you're no doubt aware, we are up to Telepathy Five now, and Samantha Rinehart Peabody, the abundantly named new lawyer of the new girl, is claiming that we tampered with the evidence—thereby admitting, by the by, that her client was trying to access a protected file, which is what we arrested her for, but that seems to be neither here nor there in anyone's eyes—and in reply I *could* take the step of assuring the judge that that's not quite what happened and that a digital proxy of the material formerly on the seized laptop remains intact, but if I were to give that assurance there is a risk that eventually I'd have to produce the files in question and as you know we need to protect the program. Or rather, programs."

"Yes."

"So we're protecting the programs and losing the cases. That's the course of action I'm letting you know about in this phone call and that we are going to be signaling this afternoon."

"You can't," Joe said.

"Well, I can, Joe. These are my cases. And anyway, as far as I can tell, we're doing this for you, if we're doing it for anyone."

"You just said you're going to signal. That means you're not really going to do this, are you."

"No, Joe. No no no. When you're a grown-up, which is something you wouldn't know about, you try not to surprise the people who are on your side. You give a signal so that your allies have a chance to adjust their positions, and then you read the room, and only once you see that everyone's ready for the change in strategy do you follow through."

Currying favor with an establishment would of course be mistaken by a man like Somerville for maturity.

"You'll notice," Somerville continued, "that I'm not asking who it was that was so ham-handed that they managed to delete a piece of evidence in a way that was observable remotely. I'm not asking who gave the defense a plump, juicy cut of premium-grade graymail. I'm assuming that the person or persons who executed this deletion were only trying to protect the surveillance programs, too, in their own ass-covering way, and happened to be unaware that they could be held in contempt of court, and I imagine that you have one or two friends at the state level who will be very relieved to hear that this is the assumption I'm going to be making. Ham-handed but obliging friends."

A man like Somerville thought exclusively in terms of who was on top and who was loyal, but as the future came into being, status and allegiance were going to shift so rapidly that it made more sense even now to be indifferent to them.

"I am curious, though, what kind of genius would bait his trap with files that couldn't under any circumstances be presented in court."

"It had to be something they wanted," Joe explained.

"It only had to be something they thought they wanted."

"Not with these kids."

"I have to get off the phone with you now. It's been lovely chatting with you, as ever. Someday soon I hope you'll show up in my docket arrested for whatever you're smoking so that I can find out what it is."

"It's yoga."

"We're all sorry we ever met you, Joe. Including, very soon, if a word from me can have any effect on the rest of her career, your girlfriend in the city innovation office."

"I'm not sleeping with Charlotte."

"I don't care who or what you're sleeping with. It's been great talking with you, as I say. Don't sell any more wooden nickels."

The moment the attorney hung up, the attorney's executive assistant briefly returned to the line: "Hello?" When Joe failed to respond, she hung up on him, too.

In the silence that followed, Joe looked out his window at the morning sun, which was hitting a quadrilateral of yellow bricks in the air shaft. A few weeks ago there had been a slant of snow leaning against the bricks, and by repetition of itself the sun had fused the snow and then hollowed it and then riven it and then sublimed it away. That was the power of repetition of even something as pale as winter morning. Repetition was one of the forms of number in the world.

It would be too dangerous to allow the members of the group to get away. He was going to have to force Somerville's hand.

He remembered when he had first recognized the danger. Something odd, Charlotte had said, had been passed on to her by analysts in the Special Operations Division. *Do you have any idea what this is about?* the analysts had wanted to know. The analysts were tasked with looking for indications of drug trades, but as dealers began to camouflage their wording, the weave of the analysts' nets grew correspondingly finer and subtler until in the end they were selecting for disguise itself, because the AI had become trained to find language that was doing any kind of hiding. Of course it had alerted them when it detected someone talking cryptically about a new kind of decryption. It wasn't what the Special Operations Division was supposed to be investigating, but it was the sort of thing that as professionals all of them lived for.

Someone, the system had discovered, was approaching hackers on chat channels (and approaching a few online tulpas that had been set up on chat channels by the division in the hope that they would be mistaken for hackers) to ask how much better than random a wholly new kind of guessing algorithm would have to be in order to be valuable. The person had been vague about what he had, but he had let drop that he had something to do with Occupy and that the algorithm was somehow analog, with a somewhat jerky variance in its margin of error. How would the black market go about pricing such a capability? The person had said he was asking about price only to find a way to assess value. The thing itself, he had insisted, was not for sale.

The disavowal had been as much of a red flag as the question.

That was the first sign of the Working Group for the Refinement of the Perception of Feelings, though of course at that point no one knew the group's name. The group probably hadn't even come up with it yet. Joe had felt certain that their algorithm was some kind of bioinformatics. He knew that in the future everyone who manages to survive will be a chimera of biology and technology—a compound of human and computer—and he had always known that the first buds were eventually going to be identified on somebody's shoulder blades someday.

The day had come.

He couldn't say as much aloud, of course, not even to Charlotte. The key to the professional environment that he worked in was parallel construction: it's okay to know, but only once you find other, public grounds for your knowledge is it safe to say that you know. Those were the terms on which the Special Operations Division had shared emails and chat transcripts with Charlotte, who was the city police department's chief innovation officer, and those were the terms on which Charlotte had in turn shared the communications with him.

Charlotte had said only that she thought she saw here an opportunity for Joe to try out the business model that he had been trying to sell her on. He had been sharing with her the software that he was developing, which coordinated sets of data about surveilled individuals that hadn't previously been linked. The software worked by mapping the patterns of interaction within each set against one another. It was possible that the business opportunity really was all Charlotte had seen.

He, on the other hand, had known at once. The constellation recognizes itself in you as soon as you look up into the sky.

He had set to work trying to identify the individuals. He had geofenced Occupy and then seeded his software with the social media profiles of regular visitors and then mapped those profiles against the dark information, the data sets that he wasn't allowed to acknowledge had been passed on to him. It was a first try; it hadn't worked. After Charlotte loaned him an IMSI catcher, however, he was able to add the details of a mass of calls made by cell phones at the encampment, which his software had been able to parse into component social groups—people who often called or texted one another just before their cell phones appeared together at the site. The breakthrough had come when Charlotte had shared with him a file she had found in a multiagency antiterrorism database of persons of interest who had been tracked to Occupy. One of them was Chris Finn. Apparently in 2010 he had gotten too enthusiastic about an anticapitalist group in Toronto. He had only been cautioned, but the agencies' computers had kept watch on him ever since.

The identification of Finn had lined up the dials. And then Joe had added a layer of parallel construction of his own. A government official is only allowed to use an IMSI catcher to track who called whom, from where, for how long. The device, however, is also capable of listening to calls and reading texts, and Joe wasn't an official employee of the government. Why had they built the functionality if literally no one was supposed to use it? Joe told investors that his software linked data sets—such as social media accounts and call detail records—by finding congruences between the patterns within each set, but he didn't think that it in any way falsified his claim if at the start of the process he trained the homology-finding engine with a few identifications that he made by hand, using as clues the texts and call recordings that the IMSI catcher, its settings changed, picked up. It was just a way for the machine to make progress in learning; there was nothing wrong with learning. The dark information couldn't be acknowledged, but a Bayesian net refined by dark information was an entity distinct from the dark information itself. It was no drawback to Bresser Opsec's business model that in the future Joe might continue to need an initial supply of such identifications in order to bring a net up to speed because he was always going to be selling *in*. He was always going to be selling to clients who collected information. If not to a triliteral government agency then to one of the big five in the private sector, who were for the most part way ahead of the government in any case.

In fact, on low days he even worried that the lag between government and the private sector was all that he was leveraging: that because it was still possible at the moment for a contractor to do what it wasn't currently legal for the government itself to do, all he was selling to the government was the blindfolded untying of its own hands, and once change agents in the government saw what he was able to do with the combination of his freedom and their borrowed power, they would be incentivized to make it legal, or at least to declare formally that they were not going to make it positively illegal, which would shrink his margins by opening the market to all comers.

For now, though, there was still enough legal ambiguity to constitute a business opportunity. If he succeeded, stakeholders now invisible to him would surely move to consolidate what he had pioneered. It was therefore unlikely that he personally would ever be in legal jeopardy. No ruler ever forswore a weapon after wielding it. All he had to do was get the weapon into the rulers' hands, at least briefly.

His phone. "Um, Joe?"

"I'm on my way," Joe said. "You go ahead on in."

"Are we meeting there?"

"What did we say?"

"I don't think we—"

"Are you still at the office? I want you to send a press release."

"Right now?"

"Tell them I'm going to be holding another press conference. In the atrium."

"But last time the building manager said—"

"Then what do we pay rent for? Come on, Lloyd. Tell them it's going to be at one o'clock."

"Today? But what if our meetings don't—"

"This isn't about the meetings. Somerville wants to quit, and I'm not going to let him."

Lloyd was silent. Joe knew, however, that he was obeying. He knew that Lloyd was writing down the instructions. He heard Lloyd mutter, as if speaking to himself, "But the government's still going to pay us."

"Why wouldn't they pay us? And can you call a car for me?"

"To your apartment?"

"How else am I going to get there? I'll be downstairs in ten minutes."

In the event, since he was already dressed, he was downstairs sooner than that, before any town car arrived, and he hailed an SUV-size taxi that happened to be turning the corner.

It wheeled downhill heavily, and on the road that circled the city along its shore, it fitted itself into the traffic like a knife into its sheath. Like a knife into a wound that it had previously made. He had been waiting for all of this for years. The only doubt that had ever been in his mind was on whose side the first chimera was going to be born—the side of force or the side of order. Force was what he called the side without law. The side prior to law. A creature of any power was almost always born there first, in the greenwood, as it used to be called, and was only later captured and harnessed and put into the service of the side of order by someone like him.

As the taxi swung up a tight, cantilevered bend, he felt his insides sink within him and then rise, on the recoil.

He called Lloyd. "Did you send it?"

"I'm going to send it from my phone. I'm in a car."

"Bcc me."

It was possible that he hadn't thought through carefully enough the contents of the lure he had set for the RPF group, but if he had put in more than he should have, it had been because he had wanted them to know that he knew. He had wanted to suggest that he was aware that they were ahead of him and that he therefore felt free to be careless about letting them see what he had on his side—that he knew that they were going to see what he had anyway. It had been meant as a provocation and you could even say as a statement of his faith in them. The mistake had been in his imagining that they would have only a few hours with the files. It used to be that a pawn once captured was taken off the board, but under the new dispensation every piece, captured or not, remained available for play indefinitely. Sequence was no longer limited to progress, which was hard at first to keep in mind when planning a strategy, but a fighter always trains himself to think according to the new laws of combat.

Thanks to the Farrell girl, he himself was already holding the piece in question again. It had been transformed by its fall and recovery; the girl had locked it and therefore silenced and in a way perfected it. So many people were in the habit of leaving weapons where he could pick them up, perhaps because almost no one saw him for who he was, or perhaps because almost no one ever stopped to think how a weapon could be used against someone other than themselves.

The car slowed and halted outside a building that a hundred years ago had been erected as a warehouse. He touched the side of his face in order to make contact with his outer self. He had omitted to shave; he hadn't wanted to look too much as if he needed anything. He was wearing his gray suit with a white shirt but for the same reason hadn't put on a tie.

His phone again. But it was only the press release from Lloyd coming through.

A wall of newly cast concrete and a stumpy man-bun of wires had been left exposed in the lobby of the former warehouse, either because renovation was incomplete or because the design was meant to induce a visitor to think that it was.

He punched 4 for Planchette and rode up. The elevator opened onto a hallway of jagged bricks, at the end of which he found a glass door stenciled with the name.

Lloyd had got there first and stotted up out of a chair.

"I'll let Mr. Weld know you're here," said a blond woman in a suit.

It was twelve minutes past the hour.

"Is that what you wanted?" Lloyd asked.

"I haven't read it yet."

After exactly twelve minutes more, the door to an inner room opened.

"Joe!" a man said. "Hilary Weld. Come on in." The door was crazed glass, like a wreck's windshield. Weld shook Joe's hand and then Lloyd's.

The scale of the room inside was so grand that it registered, at first, as empty, even though it held a desk; a white sofa in the middle of one wall; and, near a window, a rowing machine. Weld led them to a cluster of stools around a black table. The seats of the stools looked as if they had been salvaged from old rideable agricultural machines, but they were more comfortable to sit on than they looked.

"Can I ask Veronica to get you something?"

"A seltzer?" Joe suggested. "So you're going to be our angel investor."

"I don't know if I'd call myself an angel, Joe."

In Weld's faux-hawk, the raised central comb was dyed blue. His nose, pierced, was unambiguously male, even aquiline, but there was a dusting of kohl around his eyes. What did Joe care, it was business. Between the wiry hairs of the man's left forearm began the tracery of what looked like a whole sleeve of tattoos.

The blond woman in the suit set one glass of seltzer in front of Joe and another in front of Lloyd.

Joe made a winding gesture. "Lloyd, do you want to . . . ?"

"So if you'd like, Mr. Weld, let me give you a presentation about the suite of products that we—"

Weld held up a hand. "I wouldn't be talking to you principal to principal if I didn't know the product. And read the newspaper, too. Congratulations on that, by the way. It makes me as a potential investor nervous, because what other dogs will it call out, but for you—you can't buy press like that. What I think would be productive is if I talk to you a little about the vision that I have for the world that I think your work could lead to."

"Awesome," Joe said.

"What I see, when I close my eyes," Weld said, not closing his eyes but matching the pads of his fingers together like a praying mantis, "is a world where no one is ever lost, where because of the functionality that you've developed, the not quite overlapping, not always intersecting multiple data sets that people create every day, every hour, every minute, with their phones and their emails and their credit cards and their smart TVs and their social media accounts and their streaming music services and their employee ID badges and the toll-paying devices in their cars and their cars' navigation systems and the loyalty barcode dongles on their keychains are all constantly, quietly reconciled. And therefore no gesture goes unnoticed. No signal goes unreceived. Don't get me wrong: I know how important the feeling of privacy is to people. I think it's central. Nobody wants a user experience where they feel exposed. In the world I'm looking forward to, all the data sets that are collected will be anonymized. What I imagine, though, is that they'll be anonymized *and* individualized. No one will feel watched, but everyone will feel, what's a good word, *appreciated.* No one will have the feeling that there is a smelly human on the other side of the screen somewhere, totting up merits and demerits. They will instead be liminally aware of a bank of benign machines noticing, nonjudgmentally, the steps they happen to be taking. And by liminally I mean if someone wants to sock-puppet, for example—do you remember sock-puppeting? It was so cute, and there are even some people who still do it, can you believe it, who are still able in a moment of rage to convince themselves that their cell phone doesn't know what their laptop browser is doing—anyway, we're never going to let a sock-puppeteer know that we've caught on to him. If someone wants to be two people, he probably has a good reason. You can learn so much more about someone if you don't moralize. Let him be two people, and watch those two people. Or three, or four. Knowing, as only a nonjudgmental observer is free to know, that all of them lay the same head on the same pillow every night, believing in their distinctness. What I'm imagining will be like a glove that fits so well that most people will forget they're wearing it. If you don't like it that after you search for swimming goggles on one site you see ads for swimming goggles everywhere online—or even, soon, offline—the machines should know that about you, too. They should keep track of even your threshold for perception. They should know exactly, sensitively, the depth that they need to retreat to, in order not to alarm you, where they can wait for you, unseen, patient. What I'm imagining, really, is that observation will be gentle, not constraining choice or even guiding it but merely informing it. Maybe a consumer doesn't know that he can buy a wallet that looks as chic as leather but is made of recyclables, and once he does know it, that's what he's going to want, and the machines will know he can afford it or they wouldn't be bothering to present it to him. Not Big Brother but Little Brother, as it were. Nonthreatening, noninterfering. Tactful."

"That's beautiful," Joe said. "We'll know more about them under their anonymized identifiers than their mothers know about them under their names."

"But it won't be 'we' who know. It won't have the odor of human knowing."

"You don't want to be able to open the black box."

"No, exactly, I don't want to. That's where I'm not like your current client. I don't want to ever need to. I believe in discretion. I believe in letting people be themselves. Letting them be, if possible, even *more* themselves."

"I'm definitely interested in your future," Joe said.

"Now, you have patents?" Weld asked.

"Funny you should say that, we were talking about it recently, but I thought it would be premature," Joe said. "At this stage the company is really just me."

"Who's this?" Weld asked, pointing at Lloyd.

"Lloyd would never take anything."

"Lloyd can't quit tomorrow and go into business for himself?"

"I would never do something like that," Lloyd said. His eyes were bugging out somewhat at the sudden pivot of attention to him. It was Lloyd, of course, who had suggested, just before the RPF case began, that Joe ought to apply for patents.

"Don't you like money?" Weld asked Lloyd, uncoiling the fingers of his right hand. There was a ring on the index finger. "We can buy you some balls if that's what's missing."

"Hey," Joe said.

"So what you're telling me," Weld said, "is that you don't have any ownership of your ideas."

"What's going on? I thought you wanted to invest."

"Not in wishful thinking. And to be honest, what I wanted was to buy your company, kill it, and plunder the corpse of its internal organs." He smiled. He knew that Joe wouldn't mind the imagery. He had recognized him as a fellow hunter. "But you're telling me there's nothing inside."

"That's not true," Joe said. "What we have is what we call contextual expertise squared: contextual expertise about how to acquire contextual expertise."

"And I just explained to you that I'm not interested in knowledge that's all too human." He let the fingers of one hand fall like soldiers over the closed knuckles of the other. "Maybe we should talk after you've conceptualized your business a little further. It's not clear that you know what you're selling yet."

"You're an asshole," Lloyd said, rising.

"Lloyd . . . ," Joe said.

But Lloyd was already halfway across the empty room.

"We're going to keep talking," Joe promised Weld. He felt like a dog walker telling one off-leash dog to stay while another had just run into the road.

He caught up to Lloyd at the elevator. "Having someone who wants to buy us for parts isn't a bad thing."

Lloyd wouldn't look at him. "We should have done a legal review."

Joe checked over his shoulder. The hallway and the elevator were unlikely to be under Weld's surveillance if Weld was only a renter. "It's not too late."

"A full legal review. It wouldn't all be bad news. There's a case about an IMSI catcher in California right now with a pro se defendant where it looks like the government is going to argue that law enforcement has the right to keep its data out of discovery for the same reason it has the right to keep secret the identity of confidential informants."

They stepped into the elevator. "Weld's not law enforcement."

"I'm not talking about just Weld."

"Where are we meeting Long?" Joe asked.

"At our office."

"Just at our office?"

"I bought a thing of cookies for it," Lloyd said.

On the street, Joe hailed a cab. "Bresser Operational Security," he told the driver as they got in.

"Do you have an address for that?" the driver asked.

It was turning out to be a bright, hollow day. A day made of foil, teeth, and right angles. It had irritated him at first that so many of the defendants in the RPF case had thought of themselves, openly or secretly, as apostles of poetry, but he had come to realize that it had irritated him because he had never acknowledged that he had also been touched by that spirit. Once he made the acknowledgment, he was able to see that when they quoted lines of poetry to one another, the lines weren't reference texts for ciphers but places where they could meet. They allowed for a kind of peer-to-peer calibration, the operation of which depended somehow on the way that phrases from the poems sometimes got lodged in one's mind. He had read only the Wikipedia entry about the novel with the Hyacinth character, but he had read all of the poem that had inspired Saunderson's tattoo, after the press had identified it. It was an old poem; it was online. Since it was about greenery, it was probably about sex, mostly. But it also seemed to be somehow about giving up. He didn't like that part.

Members of RPF had come to the last press conference; he wondered if he would see any today. Of course everything was different for them now. They might not even hear about it; they didn't seem to talk much anymore. It was true what Weld said, that there was a sensitivity that some people had to being overheard, especially people who had been born with the little catfish feelers on their faces that this group had. There was a thing, too, where the substitution that the online world made of the real one seemed to cut people off from one another, over time. Though there were other reasons the conversation had broken down in this case: All of them facing criminal charges. The Farrell girl only getting out on bail today, after a weekend inside. The Di Matteo girl probably embarrassed. Finn probably hated by the rest. And Saunderson in a mental hospital. He had turned out to be weaker than he had seemed. The way an astronaut's bones become etiolated the longer he's in space. It sometimes worried Joe that through his own creative side, if he wasn't careful, he could develop that kind of susceptibility.

No, the defendants weren't going to be there, he predicted, as the taxi pulled up to his building. He would have the press to himself.

He saw through the glass of the taxi window and the glass of the building's front that a man was already standing in the lobby. "Is that Long?" he asked Lloyd. They hadn't been able to find a photo of him online. The man was about Joe's height and build and like Joe was also wearing a gray suit and white shirt. It was like spotting one's stunt double—a version of oneself, off to one side, waiting to reshoot the scene that one was in.

The man gave no sign of noticing Joe and Lloyd as they were getting out of their taxi.

"Ask him," Joe said.

"Mr. Long?" Lloyd asked, as they entered the lobby.

"Yes." He had rough skin. He was about ten years older than Joe.

"Warren Long, Joe Bresser. Hope we didn't keep you waiting; we're just coming from another meeting."

The man smiled.

"Come on upstairs."

The doorman nodded them through, and they took their places in the elevator like *Star Trek* crew members assembling for teleportation. Joe twisted the un-signifying ring on his ring finger.

When the doors opened, Lloyd rushed ahead. "I'll go set up."

The office door locked behind Lloyd, and Joe had to knock when he and Long got to it.

Lloyd had cleared off the card table they usually used for meetings, had found a milk-glass plate somewhere, and had put the cookies out.

"So you've had some interest," the man said.

"Talking," Joe said.

"Anyone in politics?" the man asked. "I'm sort of an advance man, myself. It's something someone like me is naturally interested in, what you do."

"That's great."

"Looking at what people do online, what they're like online. I'd be surprised if nobody else in politics has approached you yet. If only to ask what life in a group looks like."

"Of course people have asked," Joe said, temporizing.

"Are you interested in online groups because so many people online are lonely?" Lloyd guessed. He was the only one who had put a cookie on a paper plate for himself. "Is that the problem you're working on?"

"Not so much a problem as an opportunity. The way people want to be on a side—that's something we're very interested in. That's what we do in politics, after all, and we have to work the angles. Loneliness creates an opportunity for a first-mover advantage, in any contest between sides. Which side looks like it's going to be less lonely, that could be the side that's going to win. Could we automate that a little, is our question. Could we reverse-engineer the kind of observation that you've been doing and *create* an impression of being together instead of just noticing one. Create it knowing what you know, in a deep way, about what it looks like when a large group of people are in relation to one another and are going through the process of making up their minds. Knowing the structure of those relationships and that process."

"You mean, populate a discussion," Joe said.

"That might be part of it," the man said. "Can we figure out how to automate at least a little bit the impression of solidarity, so that when people are ready to choose a side, we've set up the direction they're going to fall in. The way when you're chopping down a tree, all you have to do is cut that little wedge in the far side of the trunk to determine which direction it will fall. And can we then turn that automation into a product—the kind of thing we can do without needing to know who we're doing it for. A kind of service that we can sell as if it were in a box on a shelf. I think that's a product a lot of people would be interested in."

A large part of being stronger was being faster. Sometimes what counted was being the one who got to the weapon first.

"What kind of commitment are you thinking of making?" Joe asked.

"I'd need to give you enough money that you could afford to seem not to exist, wouldn't I? Maybe you could come up with some concepts."

As the man rose to leave, Joe and Lloyd scrambled to their feet.

"Creepy," Lloyd said, after the door closed.

"Shut up," Joe commanded, looking through the peephole at the man as he receded.

"Joe, it's one," Lloyd said.

"Already?" He checked his own phone.

"Are you sure you want to do a press conference? If this guy says we're not even supposed to exist?"

It was in fact impressive that he was being asked to not-exist. He was going to be one of the people on the inside, setting up the new way things were going to be. The new way people were going to be.

"What are they saying?" he asked Lloyd.

"Who?"

"Online. Are they downstairs?"

"I'm not going to look."

"Why not?" Joe took out his own phone again. Someone had just posted a picture of the lobby, which was indeed filling up. Someone else had reposted a cartoon from last week of Joe as a villain tying himself as a damsel to railroad tracks, just as an Occupy Telepathy locomotive approached. *I'm not stupid,* the damsel was saying, which was something he had said once, online, when he had been trying to explain. His critics seemed incapable of understanding that the government would never have made its move if he hadn't arranged the honeypot. Did it really show stupidity on his part if it had worked? "Let's go," he said to Lloyd.

"I don't even know what this press conference is about," Lloyd said.

"Somerville doesn't, either."

On the way down, in the one-way mirror that shielded the elevator's surveillance camera, Joe smoothed his hair with the heel of his hand. Lloyd started clicking his pen. "Stop it," Joe said.

The gathering of journalists in the lobby had already generated by their co-presence in such numbers a sense of purposiveness so strong that they didn't at first notice the incursion of Joe, who had summoned them. Joe always felt, when he first saw a crowd like this, that it was as though he were giving a party with this many guests.

"Mr. Bresser, tell me I'm not seeing this," said the building's porter. The doorman, meanwhile, wouldn't look up.

"That's because it's not happening, Rick. And you're only going to have to not-see it for about ten more minutes."

"Just leave me an aisle through here, can you, in case the fire marshal comes."

"He won't come."

"I didn't say he would."

The crowd noticed Joe. As he and Lloyd made their way through, journalists fell silent around them, as if Joe and Lloyd were a dark spot passing across an X-ray, or a cloud detectable only by its opacity as it sailed over stars in the night sky. They stopped in front of the chewing-gum-green trees in front of which Joe had spoken last time.

"Thank you for coming on such short notice," Lloyd intoned. "Joseph P. Bresser of the Joseph P. Bresser Operational Security Consultancy would like to say a few words."

In the silence, before Joe spoke, it was as if for a moment he was holding to his lips a cornet made of wires that ran out and tugged at the sternums of every person in the room. If only the room could have been larger, grander. There were cavernous spaces under and inside the piers of the city's bridges, and Joe had had a glimpse of the inside of one of them once, while he was walking by. The city had been storing parked trucks inside it, but the volume had suggested that it was capable of containing a whole world.

"Thank you," Joe said.

At the back of the crowd, shifting unsteadily on her feet like a drunk who might be working up the nerve to heckle, was the Di Matteo girl. She had come after all. She was looking at him without acknowledging him, the way people from money are able to. The diluted beige color of her hat almost matched her skin and made her look bald. She wouldn't be very happy if they shaved her head when she went to jail.

"I want to say a few words about a turn that the case of the RPF Working Group has taken. As most of you are aware, the original charges concerned the group's illegal access to a protected computer here at our firm, and over the weekend, there was a new breach, this time of federal security, by a fifth defendant, Elspeth Farrell. There's been some chatter in the system, as they say, about the possibility that the government might prefer to drop charges in order not to risk exposing methods and sources, and what I want to emphasize today is that such a retreat would be highly inadvisable. As many of you are aware, the files that Farrell was arrested this weekend for taking were the same ones taken by the original four defendants, her comrades, and then resecured by the government. What has not been previously disclosed"—and this was like the moment when you knew you'd raised your sights to just the right amount a little bit above and ahead of where the bird had so far flown—"but which I learned from independent sources at the time of Farrell's arrest, is that before her arrest she was able to upload the same highly sensitive, contraband files, encrypted with an unknown key, to the notorious file-sharing site the Golden Cove. This is not the behavior of kids on a joyride. These are bad actors, with a skill set not well understood, who are making every effort to humiliate and even threaten the United States government."

The reporters were silent. Writing and listening. He had them. The little cornet had welded them to his grasp.

"Joe, is the government aware that this file is publicly available?" a reporter asked.

"They are now."

"And how were you able to find this out?" asked another.

"These were originally our files, and we have a procedure in place for looking for our files when they go missing."

"With tracking software?"

"We look for them, okay? The folder had a specific name." The internet was now going to make fun of him for having called this a procedure. "There was a notification that RPF-Dove-Shark was available."

"But, Joe, you said it's encrypted, right?"

"RPF what?"

"I found it," someone said.

"If it's encrypted, how do you know it's the same file?" It was a reporter from one of the tabloids, the one who always dressed like a homeless person.

("That's Jan Ridgely," Lloyd whispered.)

"Because of the file size, Jan," Joe said.

"So you had a Google alert for a file with the same name and size?"

"It's a little more complicated than that, but basically, yes."

"And what's the password?"

"How would I know? I didn't encrypt it."

The susurrus of the consultations between journalist and journalist was steady and mounting, but in deference to Joe still restrained. It was like being in a hive whose scouts had just reported a new source of nectar and the bees were with more and more agitation milling and whirring and knocking against one another. The creatures might have been dangerous to him under other circumstances, but here and now they were being organized by the information he was giving them and he knew they would stay loyal to it.

The tech reporter for the city's largest broadsheet was close enough that despite the rising hum, she was still able to speak to Joe without raising her voice. "But you probably know them better than anyone now," she said.

("That's Stacey Temple," whispered Lloyd.)

"*I'm* not psychic," he replied to her.

"Take a guess?" Temple joked. She had very sharp cheekbones.

"'A green thought in a green shade'?" Joe said. The words had popped into his head. "They used to quote that so often I thought it was code for something, but it's just from a poem."

"What did he say?" another reporter asked.

"'A green thought in a green shade,'" answered a reporter who had overheard.

"Found it," someone else said.

"You found the poem, or—?"

"Joe, sir, that password seems to work, actually."

A long icicle froze him from his throat to his groin. It removed a cone of himself from the inside of himself.

"It's not opening for me," another reporter said.

"You have to use underscores instead of spaces between the words."

"It's not downloading."

"What *is* all this stuff?"

Voices began to issue from a laptop held aloft by Jan Ridgely, at first unintelligible under the interference of the room's cross talk, and then, as the reporters succeeded in hushing one another, blotted over for a moment by a glissando of blips while Ridgely tapped the volume on her laptop upward.

"Maybe I'll write it in ballad rhythm," Leif Saunderson was saying, as the voices became distinct. "Or in one of those alliterative Icelandic things that Auden is so into."

"You'll still know," Elspeth Farrell replied.

"I know," Saunderson said. "I'll be sort of ironic about not wanting to know. I'll be sentimental for the naïve. I'm calling it the dark poem."

"Oh, Leif . . ."

"We shouldn't be—," a reporter interrupted.

Ridgely hit the Escape key.

Fortunately, Joe remembered, it wasn't at all clear that under the new laws of combat a revelation could still change the ending of a story.